The Devil's Truth

by

Paul Georgiou

Published by Panarc International 2016

First Edition

www.panarcpublishing.com

Panarc International Ltd
www.panarc.com

ISBN : 978-0-9931103-6-8
Epub:: 978-0-9931103-7-5
Kindle: 978-0-9931103-8-2

Author's Introduction

The Devil's Truth is book two of the Truth quartet.

In the first book, **The Fourth Beginning**, the Smiths set out on an epic adventure to find answers to some of life's most challenging questions. Eve desperately wants to know why her daughter had to die; Adam is looking for reasons to live.

The questors' guide on the journey is the Storyteller. Their mode of transport is a camper van, equipped with an exponential drive and a paradox device, inventions of a couple of brilliant Irish engineers, the wizened Prune Leach and the long-legged Andrew Rimzil.

As soon as the journey begins, Adam and Eve are warned by the Breaker Nick Peters and his shapeshifter side-kick Grimrose that their quest is pointless and hopeless. Undeterred Adam and Eve persist, picking up on the way an odd couple of hitchhikers, the ever-curious Uncle Rambler and his willing pupil Nephew Numpty.

The questors visit the God of the Old Testament in the Garden of Eden, near Hook off the M3. The interview with God produces no answers to the questors' questions and, indeed, turns rather nasty when Eve gives God the sharp edge of her tongue. They escape a bloody end with the help of the enigmatic blind man, Kit.

Next, the questors travel back in time to the Caucasus where they are greeted by Prometheus who has always looked favourably on man. The Titan wishes to help but has no answers, other than to encourage the Smiths in their search for the truth and in their hopes for the future.

The Storyteller then decides to give Adam and Eve a unique opportunity to witness the three great beginnings; the creation of the universe, the birth of life and the emergence of human consciousness. None of these extraordinary events provides the Smiths with answers, but they do provide a feast for thought.

When the travellers return, they find themselves in a mysland, a replica of a part of the New Forest, a virtual construct entirely under the control of the Breakers. The questors are arrested. Adam is imprisoned at the Breakers' regional office at Cadnam, where he is tested in an underground hell. The Breakers are determined to prevent the questors from initiating a fourth beginning.

After a violent and vicissitudinal struggle with Nick Peters and the Breakers, the questors, aided by Optimius, the sanguine penguin, Elsa, the imperfect seal, and the military might of the Metaphorce, seem to be victorious - and a Fourth Beginning is set in motion.

It is at this point that **The Devil's Truth**, the second book in the Truth quartet, begins.

Contents

1. Praesidium

The extraordinary meeting of the Praesidium took place on the top floor of a tall glass skyscraper in the heart of London, precisely where the Houses of Parliament stand.

Simon Goodfellow, Vice Chair of the Praesidium, a handsome man of medium build, with dark hair, hard grey eyes and a pale complexion, spoke quietly but with an unmistakable intensity.

"We have halted the aberration. Now we must make sure, once and for all, that these fanatics can never take matters so far again. And I mean *once and for all* and I mean *never*."

Manfred Bloch, the Praesidium's Technical Director, an overweight and inflexible individual, intervened.

"We really shouldn't overreact. The aberration has been diffused. Of course we need to learn lessons, but there is certainly no need to employ a Praesidium sledgehammer to crack a single aberrant nut. My own staff had concerns about the management at Cadnam well before this incident and, had they survived, the Cadnam managers would have been held accountable. But it was simply a matter of poor intelligence and communication. If they had called on us for help earlier, the aberration would have been stopped long before it reached critical mass."

Simon Goodfellow's grey eyes narrowed; his pallid lips curled inwards until they almost disappeared, compromising his good looks. The Technical Division had let them down badly. It was entirely understandable that Bloch should feel defensive, but that was no excuse for trying to obstruct the decisive measures that Simon knew must now be taken. Bloch would have been better advised to keep his mouth shut.

"Lessons will certainly be learned," said Simon, sharply, "and we should do nothing to impede Manfred as he climbs what must be for him a steep learning curve. But, in the meantime, the rest of us at this meeting had best focus on organising a definitive response to the aberration and to the cadre that conceived and then initiated it, despite..." (and this he added solely for the benefit of Manfred Bloch) "the best efforts of our technical division."

"Then we must employ the services of a practitioner."

This was the first contribution made by John Noble, the Praesidium's Chairman, a powerfully built, distinguished-looking man of above average height in his mid-fifties, a figure who exuded a natural authority. He always preferred to give Board members a chance to air their views before taking a decision – not that their views affected the decision; he simply liked to take soundings of the members' mood.

The suggestion that the Praesidium was in need of the help of a practitioner caused a general stir and not a few gasps. It was many years since the Praesidium had felt the need to summon a practitioner, and it was not a decision to be taken lightly. First of all, the services of a practitioner were expensive, very expensive. Secondly, it demonstrated that the Praesidium could not deal with a problem without help. Thirdly, and most importantly, the employment of a practitioner meant that, at least temporarily, the Praesidium must relinquish control of events.

"Do you think that is really necessary?" enquired Manfred Bloch, uncowed by Simon Goodfellow's admonition.

"I very much doubt I would have suggested it," said the Chairman softly, gently stroking his neatly trimmed grey moustache with the thumb and forefinger of his right hand, "had I thought it unnecessary."

Encouraged by the Chairman's quietly spoken but nonetheless incisive rebuke of Bloch, Simon Goodfellow decided to put the knife in.

"Our technical director seems to have failed to grasp how close we came to disaster. The Storyteller's latest cadre came within a whisker of initiating a beginning – what would have been the fourth beginning. The consequences would have been incalculable but they would certainly have included the end of this Praesidium and all we have worked for. We would have lost our grip on the nodes of power; we would have lost control of future history; to our eternal shame, we would have failed to fulfil the prime directive. This building, this magnificent parallel construct, would have been destroyed and we would have been destroyed within it."

John Noble briefly pondered whether you could endure eternal shame if you were abruptly destroyed, but Simon hadn't finished.

"All that would remain on this site would be the ludicrous mother of parliaments and the pathetic political elite of unenlightened humans who would persist in believing the fiction that they exercise any real power. There is no doubt in my mind, nor in the mind of anyone capable of clear thinking, that we need the intervention of a practitioner."

2. The end of the beginning

A week before the meeting of the Praesidium, the Storyteller was sitting on his favourite bench outside the Elm Tree pub on the outskirts of Ringwood in Hampshire, enjoying the brilliant sunlight and a fourth pint of Guinness, half of which he had already drunk.

'It doesn't get any better than this,' he mused, as he lifted the glass from the table. 'A sunny day, a pint of Guinness and, after years of trial, tribulation and failure, success at last.'

It was indeed a sunny day. The normal sunshine that fills a clear blue sky was augmented by the expanding ring of intense light engendered by the fourth beginning.

The Storyteller continued his happy musings. By now Prune Leach, the short, wizened Irish engineering genius, and his equally brilliant, but much taller, rather less extrovert, partner Andrew Rimzil must be well on their way to Wales in the questors' van. In the back of the van, Optimius, the sanguine penguin, and Elsa, the imperfect seal, would be happily consolidating their bizarre friendship despite their widely differing backgrounds and incongruous physical proportions. Above all, they would be revelling in a substantiality which neither had dreamed possible, nor thought themselves worthy of. (After all, Optimius was merely the offspring of a whimsical urge to explore an odd consonantal combination, and Elsa had quite simply been sired by an anagrammatic pun - in neither case, a favourable provenance for an existential miracle!)

Adam and Eve Smith would be back in their home in

Harrow. They would be coming to terms with what they, with the help of Rambler, Numpty and Kit, not forgetting Luke, their golden retriever, had somehow achieved. No, not coming to terms with, rather beginning to explore the extraordinary implications of the process they had initiated.

The Storyteller was pondering all these happy thoughts when the light started to flicker. Now, of course sunlight shining through a clear blue sky doesn't really flicker. I suppose if a bird flies overhead it may seem momentarily that something has interrupted the flow of light over a very small area. And certainly clouds can make the sunlight seem to flicker. But there were no clouds. And the flickering, although brief, affected the landscape - or so it seemed to the Storyteller - as far as the eye could see. When the flickering stopped, the sky was still blue and the sun was still shining, but there was something missing. The sunlight was still bright, but now it was normal; it was no longer exceptional.

The Storyteller stood up and immediately staggered forward, steadying himself by putting both hands on the table.

"Oh no!" he choked. "It's not possible; it cannot be possible."

But it was more than possible. It had happened. The fourth beginning had ended almost as soon as it had begun.

oooOooo

"What on earth are you doing?" shouted the usually equable Andrew Rimzil as Prune Leach threw the camper van across the three lanes of the M4 and screeched to a halt on the hard shoulder. The unexpected manoeuvre had given Andrew's long frame quite a buffeting.

"Didn't you see it? Didn't you feel it?" Prune Leach demanded. Prune's wrinkled brown face had gone pale.

"See what? Feel what?" Andrew asked, and then silently withdrew the question. Now he saw and felt what Prune had meant.

"Oh, Jesus!" said Prune. "Look in the back."

Optimius, the sanguine penguin, was nestling into the bulky body of Elsa, the imperfect seal. Optimius's eyes were filled with terror.

"Don't worry," said Elsa soothingly, gently patting the penguin with her flipper. "Don't worry. We're together."

She had intended to say "Don't worry. Everything will be all right," but had changed her mind, because she instinctively knew that it wasn't and wouldn't be.

"Hold on," Prune shouted. "Hold on, both of you."

Elsa nodded, to indicate she would try.

The dissolution affected Optimius first. His smaller size made him more quickly vulnerable.

"Please help me," Optimius pleaded, as holes began to appear in his body.

"Can't you do something?" Prune demanded of Andrew Rimzil.

Andrew shook his head. "There's nothing I can do," he said. "Somehow, despite everything, they've stopped it." He turned to address Elsa and Optimius. "I'm so sorry," he said. "Hold close to each other."

By now, Optimius had lost almost half of his substance, and Elsa also had large holes appearing in the fabric of her body.

"They're unsustainable," Andrew said quietly to Prune. "At least the dissolution is painless."

"It may be without pain but it's not without fear," observed Prune. He could see Optimius was now just a smudge on Elsa's failing form.

"Thank you, both of you," Prune said. "We will not forget you."

And it was over. The work of the Praesidium had made sure there was nothing to sustain the two unique aquatic creatures, given substance and life in the real world solely by the now-aborted fourth beginning.

oooOooo

Adam was at work when it happened. He had noticed the flickering light and had at first assumed it was an electrical fault in the power supply. No one else in the office seemed to have noticed anything. Then he knew. It was over.

oooOooo

Eve was at home finishing an article for a local newspaper on balancing a household budget. When the light started to flicker, she stopped typing and sat silently staring out of the window in the study for two or three minutes. The sun was still shining, but the sunlight was now no more than the light of the sun before the fourth beginning, not the light that had radiated across the world after the fourth beginning had blossomed. So it had failed; they had failed. Someone or something had stopped it. She felt a deep sadness and a profound sense of foreboding.

Just then, Luke, the ever-faithful family dog, ran into the study and rubbed against Eve's legs, trying to give them both some comfort.

"Life must go on," said Eve, without any great conviction.

"Abso-bloody-lutely," replied Luke, although of course Eve couldn't hear him.

3. The Parallel Parliament

On the Wednesday that the Praesidium had met, a session of Prime Minister's Questions had been in full swing in the identical but distinctly separate parallel location of the House of Commons.

Once the traditional cross-party tributes to young men killed in current overseas military engagements were concluded, the jousting had begun in earnest.

The Leader of the Opposition was banging on about the National Health Service which, according to her, was unsafe in anyone's hands other than hers. Without the money her party proposed to add to the existing budget (an indeterminate sum but considerably more than whatever the government finally decided to spend), the NHS, the jewel in the crown (not an entirely appropriate metaphor for a largely republican party) would be destroyed.

The Prime Minister replied that, while he loved the NHS at least as much as the honourable lady, he preferred to concentrate on the economy, pointing out that the country had so much debt that the annual interest on the debt alone was already greater than half the entire annual health service budget.

"If the national economy were a business, the country would be bankrupt," said the Prime Minister. "You could say that, without borrowing, this country would not be able to afford a health service at all, let alone a national health service free at the point of need."

"Well who's running the economy?" snapped the Leader of the Opposition. "At last we have a straight answer from the

Prime Minister. This Government believes we cannot afford a health service of any kind, much less the one we all love and which, as I have said before, is safe only in our hands."

This sally produced a roar of approval from the opposition benches.

"I see," said the Prime Minister, adopting his most authoritative voice, "that the honourable lady is determined to play politics with the Health Service. Well, it will not do. We have invested more in the NHS than any government in the entire history of the NHS and will continue to do so. The Opposition's open-ended promise to spend more on the NHS than us is palpably idiotic. We will spend every penny the country can afford. This must mean the Opposition intends to spend more money than the country can afford – a temptation to which, I might add, the Opposition invariably succumbs whenever the opportunity presents itself. That will mean even more borrowing, greater debt, still more onerous interest payments."

"There is an alternative to borrowing," replied the Leader of the Opposition. "It is time the rich took their fair share of the burden. We propose to increase taxes on the wealthy so that they will feel they truly belong to the society in which they live and from which they make their money."

Howls of delight from the Opposition benches.

"Fine chance!" muttered the Chancellor of the Exchequer. "Pull that one, and they'll all bugger off."

4. Engineering

On the day the fourth beginning ended, Prune Leach and Andrew Rimzil had a decision to make.

Prune was more affected by the dissolution of Elsa and Optimius than his fellow engineer. He had grown particularly fond of the ebullient and ever optimistic Optimius. He admired the sanguine penguin's courage and the determination with which the little fellow had thrown himself into the quest. As for Elsa, she had played a crucial role in giving them access to the Breakers' mysland domain and blocking the alarm signal. Without her help, the quest would certainly have failed.

Of course Prune recognised that both creatures had attained existence through narrative quirks. In a sense, the flatulent Gwoat, the Storyteller's now-deceased driver, had been Optimius's progenitor, the casually unaware participant in a linguistic one night stand. And Elsa, the imperfect seal, had come into being purely as a narrative and anagrammatic expedient. But such ruminations entirely failed to do either of the creatures justice. Both of them had played a crucial role in the quest. More than that, both of them had developed personalities. They had shown loyalty to the questors and affection to each other. No, their passing was a bad, a tragic, business.

"We should have done something," Prune said, addressing Andrew Rimzil, who was standing on the hard shoulder of the M4, apparently checking the tyres of the camper van.

"There was nothing we could do. There was no time.

And even if there had been time, I'm pretty sure there was nothing we could have done. The fourth beginning was terminated. Just imagine the power of those who stopped it, whoever or whatever they are."

"Really?" replied Prune, the lines on his wrinkled brow adopting a predominantly vertical mode "Really? So you're saying the inventors of the exponential drive and the paradox device – two inventions which, if made generally available, would at least speed up, if not radically alter, the course of human history – could do nothing to save the lives of two harmless, benign and entirely positive animals."

"Yes," replied Andrew, patiently. "I know you're upset. I'm upset. But the moment the fourth beginning faltered, their fate was sealed. Don't blame yourself, and don't blame me. Why the fourth beginning failed, I don't know. It seems the Breakers – assuming it was them – are more powerful than we thought. If you feel the need to blame anyone in our group, blame the Storyteller. He knew that Optimius and Elsa depended for their continued existence on the fourth beginning and that, if the quest failed, they would be destroyed. And yet he ushered them into being."

"If you continue to stand on the hard shoulder," said Prune, frustrated that he had no answer to Andrew's reasoning, "you're likely to be ushered out of being - or at least arrested by the police."

Andrew climbed back into the van, settling his long frame into the passenger seat.

"So what do we do now?" asked Prune. "We could go on, but my heart's not in it. The whole point of racing off to the Welsh coast was to let Elsa and Optimius cavort in the Irish Sea. I can't see you or me cavorting at the best of times, and I certainly don't feel like cavorting now."

"I think we must return to Ringwood. I'm hoping the Storyteller is still there. We need to know why the fourth beginning was aborted."

"Do we?" asked Prune grumpily. "I'm not sure it's any of our business. We joined the questors because Kit asked us to. It wasn't our quest. We were just doing Kit a favour. What's more, whatever stopped the fourth beginning seems to be pretty powerful and pretty determined. It eliminated Elsa and Optimius without a second thought, and I suspect it wouldn't hesitate to destroy anyone else who upset it."

"Not like you to back away from a fight," Andrew opined. "It's me who is usually the cautious one."

"I'm not backing away from a fight," said Prune. "I'm just asking whether it's our fight. And even if, in some way, it is our fight, whether the fight isn't already over? And we lost."

"There's only one way to find answers," said Andrew. "We need to talk to the Storyteller. So let's come off at the next junction and head back to Ringwood. The first pint of Guinness is on me."

5. Conference at the Elm Tree

When Prune Leach and Andrew Rimzil reached the Elm Tree pub in the late afternoon, they found the Storyteller sitting where they had left him, on one of the benches outside the pub. He had a single empty glass on the table in front of him.

"I thought you might come back."

"What happened?" asked Prune. Surely, if anyone knew the answer, it would be the Storyteller.

"It stopped," replied the Storyteller.

"I know it stopped," said Prune. "But why did it stop? What stopped it?"

"I don't know," the Storyteller replied.

"You know Elsa and Optimius were destroyed," said Prune. It sounded like an accusation, and indeed it was.

"I guessed as much. I'm very sorry; I was sure we had done it. I know there can be false beginnings, but I was certain we had succeeded this time. I really thought we had put everything in place."

"How about a drink?" suggested Andrew Rimzil. "I'll get the first round. Three pints of Guinness?"

Andrew set off into the pub to fetch the drinks. Prune sat down opposite the Storyteller. "So what happens now?"

"No idea," the Storyteller answered. Prune realised the man was deeply depressed.

"Well do we try to restart the beginning, or do we just walk away?" Prune probed.

"A beginning is not like a car or a van," the Storyteller answered. "You can't just restart it. The chances of initiating a beginning are one in a million, one in a billion, one in a trillion. The odds against being able to put everything in place are astronomical. That's why I was so happy when it seemed we had succeeded. Of course I had hoped to see a beginning in my life time but I had not expected it. No one has a right to expect it. And yet we came close, so close."

"There we are," said Andrew, carefully putting the tray down on the bench. "One pint apiece."

All three picked up a glass and drank.

"So what do we do?" asked Andrew.

Prune answered. "Well it seems we do nothing. It seems we failed and there's nothing we can do about it. We put in an enormous amount of effort, gave it our best shot, made full use of the exponential drive and the paradox device – in short, did everything we could – and it still just wasn't good enough."

"I'm not blaming you," said the Storyteller.

"That's big of you," snapped Prune. "I wasn't planning to take the blame. If we're going to blame anyone..."

Andrew interrupted: "Blaming anyone is pointless. We simply have to decide whether there is anything worth trying now and, if there is, whether we want to try it."

"There isn't. So we can't." said the Storyteller.

"So that's it. Andrew and I pop back over to Ireland and carry on as though nothing has happened."

Prune Leach finished his pint and banged the glass down onto the wooden table with some force. The glass shattered. There were shards of glass everywhere.

"Bugger!" Prune exclaimed.

"That's certainly no way to treat a chalice of Guinness, a cup of black gold, or a goblet of the divine nectar," said a voice that all three of them recognised. "And 'bugger' is no way to greet an old friend."

My God," said Prune and Andrew in unison, "Kit, it's you."

"I think it's probably your round," said Kit, addressing Prune.

Kit settled himself on to the bench beside Andrew in the only available space with an ease and accuracy that belied his sightless eyes.

"It's great to see you," said Prune, getting up, "although I've no idea what all that drivel about chalices, etc. was about."

Andrew and the Storyteller also stood up, and, with feigned reluctance, Kit arose to give each of them a warm embrace.

"It's good to be with you all again," he conceded as he resumed his seat, "although it could have been in happier circumstance."

Prune trundled off to buy the drinks.

"We were discussing what we should do now," said the Storyteller. "I was explaining to our Irish friend that it is hopeless."

"I'll admit we have had a setback," said Kit, "a major setback. But hopelessness is a state of mind. Feeling hopeless guarantees failure. What about the three beginnings: the universe, life and consciousness? Looking for them to happen before they had happened would have seemed hopeless – but they happened."

"Are you saying we should hope for a miracle?" asked Andrew, who was by no means dismissing the possibility out of hand.

"You can hope for a miracle if you like but such a leap into the supernatural is unnecessary. The first three beginnings were not miracles; they were just incredibly unlikely. Take this glass," said Kit, proudly displaying a perfectly clean glass. "See its flawless, stable form; see how perfectly if fills the space it occupies; see how it precisely delineates the boundaries between what it contains and everything else. It's all unlikely but nonetheless real and true."

"Have you been drinking?" asked Andrew. It was not like Kit to ramble.

"I may have taken a little refreshment at the last hostelry I passed, or rather patronised, in the course of my travels," Kit replied.

Just as Prune was returning with the four pints of Guinness, one of the bar staff, a young lad on work experience charged with clearing the tables outside the pub, collected four empty glasses from the table, making room for Prune's round.

"So what are you suggesting?" asked the Storyteller.

"In my opinion," said Kit, with only the slightest hint of a slur, "we should sit here and drink until the pain of failure is assuaged, and the flickering candle of hope burns more brightly. Tomorrow, we should make plans to contact the Smiths after allowing them a reasonable period of time to adjust to the new situation. When Adam and Eve are ready, we need to take soundings. But, for now, let us drown our sorrows in the sea of experience until some flotsam of optimism bobs to the surface. "

So, persuaded by Kit's metaphorical flourish, that is exactly what they did. Only Andrew Rimzil noticed that there were no shards of glass on the table. And even Andrew had failed to notice how many empty glasses the lad had taken away.

6. The Job Opportunity

A month after the fourth beginning had been terminated, Adam Smith returned home from work in good spirits. Eve was surprised. From the moment the fourth beginning had failed, their lives had sunk back into a dull, humdrum routine, a routine that had seemed tolerable before they had set out with the Storyteller on the quest, but which now seemed deeply depressing and pointless.

"You seem happy," said Eve, as though she was accusing him of inappropriate behaviour.

"I've been head-hunted," said Adam proudly.

"You've been what?"

"I've been head-hunted. You know. A firm of consultants wants to talk to me about a job – a much better job, with a lot more money."

"Are you sure?" asked Eve.

"There's no need to sound quite so surprised," Adam responded with mock-petulance. "Of course I'm sure. A chap called David Minofel contacted me on my mobile. He said he wants to meet me. I checked out his credentials, and he's a partner in Slievins, a leading head-hunting consultancy in the City."

"Well, I suppose that's good news," said Eve.

"Don't overdo the joy thing. I thought you'd be pleased. Quite a lot has gone wrong recently. This has to be good news."

Eve sighed. Perhaps Adam was right but she still couldn't muster any enthusiasm. In the company of the Storyteller, they had been on a mind-enlightening, soul-challenging, spiritually-uplifting quest that had included an interview with God; a sojourn with Prometheus; an excursion through space and time; and, for Adam, a spell in hell. In the end, with the help of Rambler and Numpty, and of course the blind man Kit, they had seemed to prevail. They had somehow initiated the fourth beginning. OK, the fourth beginning had been stopped, aborted by people unknown, probably Breakers. But the attempt had been heroic, noble, truly inspirational. Adam's news of a possible promotion and enhanced salary, while welcome enough, was not really in the same league. Indeed there was something rather demeaning about it. They had sought the truth. They had glimpsed the truth. They had achieved something remarkable. No, a better job and a salary hike were not the stuff of which great stories are made. No, not all. Or so Eve thought.

"Come on, Eve," Adam interrupted Eve's thoughts. "Give a man some encouragement. They're a top consultancy, dealing in top jobs. They wouldn't have contacted me if they didn't have something pretty impressive in mind."

"Yes," said Eve, desperately trying to sound more positive than she felt. "Yes, of course. It's good news. Well done. So what happens now?"

"Well, it's all a bit of a rush," Adam replied, relieved that Eve seemed to responding positively at last. "I guess they have a post they want to fill pretty urgently. This Minofel chap wants to meet me tomorrow – here, at home. He wants to meet both of us, wants to see that we're a stable partnership, have all the right values – you know what these consultants are like."

'Oh dear,' thought Luke, the golden retriever. 'Eve won't like that: having to put on a show for a business consultant intruding into her home. What had their home life to do with a stranger? What right had he to assess them? What did he know about what they had been through?'

But Luke was wrong. Eve didn't want an argument. To be honest, she didn't feel up to it. If Adam wanted the job, she would put up with it, even do her best to help.

The collapse of the fourth beginning had taken more out of her than she or Luke had realised.

7. Practitioner selection

John Noble, Praesidium chairman, sat silently in the chair at the head of the boardroom table. He was awaiting the arrival of the practitioner who had answered the Praesidium's appeal. This was the day of the signing of the contract that he had agreed in order to retain the practitioner's services. There was fresh coffee in the coffee machine at the refreshment table; fresh cream and milk in chilled jugs; and, laid out in perfectly symmetrical form, the special dark chocolate-chip biscuits reserved for the most distinguished of boardroom guests. Behind the table was an impressively stocked drinks cabinet but, given the time (mid-morning), the cabinet doors were locked.

Although confident that he had made the right decision, John Noble still had mixed feelings about calling in a practitioner. It was, after all, an admission of weakness, and no chairman likes to appear weak. And certainly no chairman of the Praesidium could afford to appear in any way vulnerable.

That was why seated at the chairman's right hand was Simon Goodfellow, the vice-chair. Goodfellow had never shown the slightest sign of disloyalty to the chairman, which had immediately made John Noble suspicious. At least Manfred Bloch, the only other obvious contender for his position, had, from time to time, argued against the chairman's decisions – but not Goodfellow.

The present case was a good example. Noble had decided that the Praesidium needed help from a practitioner. Goodfellow had unreservedly supported the Chairman.

Bloch had dismissed, even sneered at, what he implied was the Chairman's over-reaction to a danger that had already passed. He had really been quite irritating: "If we are to call on a practitioner when the danger has been averted, what are we to do, and what will it cost, when the danger is real and imminent?"

The only excuse for the technical director was that he was so insensitive, so thick-skinned himself, that he probably had little idea how offensive he could be to others. If Bloch was ever foolish enough to challenge for the presidency, John Noble would certainly have every opportunity to see it coming – and to deal with it.

Manfred Bloch's weakness was his exceedingly pretty wife Kathrin, a moderately successful actress. Sadly her physical beauty was not matched by an equally high standard of morality. What she had ever seen in the overweight, ponderous, tactless Manfred – apart, of course, from his substantial income as Technical Director of the Praesidium – was anyone's guess. But, whatever it was, its appeal had evidently faded, as a series of furtive affairs with fellow luvvies and even once or twice with Manfred's underlings, both male and female, amply demonstrated. Well, amply demonstrated to everyone that is, except Manfred who doted on Kathrin and who seemed blissfully unaware of her numerous peccadillos. If Manfred were ever to nurture thoughts of seizing control of the Praesidium, revelations of his wife's lubricity would certainly deflate his ego, his self-respect and, more importantly, his ambitions. Why had no one told Manfred of his wife's promiscuity? Well, in such cases, the injured party is often the last to know and, in Manfred's case, his short temper, violent disposition and brute strength were certainly contributing factors to the general reticence.

Simon Goodfellow, on the other hand, was a different matter. Simon, John Noble was sure, would be totally loyal up to the moment that he slid the knife between the Chairman's shoulder blades. Of course, he might remain totally loyal forever but it was always best to err on the side of caution in matters of security. In any case, you could never wholly trust a man whose thin lips had a habit of disappearing completely at moments of heightened emotion. So the file John Noble held on the dubious business dealings and the peculiarly unsavoury sexual predilections of his deputy constituted a useful insurance policy. Even so, if either of his subordinates were to stand against him, John Noble was sure that it would be Simon who posed the graver threat. The problem with the insurance policy was that there were few members of the Praesidium who had not engaged in dubious business practices, some of them in cahoots with Goodfellow himself. Even the revelation of Goodfellow's deviant sexual appetites might not prove decisive, since there were rumours Simon was merely a leading member of a sexually deviant ring within the Praesidium.

'Dear, dear!' John Noble mused, 'what a piece of work is a man!' by which he meant to indicate that he had a rather less favourable assessment of man's attributes than Hamlet.

Anyway, as part of John Noble's general policy of caution, Simon was seated beside the Chairman in the boardroom on the Chairman's right hand to make it clear to all the members of the Praesidium that the vice-chair had not merely supported the chairman's decision to seek outside help but had also been involved in formulating and, crucially, had approved the terms of the contract they were about to sign.

And what they were offering was quite a deal. In terms of

remuneration, the fees would stretch even the Praesidium's commodious budget, but it was not so much the money that would cause controversy as the terms. The practitioner had demanded total control of the case until its successful conclusion.

'Complete control' worried the Praesidium's lawyers. This phrase would allow the practitioner to interfere in any and every way, at any and every level, of human society. But John Noble had overruled the lawyers' concerns by pointing out that, if the practitioner failed, the Praesidium would lose control of humanity anyway.

The other condition that caused panic bells to ring in the collective mind of the Praesidium's enormous legal department was 'until the successful conclusion of the case'. On a first reading, this had sounded perfectly reasonable. They were hiring an expert; the expert needed the freedom to exercise his skills. He needed complete control. He would relinquish control as soon as the job was done.

On a second reading, someone queried what would happen if the practitioner wasn't able to succeed. Did that mean he would retain complete control despite a temporary, or even a permanent, failure? Indeed, another lawyer tentatively suggested that, if the Praesidium signed such a contract, the practitioner might be tempted to fail, or at least to delay success, in order to retain control. This suggestion persuaded the legal team to revisit the definition of success.

The original draft had defined success as: "the elimination of any possibility that the recent cadre, led by Terence Torrance, a.k.a. the Storyteller, which had set out on a quest to answer the questions of Adam and Eve Smith, a married couple currently resident in Harrow, would regroup and resume their efforts to initiate an anathema."

An anathema was the legal term for any major event which was not in the Praesidium's interests.

The practitioner had insisted 'anathema' should be changed to 'fourth beginning.' He had argued anathema was too general and too vague. His job was to ensure Adam and Eve and their friends, who had come so close to triggering the fourth beginning, would never again embark on such an enterprise. If the cadre found some other way of upsetting the Praesidium, that would be a separate issue and would be subject to a separate contract, either with him or a fellow practitioner. And, of course, further remuneration.

John Noble tried to keep out of the detailed negotiations, insisting these were primarily legal matters. He sent Simon Goodfellow to act as his representative at these interminable legalistic wrangling sessions.

"I think you should remind our lawyers that they are not being paid by the hour," he had exploded one morning, when Simon reported to him that he and the legal team had worked until midnight the previous evening. "I know many of them have been recruited from private practice, but here they have no need to work long hours to inflate the invoice."

"We are simply trying to arrive at a wording that, while meeting the practitioner's requirements, also protects the Praesidium's interest," Goodfellow replied, somewhat hurt.

"Yes, yes. I know," the Chairman sighed. "But, let's face it, when you hire a practitioner, he dictates the terms. Our protection is simply that he and we are on the same side."

In the end, John Noble was proved right. The contract they had come to sign today was, in essence, the one drafted by the practitioner. His one significant concession was that instead of full payment up front (the usual terms of business required by practitioners), in view of the length of time fulfilment might take and to allay any concerns that he might not expedite the matter as quickly as possible, he had agreed to take just 50% on signing; he would receive the other 50% on satisfactory completion of the task.

"He's late," said John Noble.

He hated unpunctuality. It was a sign of incompetence or rudeness or both. He started to pull his papers together, as though preparing to leave. Yes, practitioners were highly skilled and therefore very important but that did not entitle them to be discourteous to others of equal rank.

There was a crisp knock on the boardroom door, but before either Noble or Goodfellow could answer, it swung open and a voice said "Good morning, gentlemen. Let's get on with it."

8. An eventful evening

"It must be Minofel," said Adam. "He's early."

It was 6.00 p.m., and David Minofel of the Slievins Consultancy had set the time for his visit at 6.30 p.m.

"He's probably trying to catch us out," said Eve helpfully. "Come early while they're trying to tidy up and put everything in order. Good way to put us off balance."

"I doubt that," replied Adam. "He's here to sell me a job."

Adam stood up. "You'd better shut Luke in the dining room. We don't want his hairs all over Mr Minofel."

Obligingly, Luke trotted into the dining room, and Eve closed the door. She then went through to the kitchen to check on the casserole. Since they didn't know how long Minofel intended to stay, Eve had prepared a slow-roasting casserole which could be eaten at any time in the evening.

Adam opened the front door, ready to greet his visitor.

The pepper hit his face and burnt his eyes before he could take in the shapes of the two burly men outside who shoved him back into the hallway, strode into the house and slammed the door behind them.

Eve heard Adam's muffled cry as he choked on the pepper in his throat, and she heard the door slam. "What's happened?" she asked, as she ran through from the kitchen.

One of the intruders immediately grabbed her by one arm, swung her round and slapped her hard across the face. Eve fell to the floor. Adam was already lying on his back, pinned to the floor. The other man was kneeling heavily on Adam's stomach while wrapping duct tape across his mouth.

"OK Darren, tie her up and gag her," said the man who

was kneeling on Adam. He threw the roll of duct tape to his accomplice. "I'll see what they've got."

"Check the bedrooms for a safe, Kev," said Darren. "That's where they'll keep anything worth having, i'n'it?"

Kev thought of rebuking Darren for stating the blindingly obvious, and, of course, for addressing him by name. But then he remembered he had already called Darren by name, so he let it go. Kev emptied every drawer in the bedrooms. He found Eve's jewellery and stuffed it all into a duffel bag he had brought with him. He found some cash in the bottom of a drawer in Adam's bedside table, and that too was thrown into the duffel bag.

"Ask the wanker where the safe is," Kev shouted down to Darren.

"You heard him," snarled Darren, ripping the duct tape away from Adam's mouth. "Where's the safe?"

"I can't see," said Adam. His eyes felt like two poached eggs.

"You don't need to see," snapped Darren. "You just need to talk. You can talk, can't you? Where's the fucking safe?"

"We don't have a safe," said Adam.

"He says they don't have a safe," Darren shouted up the stairs to Kev.

"Well he would say that, wouldn't he, you moron? Make him tell you where it is."

"You heard the man," said Darren, taking out a knife. "You'd better tell me."

"I can't tell you, because we don't have safe," said Adam. His sight was beginning to clear a little and he could see his tormentor vaguely through a red haze.

Darren pressed the knife against Adam's stomach, hard enough for the point to penetrate the skin.

"If you don't start talking, I'm going to push this knife

right in, up to the hilt. I saw a bloke do it in a film and he said it would take an hour to die. So how do you fancy that for a game of soldiers?"

"We don't have a safe but we do have some cash. There's some in a drawer beside my bed, and there's more in the wardrobe. The floor inside comes up, and there's a couple of thousand underneath. That's it. Everything else is in the bank."

"Did you hear that?" Darren shouted up to Kev. "There's some money in the wardrobe."

"OK, I've got it. I've already found it," said Kev, as he thudded down the stairs.

"So what have we got?" asked Darren, still holding the knife to Adam's stomach.

"A load of jewellery and about two and half k. Not much for all the effort."

"Better than a kick in the teeth," observed Darren wisely. "Time to go, i'n'it?"

"*Time to go, i'n'it* ?" Kev mocked his companion. "No, it's not time to go, not yet. There's still the little lady to think about. She hasn't given us anything – not even a cup of tea. In fact, she's been a bit tight-lipped since we got here. But I'm pretty sure I can get her to open up."

Adam started to struggle but Darren pressed the knife half an inch into Adam's stomach.

"You stay where you are," warned Darren.

"I think the little lady should show us a bit of hospitality." Kev was now kneeling beside Eve. "She's not a bad looker. Probably pretty tasty if you hadn't smacked her in the face. She's got a good body," he added, running his hands over her breasts."

"Get your hands off her," screamed Adam, struggling to

rise despite the knife in his stomach.

"It's a pity you didn't take her knickers off before you taped her legs together," observed Kev. He looked into Eve's eyes, hoping to see fear. In fact, he saw nothing. Her eyes were blank, which was just as well because, behind the blank, there was only one emotion - pure hate.

"You and I are going to get better acquainted," sneered Kev, starting to tear Eve's dress off.

Darren himself was quite excited. "*Acquainted!*" You had to hand it to Kev, he thought to himself, he didn't half have a gift for words.

Kev was undoing his belt when the doorbell rang.

"You'd better deal with that," said Kev.

"Why me? Why can't you?" Darren responded. "I'm holding this one down."

The doorbell rang again.

"Just answer the fucking door," snapped Kev. "He's tied up. Stick the duct tape back on his mouth. And get rid of the visitor. I can't answer the door with my trousers round my ankles; it wouldn't be appropriate."

Darren got up to obey his friend. 'There he goes again,' he thought, "a*ppropriate*". Lovely choice of words! What a gift!'

Darren opened the door. On the step was a very well-dressed man, a little under six foot tall, in his late thirties or early forties.

"My name is Minofel, David Minofel. I have come to see Adam Smith."

Darren looked at David Minofel and decided the visitor was a bit of a prat. With his dapper dark grey suit, pink shirt and red tie, he looked like a bloke from the city. He probably earnt more money in a year than he and Kev had stolen in their lives.

"He's not available," said Darren.

Darren was used to telling people Kev was 'not available'. One of the things Darren enjoyed about working with Kev was the chance to expand his vocabulary. 'Not available' was so much classier than 'not here'. 'Not available' meant Kev was probably doing something important. 'Not here' just meant he wasn't there.

"Are you sure?" asked the City prat.

"He's not in," explained Darren, disappointed that his first answer had failed to settle the matter. "So he's not available."

"I see. Then please tell him I called and that I will see him soon."

With that, David Minofel turned around and walked down the path.

Darren closed the door and went back inside. Kev, his trousers round his ankles, was standing with his foot on Adam's head.

"Here," said Kev, "you take over. He was trying to get up and was making a noise, so I had to put the boot in. I want to get on with missy over there."

Kev went over to Eve and knelt beside her.

"Think of this like a trip to the dentist. It's going to hurt you a lot more than it's going to hurt me."

Kev was so intent on stripping Eve, at least sufficiently to facilitate penetration, that he heard neither the front door swinging open, nor the sure-footed manoeuvres of the figure that shot silently into the room. The first he knew of the arrival was a cracking sound and a voice saying: "I think you may have miscalculated who is going to feel the most pain."

Kev turned round. Darren was lying on the floor, his head at an unusual angle. Kev stood up, the blood draining immediately from his erection. “Oi! Darren, what’s going on?” he shouted. Then, realising he was unlikely to receive an answer, he addressed the stranger. “Who the fuck are you, and what have you done to Darren?”

“Taking your questions in reverse order, I have made the world a slightly better place,” Minofel explained affably.

Kev pulled up his trousers and tightened his belt. He didn’t know who the stranger was and he certainly didn’t understand how he had found his way into the house. Surely Darren hadn’t left the door open when he got rid of the visitor. Well, none of that mattered now. The stranger had to be dealt with. Kev was a big man, a fit man who could handle himself. The stranger looked fairly spry, but he was shorter and lighter than Kev and, in any case, he looked as though he’d be happier pruning the roses of an evening, rather than going three rounds with an ex-light-heavyweight who had been fancied as a good championship prospect a few years back.

Kev eyed Minofel. “You shouldn’t be here,” he said, opening a flick knife that he kept in his trouser pocket.

“Oh dear,” said David Minofel, “I really don’t respond well to ‘should’ and ‘shouldn’t’. They smack of some kind of moral judgement which, in your case, is peculiarly inappropriate.”

Kev didn’t really understand what the intruder was saying but he realised the man was talking down to him. He needed a lesson. A well-aimed slash with the knife across the throat would shut him up. Kev moved forward.

With extraordinary speed, Minofel kicked Kev just above the knee, shattering the joint. Kev fell to the ground, emitting an all-but-silent shriek of agony. “I know,” soothed David. “Excruciating, isn’t it? You might like to revisit your earlier pain prediction.”

Leaving Kev writhing on the floor, Minofel turned to Eve, untied her and put his jacket over her torn dress. Then he released Adam. Both Adam and Eve were shaking uncontrollably. "It's over," he said, and his voice had such authority that both Adam and Eve knew that, despite the horrific and bizarre circumstances, everything was under control.

Eve spoke first. "We don't know how to thank you," she said.

"No need for thanks," replied their saviour. "No need at all. We do, however, have to decide what to do now."

"We'd better call the police," suggested Eve.

"And an ambulance," hazarded Adam, who was bleeding from the flesh wound to his stomach.

While Eve and Adam were making their suggestions, David Minofel knelt beside the weeping Kev, who was passing in and out of consciousness because of the intensity of the pain. "I think you have probably suffered enough," whispered Minofel into Kev's ear as he pressed his thumb firmly into Kev's carotid artery, adding "I'll be having you cremated. I hope that's OK with you."

Kev looked up at his executioner. He knew he was going to die. He knew there was no point in appealing for mercy. He realised he was going to hell. He had no preferences regarding burial or cremation, so he simply nodded his assent before fading into final unconsciousness.

"I'll phone the police," said Eve, still shaking.

"I should wait a couple of minutes," suggested Minofel. As soon he was sure Kev was dead, he stood up. "What a pickle. Right, if you want to phone the police now, go ahead, but I must point out that if you do, our lives are going to be seriously disrupted for several months and the outcome may not be entirely happy." He paused for a moment, before adding, "For you or for me."

Both Adam and Eve were confused.

"First things first, let me look at your wound," David continued, addressing Adam.

Adam showed Minofel where Darren had cut him.

"It's a nasty incision, but fortunately, it hasn't penetrated the stomach lining. I have a first aid kit in my car outside. We can sort this out ourselves. No need for screaming sirens and raucous bells – unless you really want them."

"Hold on," said Eve, regaining a little composure. "We have two burglars, both seriously injured, lying in our sitting room. Where I come from, that's the kind of thing for which you call the police."

"Of course, I understand," David responded. "Just on a point of fact, though. They're not injured. They were injured. Now they're dead."

Adam was not surprised the burglar Darren was dead. He hadn't seen everything but the extraordinary ease with which the stranger had come out of nowhere, descended upon Darren and broken his neck, was imprinted on Adam's mind. Kev on the other hand had only sustained a kick to the leg and, however painful the shattering of the knee joint, such injuries rarely proved fatal.

Minofel seemed to read Adam's mind. "I put him out of his misery," he explained simply. "By the way", he added. "My name's Minofel, David Minofel."

"You killed him?" said Eve. She was much less horrified than she felt she should have been. This man, who had saved her and Adam, had done exactly what she had wanted to do to the burglars.

"Look", said David, "I need to explain a few things. "I

came here tonight to discuss a job opportunity, a really exciting job opportunity, with your husband. That's what I do. I'm a head-hunter."

"I know, said Eve, "Adam told me."

"But I haven't always been in business. After university, I spent seven years in the SAS. After that, I was employed for another ten years as a mercenary. I worked in Afghanistan, Iraq, Libya, Mali and Sudan. I'm telling you this because it complicates what happened here this evening."

Adam and Eve said nothing. They were trying to process what had happened and what Minofel was saying.

"Look," David continued. "My chauffeur, Mr Boon, is in my car outside. If I give him a call, he'll sort out your wound – he's an expert first aider. He can clean up in here as well; within an hour or so, everything will be back to normal."

Adam laughed, despite the traumatic experience he had just been through. Back to normal? What kind of a world did this man live in? As if you could kill a couple of human beings (albeit burglars and rapists), 'clean up' (whatever that meant) and be back to normal in a couple of hours. Adam thought he could hear the Storyteller's voice in his ear saying: "Hang on in there".

"I still think we should call the police. There's no reason not to," Eve argued.

"That's not entirely correct," said David. "There are likely to be some problems, believe me. The police don't like dead bodies, but they do like to arrest the people who caused them to be dead. Of course, there are mitigating circumstances. The public are understanding when decent folk take the law into their own hands, but the police and the justice system can be less accommodating. There will be questions about whether I used reasonable force. And there's a further problem: I've been trained to kill. Seven years in the SAS; ten years as a mercenary. I'm supposed to show special restraint and to use the minimum amount of force. I probably used a bit more than the minimum here."

"But we can't just forget about the whole thing," Eve persisted.

"When you say 'clean up,' what exactly does that mean?" asked Adam.

"Let me show you," replied David, pushing a fast dial button on his phone. "Jedwell, there's a couple of bodies in here that would be better elsewhere. Oh and bring the first aid kit." He then addressed Eve: "I'm sure you want these bodies removed, whatever we decide to do. No one wants corpses in their living room."

Eve was about to object, to point out they would be disturbing a crime scene, but, before she could speak, the door-bell rang. David opened the door and Jedwell Boon, a man of medium height but almost as wide as he was tall, entered. He nodded his round, bald head to Adam and Eve and looked around briefly, stroking his immaculately trimmed circular, brown beard, while taking in the scene with impassive grey eyes.

"They're all yours," said David to Jedwell. Then he added quietly so only Jedwell could hear: "Usual procedure, including blood samples."

Without a word, Jedwell rolled out and unzipped the first of two body-bags and expertly rolled the body of Darren into it. "Neat," said Jedwell. It was unclear whether he was referring to Darren's broken neck or to his own body-bag rolling and zipping techniques. Within two minutes, Kev was similarly enveloped. With surprising ease, Jedwell Boon then flipped Kev's corpse over his shoulder and trotted out of the house. Within another minute, he was back, and Darren too was gone.

"There," said David Minofel cheerfully. "All done. No bodies and no blood. Sorry about the broken furniture. A coffee table had been damaged when Adam fell on it.

"But what are you going to do with the bodies?" asked Eve, who now realised that the question of whether or not to contact the police had already been settled.

"You really don't have to worry about that," said David. Within the hour, they will be anonymous particles floating in the air. Earth to earth, ashes to ashes, dust to dust; although, in their case, in the interest of effective time management, we will be skipping the earth to earth bit."

Jedwell returned, the second body now loaded into the estate. "Will there be anything else, sir?" he asked of Minofel.

"Yes, could you take a look at Adam's stomach? It's a flesh wound but a bit of TCP, not to mention TLC, and a large plaster wouldn't come amiss."

While Jedwell, with a surprisingly gentle and sympathetic touch, bathed and disinfected Adam's wound, David Minofel turned his attention to Eve.

"Not quite the evening you were expecting," he said soothingly. "Not the one I expected either, to be honest."

"Two people have died here," said Eve, who felt very uneasy about all the events of the evening. First of all, when Kev had been preparing to rape her, she had felt a hatred she had not thought herself capable of. Then, when this stranger had saved her, she had not only felt grateful; she had also fully endorsed the efficiently brutal way in which he had dealt with the intruders. He had done what she would have wanted Adam to do, what she herself would have wanted to do, if either of them had been capable. Again, she was surprised at the ease with which she had endorsed the intruders' deaths. Finally, she and Adam had lost control of the situation. This David Minofel had not just saved them; he had also effectively erased the entire incident. Her feelings about that were ambivalent. It was wonderful that someone could 'put things right' so comprehensively. And yet what David Minofel had done was also wrong; he had broken the rules.

And there was something else that worried her. No one dies from a broken leg – or at least only a very few - and never so abruptly. Eve was troubled by the thought that, when this David Minofel had knelt beside the man Kev and had seemed to be whispering something in his ear, he might have been deploying some subtle technique to end the man's life – and that would have been murder, cold-blooded murder.

"I guess this isn't the best time to discuss the job," said David. "Look, you need to take all this in. I'm really sorry this happened to you. It's not the kind of thing you're used to. It's not the kind of thing anyone should be used to, although I have to say it's not that uncommon in some of the places I've been posted. Anyway, I'll come back tomorrow, at the same time, and we can talk business. In the meantime, have a good evening." With that, David Minofel made to leave.

Adam and Eve saw him to the door. Parked in the road outside was a Bentley.

"Have a good evening," Eve echoed David Minofel's last remark. "Is that some kind of weird sense of humour?"

"My God!" exclaimed Adam. "That's a Bentley Flying Star: the most exclusive and expensive estate car in the world."

Eve didn't say anything - but she thought "*Men!*"

9. Uncle Rambler and Numpty

Numpty was really excited. "You're right, uncle. You're absolutely right." Numpty had been performing long division on a 12 digit calculator.

The previous day, Uncle Rambler had been explaining some numerical quirks, mainly in order to give his nephew a break from the undoubtedly demanding challenge of calculus. "Take a break, lad," he had said, "and see what you make of this. Divide any number by seven and, if it is not exactly divisible by seven, it will always produce a six-digit recurring series after the decimal point, consisting of the numbers 142857. The sequence may start anywhere in the series but will then continue indefinitely."

Numpty had spent an hour testing the proposition, and, so far, had found no exceptions. He showed his working to his ever-attentive uncle.

1	÷	7	0.14285714285
2	÷	7	0.28571428571
3	÷	7	0.42857142857
4	÷	7	0.57142857142
5	÷	7	0.71428571428
22	÷	7	3.14285714285
33	÷	7	4.71428571428
44	÷	7	6.28571428571
55	÷	7	7.85714285714
123	÷	7	17.5714285714
456	÷	7	65.1428571428
789	÷	7	112.714285714

“Well done, my boy,” said Rambler. “As my father used to say, ‘There are patterns everywhere, but to find them you must be a gouger, not a skimmer.’

“I was concerned,” Numpty responded with relief, “that you might feel I had been spending too much time on my calculator“.

“Never entertain such thoughts, my boy. You should test every hypothesis as much as you can. Always remember that, while every positive result strengthens the hypothesis, just one exception will destroy it. There are many idiosyncrasies in our number system. I will share more with you another day.”

“And what have you been doing, uncle, while I have been finding patterns in our numbers?” asked the ever-inquisitive Numpty.

“Well, my boy, I have been doing a little gouging of my own. I’ve been trying to find out why the fourth beginning ended almost as soon as it began.” Rambler was sitting in his favourite armchair, a massive leather-covered seat of learning, with broad flat arms that warmly embraced its occupant and provided the perfect resting place for his ever-present notebook.

“And what have you concluded?” asked Numpty.

Rambler stared out of the window which provided an excellent view of the crescent. He had lived in Maida Vale most of his life: first with his parents; then when they had died, alone; and, for the last couple of decades, with Numpty, whom he had ‘inherited’ when his nephew’s parents had both been killed in a car crash. Rambler took great pleasure from the self-assertive architecture of the area and in particular from the noble sweep of the crescent, which was visible from the large window of his first floor flat.

"Well, uncle, what conclusion have you drawn?" Numpty's confidence had grown immeasurably since the quest and the initiation of the fourth beginning. The relationship between him and his uncle was not equal; that was not what Numpty sought or desired anyway. But he had reached a stage where he could use his mentor's intellectual techniques himself and take some pleasure from applying them to their source.

"Uncle?" Numpty persisted.

"I'm sorry, my boy. I was trying to consider all possibilities of which there are many. Two stand out as favoured hypotheses. Either we failed to trigger a full beginning and it simply lost impetus and petered out, or someone or something stopped it. I cannot believe the former is true, because all of us who had experienced and survived the quest knew we had succeeded. I therefore conclude that someone or something stopped it. That prompts a further thought: the fourth beginning, once initiated, was more powerful than we could have imagined; what then must be the power of whatever stopped it?"

It was a question which did not need an answer.

So Numpty remained silent, but he did ponder whether his uncle's use of the expression 'peter out' could be a subconscious reference to the breaker, Nick Peters, who had impeded Adam and Eve at every stage of their quest. The expression 'peter out' had always puzzled Numpty. He had tried to discover its origin but its provenance was uncertain. Some thought it a reference to St Peter whose faith, immediately after the crucifixion, had dwindled; others suggested it was derived from the French verb *peter*, to fart or to fizzle which Numpty favoured because anything connected with flatulence amused him. When he had raised the matter with his uncle, Rambler had gently rebuked him, telling him the phrase was most likely an American mining term derived from saltpetre which had been used as a fuse for explosives'. Seeing he had deflated his nephew somewhat, Rambler had then commended his nephew on his determined efforts to discover the origin of the expression. "A fine example of etymological gouging," he had remarked, patting Numpty on the head.

10. Post-Traumatic Stress Enquiries

Adam and Eve Smith spent the day after the attempted burglary trying to come to terms with what had happened. Adam took some leave that he was owed so he could be with Eve.

"We owe an enormous debt of gratitude to Minofel," said Adam. Images of the brutality of the burglars kept flashing into his mind. "I wanted to save you but I couldn't. If Minofel hadn't intervened – well, I can't think about it."

But Adam couldn't stop thinking about it. He had, of course, faced unbelievable brutality on the quest for the fourth beginning, but this was something else. This was so personal. They had invaded his home, beaten them, rendered them powerless, and one of them had come close to raping Eve. While Adam was unequivocally grateful to his saviour, it rankled with him that he had not been able to protect his own wife – or himself, for that matter.

"You did what you could. We both did," Eve replied, picking up on her husband's anxiety. "We had no chance. We just have to thank our lucky stars that your head-hunter turned out to be a cross between Rambo and Superman."

"That's for sure." Adam had never seen anything like the absolute authority with which David Minofel had resolved the situation – absolute authority and extraordinary, not to say ruthless, efficiency. He had rescued them from a situation in which they had been entirely at the mercy of two sadistic thugs. If Minofel hadn't intervened, Adam knew that, at best, he and Eve would have been traumatised so badly that they might well have never fully recovered. At worst, they might well have been killed. Indeed, since neither of their attackers had made any effort to conceal their faces, it seemed unlikely they would have been allowed to survive the ordeal.

"How did he get in?" Eve asked, interrupting Adam's speculation.

"I don't know. I guess Darren didn't shut the door properly. It's a bit stiff, if you don't push it hard. I've been meaning to give it a bit of oil."

"And why did he come back?"

"Well, he must have been suspicious. Darren wasn't exactly the kind of person we were likely to have as a house guest. And, in any case, it would have been very odd if I hadn't been at home to keep an appointment with someone who wanted to offer me a top job."

"No, I mean why did he involve himself? If he thought we were in danger and he wanted to help, why didn't he just phone the police?"

"Well maybe he thought there wasn't time. And he was right. If he hadn't arrived when he did..." Adam trailed off.

"Yes," said Eve thoughtfully, and then added: "he killed them both" – as though that needed to be said.

Adam frowned momentarily. "That's right. And if he hadn't killed them, they would have killed us."

"But did he have to kill them?" Eve asked. It was a question that had been troubling Eve all night.

"There were two of them," said Adam. "What else could he do? He had to eliminate one of them as quickly as possible, just to even the odds. Then the other one pulled a knife on him."

"I realise he had to disable them," Eve conceded, with just a hint of irritation in her voice. "But did he have to kill them?"

"I think he did what had to be done," said Adam. "He

had to be sure the thinner one was permanently neutralised, and the one called Kev was too big to take chances with."

"But he killed Kev," Eve persisted, "He killed him when he was no longer a threat, when he was lying on the floor whimpering with pain."

"What are you getting at?" It was now Adam's turn to show some irritation. "We were in a terrible situation. We were completely helpless, vulnerable. I don't know if he used precisely the right amount of force, and, frankly, I don't care. Those burglars were evil, sadistic scum and the world's a better place without them. In any case, it doesn't matter. They're gone, just as Minofel promised. It's as though they weren't ever here and that's how we should try to see it. That way, we'll get over it more easily and more quickly."

"Have you really thought this through?" Eve asked. "If he killed the big one when he was no threat, that's murder. There are no extenuating circumstance, no mitigating plea of self-defence. More to the point, if it was murder, we are accessaries. We are accessaries to murder."

Adam was silent for a while. Of course Eve was right but the truth was that David Minofel was a hero who had saved them both from violence and possible death. Yes, in today's litigious world an unprincipled lawyer would see a chance to make his name and simultaneously a shed-load of money by prosecuting them. Yes, no doubt, as Minofel had suggested, their lives would be turned upside down, and David Minofel himself might well end up as the villain of the piece, but, in reality, Minofel had done the right thing, and he had done the right thing brilliantly. He and Eve might be accessaries to murder but where was the evidence, where were the witnesses and where were the bodies?

"I don't think it will come to that," he said quietly.

11. An extraordinary offer

On the day following the aborted burglary, Adam and Eve Smith spent several hours trying to absorb the bizarre events of the previous evening.

At 7 o'clock precisely, the doorbell rang. Both Adam and Eve jumped. Neither of them had yet fully realised the damage the burglars had done to them. The intruders had destroyed the complacency which is the means whereby most people manage to hold themselves together. The brutal, moronic criminals had made Adam and Eve aware how vulnerable they were; how, at every moment of every day, they were no more than a kicked-in door or forced window away from violence and death, even in the supposed security of their own home on a summer's evening when they were planning a peaceful slow-cooked meal.

"That'll be David," said Adam.

"Yes, of course," Eve agreed. "I'm not sure I want a visitor this evening."

"Well, he's here now, and we can't very well turn away the man who saved us last night, now can we?"

"I'm not suggesting we turn away. I'm just sorry he's here."

Adam went to the door. Through the glass, he could see David Minofel waiting on the doorstep. He opened the door.

David nodded and gave Adam a quiet, understanding smile. "How are you?" he asked.

"Come in," said Adam. "I'm fine. We're fine."

"Hello, Eve." David took Eve's hand. His hand was gently warm. She felt better, a little more secure – why, she couldn't explain. After all, this was the hand of a man who had killed two people in her living room the previous evening.

"I know what you're thinking," said David. "You're worried that what happened last night isn't over. That the police will become involved. There will be knockings on the door, statements taken, even charges laid."

That wasn't what Eve was thinking and somehow that made her feel even more secure; that this stranger who had entered their lives so emphatically didn't know what she was thinking, even if he thought he did.

"Well let me set your mind at rest," David continued. "Darren and Kev are no more. I don't just mean that, in material terms, there is no trace of them. I also mean that we have checked out their social network, family, friends, associates, etc. and their digital presence – bank accounts, credit cards, employment records, passports etc. and have satisfactorily eliminated any possibility of repercussions. I won't go into detail but no one is going miss them. It will not surprise you to learn that the dominant feeling about their disappearance amongst those who knew them is relief rather than concern. If, by any chance, we have missed something, which I assure you is most unlikely, there is no way that anyone will be able to trace them back to you. It is as though last night had not happened. Indeed, apart from us, and of course Mr Boon, no one knows what did happen.

"*We* don't know *exactly* what happened," Eve interrupted. "What did you do to the man Kev?

"Would it not be better to move on?" David responded easily. "If you want the details, I will of course give them to you, but surely it's best to look to the future. I'm here to talk to Adam about a job offer. Indeed, it's more than a job offer; it's a new and exciting career path."

"That's sounds sensible to me," Adam joined the

conversation, addressing his remark to Eve. "There's nothing to be gained by dwelling on what happened yesterday." and here he turned to David, "except for me to say how grateful we both are for what you did."

Eve considered persisting in trying to find out exactly what Minofel had done, but she let it go. After all, perhaps it was better to leave some of the details unknown or at least unclear.

"I should begin by telling you a little about my organisation." Minofel took Eve's silence as acquiescence. "Slievins is an old company. It was founded at the end of the 19th century, which makes it the oldest consultancy firm in the country. It began as a modest operation, serving a small number of select clients in the City. It tottered on through the 20th century, surviving wars and recessions, gradually expanding its client base at home and, from the 1960s, abroad. That's when it really took off. Today it is a global player in its field, widely respected and admired."

"In its field?" enquired Adam.

"Yes, that too calls for an explanation. We search industry and government for people we believe have potential. I don't just mean people who are very good at what they do. Very often, people who are merely very good at what they do are, for obvious reasons, best left exactly where they are. I mean people who can go further; more than that, people for whom there is no limit as to how much further they may go. We search high and low for such people. We review maybe 100,000 executives to find one possible serious candidate. We then carry out one or two further checks to make sure we are right. And then we make an approach."

David paused.

"And..." Eve prompted.

"We believe your husband is such a one."

Eve's eyebrows lifted a little, but she said nothing.

"I need to make something clear," David continued. "We are not conventional head-hunters. Conventional head-hunters start with the job and look for the man or women to fill the post. What we do is rather different. We start with the man or woman and then we find them the jobs that will progress their career.

"Jobs?" queried Adam.

"Yes, jobs," Minofel replied, stressing the plural. "This is not about placing you in a single job. We want a continuing relationship with you. We want to manage your career, and, believe me, when we manage a career, we make sure that it's a career both our protégés and we can be proud of."

"So what's the deal?" asked Eve. She realised that David Minofel was talking to Adam, but, all the same, she was present too, and she felt Minofel had no objection to her participation. Adam was less pleased with Eve's intervention but said nothing.

"We have a job for you as Marketing Director of Zacher Donos Pharmaceuticals, the Swiss Pharmaceutical company. You will be based in Geneva."

"But I know nothing about pharmaceuticals," Adam objected.

Minofel ignored Adam's objection: "If you decide to work with us, you will pay Slievins 15% of everything you earn..."

Eve interrupted immediately. That sounded to her like a scam. "Hold on. You have come to Adam, not he to you. Why should he pay you? Surely you are paid by your client?"

"You have a fierce negotiator on your side," Minofel laughed. "Yes, we are paid by the client and paid handsomely, but that is not how we make our money. Let me explain. Adam, your starting salary will be 200,000 euros a year."

Adam gulped. That was about double what he was earning.

"You pay us 15% on everything you earn above 100,000 euros. In other words, you keep all your earnings up to 100,000 euros and 85% of everything you earn above 100,000 euros. That means you will keep 185,000 euros from your 200,000 euro starting salary. I must make this clear: you will pay us this 15% on all earnings above 100,000 euros a year from any jobs we find you, until our contract with you ends."

"And when does the contract end?" asked Eve.

"Whenever Adam gives us three months' notice."

"On what grounds can he terminate the contract?" Eve persisted.

"On any grounds or no grounds," Minofel replied affably. "We have no wish to sustain a relationship with a chosen one if the chosen one wishes to be deselected."

"If I agree, when would I start?" Adam asked.

"We will want you to start as soon as is practical after you sign the contract. I'll leave the contract with you. When you have decided one way or the other, call me on my mobile. I'm going to leave you now. You have had two eventful evenings, and I guess you would like to be alone. Read the contract; discuss it with Eve; take your time. When you are ready, give me a call. That's it."

With that, David Minofel, senior partner in Slievins Consultancy, took his leave, returning to his Bentley Flying Star estate where the faithful Jedwell Boon was waiting patiently for his master.

"Take me back to the office," he ordered Jedwell. "Did you take a blood sample from the man Kevin?"

"Yes, of course," Jedwell replied. His master was most particular about taking blood samples of the most egregious, violent and malicious offenders, for analysis and other uses.

"Good," Minofel continued. "Now I suggest you deal with Darren's mother. Why anyone should want to know the whereabouts of a toe-rag like Darren is beyond me but I guess it's that maternal thing. Anyway, she's a junkie, so it should be fairly straightforward."

12. Sorted

After dropping his employer and the Bentley estate off at the Slievins office in the City, Jedwell Boon changed into his casual clothes, climbed into his more modest Ford Mondeo and drove to Wembley.

Darren's mother lived with her latest partner in a high rise apartment in the poorest part of the suburb. The block of flats was predominantly grey, but the balconies of the more civilised tenants who still maintained some level of personal hygiene were bedecked with multi-coloured washing. The building looked dilapidated but the chaotic colours of the washing lifted it, making it seem a little less intimidating to those of a more mainstream disposition.

"I'm looking for Flat 38 in Mangosuthu Heights – a Mrs. Tracey Fisher." Jedwell had little hope of a helpful response. Everyone he had seen on the estate seemed to be either high on drugs or engaged in planning or implementing some criminal scheme. Jedwell hoped his car would still have a wheel at each corner when he returned.

"Manky Sod You Heights, s'over there, i'n'it," said the sallow hooded youth whom Jedwell had addressed.

Jedwell climbed up to the third floor of the block, the lift being out of order and in need of defuming. He knocked on the door of number 38 – or 8E as it appeared on the door, the number plate having been screwed on upside down. Someone might have noticed had the 8 not been symmetrical, he mused. There was no answer. Jedwell gently pushed the door and it swung open. Inside there was a heavy smell of cannabis.

"Anyone at home?" Jedwell hazarded.

Of course, this wasn't a home in any conventional sense of the word. It was a tip. Dirty plates, a couple of empty gin bottles, a more than generous sprinkling of crushed beer cans, overflowing ash trays, unwashed laundry, several used syringes – no need to go on.

"Who are you?" asked a spaced-out individual in a dirty T-shirt and jeans, reclining on a ragged sofa. He was unsure what to make of the heavily built stranger but he didn't seem threatening.

"I'm looking for Tracey Fisher."

"Are you the social?"

Jedwell Boon laughed. "Not really. I'm more your anti-social." He sniffed the air: "What are you on?"

"Are you the filth?"

"That wouldn't be a very smart question if I was, now would it? No, I'm not the social and I'm not the filth." With that, Jedwell tossed his inquisitor a wad of cannabis. "That should establish my credentials."

"Oh man, you're a diamond," exclaimed the recipient. "I'm Skunk." he added, to cement the new friendship. Skunk offered Jedwell his hand.

"Was Skunk a birth name?" asked Jedwell innocently.

"No, it's a kinda nickname..." Skunk's voice tailed off as he realised his benefactor's question might not have been entirely serious.

"Jolly good," said Jedwell. "Now where's Tracey?"

"She's popped out to get some booze. She'll be back any time."

"I'll wait," said Jedwell, settling his stocky frame into a large armchair with stained and torn upholstery.

"So tell me, Skunk, what kind of work is it that you do?"

"I'm between jobs at the moment," said Skunk, rolling himself a fresh spliff.

"Well, what kind of jobs is it that you're between?"

"You know, this and that," Skunk replied evasively.

"No, I don't know. If I knew, I wouldn't be asking."

"Like I said, this and that," Skunk repeated.

"Don't take this personally, but you're not really a great conversationalist, are you?"

Skunk took a long drag on his pristine spliff, smiled benignly and said "I don't rate words; they're pretty meaningless."

"Gotcha," said Jedwell. "So let me guess. You haven't worked for years. You're not very good at reading or writing and you don't do numbers. You live off the social, with your benefit money, supplemented by a bit of thieving. In short, Skunk, you're a terminally lazy, parasitical scumbag. Am I close?"

"Cool it, man," said Skunk. "I'm picking up some negative vibes here."

"I'm not criticising; I'm just describing. In my line of work you have to be able to sum up people and situations on the hoof. I need to know who and what I'm dealing with."

"And what is your line of work?" asked Skunk, his voice slurring the words together.

"I guess you could say I'm a cross between a weaver and an undertaker. I tie up loose ends and I undertake to clear up other people's messes."

Before Skunk could formulate a follow-up question, Tracey came through the door of the flat, carrying two plastic carrier bags full of bottles. She was in her early forties, but she looked ten years older. Smoking, alcohol, and soft and hard drugs had left their mark.

"Let me help," said Jedwell, leaping out of the armchair with remarkable alacrity for a man of his bulk.

"And who are you?" asked Tracey. She liked men with neatly trimmed beards, unlike the straggly unkempt apology for a beard sported by Skunk.

"I'm Skunk's new best friend," said Jedwell as he carefully placed the bags on the table. "These plastic bags are useless. You were lucky they didn't split."

"Have a spliff," suggested Skunk to Tracey. "He's all right. He's a bit odd, and I think he's a bit rude, but he's cool."

"I'm a friend of Darren's," said Jedwell to Tracey. He asked me to give you a message. He's really sorry he couldn't make it for your birthday but he's sent you a little present." Jedwell opened a pouch on his belt and took out a syringe. "This is the real stuff," he said. "Pure heroin."

"So he's all right then," said Tracey. "I was worried when he didn't phone me yesterday. I tried his mobile but it was on voicemail."

"He's fine," Jedwell assured her. "He's in a really good place. Anyway, he asked me to give you this." He handed Tracy the syringe. "And he said he'd see you soon. There's really nothing to worry about."

Jedwell made as though to leave, and then stopped. "Oh, and given my new found friendship with Skunk here, there's a present for him too." He dipped into his pouch and took out another syringe. "Have a very good evening – what's left of it," he said with a smile and a laugh.

As he left, Tracey and Skunk were tightening bands around their arms to find receptive veins for the more than lethal dose in each syringe.

Back in his car, which, to his surprise, was much as he had left it, Jedwell phoned David Minofel. He gave his master a brief report.

"Good," said David Minofel.

13. A canine call

Uncle Rambler and his nephew Numpty were taking their morning stroll along Warrington Crescent in Maida Vale. It was a bright, clear day, with sunlight filtering through the leaves of the trees to play chaotic hopscotch on the pavement. Numpty was fascinated by the process of photosynthesis which, as his uncle had explained, was the process whereby plants turned light from the sun into chemical energy within the plant. He had grasped photosynthesis fairly easily but was having some problems with the process of osmosis which, according to his uncle, explained why a potato immersed in water with a high salt content would shrink in size. The water abandoned the potato to dilute the salt solution, or something like that. Anyway, without osmosis, plants wouldn't be able to extract nutrients from the soil.

"You seem very thoughtful today," said Rambler to his nephew. "Is there anything particular on your mind?"

"Well," Numpty replied, before pausing to formulate his response, "I am full of thoughts every day, uncle. Indeed, sometimes I think I am just my thoughts."

"I see you are in a philosophical frame of mind," Rambler replied, happy to embark on an existential dialogue with his protégé. "When you say you sometimes think you are just your thoughts, are you not forgetting there must be a *you* to have the thoughts? *Cogito ergo sum*, my dear boy, *cogito ergo sum*."

"I suppose so," Numpty replied uncertainly, "but when I try to explore the bit of me that is doing the thinking, all I find is the thought of me wondering who is doing the thinking, which is really just another thought."

"Sometimes," suggested Rambler, "when wrestling with such questions, it is better to bide your time, to allow the answer to come to you, rather than to keep digging in the hope of unearthing the truth." Rambler was certain that Numpty had been permanently affected by the fourth beginning. His always-enquiring mind had a sharper edge to it. His questions now were as likely to be challenging as irritating. Rambler was not a conceited man; for all his knowledge, he was well aware of his limitations. But he did take some pride and no little satisfaction from the progress his nephew had made since coming into his care.

"You could try both," said a voice inside Numpty's head.

"Pardon?" Numpty knew the voice wasn't his uncle's but, since he was the only person within earshot, it seemed reasonable to ask for a repeat.

"I didn't say anything," Uncle Rambler replied.

"You don't need to speak. Just think your thoughts to me," said the voice.

"It can't be," thought Numpty.

"Oh yes it is," said Luke.

Of all the changes wrought by the quest and the fourth beginning, only three had persisted after the beginning had been aborted. The ageing of Adam, ensuing from his ordeal in hell at Cadnam, had not been reversed; Numpty's mind had been given and retained that sharper edge that his uncle had observed; and Luke – well, Luke, the golden retriever belonging to the Smiths, the god of dogs who had subdued the hounds of hell at Cadnam, had become an even more exceptional canine than he had been before the beginning.

Numpty recognised Luke's voice. "Luke, it is you. It must be you."

"Make up your mind," Luke responded amiably. "One minute it's 'it can't be you', then it's 'it must be you'. Well, you were right the second time. After all, everything either is or isn't. Anyway, as I said, you could try both."

"Both what?" asked Numpty.

"I was referring to your uncle's advice about the *cogito ergo sum* issue and his suggestion you should allow the answer to come to you, rather than keep digging. I was merely pondering whether you couldn't do both. You could continue to burrow and delve away into your consciousness while also waiting and hoping for an answer to emerge."

"What? Be a kind of osmotic gouger?" suggested Numpty excitedly.

"Precisely," minded Luke, with a laugh.

"An osmotic gouger!" exclaimed Uncle Rambler.

Although Numpty had conducted the rest of his conversation without speech, thought to thought, he had been so inspired by the idea of an osmotic gouger that he had spoken the phrase out loud.

"What a splendid concept! What a fecund image!" Rambler enthused, eagerly endorsing his nephew's utterance, although unclear as to its provenance. "The plant burrowing into the ground in a relentless search for buried treasure while absorbing whatever it needs from its subterranean surroundings. It calls to mind the tree of knowledge of good and evil in the Garden of Eden, a tall, majestic and relentless plant, probing the depths of the earth to find the darkest secrets and turning what it finds into a regal canopy of light-absorbing leaves - a perfect symbol to represent the osmotic gouger."

Numpty preened himself a little in response to his uncle's enthusiastic endorsement.

"Enough self-congratulation," Luke minded to Numpty. "There's work to be done. The fourth beginning was somehow aborted but that's not the end of the matter. We began something. You and I know it. It changed us. Whether we like it or not, the quest remains unfinished business."

"I was wondering," said Numpty, addressing his uncle, "what we must do now."

"I think we should continue our walk and our talk, my boy," said Rambler. "And explore the implicit paradox in the concept of an osmotic gouger – osmosis being a fairly passive process compared to the more aggressive, assertive character denoted by gouging."

"No," said Numpty. "I don't mean what we should do this morning. I mean, what we should do about the quest. What should we do about the fourth beginning? I know the fourth beginning has been stopped. But shouldn't we try to find a way to restart it?"

Rambler was a little taken aback. "Where has this come from, my boy? I have been as disappointed as anyone but we have to accept what happened."

"Tell him that accepting what has happened in the past doesn't mean we can't change it in the future," Luke thought to Numpty.

"Couldn't we at least do a bit of gouging?" Numpty asked hopefully.

"Well," said Rambler slowly, "I suppose it would do no harm to investigate what aborted the beginning. We should be cautious because whatever stopped the beginning was evidently very powerful and will probably take a rather dim view of anyone trying to restart it. But we could undertake some tentative enquiries and perhaps we will learn something useful."

"A little bit of gouging, then, and just a tad of osmosis," Luke minded to Numpty.

"Good," said Numpty.

Neither Rambler nor Numpty noticed the figure of a stocky man, almost as wide as he was tall, who had been walking some yards behind them and who, with the benefit of extraordinarily acute hearing, had heard every word the two of them had said, although not, of course, the thought-to-thought intercourse between Numpty and Luke.

14. Geneva

Geneva is a wondrous place. It reeks of money. Even the beggars wear Gucci shoes.

Adam had been to Geneva before on short business trips. He had always enjoyed his stays at the Intercontinental. He admired the cool Swiss efficiency. If one of the bulbs burnt out in his room in the morning, he never needed to call reception: the defunct bulb would be replaced within a couple of hours when the room was next serviced. Yes, Geneva was a fine, efficient, affluent place – but not one where Adam had ever expected or wanted to spend a great deal of time. It was too well-ordered, too complacent, too materialistic.

Nevertheless, there he was, back in the Intercontinental, waiting for Human Resources at Zacher Donos – or ZeD as most people called it – to finalise arrangements for his apartment.

He had asked Eve to come with him, but she had pointed out all the logistical and other difficulties of uprooting themselves for what might be a relatively short stay in Switzerland. After all, Minofel had talked about jobs, not a single job, and who could tell whether the next move would be in Switzerland, or back to the United Kingdom, or somewhere else entirely. Eve had also pointed out that, although Adam's new salary seemed generous, the cost of living in Switzerland, if they set up home there, would certainly take some of the shine off it.

So they had agreed that Adam would spend a five-day week in Geneva and fly back to Heathrow every Friday evening, returning to Geneva each Sunday evening; they had even discussed the options with Minofel. He had said the decision was of course theirs, but he thought commuting to Geneva once a week was eminently practical and there could be some very real advantages to keeping their base in the UK.

Adam himself had mixed feelings. On the one hand, he had a sense of liberation – not that he felt in any way imprisoned by Eve or their life in Harrow; no, it was just that, for the first time for a long time, there was no one else to take into account. What he did and where he went was entirely up to him. On the other hand, he missed Eve's company and the time they spent together, the small but priceless routine pleasures of loving company.

The bedside phone rang. Adam sat down on the bed and picked up the white receiver.

"It's Minofel here," said a familiar voice. "I'm in reception. May I come up? I have someone I want you to meet."

"Yes, of course," Adam replied. He had been expecting someone from ZeD to contact him so Minofel's arrival was a surprise, a pleasant one. Adam was feeling the trepidation that normally precedes starting a new job, and the presence of his sponsor was somehow comforting.

There was a knock on the door. Adam opened it. There was the smartly dressed Minofel and, beside him, a perfectly presented, extraordinarily beautiful woman.

"Hello Adam." Minofel was full of bonhomie. "Good to see you. Hope everything is satisfactory. By the way, allow me to introduce Miss Tomic. She will be your mentor."

After shaking David Minofel's hand, he took the manicured hand of Miss Tomic. It was soft, warm and welcoming.

"Miss Tomic is Croatian," Minofel elaborated. "She has a PhD in pharmacology and she speaks six, or is it seven, languages? Croatian, Bosnian, Serbian, English, French and German."

"That's only six," said Adam, still holding Miss Tomic's hand.

"He forgot Italian," Miss Tomic murmured, without the hint of an accent.

"Yes, right," Minofel agreed, with a laugh. "I forgot Italian. Anyway, Miss Tomic will be invaluable to you in your position with ZeD. She knows the company and the pharma industry inside out. She will be able to help you with any technical, medical or legal issues and she has a very good business brain."

"Sounds as though she should be the Marketing Director," said Adam.

David Minofel laughed again. "Oh dear, no! We have much more important things lined up for Miss Tomic – and indeed for you."

Adam looked confused.

Minofel continued. "You and she are two of our chosen ones. You are members of our team. We have high hopes for all our players. Very high hopes. Miss Tomic's current task is to make sure you are a success at ZeD. She has already undertaken considerable preparatory work; she is as keen as we are for both of you to move on to your next assignments. But wait, I am getting ahead of myself. First, you and she must learn to work together. You start tomorrow. Are you ready?"

"Will you excuse me?" Miss Tomic interrupted. "As you say, Adam starts at ZeD tomorrow, and I still have one or two last minute adjustments to make."

"Yes, of course, my dear," David Minofel replied, taking

her hand and patting it in an almost paternal fashion. "I'll be in touch."

Miss Tomic gave Adam a faint smile and a nod. "Sorry our first meeting has to be so short, but we will have much time to get to know each other in the coming weeks."

When Miss Tomic had gone, David turned to Adam. "Well, what do you think?"

"What do I think? Well, I think she's an amazingly attractive woman."

Minofel smiled: "Clearly you have a gift for stating the blindingly obvious but that's not what I meant. Do you think you and she can work well together?"

"Well, apart from the fact that I think I should be assisting her, rather than the other way round, I think we will get along famously."

"Good," said Minofel. Then he added: "Let's face it, you wouldn't be much use as an mentor to Miss Tomic."

Adam was unsure whether Minofel was serious or joking. After a moment, Minofel said helpfully. "I'm, joking."

"What do I call her?" Adam asked, moving on. "I mean what's her first name?"

"I'm glad you asked me that," said David. "There's a bit of a story in the answer. Her first name is Gorgeous. Yes, she's Miss Gorgeous Tomic. Perhaps not surprisingly, she's not very keen on her first name. She prefers to be addressed as Miss Tomic."

"So how did she get christened Gorgeous?

oooOooo

"Well, the story goes that, when she was born in Dubrovnik of mixed Croatian/English parentage, an imp came to her father and offered to grant him three wishes for his daughter. Her Croatian father was understandably worried that it was an imp making this generous offer so he was wary. He had heard persistent rumours of a local revival of the Devil's Twister (three wishes involving some terrible existential repercussions) scam, so he told the imp to be gone.

The imp departed but, as soon as the father set off for work, the imp returned and made the same offer to the girl's English mother. Although the mother knew her husband had sent the imp off with a flea in his long, pointed, floppy ear, she couldn't resist taking the imp up on his generous offer. First, she asked if there were any special terms or conditions. The imp replied there was only one condition, namely that, once a wish was accepted, any attempt to modify it would reverse all three wishes to bring about the opposite of the original desired outcome. That seemed fair enough to the mother, so long as she came up with solid, unambiguously benign wishes.

She thought as hard as she could, to try to make sure that, whatever she asked for could only be for the good. Her first wish was that her daughter should enjoy good health. The imp said he would make sure she was healthy all the days of her life. The mother's second wish was that she should have a good mind. The imp agreed to ensure she had a first-class brain. Finally, the mother asked that her daughter should be gorgeous. The imp laughed. He had been taught at Imp school that, when devising a Twister, you always had to wait for the third wish before springing the trap. "Very well," he said, "she shall be gorgeous. Let her name be Gorgeous, Gorgeous Tomic. But she shall be gorgeous in name only. I shall make sure her face is profoundly ill-suited to her name. I shall make her as ugly as sin, as ugly as sin, as ugly as sin."

With a wholly impious laugh, the imp departed.

When the imp reported his good work to his master the Devil, he was hoping for fulsome praise; instead, he received a demonic clip around the aforementioned long, pointed, floppy ear.

"What was that for?" asked the indignant imp.

"Why did you say you would make her as ugly as sin? Are you mad?" barked the Devil. "Sin is the most beautiful thing in the world. Have I not made everything that is desirable a sin? Are not all pleasures sinful?"

The enormity of his error gradually dawned on the imp. "What can I do to make amends?" asked the now-contrite imp.

"There is only one thing you can do, you blithering idiot. You must make her beautiful, you must make her the most beautiful of women, so that all men will know sin is beautiful."

"Shall I also change her name then?" suggested the imp.

"Certainly not," said the Devil. "Let her carry that name as a burden, as a curse of arrogance and haughtiness so that, while inevitably popular with men, she shall be detested by women."

"Shall I tell the mother of our change of plan?" asked the imp.

"You're really not very good at twistering, are you?" responded the Devil, making no effort to disguise his contempt. "Let the woman suffer for years, terrified that when her husband discovers she went against his wishes and inadvertently brought the curse of ugliness upon his daughter, he will desert her - or worse."

"But she's not going to be ugly. You just said she would have to be beautiful," the imp persisted, obviously unwisely, given the Devil's notoriously short temper.

"No, her daughter's not going to be ugly, but so long as you don't tell her, the mother will spend all her days waiting for the imposition of your curse and studying her daughter's features for fear of a wart or a carbuncle. And she won't dare to modify her third wish for fear she will bring ill-health and dementia upon her daughter. At least we can have some fun with the mother. As for you," said the Devil coldly, "your twistering days are over. You can spend the next couple of decades making buttered bread hit the floor butter-side down."

So it was that Miss Tomic was stuck with the name Gorgeous. Of course, as soon as the negative effect that her name had on the girls she met became apparent, she wanted to change it, but her mother, mindful of the imp's warning of the dire consequences of wish modification or retraction, made her promise not to. After all, as the mother decided, it was far better to be beautiful and smart, with a mildly provocative name, than sickly and stupid with a name like Beryl.

oooOooo

Adam listened to Minofel's explanation, rather like a child might listen to a quaint, family anecdote. "Is any of that true?" he asked eventually.

"Well, that's the story," Minofel replied. "I can't vouch for every detail but Miss Tomic certainly has the forename Gorgeous and it sounds like as good an explanation as any."

"But you don't believe in imps," Adam challenged. Was he taking it all too seriously, he asked himself. Increasingly, he found it difficult to tell whether his sponsor was serious or joking. "Isn't it more likely she was named Gorgeous simply because she had doting parents?"

"It may be more likely but that's not the story, or at least it's not as good a story. And I was under the impression you were rather fond of good stories."

Once again, Adam felt wrong-footed. He wanted to ask: "What do you mean by that?" but something told him to show a little caution, so he just smiled tentatively and said nothing.

"I must be going," said Minofel, getting up. "You have a big day tomorrow. When I next see you, I'm sure we will have much to discuss.

oooOooo

When David had left, Adam phoned Eve. After the usual pleasantries, Adam told Eve about his conversation with Minofel and his introduction to the extraordinary Miss Tomic.

"It seems she's to be my personal assistant. She has a PhD in pharmacology and speaks seven languages," Adam enthused. "According to David, she's going to be the secret of my success."

"Sounds like she's better qualified for the job than you are," said Eve.

"I don't think there's any doubt about that - except of course for my extraordinarily incisive business acumen and my sterling leadership qualities."

"What does she look like, this Miss Tomic?" Eve asked

"She's about five foot seven, a bit above average height, dark hair, medium build, I would say."

"And how old is she?"

"Difficult to say, I guess in her thirties." Adam was asking himself why he was being so evasive. So was Eve.

"So, on a scale of one to ten, where one is a dog and ten is beyond every man's wildest dreams, where would you place her?"

"OK, you win," Adam laughed. "She's a very attractive young woman – not in your league of course – but, for those with a taste for the more obvious, she would undoubtedly have some appeal."

"So that's a ten," said Eve.

"Maybe an eight," Adam conceded. "But there's something else."

Adam recounted David Minofel's explanation of how Miss Tomic had acquired her Christian name.

"How bizarre," Eve responded at the end of the tale. "I didn't take Minofel for a storyteller."

Both of them were silent for a moment. Then Adam asked: "Are you thinking what I'm thinking?"

"Quite possibly," Eve replied.

"What's more," Adam continued, "when I suggested the imp story was a bit off the wall, he said he was surprised by my scepticism because, as he put it, he thought I enjoyed a good story. Now why would he say that?"

Eve thought for a moment. "Well, given that he sought you out as one of his chosen people, he must have done a fair amount of research before approaching you. If he did, he would probably know about our time with the Storyteller."

"I've been thinking about that too," said Adam. "As you know, I'm not given to excessive modesty but I have been wondering why I am one of his chosen people. I mean, I'm pretty good but I can't think of any reason why Slievins, the top head-hunters in the City, should single me out."

"Unless it's because of the journey we took with the

Storyteller," Eve suggested.

"Exactly. I'm thinking it's the quest that makes me different. I know a lot of it took place in some other existence, in a parallel world and, in the end, in the Breakers' mysland, but I did survive the interrogation at Cadnam. And I did come out on top in my ordeal in hell."

"With a little help from your friends," Eve added.

Adam laughed. "Not much chance of me becoming overweeningly self-confident with you around. Yes, with a little help from my friends."

"Well I'm not around at the moment, so you'll have to curb any overweening self-confidence tendencies yourself," Eve responded.

"Do you think I'm right? Do you think Slievins recruited me because of the quest, because of the qualities I showed on the journey?"

"It's certainly possible the quest had something to do with it," Eve replied. "I think you should keep an eye on Minofel, as well as on any pride and/or complacency issues you might be developing."

They both laughed, then formulaically affirmed their love for each other and said good night.

15. Day One at ZeD

Adam had asked reception for a wake-up call at 6.30 am. He had also set the alarm on his mobile phone, just to be sure. He wanted time to prepare himself for his first day at ZeD. Given he was not at his best in the mornings, he thought he should give himself a good hour after showering and shaving to drink enough coffee to ensure he was fully awake for the start of the working day at 8.00 am.

He had reckoned without Miss Tomic. When he answered the phone at 6.30, it was Miss Tomic's voice at the other end.

"I am at reception. When you are ready, come down and we can start your briefing over breakfast."

"Right," said Adam. "I'll be with you in 15 minutes."

When he joined Miss Tomic in the Woods Restaurant on the terrace, she was sitting at a table, drinking a glass of water.

"I have ordered you a jug of coffee and a selection of croissants. I understand you like a light breakfast and a great deal of coffee."

Even though he was still half-asleep, Adam noticed how smartly dressed, how self-possessed and how beautiful she was. He was tempted to compliment her on her appearance – she deserved, indeed almost demanded, a compliment – but he thought better of it.

"What a lovely day," he said as he poured his first cup of coffee. "Evidently you have done some research on me. It's always good to know what a man likes for breakfast."

Whoops!' he thought. That could be misconstrued. Probably best to shut up and let her do the talking.

If he had spoken out of turn, Miss Tomic ignored it. "This morning I will introduce you to the president of the company and the medical director. The president is Yves Dubois. He is a very clever man. He was educated at the L'Ecole Normale Superieure in Paris, and has worked for ZeD for more than 20 years. He started in marketing and made his way up various departments until, at the age of 36, he became vice-president; then, two years later, following a tragic motorcar accident in which the then-president died, he took over the company."

Miss Tomic paused, not because she needed to catch her breath but to allow the succinct biography of Dr Dubois to register.

"The medical director," she continued, "is Dr Geoffrey Reed, an Englishman, with qualifications from half a dozen European universities. ZeD employs only the best."

oooOooo

After breakfast, they set out for ZeD's head office, a sprawling landscape of glass buildings set in an undulating landscape of perfectly maintained lawns.

"My God," Adam exclaimed, "it looks more like a garden city than a head office."

"ZeD is the biggest of all pharmaceutical companies and, with its chemical and petrochemical divisions, is one of the world's top 100 corporations. Our turnover is bigger than the GDP of 130 countries. Our closest rival in the pharmaceutical sector, Pharma BioSolex, or PBS for short, has just a third of our pharmaceutical turnover. We are a truly mighty company. In that context, our head office is wholly proportionate."

Adam smiled. She was very serious, very focused and, no doubt, very driven. Despite himself, he wondered what she was like off-duty, relaxing with friends or in bed with a lover.

Miss Tomic parked her car in a space close to the main entrance. Given the size of the car parks, Adam surmised that Miss Tomic was a very senior employee indeed.

After various formalities, including an eye scan and the issuing of a security pass, Adam and Miss Tomic took the lift to the ninth floor. They entered what Adam assumed was Dr Dubois's office. It was the size of a tennis court.

"Would you like to freshen up?" Miss Tomic asked. "I have an *en suite* facility in my office."

"Your office? This is your office?"

"As personal assistant to Dr Dubois., I need a large office to accommodate various meeting and functions which it is not appropriate to hold in Dr Dubois's office or in the board room."

"Right," said Adam.

Once again, Adam asked himself what he was doing there. Why had the head-hunters picked him? What had he to offer a mega corporation specialising in a field about which he knew nothing in a job for which he was entirely unqualified?

"You wouldn't be here if you were not the perfect candidate for the job," Miss Tomic assured him.

So, in addition to her unnerving efficiency, she could read minds.

"All of us who are chosen by Slievins have doubts at the beginning," Miss Tomic explained. "Very soon the doubts fade away."

"Jolly good. I look forward to it," said Adam, and then added, "I don't need to freshen up."

"Then I'll see if Dr Dubois is ready to receive us."

oooOooo

Dr Dubois was a bald man with what was left of his hair neatly arranged in the form of a ring of silver fitted around the back of his head and neatly looped over each ear. He sat behind a large desk, clear of all the normal detritus of office work. Adam noticed he didn't even have a phone. At his level of seniority, Adam thought, he probably communicates telepathically. Behind the desk was a large arched window through which so much light poured that Adam could only dimly discern Dr Dubois's features.

"So you are our new marketing director," said Dr Dubois., shaking Adam's hand. "I hope you have found your hotel accommodation satisfactory."

"Very much so," Adam responded. A suite in a top Geneva hotel was unlikely to disappoint.

"And Miss Tomic is looking after you?" Dr Dubois enquired.

"I couldn't ask for a better carer," Adam responded courteously.

"A carer. I hadn't thought of Miss Tomic as a carer." Dr Dubois's laugh had no humour in it. "Nor, I hope, should I think of you as someone needing care. As a pharmaceutical company, we are of course here to help the sick. But, to help the sick, we ourselves have to be particularly healthy, eminently fit to survive in a difficult, highly competitive and over-regulated world. Your task here is especially demanding. ZeD has many strings to its bow. We are one of the world's largest chemical companies, but the jewel in our crown, indeed the crown itself, is our Pharma Division. I assume you are familiar with our range of ethical pharmaceuticals."

It didn't sound like a question, but Adam nodded just

in case it was, and then was unnerved by the thought that Dr Dubois might decide to quiz him on one of ZeD's many products. He need not have feared; Dr Dubois was in full flight.

"You join us at a critical time. Two of our major drugs are about to come out of patent. This means that in the course of next year, we will lose a substantial proportion of our pharma income. When I say substantial, I mean several billion dollars of turnover. Fortunately we still have some years to run on Migrofin, our migraine product and Pacifa, our minor tranquilliser. And, with luck and your help, well before then, we will have MC57, our new beta-blocking agent."

Adam nodded somewhere between wisely and enthusiastically.

"I understand from Miss Tomic that we are throwing you in at the deep end. You are to meet Dr Reed, when you leave here. I am most keen that you and he develop a constructive working relationship. Miss Tomic will look after you at lunch. I myself intended to have lunch with you, but unfortunately an important meeting with some government officials has come up. Another time."

Adam realised he was being dismissed. Dr Dubois rose from behind his desk and came round to shake Adam's hand a second time. "I'm sure you will find your work here rewarding – challenging, of course, but rewarding. You come highly recommended. I look forward to seeing what you can do to sharpen the cutting edge of our marketing."

"I shall certainly do my best," said Adam.

oooOooo

Miss Tomic led Adam to the lift and down to the sixth floor. "This floor houses the medical department and the medical director."

The sixth floor was beautifully appointed, with an open-plan central area and overlarge individual offices at each corner. Adam guessed the main reason that so much space had been allocated to the medical function was simply in order to indicate how much importance the company attached to it.

Dr Reed was a tall man with a crop of black hair and a world-weary look in his eyes. He greeted Adam amiably enough but with an almost imperceptible sigh, as though he already knew exactly how things would work out between them.

"I hope you have settled in well," he offered in a faintly Scottish accent.

"Very well," Adam replied. "The hotel is excellent and Miss Tomic is looking after me. I'm hoping to find an apartment in the next few days."

Dr Reed nodded. "Whenever you are ready, we can begin to talk about MC57. I don't want to rush you but Dr Dubois has emphasised the need to get you up to speed as quickly as possible."

"Well why don't we make a start now?" Adam suggested.

"I will excuse myself," said Miss Tomic. "I have to put some papers together for Dr Dubois's lunch time meeting."

"Of course," said Adam and Dr Reed in unison.

Adam settled into one of two armchairs in Dr Reed's capacious office. Dr Reed sat in the armchair opposite.

"So, Dr Reed, MC57 is the great new hope for ZeD's pharma division," Adam hazarded.

"Call me Geoffrey," Dr Reed responded and then added.

"Yes, MC57 is a beta blocker – a new-generation beta blocker – and a great deal depends on its success."

Adam felt exposed. He was no marketing expert and he knew considerably less about ethical pharmaceuticals than he did about marketing. "So when do you expect to launch the product?"

"We are hoping to get approval within the next three months. Then it's really up to you. I believe your predecessor has done all the necessary preparations for the marketing but you will want to review his work and put your own stamp on the launch. I understand you have an extraordinarily good track record."

Adam felt inclined to give up. Why did everyone have such a high regard for his talents? What on earth had David Minofel told them? He was a middle-ranking executive who had reached the age when the career road forked. He was either going to make it to board level, or he would plateau and spend the rest of his working life desperately hoping to hold on to his position and his salary. In his previous job, attaining a directorship was not out of reach, but time was passing and he knew, if he didn't make the grade within a year or two, his chance would be gone.

And then along came David Minofel. David had changed Adam's life chances. David had decided, for reasons best known to David and deeply obscure to Adam, that Adam had a bright future. No, not just a bright future – a stellar one.

But why?

Adam knew well enough that many of those who enjoyed success did not really deserve it. They had been at the right place at the right time. They had made good contacts with those who could help them. Their face fitted.

They had sucked up to the right people. There are many reasons unconnected with merit or talent that could explain success. So Adam didn't feel he didn't deserve success. He just felt that you had to be lucky to be successful and that in the past he'd not been particularly lucky.

"Well that seems pretty straightforward," said Adam.

"So long as we get the product licence," cautioned Dr Reed.

"Is that in doubt?"

"You can never be certain. The European Medicines Agency has to balance the advantages of the drug against its side effects, and they then set that assessment in the context of the alternative therapies available. MC57 is another beta blocker; there are a dozen or more on the market. We can show that ours is as effective as the best and that it has fewer and milder side effects than others, but it's still going to be expensive, so there will always be an element of doubt. It's just possible they might take the view that the advantages are marginal and not sufficient to justify the price differential."

"Wow!" said Adam. "You mean there's a chance ZeD's great new hope might never reach the market?"

"Well, yes," Dr Reed replied. "I assumed you had been told. That's really why they've brought you on board. That's why they paid off your predecessor. We're counting on you."

Adam tried to give nothing away. His face remained intelligently non-committal. But his brain was whirring like a demented, unbalanced top. Why had nobody told him? Why hadn't David briefed him? Why hadn't Miss Tomic explained the situation?

And there was something else. He had been taken on for his supposed marketing expertise. How would he be able to demonstrate his ability if the product didn't even receive a licence, didn't reach the market? It wasn't up to him to persuade the EMA to approve the drug. Surely, that was Dr Reed's problem?

"I guess I need to work through my predecessor's plans for the launch." What else could he have said without exposing his ignorance or revealing his growing conviction that everyone's confidence in him was profoundly misplaced?

"Miss Tomic will introduce you to the senior people in the marketing department this afternoon," said Dr Reed. "There's an entire product management team dedicated to MC57. They'll be able to bring you up to speed on the marketing side. I'm sure everything will go well."

Adam shook Dr Reed's hand. "Thank you, Geoffrey. Of course it will."

oooOooo

Miss Tomic picked Adam up from Dr Reed's office.

"You've sorted out Dr Dubois's lunchtime paperwork?" Adam enquired.

"Yes. He has everything he will need. How did your meeting with Dr Reed go? I hope he explained to you the importance of MC57."

"He certainly did that. I couldn't be more certain of the importance of MC57, but I do have some questions, which I'm hoping you will answer."

"Of course. We can talk things through over lunch. We all eat in the staff canteen. We're a little early but we can find a table and have a coffee before lunch."

oooOooo

Having observed the palatial splendour of the grounds and the offices of ZeD, Adam was prepared for something at the top end of the canteen excellence spectrum. Even so, when they entered the open-plan space on the second floor, he gasped.

"It is impressive," Miss Tomic offered. "I should be used to it by now, but it still takes my breath away."

It was obvious that the designer of the canteen had been gifted with great talent and an unlimited budget. The whole area was brilliantly lit to give the impression of sitting outside on a sunny day. Large palm-like plants and acoustic screens were judiciously placed to add colour and break up the area into more intimate spaces where groups, or couples, could sit and converse in comfort without disturbing others. The floor was tiled but the tiles were of a material that gave the impression of softness underfoot.

"Let's sit here," suggested Miss Tomic, selecting a large low round table with two armchairs, into which she and Adam settled. "Now what questions do you have?"

"It's difficult to know where to begin. I guess the most urgent is about MC57. It seems there's some doubt about whether it will get approval from the drugs committee. Is that right?

"It is true that we are waiting to hear whether the EMA has approved it. It is not yet approved. We have to make sure it is approved."

"And how do we do that? I mean, I assume we have submitted an application. Surely now we have to wait to see what they decide."

Miss Tomic seemed a little uneasy. "You had best talk to David about that. He will tell you what you have to do."

"What I have to do!" Adam exclaimed. "Isn't that Dr

Reed's department? I don't know anything about MC57, except that it's a beta blocker. I'm not even sure what a beta blocker is; I'm the marketing guy."

"You can't do your marketing thing without a product, and ZeD needs MC57. Yves judges everyone not on their ability to identify problems but on the speed and professionalism with which they solve them."

"I still don't see how that's my problem," Adam persisted. He wasn't an expert in pharmaceuticals, far from it, but even he knew that the best person to persuade a drugs committee of the value of a drug was the head of the medical team who had developed it.

"As I said, this is something you need to discuss with David,"

Adam decided to try a different tack. "So how good is MC57? I mean you know more about these things than I do. Is it a winner?

"It's an effective beta blocker," Miss Tomic replied.

"That doesn't sound like an enthusiastic endorsement."

"I'm not much given to enthusiasm in such matters," Miss Tomic replied. "I tend to favour scientific objectivity."

"OK, speaking scientifically and objectively, how does it match up against the competition?"

"The main competitor and currently the best product on the market is Angiax, a Pharma BioSolex drug. In my opinion, our product is as effective as Angiax".

"As effective but no more effective," Adam queried.

"As effective means no more effective,"

"What about side effects?"

"There are some side effects - but then all effective drugs have side effects. The only possibly serious side effect with MC57 is that it is might be implicated in triggering migraine attacks."

"Might be?" Adam queried. He was becoming increasingly worried. His first assignment was to manage the successful introduction of ZeD's new beta blocker but, as he understood it, the drug was no better than the competition and might have been implicated in causing a fairly serious side effect. Before he could introduce such a drug, he needed to make sure it was registered and, although he was no expert in drug registration, the facts, as presented by Miss Tomic, seemed discouraging.

"There have been one or two reports in the clinical trials that some patients with a history of migraine have suffered slightly more frequent and slightly more acute migraine attacks when on MC57 for extended periods."

"Wow!" said Adam. "So, in your professional view, what are our chances of even being able to register the drug?"

"Don't be despondent," Miss Tomic spoke as though she were speaking to a child. "It's certainly as good as its best competitor and, as I said, all effective drugs have side effects. Its main competitor, Angiax, is thought by some specialists to increase the chances of dementia."

"Well I suppose a migraine is better than dementia," Adam muttered.

"That's the spirit," said Miss Tomic. "David will fill you in on what you need to do and how best to do it. He is very professional and very effective."

"Well let's hope I can meet his exacting standards," said Adam, without conviction.

16. Of the glory that is past

The Storyteller arrived at the Smith's house in Harrow at 3.00 in the afternoon. Everything looked as it had done when he had visited before to invite them to join him on the quest. The hedge in the front garden was neatly trimmed; the small lawn neatly cut.

Eve was just putting the finishing touches to an article on conservation for the local newspaper.

The last few months had been pretty awful for Eve. The aborting of the fourth beginning had upset her deeply. Just before the initiation of the beginning, she and Adam had resolved their differences and had touched each other more profoundly than ever before. Even Bella's death had ceased to gnaw away at her heart. She had felt as she had when she and Adam had first fallen in love, but this time it was far more intense. It was as though they had found a secret that made love invulnerable – not just to the day-to-day attrition of living but to the normal and seemingly inevitable depredations of time. It was a selfless, all-encompassing euphoria which had made her feel whole. The feeling of loss, when the fourth beginning had collapsed and taken that secret with it, had left her empty and exposed.

Then there had been the recent incident when those two thugs had broken into her home, beaten up Adam and attempted to rape her. Apart from the trauma of the attacks, there was the feeling of hate she had experienced when the man called Kev had prepared to penetrate her. The hate she had felt had shocked her. It was a cold, implacable, merciless hate. At the time, if it had been within her power, there was no abuse she would not happily have perpetrated against her assailant. She would have castrated Kev without a second thought before beheading him; she would have delighted in pinning his arms to his sides with a rubber tyre soaked in petrol and then in setting the tyre alight. She would... There was no end and no limit to what that hate would have made her do. And her hate had shocked her to the core.

Then there was the extraordinary way the incident had been brought to an end. David Minofel's timely arrival and ruthlessly efficient method of resolving the situation had aggravated rather than assuaged the trauma. First, he had done what she had wanted to do. It meant she was somehow complicit in what he had done. And then he had made it all go away. Minofel had killed two men. The first killing, of the man Darren, might have been excused on the grounds of self-defence or defence of others. But the despatching of Kev was a different matter. Kev had been defenceless. Minofel had been judge, jury and executioner. And as she, Eve, had done nothing to stop him or report what had happened, she too had taken the law into her own hands – or, perhaps more accurately, disregarded the law altogether.

On top of all these causes for stress, Adam had taken a job in Geneva. Of course they had discussed the job offer at some length. But they had discussed it as the people they had been before the quest, not as the enriched and enhanced individuals Eve had thought they had become when the fourth beginning began. They had talked of the salary, of the doors the tutelage of Slievins would open, of what Adam might achieve – but these were all humdrum, worldly considerations. With the Storyteller, she and Adam had set out on a quest to find meaning. In contrast, Adam now seemed to be settling for an attractive employment package offered by a Swiss pharmaceutical company and, to some extent, she was doing the same.

When she heard the bell ring, Eve felt a momentary pang of fear. Cautiously she peered through the thick glass of the door panel. She recognised her visitor at once.

"Hello Eve. I hope you are well."

It seemed such a banal greeting. The last time they had been together, they had been full of the joy engendered by the fourth beginning.

"May I come in?"

Eve stood aside from the door to allow the Storyteller to enter. She had wondered whether they would ever see the Storyteller again. Part of her had hoped he would turn up at some time, if only to explain what had happened; but part of her feared what he might have to tell her. Perhaps he would tell her they were under observation by whatever powers had stopped the fourth beginning. Since these powers had disapproved of whatever event they had initiated, they would probably look unfavourably on those who had triggered it. And it might be worse than that. Perhaps these powers were planning to sanction her and Adam, to punish them for challenging the existing order – the order they represented. It was with mixed feelings she showed the Storyteller into the drawing room.

"Where is Luke?" asked the Storyteller. "I expected a fulsome canine greeting."

"He's in the garden," said Eve. "Would you like some coffee?

"That would be kind."

There was a silence.

"I should have phoned," said the Storyteller.

"No need. Not a problem. I've just finished an article

I've been working on."

"Still earning an honest journalistic crust?"

Eve put down the coffee pot. "What happened? What on earth happened?" She had had enough of banalities.

The Storyteller took a deep breath. "Well, obviously the fourth beginning was aborted."

"Yes, obviously," Eve replied, showing some impatience. "But who stopped it? How did they stop it? Why did they stop it?"

"Hold on," the Storyteller interrupted. "At least let me have some coffee, and I will tell you all I know. Although I should say at the outset, all I know is not very much."

There was a violent scratching at the back door. Luke had been expecting the Storyteller, but, like his mistress, he viewed the man's arrival with a mixture of emotions – in his case pleasure and trepidation. He liked the Storyteller well enough, and, being a dog, was always delighted to meet old friends. On the other hand, Luke enjoyed his home comforts, and the Storyteller had the habit of inviting people on extraordinary journeys – journeys which rarely afforded regular meals, comfortable rugs or warm and welcoming fires, even when it turned cold,.

"We'd better get the reunion over," suggested the Storyteller.

Luke entered and padded over to the Storyteller. "What kept you?" Luke minded to the visitor.

"It's a long story," the Storyteller minded back, patting Luke's luxuriant white and golden coat. "Eve is going to ask me lots of questions, so you had best wait until we've settled down, and then you can share the answers I give her."

"Well?" said Eve. She plonked the freshly poured mug of coffee down in front of the now-seated Storyteller.

"Do you have any sugar?"

Eve scarcely concealed her irritation. "Will you be wanting any biscuits?" she enquired threateningly as she placed the sugar bowl before her guest.

"Has something happened here?" the Storyteller asked suddenly.

"What do you mean?"

"I just have a feeling something intense happened here. I have a nose for these things."

"I should leave it alone," minded Luke, "You're right but I shouldn't pursue the matter. I'll explain later."

"Forget it." The Storyteller took Luke's advice. "It's just me being silly. I've been on edge since the fourth beginning ended."

"Since the fourth beginning ended…" Eve repeated. "It didn't end; it was stopped; it was aborted. How could something so good and so powerful just fizzle out. I thought you said that if we could somehow initiate the fourth beginning, nothing on earth could stop it."

"I didn't actually say that, although I may have implied it, and I certainly believed it."

"Well, what's the answer?"

The Storyteller shook his head, as though hoping to put his thoughts into good order. "Throughout the quest, we were impeded at every turn by Nick Peters. Nick's an old adversary of mine – known him for longer than I choose to remember. Now Nick, as you know, worked for an organisation called the Breakers. Adam will remember well enough their regional head office at Cadnam. By the way, when will Adam be back?"

"Adam's not here. He's in Geneva."

The Storyteller was stunned. He had assumed that, after

the ordeal of the quest, Adam and Eve would wish to resume a fairly dull routine, at least for the first few months. After all, they had been through experiences vouchsafed to very few – very, very few – and had surely done enough travelling to last them a lifetime. He had also assumed that Adam and Eve would be together. They had no one else with whom they could discuss what they had been through. No one would have understood; no one would have believed them.

"What's he doing in Geneva?"

"He's working there. He has a job with ZeD, the Swiss pharmaceutical company."

"Does he? I didn't know he'd worked in pharmaceuticals."

"He hasn't," said Eve, sharply. She wanted the Storyteller to answer her questions, not to spend time answering his.

"I should leave that alone, too," Luke chipped in. "Again, I can fill you in later. Best answer Eve's question before you feel the sharper edge of her tongue."

"I thought Adam would be coming in later. You see, Kit is planning to visit in an hour or so. We wanted to talk to both of you. Do you want me to put Kit off?"

"What I want is for you to answer my questions. Adam isn't here but don't let that prevent you, or Kit for that matter, from giving me some answers."

The Storyteller decided it would be best to continue with his rather sketchy explanation of what had happened. "As I was saying, we know that the main opposition to the fourth beginning was mounted by the Breakers. As well as Nick Peters and Grimrose, we had some dealings with the Chief Dawk, Despiro Niholopificus. You and Rambler made short work of his attempts to block the beginning, I seem to remember."

"Is this going anywhere?" Eve snapped. "I remember everything that happened on the quest. Let's face it, every moment is seared into my memory. I don't need to be reminded of what happened. I want to know why, when it seemed certain we had succeeded, when the organisation at Cadnam was defeated – no, destroyed – why the fourth beginning fizzled out."

"Well, as I said, I'm not sure I have an answer, except to suggest that behind the Breakers, there must be a more powerful organisation, an organisation so powerful that even when a beginning has been initiated, they can stop it."

"Do you know who they are? Do you know how they operate?

"Not really."

"Do you have any evidence at all that these very powerful people or their very powerful organisation actually exist?"

"I think it's a reasonable assumption," the Storyteller responded, a little petulantly.

"Well, I can make assumptions myself: I can assume that whatever stopped the fourth beginning is not best pleased with those who started it; I have good reason to assume Adam and I could be under threat. And, although I can see it might not be much help, I should like to know who is doing the threatening."

"That's why I am here," said the Storyteller. "We've been discussing the situation and we all want to know more. Like you, we want to know who stopped the fourth beginning. We want to know how they stopped it. And, most important of all, we want to talk to you and Adam about the possibility of trying again."

17. Meeting McFall

The afternoon of Adam's first day at ZeD Pharmaceuticals was taken up with meeting with the marketing department. Miss Tomic escorted him to the fifth floor.

Each of ZeD's products fell into one of the major therapeutic groups. The company was particularly well-represented in psychotropics: in addition to Pacifa, a minor tranquilizer, it had a number of powerful psychotropic medicines for the treatment of schizophrenia and other psychoses. In addition to psychotropics, the company had significant shares of the market for appetite suppression, as well as cancer, diabetes and cold treatments – all either large markets or ones where high prices could be justified or both.

The marketing department employed some 70 executive and ancillary staff. Each major drug had its own product manager, who was responsible for all aspects of his charge. The product manager could call on the expertise of the medical department, research and development, the technical services department, the market research people and even the factory manager, but, at the end of the day, the product manager was responsible for its success and the one who would be held accountable if it failed.

"Hi," said a cheerful-looking individual with unkempt hair and sleepy blue eyes. "I'm Guy, Guy McFall. And for my sins, I'm the Product Manager for MC57." He was playing nervously with a silver paper knife.

"Good," said Adam, shaking Guy's hand. Thank God there was someone who specialised in the company's great new drug, someone who could answer all his questions, bring him up to speed, and perhaps make up for any deficiencies that Adam's own lack of experience might expose.

"I expect you'll want to review where we are with the marketing," Guy suggested. "Nothing is fixed, obviously. You can make any changes you want, of course, but you might as well see our initial ideas."

"I'd like that."

Guy relaxed a little. He put the silver paper knife away. He was pleased that Adam was not suffering from 'new broom' syndrome. ZeD had little patience with failures, so there was a fairly high turnover of marketing directors. In his twelve years with ZeD, he had seen three new appointments to the post before Adam. All three had insisted on scrapping past plans and starting from scratch. Indeed, one of them had refused even to discuss existing strategies. It was encouraging to have a director who was prepared at least to look at the work that had already been done.

After meeting Guy's two assistants and the other product managers, Adam settled down in Guy's office to review the draft marketing strategy for MC57.

"One thing that is fixed for MC57," Guy began, "is the brand name, Angeloma. We started with about 20 suggestions and tested them all extensively. Angeloma passed all the tests. It had either positive or neutral connotations in all countries. The 'ang' pointed towards one of the main indications for MC57, angina, but then turned away with 'loma' to suggest a soft, painless conclusion."

"You don't think the 'angel' at the beginning might suggest a not entirely happy outcome for someone suffering from a heart condition?"

Guy was taken aback. "I hadn't thought of that. You get so close to something you miss the obvious. Now you've got me really worried."

"Don't," said Adam. "I was joking. I'm sure the brand name will do very well. Everyone loves an angel. They are messengers almost always bringing good news. What more could you want if you have angina?"

Guy relaxed again. Clearly the new marketing director had a sense of humour, and, more importantly, could see both sides of an argument. Guy had had enough of the driven, myopic types who were favoured by boards for such appointments. How often had he heard 'We'll do it my way because my way is the right way" or "I didn't get where I am by listening to others" or "If your ideas had any merit, you'd be sitting where I am and I'd be listening to you". When making appointments as marketing directors, boards seemed to prize unreasoning arrogance above all other qualities, on the grounds that it demonstrated leadership qualities – the same kind of leadership qualities, Guy surmised, that were responsible for the Charge of the Light Brigade.

Guy then outlined his provisional marketing strategy for MC57. "Obviously, we'll be majoring on the 'There is no better beta blocker' theme. Dr Reed will go along with that. It's not as strong as we would like. We'd like to claim it was the best, but the Medical Department say the evidence won't support such a claim. Our main competitor, the brand leader, is Angiax, a Pharma BioSolex product. I think we could still argue the 'best beta blocker' case. If it is as effective as Angiax and has fewer or milder side effects, surely we can say it's the best? But Reed says the claim would suggest that MC57 was the most effective beta blocker in its primary indication, and that would be misleading."

Adam realised Guy expected a comment from him, so he said: "I'll discuss it with Dr Reed."

Guy seemed satisfied. Then, with the aid of a slide projector, he took Adam through the entire campaign: an analysis of the market; the main competitors; a comparison of strengths and weaknesses of the competitor drugs; a review of competitor claims and promotional material; key propositions for MC57; the visual approach; draft advertisements and mailings; the text to be learned by all company reps promoting the drug – even the technical data sheet. It took the best part of two hours.

"That seems pretty comprehensive to me," Adam said at the end. This was an understatement: it was a masterly presentation; it was coherent and professional; and it had answered every question Adam had thought of asking. "Well done," he added.

Guy decided he liked his new boss.

18. Filling in

No sooner had Adam returned to his hotel room at the end of what had been a challenging and tiring day than the phone rang. It was David Minofel.

"We're having dinner together. You must have many questions. We'll eat in the hotel. I'll meet you in the dining room at 7.30."

Adam spent the hour before dinner writing up notes on the people he had met and what they had told him. He prepared brief lists of questions for Dr Reed, Guy McFall and Miss Tomic. He had just one question for David Minofel. How was he supposed to influence in any way the registration of MC57?

When he entered the main hotel restaurant at 7.30 sharp, David Minofel was nowhere to be seen. Adam told the head waiter he was expecting company. The head waiter was polite but showed no special interest until Adam told him the name of his dining companion. Adam was unsure of the precise nature of the effect that the name had, but, for sure, it was dramatic and instantaneous. He certainly now had the head waiter's full attention.

"Mr Minofel is waiting for you. He is in one of the alcoves just off the main restaurant. You will not be disturbed."

"I hope that will not preclude a waiter from taking our order."

The head waiter saw nothing amusing in Adam's quip. "I can assure you of the highest levels of service at all times."

"I'm sure," said Adam, in a failed attempt to put the man at ease.

The alcove was really more of a private room, furnished with a dining table – laid for two but large enough to have accommodated four – beautifully carved dining chairs, a coffee table and four armchairs. There was a crystal chandelier over the table and standard lamps beside each of the armchairs.

"Let's have a drink before the meal. I have ordered a bottle of champagne. We must celebrate the first day of your new life."

"You're very kind," said Adam. "It's a little early to celebrate. I've scarcely got my feet under the table."

David smiled. "You have much to learn. Sit," he instructed, handing Adam a glass of champagne, "and listen. This is your first lesson. You have some notion that success comes though merit and effort. Well, no one would suggest that merit and effort are irrelevant, but let me tell you that you can have merit in spades and bucketsful of effort, but, if that's all you have, success can easily slip through your fingers like dry sand on a windswept shore"

Adam frowned momentarily and then smiled. Was that some kind of extended, littoral metaphor? He could imagine what Numpty would have made of it.

"I amuse you?" Minofel enquired without malice.

"No, not at all. I was just thinking of something else."

"Well, there is one thing you do need for success – and that is concentration." Now Minofel smiled, to indicate the rebuke was mild.

"Of course," said Adam.

"How was your meeting with Yves Dubois.?

"Good. It went well. At least I think it did."

"You see, there you go again. 'The meeting went well. At least I think it did.' No. The meeting went well, and that's the end of it. Of course, it's your opinion – everything any of us says is our opinion. But that goes without saying, so don't say it.

"This is really important. You are going to the top. You have to behave as though you know that is where you belong. You must speak as though you know exactly where you are heading. Above all, you must believe in yourself. If you believe in yourself, others will believe in you. Leaders and winners are not leaders and winners because they have more merit than others, nor because they try harder; they are leaders and winners because they are absolutely convinced they have an inviolable right to lead and win. Enough. End of the first lesson."

Adam hoped the expression on his face indicated complete agreement.

"There was one thing that Dr Dubois said that I didn't really understand. In my talk with him and indeed with Dr Reed, I got the impression that I would be held in some way responsible for ensuring MC57 is approved by the EMA. That doesn't really make any sense."

"Really?" Minofel's tone conveyed surprise and disappointment in equal measure. "MC57 is a crucial element in ZeD's marketing strategy. The company needs a new drug to bolster its revenues as some of their older drugs come out of patent. How can you successfully market this new wonder drug if it is not approved?"

"No, I see that. But surely it is up to Dr Reed to follow-up on the submission to the EMA. He knows all there is to know about the drug, and the trials, and the toxicology."

David Minofel smiled. "Good to see you're picking up the terminology. Of course Dr Reed and his minions have made the submission. But now we all need to do whatever we can to make sure the submission is approved. The man who is dealing with MC57 at the EMA is an Italian, Giovanni Spinetti. He's an old friend of mine, and a very nice man. You should meet him. Talk to him and find out how the submission is going. Just a friendly informal chat. Matters always move more smoothly when all those involved know each other, don't you find?"

"I suppose so," said Adam, still not entirely convinced that a meeting with an EMA official would prove productive. He had so much to learn, and a friendly informal chat with an expert, before he had even fully grasped what MC57 was for or what it could do, had to be a low priority.

"You're wrong," said David, evidently reading Adam's mind. "It's probably the most important thing you can do. I've arranged for you to have a meeting with Giovanni on Thursday evening. He will come here at 7.00 pm. I've booked this alcove for you. I shan't be there but I know you two will get on well. Now let's eat."

19. Regrouping

The Storyteller's suggestion that she should consider an attempt to restart the fourth beginning took Eve by surprise. Given that the Storyteller had no idea what implacable force had stopped the fourth beginning, it seemed doubly stupid to consider reengaging with the project.

And yet the idea of a second attempt gave Eve a spark of hope for the first time in months. When the fourth beginning had collapsed, Eve had felt a terrible, profound loss. They had set out on the quest to find answers, answers to the questions that everyone asks themselves at some point in their lives. In particular, Eve had been desperate to know why her daughter Bella, her beautiful, vivacious daughter, had died.

The journey they had taken with the Storyteller had been extraordinary. She had been able to ask her questions, and, although no one – not God, not Prometheus, and certainly not Nick Peters or the Chief Dawk, Despiro Nihilopificus – had been able to give her answers, she and Adam had made progress.

They had persisted in the quest and survived the most determined efforts of their enemies to destroy them. They had found a new purpose in the possibility of initiating a fourth beginning, and it had seemed they had succeeded – indeed, they had succeeded.

Then, the fourth beginning had ended almost as soon as it had begun. The quest had failed; their progress somehow invalidated. She and Adam had sunk back into normality – that grey, dull, monotonous land of the pointless passing of time.

"Why don't you make her a cup of tea?" Luke minded to the Storyteller. "Kit will be here soon and I think she is going to need some refreshment."

"I'll make some tea," said the Storyteller.

"No, I'll do it," said Eve, snapping back to the present.

As she stood up, the doorbell rang. Eve opened the front door.

"Hello, Eve, what a great day for a fresh start!"

Eve laughed. "Hello, Kit. It's really good to see you. Come in."

Luke ran to Kit, tail wagging. "Hello, Luke, it's good to see you too, or would be if I could," said Kit, patting Luke.

"You took your time," minded Luke. "I thought you'd come weeks ago, as soon as you knew the fourth beginning had failed."

"There's a time for everything and everything in its time," Kit said soothingly, words which Eve took to be a mild reproach to Luke for his over-enthusiastic greeting.

"Calm down, Luke. At least let Kit sit down."

Luke offered to lead Kit into the sitting room, but it was evident the blind man needed no help.

"I was just about to make a pot of tea," said Eve, withdrawing to the kitchen.

"Have you raised the matter with her?" Kit asked the Storyteller when Eve was out of earshot.

"Yes. I've told her we would like to discuss the possibility of trying again. She hasn't responded. I think she's letting it sink in."

"Does she understand the risks?"

"She hasn't said anything but I think we can assume she is only too well aware of the risks. Both she and Adam were badly hit by the collapse of the fourth beginning. Eve, in particular, has grasped that, whatever aborted the Beginning, it was more powerful than all of us, more powerful than we could imagine. We'd already seen how ruthless the Breakers could be. They tortured Adam, killed Gwoat and tried to kill the rest of us. And yet we won against the Breakers. So whatever stopped the fourth beginning is likely to be much more powerful and more ruthless than the Breakers."

"Quite so," Kit agreed.

Eve returned with the tea. "I'm afraid Adam's not here. He's in Geneva. He has a new job with ZeD Pharmaceuticals."

"That's not a problem," said Kit. "Obviously, before we decide anything, we need to talk to both of you and we all need to agree, but we're not at that stage yet. We need to know more about our enemy before we could possibly take any decisions. Let's just talk about what we've been doing since we last met, like old friends catching up with each other. After all, that's what we are and what we should do."

Eve felt relieved. She certainly didn't feel up to taking any decisions.

The three of them chatted easily about the time since they had last been together. Two pots of tea and a light meal later, Eve asked: "Where are you two staying?

"I thought I would find a local hotel and take a room for a few days," Kit replied.

"I might join you," said the Storyteller. Prune and Andrew are holding on to the camper van, so I'll need a room too."

"I won't hear any such thing," said Eve. "You're both staying here. We have two spare bedrooms; you can stay as long as you like."

"We can't impose on you," said Kit.

"You're not imposing on me. I'll be grateful for the

company. And, if we're seriously thinking of resuming the quest or reactivating it, we need to think things through. And that will take some time."

20. Giovanni

Adam's second day at ZeD began, as had the day before, with the arrival of Miss Tomic at the hotel at 6.30 am.

"Good morning," she had said when he had picked up the house phone. "I'll be in the restaurant. I'll order coffee."

When Adam joined her, Miss Tomic was sitting by herself at the same table they had occupied on the previous day. She looked stunning.

"How do you do it?" Adam asked.

Do what?"

"Look so," Adam paused, and then said it anyway, "beautiful. At this time in the morning," he added, in an attempt to take some of the intimacy out of the observation.

Miss Tomic frowned. "What I look like is irrelevant, as is the time of day. I like to look presentable at all times."

"I'm sorry. I didn't mean to be personal."

"It is difficult to see..." Miss Tomic began before pausing; for a moment, Adam thought he saw half a smile, "how an observation about someone's appearance can be anything other than personal."

Adam seriously considered arguing the point. After all, you could look at a painting or indeed a landscape and say that either or both were beautiful, so aesthetic appreciation need not be personal. He decided against it because, of course, she was right.

"You met with David Minofel last night," Miss Tomic said. He told me you are meeting the man from the EMA, Giovanni, on Thursday evening. David gave this envelope for me to give to you. As you will see, it is for M. Spinetti.

It is a letter from David, introducing you and emphasising how important you are to ZeD."

"Do you know this Spinetti character?" Adam asked. He still felt uneasy about meeting an expert from the European drug licensing authority while still relatively ignorant of the drug which, if not the main topic of conversation, was certain to come up in his meeting with Spinetti.

"I have met him once or twice before. He seems a nice enough man."

The waiter invited them to visit the buffet. Miss Tomic declined but Adam felt hungry. He took a couple of croissants and returned to the table.

Adam sliced the croissants open, buttered them, and then added some marmalade from a small pot that popped when he opened it.

"What are your plans for the day?" Miss Tomic asked.

"I'm going to spend the morning with Guy McFall and learn as much as I can about MC57. In the afternoon, I'll meet some of his staff and some of the other Product Managers. I know MC57 is important but as Marketing Director I had better try to get my head round all the products in the range, at least the most important ones. There are two I've heard about already; Migrofin and Pacifa. I should get up to speed on those, and no doubt there are others."

"Yes, there are," Miss Tomic confirmed. "It's top secret but we have an anti-cancer drug in development that could be very exciting. And there are several other promising compounds in the pipeline."

"Good to know," said Adam, washing down the last mouthful of his second croissant with his third cup of coffee.

"You should not put butter on the croissants," Miss

Tomic observed. "They are butter croissants. They consist predominantly of butter."

Well, wasn't that a bit personal? thought Adam. Was she concerned about his health or his weight, or was she just telling him off? Or did his gluttony, his excessive appetite for butter, offend her? Perhaps she was simply correcting his manners? Didn't he know that buttering croissants was simply unacceptable in polite Genevan society?

He thought all these things, but, instead of saying them, he slipped the letter Miss Tomic had given him into the inside pocket of his jacket, then looked into his companion's lustrous green eyes and simply said: "Point taken".

21. Decon

In his private chambers in the accommodation block housing the apartments of all senior members of the Praesidium, Simon Goodfellow was savouring a particularly pleasurable moment. The heavily drugged girl was not at present conscious of the damage that Goodfellow's brutal exploration of all her orifices had caused, but, when she emerged from the dark place into which the drug and Goodfellow's perverse appetites had cast her, she would certainly need strong analgesics and possibly surgical attention, not to mention long-term counselling.

Simon looked at the girl's body, strewn on the bed. There was no discernible expression in his cold grey eyes. He assessed his handiwork. She really didn't look very attractive, not any more. She lay on her back, her legs apart. Her blond hair was a mess; the bruises were beginning to show; and the blood from the cuts was soiling the sheets.

Simon's ruminations on the satisfaction he derived from turning something beautiful and innocent into something ugly and corrupt or corrupted were interrupted by a buzzer. Simon looked at his watch. He had half an hour to shave and dress before the Decon meeting in the Presidium's main conference room. "Clear this mess up," he said to the manservant who had been video-recording Simon's perversions, "and deal with the girl."

oooOooo

The Decon meetings took place on the last Wednesday of each month. No one looked forward to them, but they were an unassailable tradition and one which John Noble, the Chairman of the Praesidium, like every chairman before him, considered essential. It was mandatory for all members of the Executive Committee (i.e. the senior members of the Praesidium and the four heads of the operational divisions) to attend.

The agenda of the Decon meetings was always the same. The main items were depravity, extremism, corruption, obfuscation and negativity. These were the main levers by which the Praesidium maintained its grip on human society and the general course of human history. The relative importance of each of these levers varied over time, but it was the purpose of the Decon meeting to review each area and to ensure that all the drives were working together and heading in the same direction.

When Simon Goodfellow reached the conference room, John Noble was already in the chairman's seat, chatting to two other early arrivals, both operational heads – or monitaurs, as they were officially titled. One of the monitaurs was Lotte Axelrod, the only female member of the committee. Lotte had overall responsibility for depravity. The other monitaur was Oliver Nates, whose remit was obfuscation and negativity.

John Noble nodded a greeting to Simon, who was taking his seat next to the chairman. A moment later, the bulky Manfred Bloch arrived, accompanied by the other two monitaurs: Edgar Exton, in charge of extremism, and Charlie Cornick, who handled corruption.

"Since we are all present, let's begin," said John Noble, calling the meeting to order. "I'm sure you will all join me in hoping we can keep this meeting short today. I have several other matters which require my attention - and I'm sure all of you are busy too."

This was a more or less standard opening remark from the Chairman. Although no one seemed very keen on the Decon sessions, they were never brief. Once the meeting began, everyone liked to have their say, regardless of whether it was on the point or not. And John Noble, despite his appeals for brevity, was extraordinarily indulgent, allowing members, both the senior members of the Praesidium and the monitaurs, far more latitude than either Simon Goodfellow or Manfred Bloch considered appropriate. But then, John Noble was the chairman, and they weren't.

"Lotte," said the Chairman, "Let's begin with depravity."

22. Of times past

When Eve awoke, she heard movement downstairs. For a moment, she froze. Then she remembered she had house guests. The Storyteller and Kit were in the house. She snuggled down in the bed, feeling safer than she had since Adam had left for Geneva. Not that she felt permanently insecure, but, after the attempted burglary and rape, she had to admit to a tremor of fear whenever the doorbell rang or she heard a noise she couldn't immediately recognise or explain.

The three of them shared a cooked breakfast prepared by the Storyteller. "I'll pop out and do some shopping after breakfast. I've used all your bacon and you only have a couple of eggs left. And you're short of milk,"

Eve laughed. "You could be very useful to have around. Cooking and shopping. I don't suppose you do cleaning as well."

"I have been known to use a vacuum cleaner, although, to be honest, it's always seemed a waste of time. I avoid battles I can't win, and the fight against dust is definitely a lost cause."

Eve laughed. "I'll settle for cooking and shopping then."

After washing up and the Storyteller's departure on a shopping expedition, Eve and Kit sat at the dining table with a cup of coffee.

"How are you?" Kit asked.

"I'm all right. No, I'm not all right. I don't know where I am. We came so close to something incredibly important. I thought we had achieved something incredibly important.

And then it stopped. I've found my life after our quest confusing, humdrum, pointless. When we initiated the fourth beginning, when we were all together in that house in Hampshire, there was a fellowship, a love that seemed irresistible and infinite. How could that end? How could that be snuffed out? I've found it really hard to adjust. In fact, I haven't adjusted. I've just gone along with things but I don't really feel part of things."

"What about Adam?" Kit could feel Eve's sense of isolation.

"That's something else. He has adjusted much more easily. He seems to have accepted that the quest failed and that we should go back to the way we were. I can't do that. I went on the quest to try to make sense of Bella's death. We succeeded in a way, or at least I thought we had. But our success depended on sustaining the fourth beginning. Now I feel worse than I did before we set out with the Storyteller.

"Do you think Adam feels Bella's death less than you?"

Eve was silent for a minute or two. "I really can't answer that. You know, when the accident happened, I thought he felt Bella's death even more acutely than I did. I thought he was going mad, or at least suffering a complete mental breakdown. He would be ranting against the unfairness of life one minute and then sobbing like a child the next. He kept rerunning the events of that day. If we had set out a minute earlier or a minute later, the accident wouldn't have happened. If we had taken a different path through the park, the accident wouldn't have happened. If I had said no when Bella asked to take Luke for a walk, the accident wouldn't have happened. If we hadn't had a puppy, Bella wouldn't have wanted to go for a walk, and the accident wouldn't have happened. He just went on and on and on."

"That must have been hard for you. Just when you needed Adam's support, you lost him."

"I really did think I had lost him at one point. A few weeks after the accident, he stopped ranting and crying. When I asked him how he was, he told me he had doubts about his own existence. I had no idea what he meant. He told me that he had thought things through and he now realised that he was simply a focal point for all his memories. Each day, he had experiences. These experiences became memories. And this ever-growing bank of memories was all that he was. He said obviously some memories were good and some bad; some gave pleasure and some gave pain. But once you realised they were just memories, and that you were just the sum total of these memories, there was no point in feeling pleasure or pain because, in reality, there was no 'you' to do the feeling. The self was an illusion."

"You think this was a defence mechanism against the pain," Kit suggested.

"I didn't know what to think. I studied philosophy at university and, to be honest, I thought Adam had picked up some half-baked ideas from somewhere and was simply hoping they would help him make sense of it all. I didn't say anything but I thought his argument was like saying that, if a broken leg was causing you pain, you could just decide it wasn't your leg. Surely, if he felt the pain of Bella's death, he felt it. In a way, he had a duty to feel it. He couldn't wish it away. That would have been a betrayal of Bella."

"Perhaps you are stronger than Adam."

"I don't think it was a matter of strength; it was a question of honesty. If I feel pain, there has to be an 'I' to feel it. There is the memory. But then there is the recollection of the memory and the emotional response the recollection elicits. The recalling and the response require an 'I' that is not simply the memory, that is more than the memory, and more, much more, than the sum of all memories. It is the self. And whether we like it or not, we are stuck with it."

Kit laughed. "You speak like a philosopher. '*Cogito ergo sum*,' or, perhaps more precisely, 'I feel therefore I am'. So how did Adam come out of his self-denying phase?"

"He just did. After a year or so, the normal routines of life reasserted themselves and Adam seemed to have come to terms with what had happened."

"And you?"

Eve smiled a sad smile. "You know me, Kit. I have never come to terms with Bella's death."

"But you came close at the fourth beginning," Kit reminded her.

"Yes, in a way," Eve conceded. "But it wasn't that I came to terms with it. There was something in what we initiated that transcended it, that transcended everything, even Bella's death. It was love, but it was more than love. It was a timeless, benign, incontrovertible force. I don't know what it was except that is was good and it was more than good to be a part of it."

"You feel the loss. We all feel the loss," said Kit. "What we achieved was beyond words. And then it was gone. We were complete; and then we were broken."

"We've done our best to manage but then we had some unpleasantness here." As soon as she had said it, Eve knew it was a mistake. The burglary and its outcome were morally and legally problematic, and she certainly didn't want to discuss the subject. And David Minofel had emphasised, that, in view of the way in which the matter had been resolved, the fewer who knew about the incident, the better.

"Some unpleasantness?" Kit queried.

"Oh, just some domestic problems, some disagreements about where we were heading and what we were doing – personal matters, you know."

Kit nodded and pried no more.

"And how is Adam now? You say he is in Geneva. How did that happen?"

"He has a new job. He was head-hunted for a senior appointment with ZeD, the Swiss pharmaceutical company."

"And he took the job and left you here?"

"They offered him a massive salary. Adam felt he couldn't say no."

Kit smiled, then shook his head. "That complicates matters. We came to discuss the possibility of trying to reactivate the fourth beginning. You and Adam are the key to that enterprise. It sounds as though Adam is now preoccupied with other things."

"I could talk to him," Eve offered uncertainly. "He is very focused on his career at the moment."

"That doesn't sound like the Adam I know, or knew. According to the Storyteller, he set out on the quest without a second thought for his career. He wanted answers to some big questions. Has he changed?"

"I think he has given up, given up on the big questions. He just wants to do ordinary things. And this job he's taken on is really rather special. He's trebled his salary."

"Wow!" said Kit. "How did that happen?"

"As I said, he was head-hunted. This chap, David Minofel, works for Slievins, the city consultancy firm, contacted Adam and told him that, if he agreed, they would manage his career. We were both a bit sceptical but Slievins is a well-established firm, and Adam's first assignment has put him in a different league. I can't pretend the money won't be useful."

"Useful for what?" Kit enquired.

"We can't all be like you," Eve laughed. "You seem to wander the countryside, without a care in the world. I think you're amazing, but we lesser mortals have to think about the future and pensions and that kind of thing. After all, Adam lost fifteen years in hell at Cadnam."

"I see," said Kit. There was ill-disguised disappointment in his voice. "So you and Adam would prefer to forget about the fourth beginning altogether."

"No, I'm not saying that. I'll talk to Adam. He's flying back this weekend. You can ask him yourself."

"That would be good. I'm not here to persuade you one way or the other, but it's important you think about what we achieved and whether we should try to do more. And, at the same time, you can tell him about the baby."

Luke, who had been lying quietly at Eve's feet, twitched and gave a small yelp.

23. A gift

On Wednesday morning at 6.30 a.m., Adam received his now-familiar phone call.

"I'll be down in a jiffy," said Adam.

When Adam joined Miss Tomic, she looked as beautiful as ever, but her expression was more serious than usual. She looked concerned. "The letter I gave you," she began immediately, while pouring Adam a coffee: "I feel I should explain."

Yes," Adam replied expectantly, tapping his jacket to confirm he had the letter safely secured in the inside pocket.

"It's not just a letter. It also contains a banker's draft."

Adam frowned. "A banker's draft? Does David owe Spinetti some money?"

Miss Tomic seemed embarrassed. "Well, yes, in a way. Or no, not really."

Now Adam was concerned. This was not at all like Miss Tomic. Miss Tomic was in control of everything. She spoke in precise, perfect English. Clearly, she was ill at ease. "Could you be a little more specific?" Adam prompted.

"David has a special relationship with Giovanni, as he has with many of his contacts. David has a way of enlisting people to his cause. People like to help David, and, when they help him, he likes to thank them."

Adam frowned and his eyes narrowed. "Are you telling me he bribes people?"

"No," said Miss Tomic, regaining a little of her composure. "Bribing is when you give someone money to do what you want. David simply thanks people after they have helped him. There is no prior agreement as to what the gift will be, or how much it will be. It is entirely up to David to give what he thinks appropriate. David is a very generous man. He often gives gifts just to make people happy, rather than to thank them."

"Why are you telling me this?" Adam asked. Why hadn't she left things as they were? He was simply delivering a letter to Spinetti. Why had she told him the letter contained money?

"I thought you should know."

"You thought, or David thought?" He didn't need to ask the question: the answer was obvious. If David had wanted him to know he would have told him. Adam just wanted her to confirm that she had told him on her own initiative.

"I thought," she said.

Adam fell silent. This needed thinking through. However Miss Tomic dressed it up, he was delivering a bribe to an official of the EMA. He was not the briber and, if Miss Tomic had not told him, there would have been no way for him to know about the bribe. But now he did know. Did that make him culpable – and if so, to what extent?

Miss Tomic had said that David's gifts were for past services, so this banker's draft was not to elicit approval of MC57. It was a thank you for a past favour. It might even have been an entirely gratuitous gift, just to make Giovanni happy – although that seemed highly improbable. If it was for a past favour, it must have related to a favour granted before Adam was employed by ZeD. That somehow distanced him from the bribery, although he accepted the reasoning was rather spurious.

And why had Miss Tomic – his mentor, the beautiful acolyte of Minofel – told him something that Minofel had not wanted him to know? He had assumed she was Minofel's creature but evidently she had a mind, possibly even an agenda, of her own. He needed more information. What was the gift or bribe for? How much money was involved? He should ask David but he couldn't, not if Miss Tomic had told him of the banker's draft without Minofel's permission. And, in any case, it would be difficult to ask David about what could be construed as a bribe. What would David say? "Yes it is a bribe. Deliver it." Or "No. it's not a bribe. Deliver it." It wouldn't make any difference either way; he would still be expected to deliver it. Unless he said no, of course.

"You are not drinking your coffee," Miss Tomic observed.

"I was thinking," he said.

"Good," said Miss Tomic. "It's always good to think."

24. The gathering-in

Luke had been lying at Eve's feet during her morning chat with Kit, listening attentively to every word. He noted that, although Eve trusted Kit, she had decided not to tell him about the burglary. There were practical reasons for keeping quiet, but Luke sensed Eve felt ashamed, ashamed of being involved in the deaths of the two men and ashamed of the hate she had felt for them.

He also registered Kit's keenness to resume the quest, to attempt to reactivate the fourth beginning. That seemed odd to Luke: after all, it wasn't Kit's quest. He had joined the quest by chance. He had made a massive contribution to the battle with the Breakers and the initiation of the beginning but he certainly didn't seem to be troubled by any questions to which he didn't have answers, so his obvious enthusiasm for taking on whatever had aborted the Beginning was surprising. Surprising and not entirely welcome to a dog who much preferred the home comforts of a cushioned bed, and, in winter, a warm fire, to the hardships and possible dangers of renewed questing.

None of these thoughts was the reason for the twitching and yelping. Eve was pregnant. *Eve was pregnant!* After the years in which Eve had said she would never have another child, she was going to have a baby. What did this mean? How would it affect the household? Luke had been a puppy when Bella had died. It was difficult to remember how things had been, except that it had been different and exciting. Now, if Eve was pregnant, it would be most unlikely she would want to risk tangling with the powers that had terminated the beginning, a thought which Kit must surely have taken into account.

For that matter, how had Kit known she was pregnant? When the fourth beginning has been aborted, all the positive effects of the beginning had been negated – all but three, that is. Adam's aging had not been reversed. The sharpening of Numpty's mind, challenged and developed not just by Uncle Rambler's tutelage but also by the demands of the quest, had persisted. And Luke's own mental powers had been considerably enhanced. He could, for example, read human's thoughts with a fair degree of accuracy when he put his mind to it. This particular faculty told him quite emphatically that the news of Eve's pregnancy, assuming it was true, had been as much of a shock to Eve as it had been to Luke.

Luke had also touched Kit's mind and knew that it was time to reconvene all the questors. Kit and the Storyteller had made contact with Prune Leach and Andrew Rimzil. That left Uncle Rambler and Nephew Numpty.

Luke padded into the kitchen and, using his enhanced telepathic powers, contacted Numpty. "How's it going? Has your uncle found out anything? Do we know who we're up against?

Numpty was in the middle of reading a philosophical treatise and was wrestling with Descartes. "Hold on," Numpty minded to Luke. "How's what going on? And when you say 'Do you know who we're up against?' don't you mean 'Do you know against whom we're up?' or 'Do you know up against whom we are?'"

Luke ignored Numpty's syntactical contortions. No change there then. "Your uncle was going to investigate the ending of the fourth beginning; he was going to find out who stopped it and how. He was going to do some osmotic gouging, as I recall."

"Ah yes," said Numpty, setting aside his copy of *Meditations on First Philosophy*. "I'm afraid Uncle has made little progress. He says there is a general denial that the fourth beginning ever started. Well, not really a denial. It's just that no one seems to know anything about it."

"No matter," said Luke. "Things have moved on. There's a gathering at the Smith's house in Harrow. The Storyteller and Kit are there already. I suspect Andrew and Prune are on their way. You and Uncle Rambler need to get your skates on. I have a feeling that we're going to resume questing."

"Sadly," Numpty replied, "my uncle is not competent on skates. I have mastered the balancing and control required but uncle, being more advanced in years, is less able to acquire new skills."

"Very funny. Just tell your uncle that Eve needs his help. She's going to have a baby."

"I fear my uncle is not only deficient in skating skills; his knowledge of midwifery is also lamentable. He may offer words of comfort, but anything more is beyond him."

"I think I preferred you when you were..." Luke paused. He knew Numpty was still sensitive about his limited but ever-expanding mental acuity. "When you were less astute," he ended.

"Okey dokey," Numpty replied happily. "Uncle and I will repair to Harrow. My uncle may not be able to offer much in the skating and birthing departments, but he will be accompanied by an accomplished osmotic gouger, which is an asset in any quest."

25. Depravity

The smile on Lotte Axelrod's face as she took the Praesidium floor seemed out of place amidst the hard lines that compartmentalised her sallow face and the dark eyes that had seen and suffered everything.

"Good afternoon, *gentlemen*," she began. She liked to start by reminding them and herself that she was the only female on the Decon committee.

"All is running smoothly in the Depravity Sector. In particular, paedophilia is progressing particularly well. With the help of Oliver Nates and the Obfuscation Division, we have now reached a point where the police talk quite happily about the paedophile community.

"I don't wish to anticipate further success in this field, but I can see a time when a combination of moral relativism and the lowering of the age of consent will make the sexual abuse of children more or less acceptable."

Manfred Bloch interrupted. "Is there not significant resistance to this trend?" For all his faults, of which there were many, the Chief Engineer still inexplicably found the abuse of children mildly distasteful.

Lotte's dark eyes changed momentarily. Her irises turned yellow and the sclera, the white of her eyes, followed suit, before reverting to their normally dark hue. "I was about to add," Ms Axelrod rebuked Bloch, "that there is indeed popular hostility to paedophiles but this resistance is effectively being undermined by the establishment consensus for liberalism in sexual matters and total relativism in morality. In passing, I might suggest to Edgar that the popular hostility to paedophilia may present an opportunity for his division. We have had one or two instances where paediatricians have been attacked by semi-literate or possibly dyslexic extremists.

"There is no greater aid to the promotion of depravity," Chairman John Noble observed, "than a combination of ignorance and extremism. Good work by Oliver and, indeed, an opportunity for Edgar."

"Back to my report," Lotte continued. "We are encouraging the establishment of paedophile cells up and down the country. In this we are helped by the multi-cultural nature of society. In some of the minority communities there is a very blurred understanding, or even outright rejection, of the traditional rules on sexual behaviour. Those running social services are frequently caught between the need to protect children and the requirement to show due respect to alternative cultures."

"The benefits of a ghettoised, multicultural society continue to accrue to our cause," the chairman remarked complacently.

"Moving on," said Lotte, a little impatiently, the yellow essence of her true form casting a jaundiced colour across her face. "Slavery. Our efforts to reintroduce slavery are meeting with some success. We are seeing increasing numbers of the very poor and the mentally challenged falling prey to unscrupulous gang-masters who pay them no more than the shelter and food that keeps them fit enough to work. In some cases, this is simply abuse of labour but in other cases we can combine this economic servitude with sexual abuse. We now have tens of thousands of girls working as prostitutes who are effectively slave labour for their slave-master pimps."

The chairman made a note to check with Charlie Cornick, head of the Corruption Division, that pimps were continuing to receive protection of their untaxed earnings.

"We are also encouraging, where we can, the practice of FGM (female genital mutilation)", Lotte continued. "There is of course the abuse inherent in the practice, the fear and pain entailed, which alone justifies our efforts to promote it. But there is a long-term benefit to this form of depravity. It instils in men the idea that women can be abused. If they can suffer the knife in their most intimate parts when they are most vulnerable and powerless, then almost any form of abuse against women must be acceptable. Suppression of the female libido, a happy consequence of the abuse, is another way in which men can be encouraged to think of women as objects to be exploited for pleasure, rather than as equal human beings."

"There is definitely resistance to FGM," said Manfred Bloch. He wasn't going to be prevented from having his say, however much his interruptions upset Lotte Axelrod. He might be Chief Engineer and not therefore directly involved in the work of the Decon Committee but, as a member of the triumvirate that ran the Praesidium, he had a watching brief, and he would not let any committee member present a distorted or partial account of their work. "The establishment is making real efforts to discourage FGM, is it not?"

"True," Lotte conceded, "and we may not win this one but, while we can keep it going, it works massively in our favour. On the positive side, there are elements amongst the Muslim population who cling not only to the practice of FGM but also to the totally humiliating and therefore obviously laudable view of women as inferior, deceitful and lascivious."

Simon Goodfellow looked at Lotte Axelrod and tried to think of her in her current form as lascivious. Perhaps when she had been young some trickle of lascivious juices might have found its way to her sexual organs, but he doubted it. That hard bony face and desiccated skin strongly suggested she had been born wizened and without desire. It was odd that she should be so effective in promoting depravity when it seemed certain that, at least in the field of sexual perversion, in human form, she had to be an observer, rather than a participant.

"Do you have anything else to report?" John Noble asked. There were still four more reports to hear, and then any other business.

"Just two more items," said Lotte. "The ill-treatment of animals is being maintained at a high level. Even in the best abattoirs many of the animals are distraught, even terrified, before slaughter. With the installation of CCTV in many abattoirs, I'm pleased to report that we now have video recordings of appalling abuses which, to be honest, can give enormous pleasure even after several viewings. Once again, we are receiving the benefit of alien religious practices which ensure that many of the animals are fully conscious when they are bled to death. We have had real success here. The greed of the supermarkets has combined with primitive religious custom to expand the supply of abused animal meat to the general public. It's cheaper for the supermarkets to supply meat from abused animals to everyone rather than have two sets of meat, one where the animal is butchered relatively humanely and one where it is killed according to Judaic or Islamic cultural practises, even though the vast majority of the population are neither Jews nor Muslims. Result!"

"You said there were two more items," the chairman prompted.

"The last item is a really big issue which the committee may feel more properly falls under Edgar's remit, but I felt I should at least mention it. We are making a great deal of progress with the perversion of Islam. All I need to say is this. The more we can encourage the fanatical Islamists to behead or burn alive almost anyone they can get their hands on, the happier we should all be. Let's face it, you can't get much more depraved than that."

Lotte reluctantly concluded her report. She had so much more to say but the chairman was obviously determined to press on.

"Thank you, Lotte, for that comprehensive review of your division's progress. It's always good to end a report on a positive note, unless of course you're Oliver." The last remark acknowledged Oliver Nates' role as the promoter of negativity. "Lotte's final item leads us naturally on to extremism. Edgar?"

If you had been looking to appoint someone to foster extremism, Edgar Exton would not have been an obvious choice. Of average height and weight, Edgar was average in these and every other respect. While far from stupid, he lacked the sharp mind and tongue of some of the other members of the committee. His face was a little pudgy, providing a slightly doughy setting for his quiet brown eyes. With his balding head and generally nondescript appearance, Edgar Exton was, indeed, in almost every way, the embodiment of moderation. The one exception was his enthusiasm for and commitment to his job. When he was engaged in work, those soft brown eyes were suffused with a haze of red, an indication of his essence. When he was expounding the principles that he used to drive extremism forward, a flush of similar hue would rise like a crimson tide up the back of his neck and then spread like an erupting volcano across his balding head."

"I'm happy to report that things are going very well in the extremism field. I'll take religion first, as Lotte has already raised the subject which, as she rightly pointed out, falls squarely within my remit." All the monitaurs on the Decon Committee had specific responsibilities, and all were jealous of their own speciality. Although John Noble insisted they must all work together, there was, inevitably, resentment if anyone strayed from their own speciality into that of another. Lotte had been careful to recognise his primary role in religious extremism, but even so Edgar still felt the need to make the lines of demarcation crystal clear.

"As you all know, for years vast resources have been devoted to the promotion of a crude and in many ways barbaric version of Islam. We have of course encouraged and exploited this process and I'm pleased to report that at last it is showing real signs of success. Fortunately, the Holy Quran is full of contradictory exhortations, so by judicious selection, we have managed to turn Islam in the eyes of many from an inclusive, compassionate, tolerant – albeit rather pedestrian – religion into a vicious and bigoted death cult."

There was a series of congratulatory grunts and a ripple of applause from the committee. Edgar felt encouraged.

"The extremists now define themselves so narrowly that they are at least as happy killing fellow Muslims as they are killing infidels. We have somehow managed to promote parochial, medieval customs into a code of behaviour for the 21st century. Although I say it myself, it's an almost unbelievable achievement. At this point I'd like to thank Charlie Cornick for all his help in ensuring the world's continued reliance on fossil fuels. Without the oil money, we could never have spread the cult so far.

"And there are consequential benefits to the turmoil that the Islamist fanatics create. We can also claim credit for the violent reaction of those who oppose and fear them. Gentlemen, we now even have Buddhists killing Muslims."

This last revelation elicited a definite round of applause. Only Lotte refrained, feeling that "gentlemen" had intentionally excluded her.

"Can you give me some idea", Simon Goodfellow intervened, "of how on earth you've managed to persuade grown men to believe some of the twaddle that forms the basis of the death cult? I mean, what is all this about every Islamist fanatic who dies in their cause going straight to heaven and enjoying the favour of 40 to 70 virgins? Leaving aside the inherent improbability of a murdering bigot going to heaven, what is all this about virgins? Where would all the virgins come from? How have you managed to persuade these fanatics, of whom, of course, I heartily approve, to swallow such nonsense? And who would want 70 virgins anyway? I prefer my women a little more experienced in the darker secrets of love, women who have learned how to pleasure a man who has complex tastes and needs, women who are prepared to allow me to delve into the dark declivities of shame..."

The chairman interrupted. "Thank you, Simon, for giving us a glimpse of your own sexual predilections but we do have a meeting to conclude. Edgar, where were you?"

26. A matter of conscience

In Geneva, Adam had spent his fourth day at ZeD with Guy McFall, whose rather laid-back appearance belied a committed marketeer. Although not a qualified pharmacologist or doctor, Guy knew MC57 inside out. He described the chemical structure of the substance, its genesis and its path over the previous ten years from inception to its submission to the EMA. He could recount precisely the details of every clinical trial and its outcome.

As for knowledge of the market for which MC57 would compete, Guy could not be faulted. He was able to quote the unit and cash sales of every major competitor, year by year, over the last decade. He knew the strengths and weaknesses of each product, its unique selling points and its record of side effects.

"I'll be honest," said Guy, at the end of his briefing on the product's pharmacology. "MC57 is the product of some molecular roulette. It's very similar to the market leader in structure, but sufficiently different to avoid any patent problems. According to the clinical trials, it's as effective as the market leader (not really surprising given the similarities), but it may just have the edge, in that it has fewer and milder side effects. That's what we think. And that's what I think we have to say in the marketing of the product."

"Not the most compelling sales pitch," Adam observed. "Obviously I'm not disputing what you say for a moment, but I'm a little disappointed. I was under the impression MC57, or Angeloma as I guess we will soon be calling it, was a major breakthrough, a real advance in the treatment of heart conditions. 'Fewer, milder side effects' is good, but it won't set the medical world alight. I can't see cardiologists or their patients breaking out the champagne or snorting cocaine."

"As it happens, Angeloma is contraindicated for cocaine users, but I take your point. You're right. It's not a breakthrough but breakthroughs nowadays are few and far between and, truth to tell, ZeD is unlikely to come up with one."

"Really?" Adam was genuinely surprised. "But ZeD is the biggest pharmaceutical company in the world. If ZeD can't come up with breakthroughs, who can?"

"It doesn't work like that. The risks involved in finding new drugs are incredibly high. It now takes at least 10 years to get a drug to market. Before it can be submitted for approval it has to pass the most stringent tests. At any point in those 10 years, it may fail. One adverse clinical trial and you can write off millions, tens of millions of Swiss francs. All the while the drug is being tested, ZeD is paying for all this." Guy indicated ZeD's head office with a majestic sweep of his arm. "They pay your salary and mine, and all the people in my department, and all the medical and technical staff involved each and every day. One bad reaction, the death of one patient who was probably going to die anyway, and all that investment is lost."

"I understand that, but why do you say ZeD is unlikely to be the one to find a breakthrough? The company's development budget is the biggest of any pharmaceutical company."

"ZeD is in the business of making money. A 'me too' drug is a much better bet. If the drug which it's based on has passed all the tests, it's pretty much certain the 'me too' drug will also pass. Given the high risk of failure with an entirely new drug, it's hardly surprising most of the big companies churn out 'me too' drugs and then rely on their marketing people to carve out a decent slice of the market. That's good news for us in marketing: it means we are crucially important to the company's success. I mean, if you've come up with penicillin, who needs marketing people? But when you've come up with the tenth version of penicillin, then you need marketing expertise to find a gap in the market."

Adam smiled. Guy was being completely honest. He was also doing his best to bring Adam up to speed. That was a relief. After all, Minofel had somehow parachuted him into a senior and highly paid job at one of the world's biggest companies. He knew little about pharmaceuticals and nothing about MC57. It would not have been surprising if Guy, clearly a master of his subject, had resented him. After all, it was already clear that he would have to rely heavily on Guy, at least in the crucial early months. But there was no sign of any hostility from him.

"Well let's hope our marketing expertise is up to it," said Adam, with a wry grin.

"Before we put that to the test, we have to make sure the product is approved by the EMA," Guy reminded him.

It was a needless reminder. Throughout Guy's comprehensive briefing, the question of drug registration, or rather the precise nature of the meeting with Giovanni Spinetti arranged for that evening, had been nagging away at the back of Adam's mind.

oooOooo

After work, Adam ran into Miss Tomic on the steps of the main building. "Could we have a word?" Adam asked.

"Of course. Let me give you a lift. I'm passing your hotel."

On the way to the hotel, Adam told Miss Tomic about his

day. He said how pleased he was with Guy. Miss Tomic smiled.

"I think it was your satirist Jonathan Swift who said 'all men are either fools or knaves.'"

"What does that mean?" Adam responded. "Guy's certainly not a fool. And if he's a knave, I've seriously misread him. He's seems to me to be an honest, hard-working chap."

"Why did you assume I was talking about McFall?" asked Miss Tomic in an innocent tone.

Adam smiled. Evidently Miss Tomic had a dry sense of humour. He thought of asking her whether Swift's aphorism was equally true of women but by then they had reached the hotel.

"Have you had any luck in finding an apartment?" Miss Tomic asked, changing the subject.

"Not really. I was rather hoping you might be able to help me: you know Geneva well."

"I'll have a word with Human Resources," Miss Tomic replied. "In normal circumstances, HR would have already found you an apartment. They would have made all the arrangements before you arrived. But your appointment as marketing director took us all a little by surprise. Anyway, don't you worry, I'll talk to HR tomorrow."

Adam thanked her and suggested they have a drink. Miss Tomic demurred but, when Adam told her he had something he needed to ask her, she reluctantly agreed. As soon as they were settled at a quiet table in the bar, Adam began:

"This meeting I have with Spinetti. I'm a little bit worried."

"I see. What is worrying you: the meeting itself, or what I told you is in the envelope?"

"Well, both. I don't think I'm equipped to have a meeting

with an official of the EMA about MC57 – at least not yet."

"That's nonsense," Miss Tomic dismissed Adam's concern. "Spinetti won't expect you to be a doctor, much less a specialist in heart conditions or pharmacology. You're a marketing director."

"I've always thought marketing directors should know as much about the products they are selling as anyone."

"That's really not the issue," Miss Tomic insisted. "You are showing a lack of self-confidence. That is invariably the biggest obstacle to any individual's progress."

"You sound like Minofel."

"Is there anything else worrying you?"

"Yes, there is." Adam felt angry. "David arranged this meeting despite my reservations. You then revealed that the letter he had asked me to give to Spinetti contained a bribe. Yes, I think it's fair to say, there is something else that worries me, and I don't think it's anything to do with my supposed lack of self-confidence."

"You should control your emotions and the level of your voice," said Miss Tomic quietly. "Who said anything about a bribe? There is no bribe. And, even if there were, we would not speak about it, least of all in a public place. The envelope contains a banker's draft, but, for all you know, it could be repayment of a debt. Or a present for a daughter, Minofel's godchild."

"Is David godfather to Spinetti's daughter?" Adam asked, feeling somewhat relieved. If it was just a personal matter between Minofel and Spinetti, he wouldn't need to worry, or at least not so much.

"I have no idea," Miss Tomic replied happily. "I have no idea whether Giovanni is married or whether he has a daughter. It's not impossible he is married and has a daughter and that David Minofel is godfather to his putative daughter, but I have no evidence to support those hypotheses. I'm simply pointing out that your assumption that the banker's draft is a bribe and that the bribe has something to do with MC57 is equally speculative. You need to decide exactly what is worrying you."

Adam was silent for a moment. Was she playing with him? And if so, why? The meeting was scheduled for 7.00pm, in an hour's time. He had already decided to go ahead with the meeting and hand over the envelope. He had rehearsed in his head what he would say to Spinetti at the end of their chat: "By the way, here's something David Minofel asked me to give you". He had simply wanted to share his unease with Miss Tomic. After all, she was supposed to be his mentor. But she was unsympathetic, or at least unhelpful.

In the end, Adam said: "So why did you tell me about the banker's draft?

Miss Tomic looked him straight in the eyes: "As I have already told you: because I thought you should know," was all she said.

27. An interim report

The Decon meeting in the Praesidium was taking longer than John Noble had wanted or expected. Edgar Exton had continued for some time giving details of inter-religious conflicts around the world, all of which his division had either fomented or supported.

"We have Muslims killing Hindus and Hindus killing Muslims," he announced proudly. "We have Muslims killing Christians and Christians killing Muslims. We have Muslims killing Buddhists and Buddhists killing Muslims. So far, we have been unable to set Christians, Hindus and Buddhists at each other's throats but we are working on it. Obviously, we owe a lot to the Muslims who have shown considerable initiative in stoking the fires of hate and helping us to be where we are today.

"We can also claim success in our dealings with the governments of the West, in particular the United States, the United Kingdom and France. By persuading their leaders to involve themselves on one side or another in the internal affairs of other, predominantly Muslim, countries, we have, through the resentment this interference has engendered, given real impetus to the Islamist cause. This conflict between the West and Islam is something we can be really proud of. Who would have thought that, in the 21st century, we would be able to engineer a global conflict between a scientifically advanced liberal society and a medieval religion?"

The chairman was tempted to interrupt the head of the Extremism Division, but there was no doubt Edgar Exton had a good story to tell and John Noble had often found it advisable to allow the operational heads of the Praesidium to have their moment of glory. If nothing else, it served as a useful reminder to Simon Goodfellow and Manfred Bloch that there were other members of the organisation, albeit not human, capable of assuming higher responsibilities.

"Unless there are any questions," Edgar said, eager to continue his account, "I will move on to political extremism."

"I have a question." It was Manfred Bloch, the Technical Director. "Apart from creating general mayhem, what is your long-term strategic goal with these inter-religious squabbles? Don't misunderstand me. All credit to you for the mayhem and, if interminable, bloody squabbles are your intended endgame, that's fine by me. But, if you're planning some kind of spectacular, I'd like some notice. There have been rumours you are thinking of a nuclear conflict. That will require proliferation of nuclear weapons throughout the Middle East. The Technical Division is more than happy to help, but we will need some notice."

"Some notice! That's a bit of a euphemism after the Cadnam fiasco," Simon Goodfellow chipped in. "Indulging that buffoon Nick Peters and maintaining the Ringwood mysland was an exceptional drain on our resources. We will need more than 'some notice' to restore our reserves to a satisfactory level. We're talking months at the very least."

"Not to mention the costs of retaining a practitioner to deal with a problem that, in my view, has already been resolved," snapped Manfred. He was sick and tired of Goodfellow's sniping.

Simon could not suppress a smirk. Set a trap and you could count on Bloch to walk into it. After all, it had been the Chairman's decision, not his, to enlist the help of a practitioner.

"Edgar, could you answer Manfred's question?" John

Noble intervened. Of course Bloch walked into every trap, but Goodfellow's manipulation of Bloch was at least as predictable and rather more irritating. Goodfellow's machinations were so obvious, so transparent - and did the vice-chairman little credit. Not that there was anything wrong with manipulation. It was the lack of subtlety that grated.

"I am certainly hopeful," Edgar replied, in the tone of a librarian discussing a book recovery programme, "that we can escalate the conflict to a much higher level but we currently have no plans for a full-scale nuclear conflict. I should point out that, even with the limitations of conventional weapons, we have recorded, in the second Iraq war alone, more than 150,000 deaths, of which at least 120,000 were civilians, and a further 200,000 in Syria between March 2011 and the end of 2015, not to mention a relatively modest 6,000 in Palestine."

"You were about to move on to your division's work in the field of political extremism," John Noble prompted.

"I'm pleased to report that things are turning out even better than we had hoped in that area too. As you will recall, we had some concerns that democracy might seriously impede our efforts to promulgate extremism, but we failed to take sufficient account of human nature and its propensity for division and strife. Around the world, the old party loyalties are fragmenting, a process which presents us with a wonderful opportunity to nurture all forms of political extremism on both the left and right. Indeed, we are able to generate such confusion that the old labels of left and right are becoming pretty meaningless. The ensuing chaos makes the establishment in each country more and more dependent on us, ever more eager to ensure that, whoever is running the government, they continue to enjoy our protection. Our control grows stronger as their dependence on us increases."

"So all is well on the extremism front," the chairman observed, eager to move things along.

"There is one aspect of extremism where we seem to be losing ground," Edgar conceded. "As you know, we had all hoped that racism would blossom into serious inter-racial conflict, if not open inter-racial wars. There is still plenty of racism about, but it has not flourished as we had hoped. If anything, I have to confess to the committee that on that particular issue we are in retreat. Hitler, for all his merits as a puppet of the Praesidium, did irreparable damage to the racism cause by making even perfectly objective accounts of racial differences entirely unacceptable."

"I hope you are not giving up on the particular cause," Goodfellow interrupted. "I, for one, believe that racial tensions are a fruitful branch of the extremism tree, so to speak"

"Of course we will not abandon racism," Edgar Exton responded, "but we have concluded that currently inter-religious conflict is the way to go. If we can incorporate racism into the inter-religious conflict matrix, well it's just the cream on top of the cake."

John Noble sighed. Goodfellow's clumsy arboreal metaphor was bad enough but Exton's 'cream on top of a matrix cake' was too much. These Decon meetings could be quite a strain.

"Thank you, Edgar. An excellent report. We'll leave it at that."

The chairman was about to call on Charlie Cornick to give his account of the work of the Corruption Division when Cynthia, Noble's secretary, a willowy blonde, came into the committee room.

"I'm really sorry to interrupt, but you have a visitor."

John Noble frowned. Cynthia knew not to interrupt such meetings except in the most serious of circumstances. She leant over to whisper in the Chairman's ear.

John Noble stood up. "Gentlemen and lady, this meeting is adjourned. Cynthia will let you know when we are to reconvene."

28. Meeting Spinetti

After Miss Tomic left the bar, Adam decided to go to his room and freshen up. As he passed reception, one of the girls behind the counter called to him.

"Monsieur Smith. We have a message for you. There is a copy in your room but as you are here, we can give it to you now."

Adam took the note. It was from Minofel. "Hi, Adam. Good luck this evening. Don't forget to give Giovanni my letter. We need to meet on Saturday. I hope this doesn't interfere with your plans. David"

Adam was irritated. First, because he didn't need a reminder about the letter: he'd thought of little else since Miss Tomic had told him about the banker's draft. Secondly, what did David mean by 'hope it doesn't interfere with your plans'? David knew he planned to commute between Geneva and London. This was his first week with ZeD and he had been looking forward to a really good weekend with Eve, including dinner at their favourite restaurant on Saturday evening.

As soon as he reached his room, he phoned Eve. He recounted the events of the week, omitting only the issue of the banker's draft. He learned from her that the Storyteller and Kit had turned up on her doorstep and were now house guests. When he told her that he wouldn't be able to fly back the next day, she sounded very disappointed.

"Kit and the Storyteller were hoping to talk to us. Kit seems keen to reactivate the quest. Prune Leach and Andrew Rimzil are on their way and I have a feeling Rambler and

Numpty will be joining us. It will be a real reunion."

"It would have been great to meet the gang again," Adam agreed. "I've always felt we should keep in touch. As for reactivating the quest, that's another matter. It would be completely impractical, even if we wanted to. Didn't you tell them I've just started a new job?"

"Yes, I did," Eve answered, and then added. "Kit seemed less than impressed. He was surprised that, after what we'd been through, you would be interested in taking up a marketing job with a Swiss pharmaceutical company."

"Hold on a minute. It's not just a marketing job; I'm the marketing director. And it's not just a Swiss pharmaceutical company; it's ZeD, one of the biggest and most successful international corporations in the world. I hope you explained that I've trebled my salary and that my future prospects are limitless."

"Short of telling him your actual salary and going into minute detail about all the company perks, I think I did justice to your meteoric rise, but he still wasn't impressed. He thinks we really did something amazing in initiating the fourth beginning; however much you're earning and however important you think your job is, he thinks you're now wasting your time."

"It sounds as though you agree with him."

"I'm just telling you what he's said to me. I agree with you that we should think carefully before we undertake any more questing."

"I didn't say we should think about it carefully," Adam interrupted. "I said we couldn't even consider it. Look, I've got to go. I have a meeting with this chap from the EMA. It's important because he has a say in whether we get MC57 registered. He'll be down in the lobby in a few minutes, and

I should be there to meet him. I'll phone you at the weekend. Love you."

Adam checked himself briefly in the mirror in the *en suite*, straightened his tie and went back down to the restaurant where David had booked him an alcove for his meeting with Giovanni Spinetti.

Giovanni was a tall, pleasant-looking Italian, in his mid-thirties. Dark, well-cut hair, smiling brown eyes, tanned skin, clean-shaven, he was the epitome of virile Italian manhood and therefore immediately an object of suspicion for Adam. Many thoughts passed through Adam's mind as he shook Giovanni's hand, employing a slightly stronger grip than usual. If the envelope contained a bribe, then Spinetti must be corrupt, otherwise Minofel would not have sent the banker's draft to him. If Minofel had any doubts about Spinetti's corruptibility, he would have been more circumspect. He would have checked him out, hinted at a bribe, observed Spinetti's reaction. But no. Minofel had simply put the draft in an envelope and asked Adam to drop it off. This was almost certainly not the first time Spinetti had enjoyed David's largesse.

"It's good to meet you," said Giovanni, with only the slightest hint of an Italian accent. "David has told me so much about you. You're one of Slievens' high-flyers, I understand."

Adam resisted the temptation to deny his capacity for high flight. Miss Tomic's admonition about lack of confidence had sunk in. "Good to meet you too," was all he said.

They settled in the alcove. Adam ordered a coffee and Giovanni a Negroni (a mixture in equal parts Vermouth rosso, bitter Campari and dry gin).

Giovanni sipped his cocktail and got straight to the

point. “I guess you want to know, off the record of course, how MC57 is progressing.”

Adam was a little taken aback at Spinetti’s directness. “Well, of course, we are interested. A great deal depends on MC57. I understand you are close to the registration process.”

Giovanni smiled. “I’m not just close; I am, as you say, on top of it. I am directly responsible for submitting a recommendation to the committee.”

Adam waited. Giovanni continued to smile. “You know, this Negroni is one of the most popular pre-dinner drinks in Italy. You should try it.”

“Coffee is fine,” Adam replied, trying to kill off any discussion of drinks or dinner. The last thing he wanted was to spend the evening with this venal Italian stranger who evidently wanted to play a little cat and mouse with him.

“OK,” Giovanni laughed. “I will tell you how things stand. MC57 is a good, sound beta blocker. It’s not a major improvement on the main competitor. Indeed, to be honest, it’s not even a minor improvement. But what can you expect? It’s almost identical to the main competitor. There are some minor differences in side effects but, again, not in my view enough to make a significant difference. When I say ‘my view’, I really mean the view the committee will take. As I have often explained to David, my job is to assess each drug according to the criteria set by the committee. I don’t have, as you say, any wriggle room, even if I wanted it. Do you understand?”

“Of course,” Adam answered. “I have been briefed on the product.”

Giovanni seemed pleased. He ordered another cocktail.

Adam had intended to wait until the end of the meeting to hand over David Minofel’s letter, but this seemed an opportune moment to do it. "By the way, David asked me to give you this."

Giovanni took the envelope and slipped it into the inside pocket of his impeccably cut blazer. He did not even look to see to whom the envelope was addressed.

"Can you give me some idea of when the committee will take a decision?" Adam asked.

Giovanni inhaled sharply through his nose, in the manner of a plumber preparing to explain how difficult it would be to install a replacement boiler. "It's always difficult to predict," he said, "but I'm sure there will be a decision within the next six weeks."

At least that was something.

"And with my recommendation that the drug be approved," Giovanni added casually, "I think you can be confident you can prepare for the launch."

Adam almost choked on his coffee. "That's great news," he spluttered.

Giovanni laughed. "You know I've met several of David's protégés over the last few years. When you first arrive, you're all a little nervous. But you soon get over it. David never makes a mistake."

Adam felt relieved. The meeting had been a success, more successful than he could have hoped. He could now tell Yves Dubois at ZeD that the drug on which so much depended would be approved within the next six weeks. And David would be pleased he had handled the meeting well and emerged with the perfect outcome.

"Would you like to stay for dinner?" Adam asked. He felt it was the least he could do, and Spinetti's apparent predilection for pre-dinner cocktails suggested that he might have dinner in mind.

"It's very kind of you but I have a prior engagement," Giovanni said with a smile, "with a beautiful young lady," he confided. "But another time. We will meet again very soon, I am sure."

29. All together, all but one

On the evening of the day that Adam had his meeting with Giovanni Spinetti, a red camper van pulled up outside the Smith's house in Harrow. Luke barked enthusiastically. The driver, Prune Leach, tooted the horn. Eve looked out of the front room window, and smiled. So they had come. Kit had said they were on their way. And there was Prune Leach, as brown and wizened as ever, on the pavement, kicking the van's front offside tyre, which he suspected was a little under-inflated. Beside him was a large cooler box, which he had lifted carefully through one of the side doors of the van.

From the other side of the van, the tall, lean figure of Andrew Rimzil emerged to perform some much-needed leg-stretching exercises. For the long-legged Rimzil, the van afforded insufficient legroom.

Eve made her way to the front door, so she missed two other figures dismounting from the van: Uncle Rambler and Nephew Numpty. When she opened the front door, all four visitors stood before her. Kit joined her at the door and there was a melee of greetings. As soon as Luke saw Numpty, he ran and jumped up on his hind legs and licked Numpty's face.

"The first thing to say" Andrew declared, when all the guests had settled in the now-crowded sitting room, "is that we do not have any wish or intention to stay in your house. Prune and I are more than happy in the camper van and can easily accommodate Rambler and his nephew."

Numpty nodded his approval. Rambler assented but with rather less enthusiasm. He really felt, and certainly had hoped, his camper van days were over.

"I still have one spare bedroom, so I insist," said Eve.

"Well, if you insist," Rambler responded, with indecent eagerness, "I feel it would be churlish to refuse."

"I'm with Prune and Andrew, if they'll have me. I'll sleep in the camper van," said Numpty, looking first at his uncle and then at Prune and Andrew for their approval.

"That's settled then," said Prune, who had been sitting on the box he had brought with him. "Now, how about some light refreshment." With that, he stood up, flipped open the catches on the cooler box and began to distribute ice-cold cans of Guinness.

Eve laughed. "I'll make tea for anyone who feels that 2.30 in the afternoon is a little early for a Guinness."

"It's never too early for a Guinness," was Prune's gentle rebuke.

"Well, it's too early for me," said the Storyteller, who had kept to himself during the hubbub of meeting and greeting.

"Tea for me too," Uncle Rambler chimed in. "And I suggest, Nephew Numpty, you follow my example."

Numpty reluctantly agreed.

"It's not going to be much of a party, if most of you have turned into kill-joys," Prune chided the tea-drinkers. "Still, never mind, it just means the burden of Guinness consumption will fall more heavily on Andrew, Kit and me."

"A burden we are content to bear," added Andrew.

When everyone had a cup or a can in their hands, Kit called the assembly to order. "We are here to discuss what we do next. Let's begin by finding out what each of us thinks. Eve?"

Eve was taken by surprise. Kit was so direct. "I think Adam should be here if we are going to discuss anything to do with the quest and the beginning."

"Good point," said Prune. "Where is Adam?"

Eve told them about Adam's new post in Geneva.

Prune addressed Kit. "Why didn't you mention that when you called us?"

"Because, whether Adam is here or not, we still have to discuss the situation and take a decision."

"I'm not sure we can do that," the Storyteller intervened. "Without Adam, we risk losing control."

"What control?" asked Eve and Prune in unison.

Eve elaborated. "We had no control when the fourth beginning was aborted. We have had no control since. We don't know what terminated the beginning and we certainly don't know what we can do about it."

"We didn't have much control when Elsa and Optimius were torn apart by the termination," added Prune, with anger and sadness in his voice. The deaths of the two mammalian constructs, the imperfect seal and the sanguine penguin, still rankled in Prune's mind.

"We have gathered here today, haven't we?" Kit responded. "We had sufficient control to achieve that. And we can now discuss the situation and what we can or should do about it. We are in control if we take control."

"But Adam is an essential part of our group," the Storyteller objected. "He and Eve initiated the quest. It was their decision. We need them both if we are to take any further action."

But Kit was undeterred. "Adam and Eve have been separated before, when Adam had a spell in hell under the Breakers' regional office at Cadnam. If you recall, we managed to achieve quite a lot while Adam was incarcerated. We may have to do so again."

"Why?" asked Andrew. "He's not incarcerated now. If he's in Geneva, he can fly back any time. It's only a one-and-a-half hour flight. I expect he's coming back to see Eve anyway."

"Not this weekend," Eve informed the group. "He has a meeting on Saturday so he can't make it."

"Well I guess there's no harm in discussing the situation," suggested Uncle Rambler. "I wouldn't be happy in taking any decision without Adam, but there's no harm in the rest of us saying what we think."

There was a consensus that talking would do no harm, but not, as Prune insisted, before they had something to eat. "Come on everyone, let's pile into the camper van and repair to a hostelry offering a noble repast of burgers or fish and chips."

oooOooo

As the others filed out of the house, Eve and Kit found themselves alone together for a moment.

"Did you tell him?" Kit asked. "About the baby?"

"No" Eve answered. "No, I didn't. He didn't give me a chance. He had to rush off to a meeting."

30. Spinetti's guest

After Adam had left the alcove in the hotel's restaurant, Giovanni Spinetti returned to the restaurant and resumed his seat in the alcove. Minofel had told him he had reserved the alcove for the whole evening, and it seemed a pity to waste such an opportunity. I'm expecting a guest, a very beautiful young lady," he confided to the head waiter.

Although the description was a little vague, the head waiter had no difficulty in identifying Spinetti's guest when she arrived. The woman was certainly beautiful, with fine symmetrical features and a perfect figure, but she was also extraordinarily attractive. Her green eyes were full of laughter and life. She was wearing an expensive, finely cut dress but, in the eyes of all the men who saw her walk through the restaurant, she would have looked irresistible in sackcloth.

"Miss Tomic," said Spinetti, getting up to greet his guest. "What a pleasure! I have waited for this moment for a very long time. Perhaps all my life."

Miss Tomic smiled. She took the seat Adam had vacated and they chatted amiably about what they were going eat, the wine list and the ambience of the restaurant.

"How was your meeting with Adam?" Miss Tomic asked.

"It went well, entirely as expected," Spinetti replied, tapping his blazer, where Minofel's letter nestled in an inside pocket. "I told him ZeD would have its drug within six weeks. In fact, you will have approval even sooner. The committee approved the drug for marketing almost a week ago."

They ordered their meal. Their conversation centred

on developments in the drug industry, rumours of possible breakthroughs in genetic engineering and nanotechnology, with a sprinkling of comments on the food and the wine.

When the meal was finished, Giovanni leant forward and said quietly; "Now, Miss Tomic – or may I call you Gorgeous? I think it's time I had the rest of my reward, don't you?"

31. Extreme Licence

When John Noble left the Decon meeting to return to his office, he felt uneasy. As he padded along the wide, thickly carpeted corridor, he tried to guess what kind of event could possibly have prompted such a breach of Praesidium etiquette. To expect access to the chairman without an appointment constituted inexplicable hubris. To demand that the chairman should be summoned from a major committee meeting was entirely unacceptable, even if the summoner were a practitioner.

Given that the Praesidium was retaining the services of only one practitioner, clearly the emergency must be connected with the cell that had attempted to initiate the fourth beginning. But there was surely no emergency that could justify such disregard for the organisation's protocols.

In any case, it was an absolute rule that, once a practitioner had accepted a mission, he would not trouble the Praesidium again until either he was due a staged payment or the mission had been completed. After all, that was the point of employing them. Practitioners charged extortionate fees because they took problems away and dealt with them. The last thing the client wanted was any involvement in the process of fulfilling the mission

Even if the Smith's cell was hoping to regroup, even if it was committed to trying to reactivate a beginning, the practitioner could surely make an appointment - and an appointment at a time which did not clash with the Decon meeting. Of course there were those, some even on the committee, who saw the monthly meeting as a rather tedious formality – but they were wrong. The chairman of the Praesidium himself was answerable to a higher authority, and each month that authority expected – no, demanded – a clear, concise and positive report of the Praesidium's efforts to promote depravity, extremism, corruption, obfuscation and negativity.

By the time the Chairman had reached his office, his anger had the edge on his unease.

"We have a problem," said David Minofel, unabashed by his own disregard for Praesidium etiquette. He was lounging in one of the armchairs provided for the comfort of honoured guests, some distance away from the chairman's desk.

"I see you're making yourself at home," John Noble snapped, making no effort to disguise his irritation.

Minofel smiled. "And I see you're not in the best of moods."

John Noble considered listing all the offences Minofel had committed by breezing into the building without an appointment, demanding to see the chairman, breaking up a crucial meeting before its work had been completed and then conducting himself in the chairman's office as though he owned the place. John Noble thought about it but decided against it. Minofel knew well enough what he had done. Clearly he didn't care. And since John Noble had no means of punishing his ill-manners and his arrogance, a rant would simply give Minofel greater satisfaction. Instead, he simply made a note to rebuke Cynthia for allowing the practitioner to wait for him in his office.

"You said there was a problem."

Minofel was not yet ready to reveal the reason for his visit. He rose from the armchair and walked over to the array of windows which gave the Chairman a magnificent view over much of London.

"Do you not find it odd to be at the centre of so great a city and yet not really part of it?" Minofel asked. "I mean, here you are, at the top of a giant structure, controlling the affairs of men, and yet you are entirely invisible to those whose lives you manipulate."

Noble knew at once the point the practitioner was making. Only practitioners could move between the two worlds. The Praesidium could exert influence over every aspect of human activity but only practitioners, and, to a lesser extent, the monitaurs, could be physically present in both the Praesidium and on Earth. Minofel was preparing the ground for something.

"The problem?" Noble repeated, keeping his voice calm.

Minofel returned to the armchair and settled himself. "Please don't take offence, but is it not a trifle discourteous not to offer your visitor a drink: a coffee, a cup of tea or even a glass of water? Indeed, perhaps you might find it in your heart to stretch to a biscuit."

A vein began to throb in John Noble's temple. He was not an irascible fellow; indeed, if anything, he erred on the side of placidity, but he knew that if the practitioner did not get to the point in fairly short order, he would be driven to ripping him limb from limb.

"The problem…" David began, and then paused for a moment. "The problem is that, in our negotiations, you were not entirely honest with me."

Noble frowned. In what possible way could he have been dishonest? After all, he had yielded to every demand the practitioner had made.

"You will have to explain."

"Well, as part of due diligence, you should have made clear from the start the precise nature of the task you were asking me to fulfil. Failing to reveal a key factor is just as dishonest as actually lying."

"What key factor?" John Noble truly had no idea what Minofel was talking about.

"You failed to mention that I should have to deal with what we practitioners call a sport, a deviant, a mutation indeterminate in nature."

John Noble remained puzzled. "I think we told you who had been involved in the quest. We made it clear that apart from Adam and Eve Smith, both of whom had been damaged by the death of their daughter, all the questors were rather odd. Rambler and his nephew were both, in different ways, decidedly peculiar. The late Gwoat was a flatulent oddity. Grimrose, for heaven's sake, was a shape-shifter. Leach and Rimzil were not, as we told you, your run-of-the-mill inventors or engineers. And as for the Storyteller, you knew you had to deal with him from the start – and surely he is no match for a practitioner? I think we gave a more than fair summary of who was involved and what you would be up against."

"You've left someone off your list," said Minofel. "You haven't mentioned the blind man."

"Oh, Kit Turner. Yes, as you say, the blind man. Is that the problem? You're flummoxed by a blind man! Not what I would expect from a practitioner."

"I think he may be an emergent," said David quietly.

"An emergent?" Noble queried, stunned. "What makes you think he is an emergent? He was not part of the quest originally. He joined them after they had started their journey, after the Smiths had met Rambler and his nephew.

He was a coincidence."

"I think not," said Minofel. "It was Kit, the blind man, who enabled the questors to escape the Garden of Eden; it was the blind man who struck Nick Peters and knocked him off Mount Strobilos; it was Kit, the blind man who helped Adam escape from the hell under Cadnam. And there's other evidence."

"But it's all circumstantial. He may be what you call a sport, but an emergent…? I think not."

"I am here to tell you I think he is an emergent, and you know what that means if he is."

John Noble wasn't at all sure what it meant. He knew emergents were special, that they were dangerous, that they could be taken down only by employing special measures. But he also knew they were incredibly rare: that individuals thought to be emergents had over and over again proved to be nothing of the sort. And he also knew that eliminating an emergent, if that's what was needed, was not only exceedingly dangerous but also, he suspected, expensive.

"I'm not convinced," said Noble.

"Not convinced Kit is an emergent or not convinced we need to take steps necessary to deal with him?"

"Both," the Chairman replied.

"All right, let's put it this way," said Minofel, using his most authoritative voice. "It's my call because I am tasked with fulfilling your mission. I am convinced he is an emergent or, at the very least, I am certain that to assume he is not an emergent is far too risky. Therefore, either you approve the use of exceptional measures or I will consider the contract broken."

It was always the same with practitioners. They didn't really understand the essence of bargaining. There was no give and take. You gave; they took.

"You are asking for an extreme licence," John Noble said gravely. He put his hand to his face and stroked his moustache, a sure sign that some emotion was causing a ripple through his normal equanimity. An extreme licence permitted the holder to annihilate an emergent, to erase the target so completely that there could be no record, no trace of the emergent's existence. Destroying an emergent was the greatest affront to creation. An extreme licence allowed the practitioner to use any and all possible measures to destroy the emergent – even, if necessary, allowing them to tamper with space and time. It was the greatest challenge practitioners could undertake and one which, if accomplished, marked their greatest achievement. It also necessarily involved the greatest risk. "I will have to have the board's approval." Noble concluded.

"Of course," said Minofel. "But, let's be frank, that's merely a formality. Perhaps more contentious is the matter of my additional fees."

32. Planning

It was Saturday, the day after all the questors but Adam had gathered at the Smith's house, and the day on which Adam was to have his meeting with David Minofel in Geneva.

Kit had suggested a meeting in the evening, which meant that Eve and her guests had a day to kill.

Prune and Andrew had spent the day servicing the camper van, calibrating the exponential drive and fine-tuning the arcane physics involved in enabling the vehicle to travel through time and space far faster than the speed of light, not to mention the rather less demanding task of repairing and inflating the front offside tyre. It was all pretty straightforward and routine for the two engineers. What really fascinated Prune was the paradox device. Although he had worked on the invention with Andrew, in truth, the device was a product of Andrew's genius. Nevertheless, Prune was convinced he had one or two ideas on how to develop and apply the device.

When the servicing of the van was finished, Prune decided to raise the matter.

"Do you not think we should take a look at the paradox device? You know, put it through its paces?" he suggested.

"I think it would be better if you focused on making sure your exponential drive is robust and resilient, and precisely locked into the universal positioning system."

Prune took Andrew's rebuke to be the natural response from an inventor to an intrusion into his intellectual domain, but that was not the case: Andrew had been worried about the device from the moment he had conceived the idea of creating it.

"But don't you see, we have scarcely scratched the surface of what it could do?" Prune persisted.

"I don't think you can describe a journey to the dawn of time as 'scratching the surface,'" said Andrew. "Most of the quest, including the witnessing of all three beginnings, was either made possible by the power of the device or was dependent on it."

"Yes, of course," Prune conceded. "But the device has enormous potential. I'm pretty sure it could solve some of mankind's most intractable problems. It could be a great help in the search for meaning. I think it might even answer Adam and Eve's questions."

"I agree," said Andrew. "But I fear it could also do even more, which is why it is best we don't do what you suggest."

"That van looks as though it's been round the block a few times," said a deep, strong, unfamiliar voice.

Prune adjusted the wrinkles on his face into a grin. "You could say that," he responded.

"I see you've sorted out the tyre. I noticed it was a bit flat last night."

"And you are?" enquired Andrew Rimzil, observing the substantial physical dimensions of the man.

"I'm a neighbour. I live a few houses down the road. The name's Jedwell. Jedwell Boon."

oooOooo

While Andrew and Prune were discussing the paradox device, Uncle Rambler and Nephew Numpty went for a walk. Rambler was eager to explore the environs of the house. He was unfamiliar with the suburbs of London and found the predominantly 20th-century architecture of north

Harrow fascinating, especially the relative profligacy with space, compared to the generally more densely packed accommodation closer to the centre of London. Luke had expressed interest in accompanying them and, with Eve's approval, they had taken the golden retriever with them.

"I have a horrible feeling Kit is going to try to persuade us to go questing again," Luke minded to Numpty.

"Well there wouldn't be much point in gathering us together otherwise," Numpty replied. "And I think he's right. There's unfinished business."

"I agree we should consider further action," Luke minded, "but I don't fancy another epic voyage to the Caucasus and beyond. I'm up for a run at any time but, at the end of the run, I like to go home."

Luke silently chatted on but Numpty's mind was elsewhere. He was wrestling with his uncle's latest mental challenge, designed to exercise young Numpty's brain. "You are in a room with two doors," his uncle had proposed. "One door leads to freedom; the other door leads to death. There are two guards in the room. One always tells the truth; the other always lies. You may ask one question, and then you must leave the room by one door or the other. What question do you ask?"

When Uncle Rambler had posed the question, Numpty had sought further clarification. He immediately asked whether both guards knew which door led to freedom and which to death.

"Yes, of course," his uncle had replied.

Numpty thought his uncle sounded a little irritated, as indeed he was, but it was a perfectly reasonable question. "And should I assume," he continued, "that I would prefer freedom to death?"

Uncle Rambler realised that his nephew was systematically exploring the proposed scenario. On second thoughts, he decided that the boy was doing rather well. "Yes, my boy, you can surely assume a preference for life."

Numpty thought of challenging his uncle's assumption. As part of his study of modern history, he had recently read an account of the life of Osama bin Laden. One of the quotes he remembered was: "We love death. You Americans love life. That is the difference between us two." So it was evidently possible to view death as a positive. Indeed, if you saw life as a vale of suffering and the afterlife as a haven of peace and delight, then clearly one might favour the door to death. Of course, that also required a belief in an afterlife and a further assumption that, if you opted for death, you would find the afterlife was benign – that is, you would be admitted to heaven rather than shuffled off into hell. Things weren't as simple as his uncle supposed.

Having establishing that both guards knew which door was which and that he, Numpty, the putative prisoner, preferred freedom and life to death, he had started to wrestle with the puzzle.

"You seem preoccupied," minded Luke, after realising that Numpty was no longer responding to his chatter.

Numpty told Luke about the puzzle.

"Oh, that old conundrum! Have you solved it?"

"Not yet," Numpty conceded. "Uncle set it as an exercise this morning. It's quite hard to formulate a single question that gives a certain answer."

"Do you want some help?" Luke was enjoying this.

"No, of course I don't want some help. What's the point of trying to solve a puzzle if someone else solves it for you?

That just means that you haven't solved the puzzle – and never can."

"OK, calm down. I was just offering. I won't say nothing."

Numpty frowned. And then it dawned on him. He had the question. "If I ask your fellow guard which door leads to freedom, what will he say?" The honest one would have to recommend the door to death because, if he were the liar, he would have to lie. The liar would also have to recommend the door to death because, if he was the honest one, he would recommend the door to life, but, since he always lied, he would have to recommend the door to death. So, whoever Numpty asked, he should ignore the advice and exit through the other door.

"Well done," minded Luke.

Numpty grunted. "I'm not stupid. I know what you did. 'I won't say nothing'. Double negative – pretty obvious hint."

"Only for someone with a really sharp mind."

Numpty couldn't help preening himself a little. Sure, the compliment was canine in origin, but Luke was no ordinary dog.

"Well done, my boy," said Uncle Rambler, when Numpty revealed his solution. "Your mental acuity develops apace."

Numpty smiled broadly. Two compliments in quick succession.

None of them noticed that a man with a tanned, shiny bald head and very broad shoulders had been tailing them. Despite his unusually acute hearing, he hadn't heard much of the conversation because most of it had been minded between Numpty and the dog, but he had noted the appearance and demeanour of both males. He would be able to identify them easily in future.

oooOooo

While the other questors were servicing the camper van or exploring the area, Kit and the Storyteller found themselves alone in the house. Eve had gone shopping to cater for her several guests, using a communally prepared shopping list in which cans of Guinness appeared more than once.

"Do you really think you can breathe life back into the quest?" The Storyteller sounded very doubtful.

"I have to try," said Kit. "It's not over. I know it's not over. Whatever stopped the fourth beginning will now want to be sure it can't be restarted. That means they, whoever they are, will need to negate us. They won't leave us alone. So, whether we like it or not, the story isn't ended."

"Negate us? An odd choice of word!"

"They will check us out, one by one. If we present any threat now, if we appear to be capable of offering any threat at any time in the future, they will do whatever is necessary to stop us. I don't know who or what we are fighting, but I believe it is evil and will stop at nothing to destroy us – or, indeed, anyone like us."

"Evil?" queried the Storyteller. "That's not a word you hear so often nowadays in these secular, non-judgemental times."

"For evil to succeed, good men need only cease to believe it exists."

"I suppose," the Storyteller replied, a little uncertainly. "Of course it's quite the opposite with God. When good men cease to believe in Him, good tends to dwindle."

"That's what gives evil the edge."

oooOooo

Seated inconspicuously in his car, parked not far from the Smith's house, Jedwell Boon completed his notes and then read them through, making minor corrections, before sending them from his tablet to David Minofel. He added a postscript: "*They are having a meeting tonight. I'll send you a summary as soon as the meeting ends.*" He attached a file containing the photographs he had taken of each of the questors. His master always liked to know what the targets looked like.

oooOooo

After an early dinner, Eve and her guests settled around the table in the large kitchen diner.

Kit opened the meeting. "I know some of you are not very keen on discussing what happened and are even less keen on contemplating what we should do now."

There were one or two murmurs indicating assent.

"But I honestly believe we don't have any choice," Kit continued.

"Why?" Eve interrupted. "Why do you believe we have no choice?"

"The fourth beginning was a powerful event; it promised to change history, to change the world – you know it did. You know how hard Nick Peters and the Breakers tried to stop it. They failed; we succeeded. It began."

"And then it stopped," said Prune Leach. "It stopped, and Elsa and Optimius were destroyed."

"That's right," said Kit. "And I believe whatever killed them will want to kill us."

"That's a bit of a stretch," said Andrew Rimzil. "If we're honest, Elsa's existence was underwritten by a pun and an anagram, and Optimius was dependent on consonantal opportunism. All a bit of narrative jiggery-pokery!"

The Storyteller smiled briefly, but Prune Leach was not at all amused.

"A bit of narrative jiggery-pokery! Elsa and Optimius were as human as you or me," roared Prune.

"Speak for yourself," quipped Andrew. "Elsa was a seal and Optimius was a penguin. I loved them both but they weren't human."

"As human as you or I," corrected Numpty.

"Don't start that again," said Prune.

"Gentlemen," Kit said, calling the meeting to order. "Let's stick to the point. We know two things about whatever stopped the fourth beginning. First, it was determined to stop the event. The whole quest was about them stopping us from triggering the beginning. They did everything in their power to deter us. And then, when we remained undeterred, they were prepared to kill us. They shot Gwoat without a second thought and they put Adam in such danger in their hell-hole at Cadnam that they must have been expecting him to die too."

"And the second thing?" Eve prompted.

"Secondly, we know it had the power to stop the beginning, even after it had started. We need to think about that. We won the battle with Nick Peters and the Breakers. We destroyed the Breaker regional office at Cadnam. And yet the fourth beginning was snuffed out."

"So whatever did the snuffing must have been incredibly powerful, a hyper-snuffer," suggested Numpty.

"Yes, that's right," Kit confirmed.

"That suggests to me we should be very careful," said Eve.

"Absolutely," Kit agreed. "I think we are facing an

unbelievably powerful enemy and a truly terrifying level of danger."

"Do you have any evidence of the danger?" Eve interrupted. "We know whatever stopped the fourth beginning was very powerful, but what evidence do you have that we are in danger? They have achieved what they wanted. They aborted the beginning. Why should we be in danger?"

"Because they will be afraid we might try again," said Kit quietly.

Rambler agreed with Eve. "If you're right," he said, addressing Kit, "then the biggest danger is meeting like this to discuss the possibility of trying to restart the beginning. Surely that's exactly what we shouldn't do? If we just accept the beginning failed, we won't upset the power that stopped it, and they, whoever they are, will have no reason to take any action against us."

"What do you think?" Kit asked Prune.

The inventor of the exponential drive leant forward. The wrinkles in his furrowed brow deepened.

"My god, you're ugly!" exclaimed Andrew.

There was a moment's silence and then roars of laughter, led by Prune himself.

"I never set myself up as an Adonis," said the wizened, weather-beaten engineering genius. "And you're no beauty queen yourself. As for Kit's question, I'm on his side. We know what the Breakers were like. They thought nothing of killing those they feared."

"If they thought nothing of killing, why did they kill?" asked Numpty.

"It's all right," Rambler intervened. "He's just playing a game."

Numpty smiled. There was a time when he had asked such questions because they genuinely puzzled him. Since the fourth beginning, he was no longer puzzled but challenging the logic of language amused him, as did the irritation of those he teased.

"I think they will still see us as a threat," Prune continued. "We succeeded more than they expected. We succeeded more than we expected."

"Has anyone experienced an attack or heard any threat of an attack since we last met?" Eve asked.

No-one spoke, but Kit looked at Eve quizzically.

"Oh!" said Eve. It had never crossed her mind that the burglary might have been connected with the quest. She had always assumed it was just chance that it was their home that the two thugs had burst into. But maybe some powerful organisation had decided to make sure Adam and Eve never again thought of questing – and what better way could there be than terrifying and traumatising them? What better way than making them so fearful that they would be afraid to leave their home, let alone set off on heroic adventures?

Of course, if that had been the purpose of the burglary, it had not been entirely successful. She had not been raped, the burglary failed and the two thugs had faced a just, albeit brutal, end - courtesy of the timely intervention of a stranger.

Eve had no intention of discussing that unpleasant episode in an open forum with her guests, but she decided that she and the others should perhaps listen to Kit's argument more sympathetically.

"I'll admit all the evidence so far is circumstantial," Kit continued. "But it will do no harm if we at least consider the possibility that we are at risk and discuss what, if anything, we can do if we are attacked."

"I guess there's no harm in discussing," Eve conceded, "but we certainly can't take any decisions without Adam."

oooOooo

Jedwell Boon took much pride in his reports. They were informal but carefully structured to ensure his master was fully informed of the facts and their significance. He had been meticulous in observing and describing Eve's mental state, and, on several previous occasions, he had voiced his suspicion that Kit could well be an emergent. He liked to think his master truly appreciated and acted upon his insights.

Before Jedwell sent his current report, he underlined one sentence, one that David Minofel would find both interesting and challenging. It would prompt Minofel to review every aspect of his strategy to ensure the plan remained viable. The sentence he underlined was: "By the way, Eve is going to have a baby."

33. Debrief

"So how did your meeting with Giovanni go?" enquired David Minofel when he and Adam had settled themselves down in a quiet corner of the hotel lounge.

"It went well," said Adam. "I have good news. First MC57 is approved or is about to be approved by the EMA. And secondly, because of the imminent approval, we can meet ZeD's deadline for the launch in six weeks. I've spent some more time with Guy McFall and I think I'm up to speed on the marketing."

"That's really excellent news," Minofel replied, seeming genuinely thrilled and not a little impressed. "I won't say you have exceeded my expectations because, as you know, I have the highest expectations of you and all my charges, but you have undoubtedly met them very comfortably. And Adam, I very much hope you will never again express any doubts about your ability."

Adam sat back in his armchair and sipped the cappuccino he had ordered. For the first time, he felt truly relaxed in David Minofel's company.

"By the way, did you give Spinetti my envelope?" asked David casually.

"Yes, I did," Adam replied in as neutral a tone as he could manage.

"Excellent," Minofel responded, and then without warning, he asked: "Do you know what was in it?"

For a moment, Adam couldn't help looking a little startled. Why would Minofel ask such a question? Of course he wouldn't know what was in a sealed envelope. He hadn't opened it. The only way he could know the contents of the envelope was if someone had told him. Did Minofel think he knew? Did Minofel think someone had told him?

"No, of course not," said Adam.

"You seem a little nonplussed," said Minofel.

"It was an odd question," Adam replied. That was true.

"It did cross my mind that you might have thought the envelope contained an inducement, a bribe."

"It never crossed my mind." Adam frowned. Was Minofel playing a game? If so, what game?

"Well, I will tell you what was in the envelope. It was an invitation to dinner, an invitation for Giovanni to join you and me and Miss Tomic for a celebratory dinner. It will be a very special dinner."

"That sounds great," said Adam. "What are we celebrating?" It could scarcely be the approval of MC57, since David had given him the envelope before Spinetti had told him the drug was to be approved.

Minofel smiled. "We shall be celebrating the engagement of Giovanni Spinetti and Miss Tomic. Did I not mention it before? They are an item."

34. Decon meeting continued

The Decon meeting was reconvened on Monday morning. John Noble was keen to complete his report and send it off before the end of the week, and he needed a few days to sub-edit and fine-tune the text.

The Chairman was not in the best of moods when he took his seat at the top of the boardroom table. He had just concluded a meeting with his deputy, Simon Goodfellow, whom he had briefed on Minofel's visit, its purpose and outcome. It was Simon's reaction to the outcome that had put the Chairman in a bad mood. For the first time, Simon had given him less than his whole-hearted support. He had queried Minofel's assertion that the blind man was an emergent. He had pointed out that it was hundreds of years since there had been a plausible emergent entity. He even hinted that the Chairman had been a little naïve in accepting the practitioner's assertion and then agreeing to a trebling of his already outrageous fee. He had actually implied that, although he wouldn't oppose the chairman's decision at the board meeting which would have to approve the additional expenditure, he would not actively support it.

"Lady and gentlemen," said the chairman, calling the meeting to order, "I apologise for the interruption to the meeting on Friday, but we can now press on. Charlie, let's have your report on corruption."

Charlie Cornick was large, fat and cheerful. He had a florid complexion and a knack of establishing an immediate feeling of intimacy with everyone he met. There was always a twinkle in his shimmering blue eyes which, in a seemingly entirely benign way, told you that he knew rather more about you than he should.

"It's been a bloody good month, chairman," Charlie began. "Let's start with the financial sector."

Lotte Axelrod sighed. Many of the committee members felt that the depravity brief was the easiest of all the tasks assigned to divisional heads, but really, in her view, corruption was child's play in comparison, especially when it embraced the financial sector.

"I think I can claim, without fear of contradiction, that the financial sector has now reached a level of corruption unequalled at any time in the past. Greed is so prevalent that it is now considered the normal driver of performance and efficiency, with the result that almost all the activities of the financial sector are fraudulent."

"But is it not true," Lotte enquired innocently, "that most of these frauds have been exposed and the authorities are taking action against the offenders? Won't that put a brake on future plans for the expansion of corruption?"

A less subtle creature than Charlie Cornick might have permitted himself a snigger or a sneer but that was not Charlie's way. Of course he could smack down Lotte's intervention easily enough. He had been at the corruption game long enough to know not only how to manipulate the corruptors but also how to corrupt those who tried to bring the corruptors to justice. But an abrupt rebuttal would only alienate Lotte and, far worse, imply that his stratagems were far too easy to be considered difficult. They might in truth be easy for him but his devices were extremely complex and subtle. No harm at all in reacquainting the other committee members with his mastery of his brief, not to mention his undoubted genius.

"You're right, Lotte. The authorities are taking action. The major banks are now being routinely fined so often and so much that it scarcely merits a headline. They are having to pay billions in fines and compensation. But what seems like a punishment for their misdemeanours is nothing of the sort. It's the very people and organisations they have cheated who pay the fines, through higher bank charges and higher fees. The financial institutions, I'm delighted to report, continue to make obscene profits while making little or no contribution to the actual wealth-creating process. And, most important of all, the individuals who have benefitted from the widespread fraud remain entirely unaffected by the modest penalties that governments have imposed. Their avarice continues to be rewarded; they keep their wealth while the plodding masses pay the fines intended to penalise the fraudsters."

Charlie Cornick had done it again. He was, after all, a bit of an orator. The committee thumped the boardroom table in approval, and then, led by the chairman, the other committee members stood up and gave him a standing ovation. Charlie revelled in the applause to such an extent that, for a moment, the appearance he adopted for his dealings with the human members of the Praesidium slipped a little, giving the sharp-eyed a glimpse of his true physical form. A thin line of blue lubricating slime seeped over the top of Cornick's buttoned shirt collar. Charlie didn't wait for the applause to end. He had more, much more, to say.

"It is not just the financial sector where corruption is thriving. Almost every commercial organisation is now heavily involved in deceit, in tricking its customers and clients into paying ever more for ever less. There is scarcely a single advertisement that does not involve a misleading proposition, whether it is interest rates on savings which consist almost entirely of temporary introductory bonuses, or Photoshop-enhanced pictures to exaggerate the claims made for a face cream, or entirely spurious sales reduction offers. Dishonesty is now endemic in the system. In the very place over which our magnificent Praesidium complex has been superimposed, Members of Parliament have been caught fiddling their expenses or selling their influence to lobbyists. Those MPs with anything saleable sell it by pursuing their careers outside Parliament, taking on non-executive directorships or writing books of varying literary quality, while those whose salaries as MPs far exceed their worth within or outside Parliament and who are therefore unable to supplement their parliamentary income complain bitterly about the venality of their more gifted colleagues."

There was a general round of sniggering as Charlie Cornick recounted how corruption was spreading even in the Mother of Parliaments.

Only Lotte Axerlod felt the need to snipe. "It's easy enough to tempt those with power to abuse it and to tempt those with the opportunity to cheat to seize it with both greedy hands. Furthermore, it requires little effort from the Corruption Division to persuade the entire UK population to sustain the black economy. It is routine for almost everyone to pay their servicers – their gardeners, handymen, cleaners, etc. – in cash, thereby cheating the Exchequer of both the VAT they should pay and the income tax or profit tax for which the service provider is liable? This particular and widespread scam runs into billions every year in lost tax revenue and makes the misdemeanour of members of Parliament look almost – and I hesitate to use such a distasteful word – virtuous, or at worst trivial. Is the head of the Corruption Division unable to report a deeper evil than instances of mere avarice?"

Charlie Cornick refused to be goaded. "Lotte is right. In reporting the venality of the politicians I claim little or no credit for my division. Humans are programmed to be acquisitive and avaricious. The misdemeanours of MPs have indeed been relatively trivial and, as Lotte suggests, entirely predictable. And I endorse her account of the pervasive corruption among the general population for which, again, I claim little credit. I would, if I may, make one claim for my division's achievement in this entirely appropriate self-deprecating homily: namely, the outrageous excesses of those in charge of running the financial institutions, which have happily become a cancer in the economic system.

Lotte did her best to deconstruct Charlie's last few sentences. He had agreed with her main point, and yet somehow, by the end, he had been pitching for praise in an openly brazen manner, in such a way that any further taunts from her would seem biased and ungracious.

Charlie waited a moment for Lotte to concede defeat. Then he continued: "It was, after all, the Corruption Division that encouraged the development of obscure financial instruments which were entirely divorced from the real world of production, value and wealth creation. Without being immodest, I myself played no small part in driving forward the development of credit default swaps and such like. To allow unbridled greed to permeate the financial industry, it was essential to create a gaping chasm between the real world and the financial world. Once the separation had been accomplished, perfectly decent human beings could happily bankrupt firms, create mass unemployment and spread poverty, simply in order to accumulate obscene amounts of personal wealth. I am of course using obscene in a purely positive sense. My only regret is that some of these fraudsters have been able to pretend to themselves that they are not personally responsible for the havoc they wrought. Our true purpose in the division is not merely to corrupt but to ensure the corrupted fully appreciate the splendid depths to which they have sunk. But, even if some have fooled themselves, the consensus is that their insatiable greed has ruined millions of lives, and that surely is something of which I and my division can be justifiably proud.

"In short, whether at the top of the establishment in the corridors of power, in the temples in the City devoted to money or in the humbler dwellings of the general population, I can report that dishonesty and greed are rife. The scale depends largely on the level of opportunity.

"I cannot end my report without paying tribute to one superb example of complete moral disintegration. The former British prime minister Anthony Charles Linton Blair has, as you know, been one of our most valued assets for years. His ruthless exploitation of his position since leaving government has set a very high bar for those with ambitions in the fields of overweening self-aggrandisement and pure greed. More than that, with our encouragement, but of his own volition, our subject attained levels of hypocrisy and self-delusion that, I must admit, had I any need to breathe, would surely have taken my breath away. His decision to put himself forward as a Middle East peace envoy, after spending his years in office doing everything in his power to create chaos in the Middle East, was a masterstroke. His success in persuading the quartet of countries involved in the Middle East peace process to endorse his appointment was remarkable. Of course, his success depended to some extent on the almost complete lack of interest amongst members of the quartet in making any attempt to resolve the intractable Palestine/Israel problem. Nevertheless, there was a danger that his appointment might have been impeded by the obvious idiocy of approving as peace envoy a proven warmonger who had embarked on at least one unnecessary and illegal war in the Middle East. All credit to T. Blair for his incredible gall in brazenly facing down the obvious and clearly unanswerable objections to his appointment and then systematically using his position to extract as much money as possible from those gullible enough to pay him for his highly dubious consultancy services. We need more people like him. We can forgive his attempts to salve his conscience by various acts of charity, secure in the knowledge that such paltry gestures can in no way detract from the admirable legacy of chaos, hatred and bloodshed he has bequeathed to the lands where we helped to promote him as a bringer of peace."

There was general assent to this encomium to T. Blair, an assent at which even Lotte Axelrod of the Depravity Division felt no need – indeed, had no wish – to cavil.

35. True love

On Sunday morning, Giovanni Spinetti woke early. The sunlight was gathering strength and shining through a gap in the only partially drawn curtains. He looked down at the woman who lay in the bed beside him.

Giovanni had a way with women. He was not especially good-looking but he had the famous Italian charm and a love of fun. Those assets, combined with a substantial inherited fortune, had enabled Giovanni to sleep with many women. In his youth, he had been indiscriminate, bedding any girl who was willing. As he grew older, he had become more fastidious; now, in his thirties, he took some pride in engaging in intimate relations with only the most attractive women.

But the woman beside him was in a class of her own. She was flawless. His eyes took her in: the lustrous dark brown hair; her full, firm breasts; the contours of her belly; her exquisite long shapely legs – everything was perfect. Her lightly tanned skin glistened in the sunlight.

Gently he undid the black bra she was wearing. She stirred, still half asleep and then invitingly turned onto her back. When he took hold of her black panties, she obligingly lifted her bottom a fraction to let him slide them off. Giovanni kissed the woman's full lips which parted to let his tongue tangle with hers. He caressed her breasts and she responded, her nipples firming and her legs parting. He kissed her breasts and then her stomach. Her scent was intoxicating. He kissed the inside of her thigh, intending to pleasure her with his tongue but she pulled him up so he lay over her and slid into her. Giovanni was an experienced lover, but it was only with considerable effort that he managed to prevent himself from ejaculating almost immediately.

When it was over, Giovanni lay back and pondered what divine hand had fashioned a woman who was not only highly intelligent but also extraordinarily beautiful and a mistress of the art of love. Although not much given to modesty, he did feel incredibly lucky that she had chosen him of all other men.

Miss Tomic, for her part, was simply wondering whether this particular assignment would require her to marry the man beside her or whether she had already done enough to ensure the success of the project.

36. Good news/bad news

When, on Monday morning, Adam sat down in his office on the 5th floor of ZeD's Head Office building, he planned to have a long session with Guy McFall. He wanted to go through every aspect of the draft marketing plan for MC57 to see whether there was any way they could sharpen the strategy.

He had just started to drink his double expresso, when the internal phone rang. It was Miss Tomic. "Hello Adam. Dr Dubois would like to see you in his office. Now."

Dr Dubois was seated behind his desk when Adam entered. Immediately he stood up and came round the desk to shake Adam's hand. "I hear you have some good news for me," he said, with a broad smile that made him look ten years younger.

Evidently someone had already briefed Dr Dubois on the outcome of his meeting with Giovanni. Adam wondered whether Giovanni had informed David Minofel and Minofel had passed the good news to Dubois – or perhaps Giovanni had told Miss Tomic, and she had told Dubois.

"Yes," said Adam, "I can confirm that MC57 will be approved by the EMA and that we will be able to proceed with our plans for marketing in six weeks."

"You have done well," said Dr Dubois. "Very well, given all the circumstances. I can see that Minofel's recommendation was, as ever, soundly based. This company is successful because it appreciates and rewards those who help it to succeed. If you can keep to the MC57 timetable, you will enjoy the benefits of this corporate policy. Ten thousand euros, which is ten percent of that measure of our appreciation, will be paid into your bank account today. You will receive the balance immediately after the product launch."

Adam realised the meeting was over. He thanked Dr Dubois for his encouragement and left the Chairman's office.

oooOooo

On returning to his own office on the fifth floor, he found that Guy McFall was in an agitated state, pacing around the office like a mad cow.

"Oh my God," said McFall as soon as he saw Adam. "Oh my God."

Adam frowned in surprise, sat down at his desk and drank the rest of his now barely-lukewarm coffee.

"Calm down, Guy. Just calm down and tell me what is driving you to invoke the Almighty."

Guy's hair, which was always unkempt, now seemed entirely dishevelled, rather like Einstein's hair in the photographic portrait of the great physicist taken in Princeton in 1935.

"It's Reed," said Guy. "He came here while you were out and gave me this." He waved a sheet of paper as though he wished to discard it but was prevented by an invisible adhesive.

"And this is?" queried Adam.

"It's unbelievable," Guy replied.

"Try me."

"Look," said Guy, handing the paper to Adam. "One of the patients in the Basel clinical trial has died."

Adam looked at the paper. It showed a table containing

various numbers. "What are you saying?" Adam asked, confident he would learn more from Guy than from the obscure numbers and symbols on the sheet.

"One of the patients on MC57 in the Basel trial has died," said Guy, as though he was announcing the passing of a great and much-loved statesman.

"What exactly does that mean?" Adam asked. "Was his death connected with MC57? He could have died of something else, couldn't he?"

"Obviously, we'll investigate the death in minute detail but there is no way we will get approval for the drug in time for the launch, if at all."

"It's as bad as that?"

"We can't market a drug which kills patients," said Guy, a little irritated by Adam, whose grasp of the situation was, it seemed to him, painfully slow. "The best case scenario is that they review the new evidence, find that MC57 is not directly implicated in the death and, after some further double-blind clinical trials, we get things back on track. But even if that happens, we will have lost at least one year, probably two. Even if Angeloma is exonerated, the incident is likely to cast a shadow over the drug. It's something Pharma BioSolex and our other competitors are very likely to mention and exploit. I've faced this type of problem before. Believe me, it will make the marketing of the drug even more difficult."

"Would it make any difference," said Adam slowly, "if I told you the decision to approve the drug has already been taken?"

Guy was surprised. "We haven't heard from the EMA, have we? Why do you think it's been approved? In any case, it doesn't make any difference. We have to submit the Basel trial results and the Committee will need to review their assessment."

"You told me that MC57 was a "me too" drug. If that's the case and it's almost identical to Angiax, the leading beta blocker, why would it cause a death? Angiax

has been on the market for several years and, as far as I know, it hasn't left a trail of corpses in its wake." Adam realised he probably sounded callous but Guy's attitude seemed unnecessarily pessimistic. They didn't have enough information yet to throw in the sponge. Adam was also considering the likely response of Dubois to the news of the drug's fall from grace. He certainly wouldn't be best pleased. And he wondered what David Minofel would have to say about this sudden and, if Guy was right, definitive reversal.

"Guy, Adam continued, "I want you to write a full report on the situation, including best and worst-case scenarios. Mention how you think the competition might use this against us, even if we do win approval for the drug. The full works."

Guy nodded, his normally sleepy blue eyes wide awake and full of anxiety.

oooOooo

That evening Adam moved into the apartment that Miss Tomic and ZeD's HR department had chosen for him. He was on the top floor of a building which

overlooked Lake Geneva. The apartment was spacious and tastefully furnished. It was, Adam realised, certainly the most expensive residence he had ever occupied. He was not familiar with Geneva rental prices but he suspected that HR had put him in accommodation with a rent which, had he been paying it, was too high for him to afford, even on his generous salary.

In other circumstances, Adam would have taken some pleasure from this extraordinary good fortune. He would have phoned Eve and enjoyed telling her about his success with MC57, the fine furnishings and magnificent view of his accommodation, his prospects for a large bonus, all of it confirmation that he had made the right decision. But Guy's news threatened to change everything.

So it was that the first thing Adam did on entering his new accommodation was to phone David Minofel.

"I see," said Minofel, when Adam had blurted out the report of a death in one of the MC57 trials. "I think the first thing you should do is calm down. Slievins people don't panic."

Adam thought David's response unsympathetic. "I'm not panicking, but I am naturally concerned. My job here depends on the success of MC57. The news I have had today jeopardises that success."

"So what are you going to do about it?" asked Minofel. "Slievins people solve problems. It's what we do."

"I was rather hoping you might have a suggestion or be able to help."

"I'm not the Marketing Director of ZeD, Adam - you are. You're not paid 200,000 euros a year, plus a substantial bonus, to falter at the first obstacle."

Adam noted with some surprise that Minofel knew about his bonus, a bonus that clearly was at risk, given the threat that MC57 was under.

"I'm not faltering and I'm not panicking," said Adam, a hint of irritation in his voice.

"That's better. Nothing like anger to stiffen the sinews. So what do you propose to do to resolve this problem?

"What can I do? I can scarcely resurrect the dead trial patient."

"Of course not," David laughed. "That would cause no end of problems. You can't resurrect him, but you might be able to erase him, or at least erase the results of the trial."

Adam was stunned. What was Minofel suggesting? Was it possible? "You mean we could alter or suppress the results of the trial?"

David paused before answering. "I'm not going to solve your problem for you. I want you to think logically about the situation. Start from the premise that the results of this one trial constitute a threat to your position at ZeD and to the undoubted benefits that continued employment at ZeD offers. Think of any way, however outlandish or bizarre, that could solve the problem to your satisfaction."

"Well, if we could prove the death had nothing to do with MC57, presumably registration could go ahead as planned."

"That's good. It's certainly a possibility to explore. I should warn you, however, that often it is difficult to prove a negative."

"The only other way would be to suppress the results of the trial – or at least to delay them," Adam mused.

Minofel smiled. "It may help you to know that, for various reasons, Giovanni Spinetti is – how shall I put it? – on our team, at our disposal, in our power."

"What does that mean?"

"It means he will do whatever you want him to do. Perhaps I should explain. First of all, young Giovanni is hopelessly enamoured of our Miss Tomic. Perfectly understandable, given her physical and mental attributes, wouldn't you say? As you know, Miss Tomic is one of Slievins' chosen people. She will do what we ask of her, just as the love-struck Giovanni will do as she asks of him."

"I see," said Adam, not entirely convinced that Miss

Tomic, for all her charms, could persuade Spinetti to do something that would jeopardise his career and quite possibly put him in prison.

"There is another reason," Minofel added. "It's not really fair, but there is evidence that Giovanni has been taking bribes."

A cold shiver ran down Adam's spine. Was Minofel admitting that the banker's draft that Adam had given Spinetti was a bribe? If so, Spinetti was guilty of corruption but Adam, as the bribe-giver, was equally guilty. That would mean that the first significant action Adam had taken since arriving at ZeD, an action that had earned him praise and a bonus from Dr Dubois., was morally unacceptable and legally impermissible. Far from enjoying the good life on an extraordinarily generous remuneration package, he might well end up in a Swiss prison, his name disgraced and his career ended - and all in the first week of his new, exciting fast-track career.

"As I said, it's not really fair," Minofel added easily. "It wasn't a bribe. It's just that it could look like a bribe. And, as I said, it's often difficult to prove a negative."

"Well, if it wasn't a bribe, what was it?" That was a question Adam had wanted to ask Minofel from the moment Miss Tomic had told him about the banker's draft. Now seemed a good opportunity.

"It was simply money I owed him. He and I had a bet. I lost. The 100,000-euro banker's draft was what I owed him."

Adam relaxed. A hundred thousand euros was a hell of a bet but everyone in Geneva seemed to work in hundreds of thousands. At least Adam was in the clear. Obviously Minofel felt that the possibility that someone might misinterpret the situation was sufficient to give David and

Adam a hold over Spinetti. As David said, it wasn't fair but, given Adam's current problem, it could be helpful.

"Are you saying that Spinetti could suppress the trial results or delay them?

"I'm sure, if we want him to, he could lose them altogether. It's easily done. He is responsible for presenting the final submission to the EMA Committee. The offending clinical trial has not been fully written up yet. It would be perfectly reasonable for him to omit the trial from his submission."

Adam needed time to think. Obviously, it was not ethically right to suppress a clinical trial, just because the results were bad. After all, someone had died. On the other hand, there was no evidence the death had anything to do with MC57. The patient might have died from any one of a dozen other causes. And the consequences of failing to register the drug, cancelling the launch and thus wasting twelve years of investment also had to be considered. People would lose their jobs; shareholders would lose their money. And why? Because of an over-reaction to a negative outcome in one of a dozen trials, a negative outcome almost certainly unconnected with MC57.

"I can see you need time to think this through," said Minofel. "You're certainly on the right lines, but you will need to be thorough, to make sure there are no loose ends. I can help; if need be, I will put Jedwell Boon at your disposal, but the plan must be yours and managed by you. I suggest you focus on this to the exclusion of all else. No weekend trips back to the UK. And I would advise against any contact with Eve until the situation is resolved. You have a lot to think through and a plan to devise and implement. Talking with Eve will just confuse the issue and interfere with the clarity of thought you now need to employ. There will be time for personal matters when this is over. Come on, Adam, you're a Slievins man now."

Adam was about to ring off when he thought to ask one more question. "By the way, what was the bet?"

Minofel laughed. "I bet him 100,000 euros that MC57 wouldn't get EMA approval."

37. Decon meeting concluded

When the murmur of approval subsided, Charlie Cornick leant back in his chair, well pleased with his delivery of his report and its favourable reception. His only regret was the momentary loss of concentration which had led to the mild soiling of his shirt collar.

"Thank you Charlie for a first-class report. It's good to know that the Corruption Division is not resting on its laurels but striving to build on and exceed past successes. Lastly, we come to obfuscation and negativity. Oliver, over to you."

Oliver Nates was a hard-faced disciplinarian with a straight nose, grey hair and grey eyes, framed by heavy, grey thick-framed glasses. Indeed, Oliver was grey both inside and out.

"I will deliver my report in three sections as usual:

- Education
- Reasoning
- Relativism

"I know the chairman is eager to terminate what has been an unexpectedly long meeting, so I shall be brief.

"First, education. My people continue to undermine educational standards with sustained enthusiasm. As the committee knows, it was not easy at the beginning when notions of excellence prevailed, but, by converting elite into a word with negative connotations and conflating excellence with elitism, we began to make real progress.

"We were further aided in our endeavours by the idea, one we heartily endorsed, that the only form of excellence was the academic. Apparently, the good people running the educational system failed to realise that, if they insisted in assessing everyone on the academic yardstick, the only way to avoid classifying most people as failures would be to lower academic standards to just a little below the level of average academic ability. Mathematically, this is obvious and should have been clear to those formulating academic policy, but happily a sound grasp of basic mathematics has declined amongst the teaching profession, just as much as it has among the public.

"In passing, I should like to mention if I may, a masterstroke for which I can personally claim some credit. Some decades ago, I started to suggest that grammar should no longer be taught in schools. Fortunately, it seemed an innocuous enough suggestion. After all, grammar is boring, and, in any case, the formal teaching of grammar militated against the enthusiastic advocacy of non-standard forms of language. As a result, most children and many teachers have no idea how to parse a sentence; indeed, many will be unfamiliar with the word 'parse'. The abandonment of grammar as an academic subject has happily lead to such a decline in the mastery of language that ambiguities and solecisms in human speech are now so common and widespread that the ability to communicate is being seriously compromised.

"As academic standards have fallen, examination pass marks have improved. You will appreciate this is, for us, a perfect outcome. As thicker and thicker people become academically qualified, the difficulty of trying to maintain academic standards becomes greater. Of course, there are still bright kids passing through the system, and many of them attain high levels of literacy and numeracy, but we can take considerable pride from the creation of a society that, far from valuing such accomplishments, actually tends to view them negatively, as evidence of superiority, arrogance, privilege and elitism. I can report that the BBC, in its desperate efforts to be inclusive, now favours dim presenters with regional accents, ideally from ethnic minority backgrounds, over more able applicants simply in order to burnish its non-judgemental, anti-elitist credentials.

"This leads me to report on reasoning. We have made great strides in undermining the ability of the public to reason. This has been achieved partly by undermining academic standards, especially in the mastery of language, but has been greatly assisted by another concept developed and promoted by my division, namely non-judgemental inclusiveness. We have reached a stage where respect for other people's views takes precedence over reason. People can now hold inconsistent or even idiotic ideas without fear of being challenged. Indeed, those who hold such views now expect and receive as much consideration as those who are still capable of presenting a reasoned argument. If you wish to see evidence of my division's success in this area, you need only listen to any of the discussion programmes on television to discover how inane and chaotic public discourse on key political, economic and social issues has now become.

"Finally, and closely related to our efforts to undermine education and reasoning, is relativism. This has been a major success. What began as a perfectly legitimate intellectual concept has been perverted under our guidance into an entirely uncritical acceptance of the most laudably pernicious ideas ever devised by man. Edgar has already eloquently recounted his success in fomenting divisions in Islam."

Edgar winced, and a small dark red spot appeared in the middle of his forehead, a discoloured version of the Hindu sign of the third eye. The spot always appeared whenever Edgar felt, rightly or wrongly, that anyone was criticising his work. He knew well enough that he was not the best presenter and he felt that the use of the word 'eloquently' to describe his presentation earlier was laden with sarcasm. He also considered it a little unfair, given that Oliver, although disciplined, precise and succinct, was not himself the slickest of presenters.

Oliver noticed Edgar's reaction and hastened to reassure him that no sarcasm had been intended. "We have built on Edgar's success" he continued, "by inhibiting all criticism of the barbarism of the extremists, and by insisting on the unacceptability of any absolute or universal standards of morality. We have actually been able to introduce the delightfully perverse practice of female genital mutilation into Western societies by preventing criticism of the more pernicious Islamic practices."

"But surely there are moves to ban such practices," Manfred interrupted, convinced that too often the operational heads exaggerated their successes and concealed reversals.

"Yes, you are right," Oliver conceded. "Nevertheless, we deserve considerable credit for creating such muddle-headed inclusivity that we have actually been able to foster such barbarism in what is considered to be a 21st-century enlightened liberal society - even if resistance is growing to it now. In some cases, we have even been able to engineer the death of children by inhibiting social workers to such an extent that they fear to challenge black magic or voodoo out of respect for cultural diversity."

Simon Goodfellow interrupted. "Given there is some evidence that British society is now enforcing rules against such delightfully barbaric practices, including forced marriages and other features of patriarchy, do you see much more mileage in the use of relativism to pervert moral standards? Indeed, I see things rather differently. Some of our greatest successes, at least in terms of carnage and anarchy, have come about through the opposite of relativism. The West's persistent promotion of "freedom and democracy" in Muslim countries is surely an example of asserting absolute standards on societies where such concepts are happily totally alien. The Praesidium has done extraordinarily well by encouraging the West to invade Muslim countries with the declared intent of imposing 'freedom and democracy'. Since most Muslims believe that the Quran is the revealed word of God and is definitive on all issues, and given that Islam means submission to the will of Allah, the concept of freedom among Muslims is pretty comprehensively compromised. And, since most of these countries are riven by tribalism and religious sectarianism, it is obvious to all but the most stupid or ignorant that democracy is entirely inappropriate as a system of government in such societies. By assisting the stupid and ignorant to rise to positions of power, we have managed to launch war after war against Muslim countries, with the delightfully gratifying outcome that hundreds of thousands have died and the region is in chaos. But we have achieved all this, not through relativism, but rather through ideological imperialism."

Oliver was clearly subdued by Simon Goodfellow's

incisive contribution; his always slightly grey skin tone had darkened perceptibly. Edgar made little effort to conceal a smirk. John Noble decided to give Oliver time to gather his thoughts. He summoned his secretary Cynthia to bring in the coffee and chocolate biscuits.

Simon observed Cynthia from behind as she served the coffee. She was not particularly pretty but she certainly had an excellent figure. She was slim, with trim breasts and hips. Her blonde hair made her seem bright and innocent to Simon and therefore very tempting. He had never thought of molesting her before, as he had considered her John Noble's property and thus under his protection, but now that the chairman had shown weakness by acquiescing so readily to the outrageous demands of a practitioner, this might be a good time to explore previously prohibited possibilities. He guessed that, unlike many of the others amongst the Praesidium's staff who had already attracted the vice-chairman's attentions, she would put up a determined resistance but he was fairly confident he could have his way with her without causing irreversible, visible damage. It would be exceedingly pleasurable to see the woman still working for John Noble, knowing he had defiled and damaged her as only he could.

"Please continue." John Noble was addressing Oliver but he had noticed Simon Goodfellow's lascivious look and his mind was now on his deputy. Evidently the Vice Chairman had decided to make a move. 'So it begins,' he thought. 'So it begins.'

Oliver was now recovered and ready. "Obviously relativism is only one weapon in my division's armoury. There are many ways to confuse people and prevent them from exercising their critical faculties. We have had great success in damaging communication by undermining people's ability to use language precisely. We promoted the entirely misleading saw 'a picture is worth a thousand words'. We planted that particular maxim in the United States in the early 20th century as a way of making the fair point that a diagram can often tell you how something works more quickly than descriptive text, but we then generalised it to persuade people that the plethora of emotions that a picture can engender is somehow more meaningful than words precisely used. As we moved the people from verbal to visual forms of communication, they lost the ability to express themselves incisively.

"One of our most inspired stratagems has been to encourage people to feel comfortable with holding two entirely contradictory positions on the same issue. In other words, we castrated consistency in rational debate; and we introduced 'being comfortable' as an argument clincher. You could profess a belief in the sanctity of human life but support bombing raids that killed thousands, so long as you felt comfortable about it. We made it possible for people to claim a commitment to equality between the sexes while accepting the proprietorial rights of men over women in other cultures. You could express the most profound concern for animal welfare but still consume the meat of animals slaughtered in the most appalling conditions. All this was acceptable, so long as you felt comfortable. By promoting this notion of 'being comfortable', combined with encouragement of uncritical respect for the views of others, however bizarre or pernicious, we have effectively killed off any possibility of serious debate of issues. I don't want to overstate the case, but I think I may justifiably claim that my division has stripped humanity bare and laid it on the altar ready for the Praesidium's sacrificial knife."

Oliver had spent hours honing this last metaphor. Rhetorical flourishes didn't come easily to him so he was meticulous in preparing and rehearsing his presentation. There was after all a competitive element in these monthly meetings. All of the operational heads (or monitaurs to give them their official title) were well aware that the Chairman based his monthly report on their presentations. And what he said in his monthly report determined the rewards the monitaurs received in the form of shape, colour and malign energy.

"That's a tad over the top," suggested Simon. "Our function is to corrupt and deprave people – no need for altars and knives. Let us remember, we are on their side. They must and they will fulfil, and thus destroy, themselves."

Oliver felt deflated again. A grey tear streaked his face. The Chairman felt it best to move things on.

"Gentlemen," said John Noble. "I have one more item to discuss before we conclude this meeting."

"There are no other items on the agenda," Lotte Axelrod remarked. She felt a strong need to return to the crucible of eternal light (crucibulum aeternae lucis) for sustenance.

"No," John Noble agreed. "It only came up when our meeting was interrupted. The interruption was caused by the unexpected arrival of a practitioner. He brought word of a problem: there is a possibility that we are going to have to deal with an emergent."

There was absolute silence. Simon looked around the table. Only he had known about the practitioner's claim. The others were stunned.

Manfred Bloch was the first to speak. "Are you serious?"

John Noble showed no sign of the irritation he felt.

What could he say? "No, of course I'm not serious – just kidding." He ignored Manfred's question.

No one else spoke, so John Noble continued: "The practitioner believes – no, is convinced – that the man Kit, who joined the aberrants on their quest, is an emergent."

"The blind man?" said Bloch.

"The blind man," Noble confirmed.

"And the evidence?"

"It is at present largely circumstantial but the practitioner is convinced."

Again silence.

"As a result," Noble said, "I have agreed to treble the practitioner's fee, as is customary if a practitioner's brief includes dealing with an emergent."

"A trebling of the fee?" asked a shocked Manfred.

"You really must stop repeating everything I say in the form of a question; it is not constructive."

"Whereas trebling a practitioner's already extortionate fee without first running it past the management committee is?" Manfred responded.

John Noble's eyes narrowed. So there was to be an insurrection, and it seemed both contenders for his position were ready to make a move. That was good. Since both of them wanted to replace him, he would be able to play one off against the other.

"You are of course right, Manfred. Such decisions must of course be approved by the members of the Executive Committee, which is why I have raised the matter now. I suggest the operational heads withdraw, since they are not concerned with financial matters, so that we can fully discuss the matter."

oooOooo

The monitaurs rose. All four of them found the Decon meetings tiring, even draining. They were eager to return to their accommodation and the source of their colour and energy.

Meetings with the humans involved the adoption of human form. This was not a problem in itself, although it did entail a number of physical compromises. Lotte in particular found it deeply disappointing that, as head of Depravity, she invariably had to adopt the form of an ugly, elderly, desiccated woman. She had frequently consulted the Praesidium's medical staff to find out why her attempts at a rather more attractive manifestation always failed. They told her that there was no physical or biological reason. One had speculated that her need to feed on yellow might have contributed to her sallow complexion. But what did they know? They had little knowledge of monitaur physiology and even less of the entity/human transformation process.

Edgar was not entirely happy in his human manifestation either. It was quite beyond him why the head of extremism should have to adopt such a banal, nondescript, even moderate form. Surely, he had argued, extremism should be large, powerful, terrifying. Given that he fed on red, should there not be something of fire about him? Even if he couldn't breathe fire (and that really wasn't possible since he didn't breathe at all), at least he should have had an intimidating fiery disposition. Instead, after every transformation, he assumed the shape and appearance of a bald, pudgy bank manager.

Charlie Cornick felt more at home in his human form. His large, fat and cheerful persona seemed to Charlie to be entirely appropriate for an entity engaged in promulgating corruption in all its forms. And he saw a happy irony in his inclination towards blue: being the colour of a cloudless sunlit sky, it cloaked his malign intent, creating the impression of happiness, openness and innocence.

As for Oliver, who felt he had the toughest brief and, because of the nature of his tasks, little chance for glory, his grey essence and predominantly grey aspect were the least of his worries.

More important than their concerns about the adoption of human form was their enforced separation from the Crucible of Eternal Light. The crucible itself was a geodesic sphere about a metre in diameter. It was buried deep beneath the Praesidium building, in the centre of a large chamber that formed an integral part of the parallel construct imposed on and over the Houses of Parliament. The Crucible floated in the centre of the chamber, halfway between floor and ceiling. The chamber itself was unfurnished and had no distinguishing features, other than four three-metre-wide indentations in the floor, arranged symmetrically around the Crucible.

The outer case of the Crucible sphere was constructed from thousands of very small interlocking triangles, each of which was made from two layers of titanium with a lining of graphene in between. The inner case of the Crucible, which no one had ever touched, was another sphere made of pure crystal glass, evidently of enormous strength. Originally, it had been ascribed extraordinary insulating properties until Praesidium engineers from the Technical Division decided that whatever the light was, it was not generated by consuming energy. Nothing was burned to produce this, the brightest of all white lights.

The light had been in the hands of the Praesidium for thousands of years, and yet in all that time its power had not diminished one jot. None of the members of the Praesidium had any idea what energy source maintained the light but they all knew that it was the most prized and powerful of all the Praesidium's possessions. It was, after all, the source from which they drew the power to maintain their parallel world. It enabled them to place the UK headquarters of the Praesidium in the centre of Westminster, coincident with the Houses of Parliament, yet cloaked and entirely unobservable by the population of central London. It allowed them to create myslands, complete replicas of whole areas of a city or countryside in which they could imprison unenlightened humans and impose on them whatever rules they chose.

Above all, the light provided sustenance for the monitaurs, who were the means whereby the Praesidium achieved its goals. Each of the tiny triangles of the outer case could be pivoted over its neighbour to open a window into the heart of the Crucible. Narrow shafts of light could burst through any of these windows.

Lotte was the first to reach the Crucible Chamber. She stumbled once while making her way across the floor, but finally, with a sigh of relief, she stepped into the indentation. This was her home and her operational base. As soon as she was settled, she began to morph out of her human form into her natural state, in colour currently a rather drab khaki as a result of her depleted energy reserves. Using her telekinetic powers, she flipped up one of the tiny triangles on the outer case of the geodesic sphere, and a shaft of yellow light drove into Lotte. Within minutes, she was a bright, fully charged yellow, the cells of her consciousness glistening and flashing across the surface of the glutinous substance that now entirely filled the indentation. That was better; she was free from the ludicrous constraints of arms and legs and other body parts which humans considered essential to justify their odd conviction of their individuated identity.

Lotte relaxed and activated her receptor cells. It was good to be connected once again with the human world outside and absorbing information on the progress of her numerous schemes of depravity.

The other three monitaurs entered the chamber one after another and occupied their own hemispherical indentation. Edgar and Charlie shed their human forms, settled comfortably into their wells and slid aside a single triangular patch in the cover of the Crucible to allow the red and blue shafts to feed them. Oliver, needing grey to sustain him, had to undertake a more complex feeding programme, which involved oscillating between white light and no light at speed to generate and absorb an appropriately uncertain achromatic grey. It took Oliver twice as long as the others to feed on the light.

oooOooo

After the monitaurs had departed, there was silence in the conference room for almost a minute. In the end, it was the chairman who broke the silence.

"Have either of you any idea what an emergent could do? An emergent represents a threat to everything we have worked for and everything we believe in. A single emergent could, within a few short months, entirely destroy us. The power of an emergent is potentially immeasurable and uncontainable."

John Noble was using all his natural authority to set the ground rules for what he knew would be an acrimonious session. He knew that both his subordinates would be against him. Manfred would blunder in with the finesse of enraged rhinoceros; Simon Goodfellow would bide his time, waiting to see what happened to the rhinoceros. Both would be mindful that they did not merely have to undermine the chairman; they also needed to be wary of each other, since, with John Noble out of the way, it would become a straightforward contest between the two of them to replace him. The rivalry between the two aspiring usurpers was something John Noble could use to his advantage.

"There's no need for you to explain the dangers posed by emergents," said Manfred Bloch. "That's not the issue."

"Then what is?" asked the chairman, stroking his grey moustache.

A flicker of a smile crossed Simon Goodfellow's face. There was something about facial hair that Simon found delightfully repellent. The chairman's moustache was a source of endless stimulation for Simon. Its neatness, its requirement to be caressed by its owner, its habitual hovering over the chairman's mouth: all spoke to Simon of a disciplined eroticism. He would allow Manfred to make the running while he carefully observed the Chairman's responses.

"It's perfectly simple," Manfred said, answering John Noble's question. "First, what evidence is there that the blind man is an emergent? Secondly, if he is an emergent, is it necessary to pay a practitioner the extraordinary fee you have agreed in order to deal with him?"

"What do you think, Simon?" John Noble was not going to allow Goodfellow to stand on the side-lines waiting until he and Bloch had exhausted each other.

"Manfred has asked two good questions," Simon replied. "In my opinion, the first question is the important one. If the man Kit is an emergent, we must do whatever is necessary to destroy him. If we need to pay the practitioner the sum you have agreed, then pay it we must. But first we need to be sure that what you are telling us is so."

It was typical of Simon to sit on the fence. He endorsed Manfred's first question, but, if Kit was an emergent, he supported the chairman's decision to pay the practitioner. Except of course that wasn't quite what Simon had said. His words on the payment issue had been circular and tautological. If they needed to pay the sum agreed, then obviously they must – but did they need to?

"It's not what I say," said the Chairman, "it's what the practitioner says. He has told me there is overwhelming circumstantial evidence that the blind man Kit is an emergent. Of course I argued with the practitioner; I asked for definitive proof. The practitioner conceded that there was none, but when I resisted his request for an extreme licence and, yes, a substantial hike in his fee, he asked to be released from the contract. As you know, practitioners always fulfil their contracts. A request from a practitioner to be released from a contract is unprecedented. For me, that is proof enough."

"That's all very well," Manfred replied, undeterred, "but we can't agree to pay out vast sums of money when the person who is justifying the fee is the person who is receiving the fee. It doesn't make any sense."

"So what do you suggest?"

Manfred was a little taken aback. He looked to Simon for a helpful intervention, but none came – he was on his own.

"We could negotiate; we could insist the practitioner should moderate his demands. How can he justify a fee that will leave our entire annual budget as empty as a Breaker's promise? We will need to dig deep into our emergency funds."

"It is true the fee will cause us some financial problems," John Noble conceded. "We are still recovering from the problems at Cadnam and this trebling of the practitioner's fee is an embarrassment. But there is no alternative. Simon, you and I have some experience of negotiating with practitioners."

"That's true," said Simon. He did indeed have experience of such negotiations, but Manfred Bloch didn't – definitely a point in his favour in the impending tussle between him and Manfred to succeed Noble! "They are inflexible. Unfortunately, we have little leverage. We call on them only when we are in desperate need of their services. It is difficult to negotiate from a position of desperate need."

"So," said the chairman, "it's really very simple. Either you support me when I take this to the full board, or, if you oppose me, you will be arguing that we should risk everything on your hunch that the practitioner is wrong and the blind man is not an emergent. I don't think either of you would want to take that risk. Am I right?"

Neither Manfred nor Simon could disagree.

John Noble smiled. He thought: 'First round to me, I think.'

38. Growing concerns

It was a bright, sunny morning when the questors gathered for breakfast in Eve's rather overcrowded house in Harrow. Eve had laid the dining room table and set out her full range of cereals. She thought it best not to prepare a cooked breakfast, for fear that her guests might then expect one every day.

"How did you sleep?" she asked Andrew Rimzil, who had spent the night in the camper van along with Prune Leach and Numpty.

"Well enough," Andrew replied. "Inserting ear plugs reduced Prune's snoring to a just about tolerable level for someone with seriously impaired hearing. After that, I managed to snatch the odd hour."

"That's really funny," Prune responded, "because I woke up pretty frequently, and every time I did, the only snoring I could hear was yours – and unfortunately, I didn't have any ear plugs in my travel bag."

"I pack ear plugs only because I have shared sleeping space with you before. I came prepared."

"Well, next time I'd be grateful if you could stretch to two pairs, so I too could enjoy a decent night's sleep."

"Of course, my dear fellow," said Andrew, "and while I'm at it, I'd like to try a gadget I've devised for those with a really serious snoring problem. I've tested it myself and I believe it could stop you snoring altogether."

"Well, if you were wearing it last night, it didn't work."

"Sadly, my device works only with those who have a serious snoring problem: really only those who emit noise at or above 80 decibels, which is around, for example, the noise level of a garbage disposal unit."

"Are you suggesting my snoring matches the sound of a garbage disposal unit?" enquired Prune, whose sense of humour was never at its best first thing in the morning.

"No," said Andrew, "if I were to try to think of a noise closest to the sonic effusions of your nasal passages, I'd go for the sound of a food blender."

"Sonic effusions?" snorted Prune. "You've been spending too much time with Rambler."

"And how did you sleep?" Eve asked of Numpty, eager to forestall any further bickering.

"Horizontally," Numpty replied.

"Jolly good," said Eve. "Now sit down everyone and eat."

After breakfast, Kit drew Eve to one side. "Have you spoken with Adam? When will he be back?"

"No, I haven't. He didn't phone me last night."

Kit frowned. "That's a bit odd, isn't it?

Eve shrugged. "He seems to be very busy."

"Come on, Eve. He can't be too busy to give you a phone call. Is there something wrong?"

"I don't know," said Eve. And then it all poured out: "I really don't know. I don't know why he took the job in Geneva. He seems to be obsessed with his work, his career. He's changed. I don't know him anymore. When we thought we had started the fourth beginning we were closer than we had ever been, but when it ended – or was aborted, whatever – it was as though something snapped inside him. We had set out with the Storyteller in search of the truth – or at least a truth. Adam seems to have decided there isn't any truth; that's why he's putting all his energy into his career."

Kit was silent. If Eve was right, he was wasting his time. The questors had come together to plan their next move.

Adam had to play a key role in any decision. But, according to Eve, he would not be interested.

After a few moments, Kit asked: "Does he know you are going to have a baby?"

"No," said Eve a little sharply. "I haven't spoken to him since you last asked."

"Why don't you phone him? Even if he's not interested in any more questing, he's sure to be interested that he's going to be a father again."

"I don't want to bother him. If he's too busy to ring me, I'm sure he'll be too busy to take my call."

Kit frowned again. "What is going on, Eve? You sound as though your relationship with Adam is collapsing."

Eve suppressed the urge to start crying. "We are drifting apart. We don't connect. He doesn't seem to understand how I feel or be interested in how I feel, and I can't relate to what he's doing in Geneva. We didn't really discuss his new job. He just said it was too good an offer to refuse. No discussion about what it might mean for us or for me."

"Did you tell him how you felt?"

"I didn't get the chance. There was nothing to discuss; he had decided. From the moment David Minofel, the Slievins consultant, approached him, he was gone, out of reach, even before he set of for Geneva."

Kit put his arm around Eve's shoulder. "I think you're being a bit melodramatic. A relationship like yours with Adam doesn't disintegrate unless there's some powerful destructive factor at work. After what the two of you have been through, the bond will be deep, deeper than you can imagine. Adam is still Adam. Phone him tonight. Talk to him. Above all, tell him you are having a baby and persuade him to come back this weekend."

39. Breaking souls

Jedwell Boon did not feel entirely at ease in the opulent lounge of the Intercontinental Hotel in Geneva. With its discreet islands of leather-clad furniture, it was a place for the affluent – for senior business executives, leading politicians, those at the top of the establishment. Not that Jedwell felt in any way intimidated by any of them: he was brighter than most of the guests who had ever stayed at the hotel and almost certainly physically stronger than any of them. No, his unease was caused by divergent values and a matter of degrees.

All these guests, these highly successful individuals, had one thing in common: their primary concern was self-interest. Jedwell, on the other hand, was wholly committed to the service of another, David Minofel. Serving his master was not a means to an end; it was an end in itself.

As for the matter of degrees, most, if not all, of the guests in the Intercontinental lounge, accepted limits to their scope of action. They could not pursue their goals by all and any means; they were in the end inhibited by legal or, in some cases, moral considerations. Not so Jedwell Boon. Whatever needed to be done in the service of his master would be done, without hesitation and without remorse. Some might suggest that such total subservience to the will of another was akin to some kind of spiritual slavery. Again, not so. Like others before him, in whole-hearted commitment to the service of another, Jedwell had found perfect freedom.

"How are you, Jedwell?" enquired David Minofel,

affably, joining his assistant and easing himself into a leather arm chair.

"I am well, as ever," Jedwell replied.

"That's good to hear, my friend, as we face quite a challenge. With the help of your ever-succinct and perspicacious reports, I have persuaded the Praesidium to issue an extreme licence against the blind man. The Praesidium chairman has accepted that the man Kit is an emergent. Now we must deal with him."

"Very well. How do you wish me to resolve the matter? I observed the subject at the Smith's house in Harrow. I see no problem. He is, after all, blind."

"Whoa!" said David Minofel. "If I am right, the man is an emergent. We have to tread carefully. We haven't had a true emergent for many hundreds of years. There is not a single practitioner alive who has ever dealt with an emergent, but all practitioners know it is the toughest and most difficult of all assignments. First of all, they tend to have extraordinary and unpredictable powers. Secondly, it is not enough to kill them. We have to annihilate them – literally break them down until there is nothing left."

"And how do we do that?" asked Jedwell.

"To be honest, I'm not entirely sure. The first thing to do is to isolate him. I need to spend time with him to determine how best to take him apart. I suggest you bring him here to Geneva, to my house. That way, I can get to know him and then decide how to proceed."

"And how should I do that? If he doesn't want to come, I will have to use force."

"I don't think there will be any need for coercion. The blind man will be only too eager to come to Geneva, especially if I persuade Adam not to return to the UK. And

I have done that. I've told Adam not to think of leaving here until the MC57 issue is resolved. Kit wants to reactivate the fourth beginning, and he knows he can't do that without Adam. All you will have to do is tell Kit that Adam wants to see him and then I'm pretty sure you would have to use force to stop him from coming."

"Are you sure I can't just kill him? It would be simpler, and, as you know, I can dispose of a body so completely that it is as though the person had never existed."

"There's no question about your excellent body disposal expertise, but an emergent is a non-corporeal challenge. It is not enough to destroy the body; we must break his soul."

Jedwell shrugged. Breaking souls was probably best left to his master.

40. Conscience

On the Tuesday evening, Adam settled down in his new apartment on his own, poured himself a large whisky and decided to give himself time to think. It had been a busy day. Guy had been closeted away, preparing his report on the options open to the company in view of the adverse clinical trial. Adam had spent the day on the fifth floor of ZeD's head office, meeting other members of the marketing department and familiarising himself with the various administrative procedures. He hadn't phoned Eve the previous evening and, although he had thought of giving her a call at various points in the course of the day, he just hadn't got round to it today either. On the other hand, he had found time to check his current account balance. He found that, sure enough, his account had been enhanced by 10,000 euros.

After the second sip of whisky, Adam played back David Minofel's last words to him at their meeting the previous evening

"You're certainly on the right lines, but you will need to be thorough; you will need to make sure there are no loose ends."

Evidently Minofel thought there was a way to resolve the situation, and evidently he expected Adam to find it. Minofel had implied that, if Adam explained the situation to Spinetti, he would be able to persuade him to 'lose' the report on the Basel trial. That would help, but it wouldn't be the end of the matter. The dead patient would probably have relatives, and they wouldn't be too happy if the drug that might have been responsible for killing their loved one was launched on the market within weeks without any investigation. Assuming they found out about it, that is.

Adam had learned enough about double-blind clinical trials to know that half the patients would have been on a placebo. If only the patient who had died had been on a placebo. Would the relatives of the dead patient know whether their loved one had even been given MC57? Would it be possible for Spinetti to amend the trial report by swapping the dead patient with one who had been on a placebo? That would damage the validity of the trial only marginally, if at all, while effectively exonerating MC57 of responsibility for the death. It was certainly an avenue worth exploring. Adam felt a little better. He took a third sip of whisky.

But what about Guy McFall and, still more crucially, Dr Reed? Adam was Guy's boss, so he could tell him what to do. Guy was a decent, honest man but he had a job he wanted to keep and a family he had to support. It might be difficult, but Adam was confident Guy could be persuaded to see sense in the end. After all, as Adam kept telling himself, there was no evidence that MC57 had caused the death.

Dr Reed was a different proposition. It was after all the Medical Director's professional duty to ensure that ZeD maintained the highest ethical standards. To connive in suppressing the result of a clinical trial, one that might have such important implications, would utterly negate the reason for his employment, if not his existence. Yes, Dr Reed was a real problem. It would be a lot easier if there was a way to neutralise the good doctor, to send him away, to second him to one of ZeD's offices elsewhere, to put him on sabbatical. That was another possibility to explore. Yes, if Dr Reed could be removed from the equation, a satisfactory solution would almost certainly be found.

Adam summarised his analysis:

- persuade Spinetti to delay, supress, lose or amend the trial report
- persuade McFall to forget the patient death had ever happened
- remove Dr Reed from the equation

That was a plan. It might be difficult to implement, especially the third stage, but, if completed, the launch of MC57 could proceed unhindered.

What else had Minofel said?

"I can help, and, if need be, I will put Jedwell Boon at your disposal, but the plan must be yours and managed by you. I suggest you focus on this to the exclusion of all else."

Boon's services could be useful. He would be better-placed than Adam to talk to Spinetti. Adam certainly wouldn't feel comfortable telling someone he had met only once to betray the trust of the organisation that employed him, not to mention any moral principles he might still retain. Boon, on the other hand, was a trusted servant of Minofel; he could speak with the authority of the Slievins partner and would surely find it easier to communicate Adam's requirements without embarrassment.

As for Guy McFall and Dr Reed, Adam knew he would have to deal with them himself. As David Minofel had said, it was Adam's plan and he would have to manage it.

"No weekend trips back to the UK. And I would advise against any contact with Eve until the situation is resolved. You have lot to think through and a plan to devise and implement. Talking with Eve will just confuse the issue and interfere with the clarity of thought you now need to employ."

This made sense to Adam; in other circumstances he would have been eager to discuss his problems with Eve, but this time he knew she would just complicate matters. Not that he doubted her ability or her good sense, but this situation involved issues that were outside her range. She wouldn't really understand the importance of MC57 and the disproportionate difficulties a random death in a wild card clinical trial could cause, not just to the company's management but to the thousands of employees who would be adversely affected. No, this was a problem he had to sort out by himself. If she phoned him, he would have to speak to her. Otherwise, that evening he would send her a text message explaining that in the build-up to the launch of Angeloma he would be really busy, and it would be best if he concentrated on work to the exclusion of everything else. He was sure Eve would understand, especially if he ended the message with a brief note mentioning his 10,000 euro bonus. Then she would realise he was playing for high stakes.

41. The Invitation

Jedwell settled himself into a seat in a carriage on the Bakerloo line. Jedwell was not a fat man but he was big-boned and muscular. It was a fairly tight fit.

He had chosen to travel by tube, just in case he had to use force to persuade the blind man to come with him. If he travelled by car, the ubiquitous security and speed cameras would no doubt record his journey and it was just possible they might connect him with the abduction. The police would probably not bother to check tube train travellers, especially as Jedwell planned to alight at Wealdstone, a stop before the nearest station to Eve's house in Harrow and walk the rest of the way.

The carriage was empty, apart from a pretty young girl in a floral dress who was listening to music on her mobile phone and reading a magazine.

At Stonebridge Park, a thin young man boarded the train. He looked around the carriage and took a seat opposite the girl, stretching his legs out so that they almost touched the girl's feet. "Sorry, darling," he said, giving her foot a nudge.

The girl looked up momentarily and muttered an acceptance of his apology.

"Here, love, I said I was sorry. Don't you talk to people like me?"

The girl was frightened. She looked around the carriage. The only other passenger seemed preoccupied and unaware of the situation.

The young man stood up and then sat down beside the

girl. "You've got a nice pair of legs," he said. "I could see a fair bit of them sitting opposite. That's why I moved. I was getting a bit stirred up." He nudged her. "Know what I mean?"

"Leave me alone," said the girl.

"Is that an iPhone?" the young man asked. "Can I have a look at it?"

The train pulled in to a station and the girl tried to get up. It wasn't her stop but she wanted to get away from her tormentor. The young man snatched hold of her arm and jerked her back into her seat. The girl was so frightened she didn't try to get up again. The doors closed.

Jedwell had no desire to become involved. He was on a mission, a fairly difficult and delicate mission. The last thing he wanted was to risk involvement in an irrelevant incident. On the other hand, if he didn't intervene, the situation might escalate. The young man might assault the girl, hurt her, rob her. It really was unbelievably irritating. It was early afternoon on an almost empty train heading out of town. What were the chances of this type of incident on such a train at this time of day?

"Leave the girl alone."

"Mind your own business, gramps," sneered the young man. "She's my girl now," he added putting his arms around the now-terrified child.

"I will not tell you again," said Jedwell quietly.

"I will not tell you again," mimicked the young man. "Who the fuck do you think you are?"

"I am your better nature," said Jedwell, with a smile.

"I haven't got a better nature," quipped the young man.

"Never mind. I think this is your stop," said Jedwell, as the train pulled into North Wembley. With that, Jedwell walked over to the young man, grabbed him by the hair, dragged him from his seat and hurled him through the open doors of the train just before they closed. The young man crashed into an empty seat provided for passengers awaiting a train. He lay where he had landed, shocked and stunned, not yet feeling the pain of the broken arm and the two cracked ribs.

"Are you all right?" Jedwell asked the girl, shaking from his right hand the clump of hair and bloody skin that had come away from the young man's head.

"Thank you," was all she could say. The train started to trundle on to South Kenton.

Jedwell himself felt a little uneasy about this turn of events. Saving maidens in distress was certainly not part of his brief. He liked to keep things simple and focused. His mission was to bring the blind man to his master, not to involve himself in other matters.

On the other hand, he felt surprised by the satisfaction he had experienced in saving the girl from further harassment, a satisfaction he thought best kept to himself.

oooOooo

On arriving at the Smith's house in Harrow, he knocked on the door. He had walked some way, and it was now nearly 4.00 pm. Only Eve and Kit were in the house. Uncle Rambler and Nephew Numpty had gone to the local library. Prune Leach and Andrew Rimzil had decided they needed more welding equipment and were looking for a suitable supplier. They had taken Luke with them in the camper van.

Eve opened the door.

"I'm really sorry to bother you, Eve, but I'm looking for the man Kit."

Eve was surprised but also a little relieved to see Jedwell again. Adam's new job and his move to Geneva had left Eve feeling cut off, excluded. Even if Adam hadn't been able to make it back to Harrow, at least someone connected with Slievins was still keeping in touch.

"Is Adam with you?" Eve asked. A pointless question, since it was obvious Jedwell was on his own.

"No, I'm afraid he's tied up in Geneva. I don't know much about his work, but I do know the launch of this new drug is going to keep him more than busy."

"I see," said Eve, hurt and disappointed in equal measure.

"Who is it?" asked Kit, who had followed Eve to the door.

"It's someone who works for Slievins," Eve answered.

"I expect you'll want to talk business," said Kit. "I'll leave you to it."

"No," said Jedwell quickly. "It's you I've come to see. May I come in?"

Eve welcomed Jedwell Boon into her house and introduced Kit to Jedwell. She was hoping Kit wouldn't ask too many questions and that Jedwell would be discreet. It would be difficult to explain to Kit that the first and last time she had seen Mr Boon he had been removing from her sitting room the still-warm bodies of two men whom David Minofel had just killed. No, that would take a good deal of explaining.

When they had settled down in the sitting room and Eve had provided a pot of tea, Jedwell came straight to the point. "Adam wants you to come to Geneva," he said, addressing Kit.

"Me? Why me? I would very much like to meet Adam again but surely he will be coming back here."

"He will not be able to leave Geneva for a few weeks. He has too much to do to ensure the successful launch of this new product."

"Too much to do to come back one weekend to see his wife?" Kit asked.

"Why does he want to see Kit?" Eve asked. If he was so busy with the drug launch, why would he want to see Kit? How could he spare time to see Kit when it seemed he didn't even have enough time to phone his wife?

"I don't know," said Jedwell. "It may be something to do with the launch of the drug."

"I doubt it," said Kit, with a laugh. "I know nothing of business – much less pharmaceuticals."

"Well, whatever the reason, Adam asked me to invite you for a weekend in Geneva. If you agree, I'm to accompany you to my boss's house just outside Geneva. Adam will join you there on Friday evening."

"What about Eve?" asked Kit. This was ridiculous. True, he wanted to see Adam, but, as far as he knew, there was no reason why Adam should want to see him. Adam might well guess that Kit would want to talk about the fourth beginning, but Adam had made it clear to Eve that he had moved on. He was now a high-flying, elite businessman. He really didn't have time to search for the truth.

"Adam will contact Eve soon," Jedwell replied. "Just at the moment, he's involved in resolving a delicate and complex problem, and he feels it's best if he just focuses on the issue until it's sorted."

Kit waited for Eve to say something but she just shrugged.

"If you agree, I will pick you up tomorrow at 08.00 a.m. I have two first class tickets for Geneva. We will be getting the 11.40 flight out of Heathrow.

"I'll be ready," said Kit.

oooOooo

When Jedwell Boon had left, Kit sat down beside Eve on the settee. He put his hand on hers. "Eve, you must talk to Adam. You must phone him. Find out what is going on. Find out why he wants to see me."

"And why he doesn't want to see me," Eve added drily.

"Eve, you have to tell him you're pregnant. I don't care how important he thinks he is, or how important his job is to him, you have to tell him the good news." He paused, and then added: "And perhaps that will bring him to his senses."

"I've tried to phone him. He doesn't answer. I don't know if his phone is switched off, or if he's ignoring my calls. Anyway, if you are flying to Geneva tomorrow, you can tell him my good news. And you can find out why he's decided to cut himself off."

Kit felt uneasy. Adam was behaving oddly – not just because he wouldn't speak to Eve but because he had obviously gone to some trouble to invite Kit to Geneva. Perhaps he was having second thoughts about his new job. But Kit couldn't give him much help if that were so: Kit had never taken work that seriously. Perhaps – and this seemed even less likely – perhaps he really did want to talk about the aborted fourth beginning. Perhaps he, like Kit, felt they had unfinished business, that they had come close to creating something extraordinary, and one more try, one final push, might achieve something truly remarkable.

"Tell me a bit more about the company that head-hunted Adam. This man Boon, how well do you know him?"

"I've met him once before," Eve replied. "He came with David Minofel when the Slievins' head-hunter visited us to offer Adam a job." She had no wish to explain further.

"And this Minofel," Kit persisted. "What is he like and what do you know about him?"

"All I know is that he is a senior man at Slievins, which is a highly-regarded City consultancy firm. I really don't know any more. You should ask Adam. Minofel was interested in him, not me."

Kit decided to stop his questioning; clearly Eve was upset. But there was something else. Kit knew there was something Eve wasn't telling him.

"I'll talk to Adam," said Kit, "and I'll make sure Adam talks to you."

When Kit left Eve, the first thing he did was to check that his passport, which he always carried with him in his rucksack, was up-to-date, no mean feat for a blind man.

42. The first meeting

The journey to Geneva was uneventful, apart from the fairly hair-raising flight path required to land between the mountains that surround Lake Geneva.

As soon as they left the aircraft, Kit heard someone say "Mr Boon, your car is on the tarmac. You are cleared to leave the airport."

When Kit was settled in the passenger seat, Jedwell put the car in gear and they drove out of the airport. From the comfort of the seat and the smooth-running of the engine, Kit guessed they were in a very expensive car.

"I'm surprised you don't have a chauffeur," Kit said. "You are evidently a very important man.

Jedwell laughed. "I prefer to drive myself. Always. In any case, I am a chauffeur. And I am not a very important man."

"I'm pretty sure they don't let many people pick up their car on the tarmac beside the plane and then let them leave without the normal passport and security checks."

"That is so, but we were excused the usual formalities – not because I am an important man but because I work for a very important man," Jedwell explained.

"Ah! The mysterious David Minofel," said Kit.

"Mr Minofel is a very powerful, intelligent and determined man, but he is not mysterious."

After a very comfortable twenty-minute ride, for Jedwell was indeed an excellent chauffeur, they arrived at David Minofel's Geneva home. Set in a generous plot of 3,000 square metres, the imposing house was white, with a grey-tiled roof. It boasted generous accommodation for a family, an annex with a guest suite, staff apartments and an indoor swimming pool.

More remarkable were air-conditioned offices, library, laboratory and guest suite, which were located some 50 metres under the house.

Kit, of course, was unable to see the grandeur of his host's dwelling above or below ground, but he had a blind man's sensitivity and could hear the birds singing in the old trees that rose from the well-kept lawns; and he could smell in the air the complacent satisfaction of people who could afford a house near Geneva worth more than SF10,000,000.

"Mr Minofel is not at home at present," Jedwell explained, "but he will join you for dinner this evening. In the meantime, I will show you to your suite and make sure you have everything you need."

"I need very little," said Kit, "'though it's kind of you to be so concerned. When will I be able to see Adam?"

"Very soon," Jedwell replied. "I believe my master has arranged for Adam to join us tonight."

Kit frowned. "Your master? Don't you mean your boss?"

Jedwell laughed. "Yes, of course, 'my boss', if you prefer. I should explain. I am old school. I see nothing demeaning about devoting oneself entirely to the service of another – assuming, of course, that the other person is worthy of such commitment. When I refer to Mr Minofel as my master, I am simply acknowledging his extraordinary merit and the total satisfaction I feel serving him."

Kit shook his head. "It all sounds a bit biblical to me, just a tad over the top."

"Not in the least biblical," Jedwell returned. "I have my own philosophy. All men devote themselves to something. For some it's power, others money. Some live for love. Others for food. Some simply live from day to day, with no great passion. I believe you can best fulfil yourself in the service of others."

"Very laudable, but if that is your philosophy, why aren't you working for a charity? I mean, where is the satisfaction in dedicating your life to a director of a London consultancy firm? I've no doubt Slievins is highly regarded in head-hunting circles, but it's scarcely an organisation devoted to the benefit of mankind."

"Before you make any judgments about Mr Minofel, may I suggest you wait till you meet him." Jedwell replied, sounding a little hurt.

"I'm sorry. I didn't mean to be rude or to cast aspersions on your boss. Of course I'll wait to meet your Mr Minofel before I form any judgements."

"I'm pleased to hear it," said Jedwell, a little huffily. "Though may I advise you that my boss is not someone whom many feel capable of judging even after meeting him."

Kit surrendered. "Fair enough. I take people as I find them and if, as you say, Mr Minofel is worthy of your whole-hearted devotion, I'm sure I will recognise him as such."

oooOooo

After fulfilling his promise to escort Kit to his suite in the annex, Jedwell suggested he should familiarise the blind man with his new surroundings. Kit gently declined Jedwell's offer, explaining that it would be far better for him to explore the rooms on his own, using his finely honed spatial sense to record the location and shape of objects and his acute sense of touch to reveal their precise form and function. Kit did not mention his faculty for creating in his mind's eye an almost perfect replica of any environment where he found himself, a faculty refined by his spatial sense and sense of touch but, peculiarly, not wholly dependent on them. Within half an hour, Kit could navigate the suite and use its facilities with as much ease as any sighted person.

His exploration complete, Kit sat down on the white leather-bound settee in the main living room. The sun was pouring in through the high, arched window and Kit took comfort from the feeling of its warmth on his face. He needed some time to consider how best to deal with Adam. According to Eve, Adam had changed. He was no longer interested in searching for any kind of truth. He simply wanted to pursue his career. Of course it was possible that Eve was right, but, to Kit, it seemed unlikely. After all, it was Adam who had been determined to set out on the quest. He had never faltered in his commitment to see it through to the end. True, he had suffered most. His captivity at Cadnam, his ordeal in Cadnam's underground hell, the toll it had taken on Adam's lifespan – all of this had marked Adam. But he had survived. He had solved the riddle that had held him in hell. He had escaped from Cadnam with the help of his friends, and they – Adam, Eve and the others – had then initiated the fourth beginning. It was of course possible that Adam had concluded his search was too dangerous to pursue, but it seemed inconceivable to Kit that Adam would then decide to commit himself, his life, to an office job. Yes, it was a high-flying, well-paid office job, but it was an office job nonetheless. Adam had witnessed the three great beginnings: he had seen the creation of the universe, the birth of life and the emergence of human consciousness. Surely after such experiences, no one – least of all Adam – would settle for the banality of executive prestige and material acquisition.

On the other hand, Adam was now a senior manager working for ZeD, a leading Swiss pharmaceutical company. That was a fact. He was under the patronage of Slievins, an eminent City consultancy firm that had identified Adam as a man with far to go. That too was a fact. And Adam seemed wholly committed to his new employer and his new patron, even to the extent of effectively cutting himself off from Eve in order to concentrate on his job.

It was while musing on Adam's state of mind that Luke intruded into Kit's consciousness with a mentally-transmitted bark.

"How's it going?" he enquired. "How do you like Geneva?"

"Hello, Luke. I'm fine. I haven't seen too much of Geneva. In fact, I haven't seen any of it, but it smells good, and the sun is warming. How are things with you?"

"Bored out of my head, to be honest," Luke replied. "I had no idea that there was so much to talk about when purchasing welding equipment. Andrew and Prune have been chatting to this salesman for at least half an hour – most of it gibberish, as far as I can tell."

"So is this simply a social call because you're bored?" Kit enquired, with a minded laugh.

"No, it's something serious, at least I think it could be serious. Did Eve tell you about the burglars?

"Burglars? What burglars?" asked an astonished Kit.

"A few weeks ago, Adam and Eve were attacked in their own home. Two burglars forced their way in and ransacked the house. Then one of them decided to rape Eve."

"What are you saying?" If this was true, why hadn't Eve told him? It must have been a traumatic experience. Surely she would have mentioned it when they talked. He'd asked her if there was anything wrong. "Are you sure?" he added lamely.

"Of course I'm sure. I was there. Well, I was there, but locked in the kitchen so there was nothing I could do."

"Are you saying Eve was raped?"

"No, she wasn't raped..."

"Well what are you saying?" Kit interrupted. This was utterly confusing. If Eve had been subjected to such an ordeal, why had Adam taken a job in Geneva? Adam himself must have been traumatised. And, if any of this had happened, what were the police doing? Had they caught the offenders? Was there to be a trial? None of this made any sense – and it didn't help that his informant was a mentally enhanced golden retriever in an equipment hire shop somewhere on an industrial estate in north London.

"No, she wasn't raped because someone intervened."

"Intervened?"

"Yes, intervened – and in a fairly emphatic sort of way. David Minofel killed both burglars."

Kit laughed. Obviously Luke had inadvertently consumed some magic mushrooms and was elaborating a fantasy while under the influence.

"That was good of Mr. Minofel. I guess he just happened to be passing when the burglary was taking place, and being a head-hunter from some obscure Amazonian tribe, he simply whipped out his blowpipe, inserted a poison-tipped dart and killed both criminals with a single arrow, which passed through the first burglar and embedded itself in the second, thereby causing both to die silently in paralysed agony. Am I close?"

"I'm serious," said Luke, a little hurt. "He killed them both with his bare hands. He broke the neck of one and cut off the blood supply to the brain of the other. The second one, the aspiring rapist, died in agony, but there was no poison dart. Minofel shattered his knee first, then waited a bit before killing him."

"OK, so why was Minofel there? And how was he able to eliminate two burglars so easily, without any weapons or help? And what happened afterwards?"

"That's why I'm contacting you. I understand you are about to meet David Minofel and I think you need to know a bit more about him. I'll answer your questions. Minofel was there because, by chance, he had an appointment with Adam that evening to offer him a job. He was able to deal with the burglars because he is ex-SAS and has worked as a mercenary in most of the world's trouble spots. As for what happened afterwards: as I understand it, you should ask Jedwell Boon; he disposed of the bodies."

"Are you telling me that the matter was closed – no police, no trial?"

"That's about the size of it." Luke was relieved that Kit understood.

"Well, it's good to know," minded Kit. "It's always good to know, but I'm not sure how this helps. I should really be back with Eve, not here waiting to see Adam. I need to find out what's going on in Eve's head. I need to know why she didn't tell me any of this. As for Minofel and Jedwell Boon, I'm not really interested in them. Since I'm here, I will talk to Adam as soon as I can, and then I'll return to Harrow as quickly as possible."

"You're wrong," Luke minded emphatically. "Don't underestimate Minofel. He seems to have taken control of Adam. According to Eve, the job at ZeD is just a stepping stone. Slievins has plans for Adam. I don't know what they are; I don't think Adam knows what they are either. But I have a feeling they are not plans that will be good for Adam or for Eve – and they certainly won't be good for you if you have any hopes of reactivating the quest or the fourth beginning."

"Thanks for the warning. I should be meeting David Minofel this evening, and I'm hoping Adam will join us. When I've spoken to Adam, I'll have a better understanding of the situation. In the meantime, ask Andrew if he can find out anything more about Slievins and, especially, about David Minofel."

43. Machinations

Adam had texted Eve, telling her of his need to concentrate on work and mentioning the bonus he would receive if all went well. He had heard nothing back. He was relieved that she seemed to have accepted the situation without argument, but he was mildly concerned she hadn't even acknowledged his message. He just hoped she understood. Whether she understood or not, he had work to do.

His meeting with Guy McFall had been difficult but productive. Guy was proud of the report he had prepared on the company's options in view of the adverse clinical trial. He was therefore taken aback when Adam had said it would be better if, rather than responding to the problem, they eliminated it altogether.

Adam had listed possibilities that Guy had not considered. Was it not perfectly possible the death in the trial was entirely unconnected to MC57? Perhaps there had been a mistake in the coding and the dead patient had in fact been on the placebo. Or perhaps it had not been a mistake but an act of sabotage by a rival company which had switched the dead patient's files from placebo to the active drug. It was even possible that a rival firm had poisoned the patient to damage MC57's results.

Guy had put up some objections to Adam's torrent of hypotheses, while conceding that some of the less outlandish speculations could be worth investigating and testing.

Adam emphasised that it was most unlikely there was anything wrong with MC57, given that it was almost identical to the brand leader, which had an unblemished record over the several years it had been in use.

By the end of an hour, Guy was not entirely clear on what he should do, but he now had a pretty clear idea of the direction in which Adam intended to go. Whatever happened, the death of the patient was not going to impede the launch of Angeloma. For the most part, Guy came out of the meeting happy. He'd put a great deal of effort into his report, but he had felt he had been writing the company's obituary. So much depended on Angeloma: not just in terms of the company's turnover and profits, but also in terms of its effect on the employment prospects of hundreds, if not thousands, of ZeD employees, including his own.

"If we can sort this out," Adam had said at the end of the meeting, "things will go well for you. You are, after all, the product manager for MC57."

oooOooo

After his meeting with Guy, while Adam was drinking his morning coffee, David Minofel phoned him.

"How are things going?" David asked.

"I'm working on a plan," Adam replied. "I've spoken to Guy and I think he's pointing in the right direction. I'll talk to Dr Reed later today. I'm hopeful we can sort something out"

There was a moment's silence and then Minofel spoke again. "To be frank, I'm a little disappointed. You think Guy is 'pointing in the right direction'. What exactly does that mean? And obviously you haven't even approached Reed yet – and he's likely to be the biggest problem. I thought we agreed we needed decisive action. You are 'hopeful we can sort this out'. Well, good for you. Hope is a great consolation, especially for those destined to fail. Come on, Adam. You're a Slievins man. More action, less talk. Have your chat with Reed this afternoon, and then tell me what you intend to do. I'll come to your apartment at 6.00 pm." He ended the call.

Adam frowned. That was not what he had expected. Indeed, he hadn't expected to hear from Minofel at all until he had developed his plan and was ready to act. And he wasn't happy with being treated like an indolent schoolboy. You didn't talk to senior managers like this. He was trying to sort out a really tricky problem – a problem that was not of his making. If Minofel wanted to be involved, he should be helping, not carping. Minofel wasn't his boss; he was employed by ZeD and reported to Dr Dubois.

While Adam was thinking these thoughts, his phone rang again. Adam guessed it was Minofel calling to apologise. But it wasn't Minofel; it was Yves Dubois. "I hear there could be a problem with MC57. Do I need to be concerned?"

Adam considered telling the ZeD Managing Director the truth but he didn't. Obviously Yves Dubois didn't know the details of the problem. If he had known a patient had died on MC57, he would have said so, and he certainly wouldn't have asked whether he should be concerned. This must mean that that Reed hadn't spoken to him yet. Adam still had time.

"Nothing that I can't deal with," said Adam.

"Good," said Dubois. "I just had a call from David Minofel, and he suggested I should check with you. Delighted you have the matter in hand."

oooOooo

Adam spent the rest of the morning preparing for the meeting he had arranged with Dr Reed in the afternoon. He planned to present the same arguments he had used with Guy McFall, but he recognised that Dr Reed would probably prove rather less receptive than the MC57 product manager.

At 2.30pm Adam made his way to Dr Reed's office on the 6th floor.

When Adam had finished, Dr Reed responded. "I'm really not sure what you are saying. Of course all these possibilities should be explored. Some of them have been. I can assure you the patient who died was on MC57. He was not one of the placebo patients. There was no mistake with the coding. It is perfectly fair to ask whether there is proof the death was in any way caused by MC57. In my opinion, it is most unlikely MC57 is implicated. As you say, it is a 'me too' drug and its precursor is as safe as any beta blocker..."

Adam jumped in. "So you concede it is unlikely MC57 caused the death?"

"As I said, I consider it most unlikely."

"Then we must find a way to prevent an unfortunate coincidence from threatening ten years of research, millions of dollars of investment in research and marketing, hundreds of millions of dollars in turnover and thousands of jobs."

Dr Reed was confused: "I still don't understand what you are saying. Of course, I don't want MC57 to fail, but the trial results exist and a patient has died: the unfortunate coincidence, if that's all it is, must be investigated. I'm pretty confident MC57 will be exonerated, but we have to go through all the processes. Yes, there will be a delay, but that is unavoidable."

"It isn't unavoidable," said Adam. He would have to be blunt. "For example, on checking, we might find that the patient who died was on the placebo after all. Even if the patient was on MC57, the trial result could be lost by the

EMA or misplaced. I have spoken with a representative of the EMA, and he said that MC57 has virtually been approved already. I think it would be possible for me to ensure that this particular trial doesn't interfere with the final approval of the drug."

Dr Reed seemed about to panic; he reminded Adam of a skater who has only just realised he is skating on too-thin ice. "Are you seriously suggesting we connive to suppress the trial result? Even if such a deceit were possible, I could never agree to it. Do you not understand, Mr Smith, that my role here as medical director is to ensure the integrity of our medical practices and procedures?"

"Of course I understand," Adam said, trying to soothe the clearly disturbed doctor. "I'm simply asking you to consider the implications of delaying or abandoning the launch of MC57."

"It's not my job to consider implications," said Dr Reed. "My job is to maintain and protect the integrity of the company. I have to warn you that if you try to interfere in the correct medical protocols in any way, I will go straight to the MD and lodge a formal complaint. And if, by any chance, he doesn't support me, I shall immediately go public."

oooOooo

David Minofel arrived at Adam's apartment at 6.00 pm. Adam himself had reached home only a few minutes earlier.

"Come in, come in. Would you like something to drink?

"A glass of water would be good," David Minofel replied. "Sadly Mr Boon is occupied elsewhere, so I shall be driving when I leave you."

Adam nodded and handed Minofel a glass of water.

"I hope you approve of your accommodation. If you have any complaints, however minor, they will immediately be resolved. This is a top apartment for a top executive. You are a Slievins man and must have the best."

Adam said nothing.

"Of course, strictly speaking, just at the moment you are a ZeD man, but underneath, in the deeper recesses of your being, you are Slievins through and through."

Adam poured himself a whisky. With Minofel, you never knew which direction the conversation would take. A drink, Adam thought, would help him to relax – and the drinking of the drink might give him some valuable time to think.

"I have some good news for you," Minofel volunteered, "Giovanni feels sure he can find some flaws in the trial protocol to justify him setting the report aside. Now that's good news, isn't it?"

"Yes, that's a real help."

"So all you need to do," Minofel continued, "is to make sure ZeD's medical department behave sensibly."

"I've spoken to Guy McFall and he's on side," Adam offered.

"I'm not worried about the marketing department. You are head of marketing. I think I can assume you have control of your own people."

Adam took a sip. This was not going well. Adam considered his success in persuading an honest chap like Guy to fall in with a plan which, for all its merits, was still unethical, if not illegal, had been a substantial achievement. Not so in Minofel's mind.

"Have you sorted out Dr Reed?"

"I have spoken to him, but he is adamant that the

negative trial result must form part of our submission to the EMA."

"I see," said David Minofel.

He then remained silent, as though expecting Adam to continue. Adam also remained silent, since, in his view, there was nothing more he could say.

"Well?" prompted Minofel.

Still Adam was silent. He really didn't know what Minofel expected of him.

"This is the last time I shall explain things to you," Minofel said at last. "Slievins people have two great strengths. First, when they see a problem, they always find a solution. Secondly, to solve such problems they employ a degree of clarity of thought that goes well beyond the mind of lesser mortals. Now I want you to think about the situation. Deconstruct it. Identify the facts. Then, without any constraints, consider the possible solutions. If you discover many possible solutions, pick the one that most closely meets any secondary objectives you may have. If you find only one solution, your task is easier. You have found the answer."

This sounded to Adam like some fairly obvious and certainly patronising advice until he realised Minofel was expecting him to perform the exercise immediately. "What now?" was all he could manage.

"Time is of the essence, my friend. Time is always of the essence."

Adam poured himself another drink. He was not a heavy drinker but he was beginning to feel the need for a drink at or after any meetings he had with Minofel.

"We need to ensure the successful launch of MC57," Adam began.

"Excellent," Minofel encouraged. "That is the objective. Now list where we are now and what must be done to ensure we fulfil the objective.

Adam drew up his list:

- MC57 is about to receive EMA approval.
- There has been a death in one of the most recent MC57 trials
- But we have found a way of suppressing the trial.
- So far, only two people at ZeD other than me know of the death
- One of them, Guy McFall will keep quiet
- The other, Dr Reed, will not agree to the suppression of the trial.
- Dr Reed must be persuaded.

"Very good, but your list has to guarantee success. You must therefore consider what to do if, for any reason, you are frustrated in carrying out any of the necessary actions."

"You mean: what do I do if I can't persuade Dr Reed?"

David Minofel smiled. "I'm delighted that you have picked up the Slievins *modus operandi* so quickly. As this is your first real challenge, I'm going to give you a little help. Here is a dossier on Dr Reed. You will find it both interesting and useful. I'm going to leave you now to complete the exercise on your own. It's really good experience and will serve you well in future assignments. But before I leave you, I'm going to invite you to have a bet with me, and I'm prepared to give you very attractive odds. I bet you that you won't find a satisfactory solution to this problem."

"You bet that I won't find a satisfactory solution to the problem?" Adam was confused.

"That's right. I'll give you ten-to-one odds on it. You must stake 10,000 euros. If you fail, that's what you will lose. If you succeed, you win 100,000 euros."

"You really think I can't work this out? You think I have only a one-in-ten chance of success? Is that what you're saying?"

"They're the odds I'm offering. Take them."

"I'm not really a gambling man."

"That's not true, Adam. You've taken some fairly wild risks in your life. In any case, all Slievins' operatives enjoy a flutter now and again. Take the bet. I insist."

Adam, perhaps influenced by the whisky, decided he was pretty much committed to solving the problem anyway. Almost certainly, his job depended on it. Given that he had been employed to ensure the successful launch of MC57, the company would have little need to retain him if the drug failed to reach the market. His ZeD bonus depended on success. Another 100,000 euros would make success all the sweeter. And even if he lost, he could pay Minofel out of his severance package. The real issue was how to persuade Dr Reed to keep his mouth shut.

"Fine, I'll take the bet."

Minofel finished his glass of water and left. Adam poured himself a third and unusually generous glass of whisky.

44. Kit meets Minofel

David Minofel drove back to his house in his Lamborghini Aventador. He had much to ponder on the twenty-minute drive.

As an experienced practitioner, he had dealt with some pretty tough assignments. Occasionally a person of integrity would somehow achieve a position of power without being corrupted, and then the expertise of a practitioner would be required. Blackmail was the favoured method, but, if no skeletons could be found in the closet, assassination was the preferred solution. Simply killing someone did not require the skills of a practitioner but surreptitiously ensuring the victim was denied the status of hero or martyr did. With the advent of the social media, it had become ever easier to start a false rumour that would tarnish the victim's reputation. Practitioners were particularly skilled at weaving the rumour into a web of events in order to give it credibility and enhance its probability.

Funnily enough, run-of-the-mill tasks could turn out to be more difficult than corrupting or destroying the odd honest leader or politician. Many ordinary people were capable of good thoughts and actions. They didn't matter. The Praesidium was perfectly capable of containing any such deviant tendencies.

From time to time, however, one of these do-gooders would start to exercise some significant influence over others. These influencers were practitioners' bread and butter. In most cases, it was easy to turn such people back to normality. Succeed in fuelling their vanity, their natural sense of superiority, and the job was done. If that failed, a whole armoury of corruption could be employed. Lust, avarice, even gluttony: all had their place in diluting the effect of such influencers.

In essence, Minofel concluded, practitioners were on top of their brief – unless they had to deal with a genuine emergent.

For practitioners, emergents were rather like the evil giant in a child's fairy-tale. No living practitioner had ever had to face an emergent, so the stories of these adversaries had taken on a mythic dimension. They were thought to have extraordinary powers and, in order to destroy them, it was necessary to use extreme measures: extremes of subtlety and extremes of violence.

The Praesidium had doubted whether the blind man was a genuine emergent. Such doubts were understandable: emergents were so rare. But Minofel was confident in this case he was right; and so he was certain he would have to be careful. Destroying an emergent would give David Minofel a pre-eminent position in the practitioners' hall of fame. Failure – total failure – was unthinkable. But if Minofel failed and another practitioner had to finish the job, his own reputation would be in tatters.

No, this was a make-or-break assignment, and David Minofel was determined the only one to be broken was the blind man.

45. The paradox of the paradox

On completion of their shopping expedition, Andrew Rimzil and Prune Leach made their way back to the camper van. Luke, who had returned to the van earlier, welcomed them with a bark and a wag of his tail. Neither of the engineers could hear Luke's thoughts, so he was unable to tell them he had conversed with Kit and warned him to be wary of David Minofel.

When they reached the house in Harrow, all three of them joined Uncle Rambler and Nephew Numpty, who had returned from their walk a few minutes earlier. After an exchange of greetings, Prune addressed Andrew.

"Andrew," said Prune cautiously, "don't jump down my throat, but could we discuss the paradox device again?"

"Of course we can discuss it, but if you have in mind any hare-brained schemes for experimenting with it to see what else it can do, the answer is no. I'm well aware of the device's extraordinary power, but I am not well aware, and neither are you, of what those extraordinary powers might do or what damage they might cause."

"That's my point," Prune interrupted. He was not too happy that Andrew had thought him likely to be the author of hare-brained schemes. "We don't know what it is capable of, but shouldn't we find out? It can't be beyond our abilities to devise experiments which will tell us more about the device's capabilities without running any grave risks."

"For example?" Andrew prompted.

"When we witnessed the moment of the Big Bang, we used my exponential drive to travel back in time, and then we parked in a lay-by so we could observe the moment the universe came into being."

"That's right," Numpty said, who had been listening carefully. "I recall we had to relieve ourselves in the lay-by. It had been a long journey for us all, cooped up in the camper van."

"So how did that work?" Prune persisted. "How could there be a lay-by for us to park in to observe the Big Bang? Time and space didn't exist before the Big Bang so where was the lay-by."

"Bit of a paradox," suggested Numpty

"Obviously," said Prune, a little dismissively. "But how did the paradox device create a little bit of time and space for us to park in before there was any time and space?"

No one answered.

"Because it created a parallel universe," Prune suggested.

Uncle Rambler joined the conversation. "That's certainly possible. As I think we've discussed before, some cosmologists think there may well be an infinite number of infinite universes."

"That's right," said Prune, pleased that the others were joining in – mainly because it would make it more difficult for Andrew to close down the conversation. "But this was different. If the lay-by was part of a parallel universe, it would have been completely separate, but our lay-by wasn't separate. We could see the Big Bang. It was, if you like, a superimposition. Our lay-by and the Big Bang coexisted."

"Which would mean," said Andrew Rimzil, "that the paradox device could create coexistent universes. Yes, that thought had crossed my mind. And that is why I don't want to conduct any further experiments."

"But maybe there are already coexistent universes,"

Numpty speculated, "and may be the paradox device could find them, show them, give us access to them."

"You see," said Prune, addressing Andrew, "even the lad can see the potential. Even he wants to know what the device could do."

"What do you mean "even the lad"? asked Numpty. "Under my uncle's tutelage, I have become as curious about the world as anyone. I am an osmotic gouger."

"Right?" Prune responded uncertainly, looking to Rambler for an explanation.

"It is no matter," Rambler said. He hesitated as though there was no more to be said, but then continued, realising that some explanation was required a matter of courtesy. "Numpty has been wrestling with some existential issues, and in his pursuit of knowledge, he has fashioned for himself the role of osmotic gouger: one who digs and delves continuously into the deepest layers of perception in the confident expectation that intelligible information will seep up into his consciousness, just as water and nutrients are absorbed by a plant as its roots burrow into the soil. It is quite an interesting analogy."

Prune regretted inviting Rambler to explain.

"I'm sorry," said Andrew, eager to terminate the conversation. "None of you have given the paradox device as much thought as I have and, believe me, it's best left unexplored. You want to investigate its limits; I believe there are no limits. Do you understand what that means? If we misuse it, the results are incalculable and could be catastrophic – and I mean *catastrophic*, in a universal, cosmological sense! When we observed the Big Bang, we were not in a parallel universe. If we had been, we could not have observed the Big Bang. But we weren't in a coexistent universe either. If we had been, we would have been annihilated by the Big Bang. What we did in that lay-by suggests to me that the paradox device certainly has enormous potential, but it also tells me that we should use that potential sparingly and very cautiously."

Prune shook his head, conceding defeat. "Fair enough, but one day we may need its help, and, if we haven't already tested its capabilities, the risks will then be so much greater than they are now."

46. First Meeting

When Minofel arrived home, he parked his mid-engined sports car in its allocated space in his four-car garage. Jedwell came from the house to greet him.

"The blind man is in the guest wing. He is eager to talk to Adam."

"Well I'm afraid we will have to disappoint our guest on that score. I have just left Adam, and he has much to think about."

Jedwell nodded. "I have arranged dinner for 8.00 p.m. Will you see the blind man now? Or will you wait 'til dinner?

"I'll wait. In the meantime, what else have you learned about him?"

"Very little. Obviously he has something important to discuss with Adam – or at least something he thinks is important. Apart from that, he seems very self-possessed. In some way, he reminds me of a practitioner. He is very…" Jedwell paused.

"Very…?"

"Very confident."

"Then we shall have to put his confidence to the test. Do you still believe he is an emergent?

"Yes, I do," said Jedwell firmly. "There is something about him I've not found in any of our other targets. And I can't identify what that something is. Of course, he could be shielding it, but I don't think he is. I think it's simply that he has something I can't comprehend. And I'm pretty sure he doesn't understand it himself. But I will say this: if this something matures and he takes possession of it, or it takes possession of him, I think you will be facing an emergent."

"Then I had best freshen up for our first meeting. We'll have dinner on the terrace. I'm sure our guest will feel more at home outside where he can hear the birds singing and feel the warm breeze on his face."

oooOooo

At 8.00 pm Jedwell escorted Kit to the terrace. David Minofel was seated at a glass-topped metal table. He rose as Kit approached, and said: "I'm delighted to meet you. I know so much about you. Are your rooms comfortable?"

"Thank you. My rooms are more than I expected or need. As you know, I have come to Geneva to talk to Adam."

"Ah yes," Minofel responded at once. "I was hoping Adam would be able to join us for dinner, but I have just been with him, and he is really caught up in some complex business issues."

"So caught up that he can't take a phone call?"

"No, of course you could phone him. But he is now in a meeting that is likely to last most of the evening, and, when it ends, I'm sure it would be best if we let him get some rest. You can have a good long chat with him tomorrow."

"So they work long hours at ZeD?" said Kit, not entirely satisfied with Minofel's answer.

"Yes, they do work long hours at ZeD, but Adam is not merely a senior executive at ZeD. He's a Slievins man, one of our chosen few. We expect real commitment from our people."

"I see," said Kit. "And Adam's happy to give that commitment?"

"Absolutely. He's doing very well. Coming along nicely,

one might say. Indeed, Adam and I have become quite close, and I'm hoping that while you're here, we too might become friends. After all, the friend of my friend is my friend."

"I tend to find it takes longer than a weekend to forge a friendship," said Kit. He thought of adding that he liked to choose his friends very carefully but decided that would be a little too unsubtle. "In any case, isn't the saying 'the enemy of my enemy is my friend?'"

"Let's have no talk of enemies on our first meeting," David Minofel laughed. He saw now what Jedwell had meant. "Let's drink to this meeting. I have a rather special bottle of wine. Nothing too expensive – it's a 2006 Chateau Cheval Blanc, a Saint Emilion Grand Cru. I'm not an expert, but it suits my palate."

Minofel poured the wine, and they both drank. After a couple of seconds, Minofel took the glass from his lips, a look of disgust on his face. "I must apologise. The wine is not good." He summoned Jedwell. "Take this away."

Jedwell departed, instructing the girl serving the dinner to provide a replacement immediately.

"I'm so sorry," said Minofel to Kit. "And after I had introduced the wine as something special."

"Don't worry," said Kit easily. "In any case, it wasn't so bad – just a little watery."

47. Thinking the Slievins way

Adam decided to devote Saturday morning to reading the dossier on Dr Reed and preparing for the difficult meeting with the good doctor, scheduled for the next Monday morning. He settled into one of the comfortable recliner chairs in the sitting room of his luxurious apartment and began to read.

Dr Geoffrey Reed was 42 years old. He had been born into a medical family (both his mother and father were doctors) so his career path had largely been set from birth. He had spent five years at the University of Edinburgh studying medicine, taking a variety of placements in the city's medical institutions. He had then moved to London to undertake his two years of foundation training. He had always had an interest in cardiovascular diseases, an interest reinforced by knowing that heart problems ran in his family. When Geoffrey was 21 and studying at Edinburgh University, his father had died of a heart attack.

On completing his studies and training, Dr Reed had taken up posts in various hospitals in the UK and Europe where he had been happy in his work. His personal life had been eminently satisfactory as well. He had met Sarah, a dental nurse, while studying at Edinburgh University. They had married the year after Geoffrey had become a fully qualified doctor. They had three children: two girls and a boy. Sarah had given up work on the birth of their first child. As she had said at the time: "I'd rather look after our children than other people's teeth".

Sarah's decision to make a home rather than follow

a career was made possible by the generous salary that any hospital doctor with Dr Reed's qualifications could command. That generous salary was, however, revealed as derisory when ZeD approached him with an invitation to become ZeD's medical director. Adam gulped when he saw what Dr Reed was earning. Even with the cost of educating three children at one of Switzerland's most expensive private schools, the good doctor would not be short of a penny or two.

All this information, apart from the size of the good doctor's salary, was exactly what Adam had expected. It was good to know a little more about the man but everything he read suggested he would find it very difficult to persuade Dr Reed to agree to the suppression of the Basel trial. It was too early for a whisky, but a double expresso from the Gaggia fully automatic machine seemed like a good idea.

Adam settled back into his recliner, sipped his coffee and read on. He came to the end of Dr Reed's potted biography and turned the page. There was a new section, entitled: "Character and Stress Points".

"*Dr Reed sees himself as a good man. He has worked hard in a field which he believes is essentially benign. He has come from a stable background and has enjoyed all the advantages of a solid upper middle-class upbringing. He is not particularly ambitious but he is proud. Although not avaricious, he is attracted by money, not as an end in itself but as a means of measuring his worth. Despite his high salary, he is stretched financially. Aside from the costs of educating his children, he has a mortgage of SF2,000,000. He also has additional costs associated with his domestic arrangements. See below:*"

Adam paused. This was an extraordinary analysis, certainly unlike anything produced by a conventional

Human Resources department.

"Dr Reed is heterosexual, and his sexual drive is of an average level. His sexual liaisons before marriage were all long-term, lasting between six months and two years. He has slept with five women, including his wife Sarah. He has been married to Sarah for nine years.

"Since marrying his wife, Sarah, he has had only one affair. This affair, which is currently active, is with a ZeD employee and has been running for three years. Dr Reed pays for his mistress's apartment, a substantial cost which increases the strain on his already stretched finances. His wife is entirely unaware of the affair."

Adam paused. He was shocked. How had Minofel acquired the document? How had the author acquired the information? Did ZeD or Minofel have a dossier on every employee? Did they have a dossier on him? And what might they find to put in his "Character and Stress Points" section, if so?

It was fairly obvious why Minofel had given him the dossier. In the language of the dossier, Dr Reed had two identified "stress points": money and sex. It was clear how Minofel expected Adam to persuade Dr Reed.

Adam had a good deal to ponder. He was about to set the dossier aside when he noticed that there was a one-page appendix at the end of the document, which contained brief details about Geoffrey Reed's wife and children. It was the final paragraph, consisting of just one sentence, that elicited a gasp from Adam. He read the sentence twice; it simply stated:

"Dr Reed's mistress is Miss G. Tomic, personal assistant to Dr Yves Dubois, MD of ZeD Pharma."

48. Second meeting

While Adam was studying the dossier on Dr Reed, David Minofel was chatting to Kit.

"I hope you slept well," Minofel had said when he entered Kit's suite. He looked around the room and saw that it was perfectly tidy. "Evidently you have found your bearings. I hope all is as you could wish it."

"Thank you," returned Kit. "I slept well enough. I am used to moving from place to place, so I find it easy to sleep in a hotel room, on a bench or even on the ground. I am aware that what you are providing for me here is the height of luxury."

Minofel smiled. "You seem a little prickly. I'm simply asking, as your host, whether you have everything you want."

"I want to see Adam. I want to have a private chat with him – that's all I want. That is why I came to Geneva. As soon as I've talked with Adam, I shall leave."

"You will see Adam this evening. He is coming to dinner."

"That's good to hear. Let's hope he makes it. I was disappointed not to see him last night."

"Yes, I know," said Minofel. "Don't worry. He will join us tonight. In the meantime, let's talk. You say that the only thing you want is to have a chat with Adam. Is that really all you want?"

"I don't know what you mean."

"Well, when you agreed to come here, were you not at all curious about Geneva, about the place where Adam was living or about ZeD, the company he was working for? Were you not perhaps a little curious about me, the man who had set Adam on this new and exciting career path?"

"As for Geneva, I have been here before. For the rest: I am surprised at the course Adam's life seems to be taking. That is one of the reasons I want to talk to him. In so far as you seem to be the driving force behind Adam's 'new and exciting career path', I guess I am a little curious about you."

Minofel looked at Kit. He was beginning to wonder whether he had made a mistake. The man seemed ordinary – perhaps a little odd, but not exhibiting any signs that he was a potential emergent. Either he was suppressing or concealing his power, or he was just a mildly eccentric blind man who had been accidently caught up in the quest that had initiated the fourth beginning.

"Tell me a bit about yourself. How did you meet Adam?

"I met Adam's dog before I met Adam. In fact, it was Luke, Adam's golden retriever – a remarkable animal – who introduced me to Adam. Adam had got himself into a spot of bother, and, like any good, intelligent dog, Luke brought his master some help. As it turned out, that help was me."

"What sort of bother?"

"It's a long story. Let's just say Adam had upset someone with whom I had some influence. I called in a favour and solved the problem."

"So you became friends."

"We found we had some interests in common but we went our separate ways. It was some time before I caught up with Adam and his wife."

"Your separate ways?" Minofel queried. "What is your way? I mean what do you do for a living?"

Kit laughed. "I've found that you don't need to do anything for a living. Life is a gift, and, so long as you don't hanker after expensive cars, exclusive watches or highly prized vintage wines, you can just enjoy it. There's no price to pay for the gift of life."

"Really? So how do you eat? How do you find shelter?"

"It's difficult to say. It just happens. I meet people. When I can, I help them. I look after them and they look after me. They give me food and shelter, and, yes, sometimes they give me money. It's not a deal; it just happens."

"Well, you are blind, so I suppose that helps. But don't you feel you're living on charity, taking advantage of people's sympathy?"

"No, I don't feel that at all. You must ask those who help me if they feel exploited. I hope and believe that, in your terms, they think I'm good value for money. You see, when I help someone, I give them everything I've got. What more can I give?"

Minofel frowned. "I don't mean to be rude, but, since you have nothing, giving everything you have is not quite as altruistic as it sounds."

Kit smiled. "You are not rude, but you are curious. And I'm perfectly happy to satisfy your curiosity. There is no mystery. I had a good childhood. My dad, Joe Turner, was a welder. My mother, Mary, did some part time work but she was really a stay-at-home mum. Because I was blind, my parents were over-protective, but it soon became obvious, even to them, that I was independent-minded and rather good at looking after myself. Even as a youngster, I loved to travel. When I was thirteen, I hitch-hiked from London to Edinburgh and back again. Every school holiday, I visited a new part of England. And, when I left school, I set out on my international travels."

"You set out on your international travels? How did your parents feel about that? You were a young lad, blind, with no money – weren't they worried sick?"

"I told them it was what I wanted to do, and, being good parents, they encouraged me."

'Probably glad to see the back of you, you pompous, self-satisfied, parasitical little prick,' Minofel thought, but he didn't say it. He decided to try another tack. "If you could have anything you wanted, what would be your first choice?"

Kit seemed resigned to humouring his host. "What, do you mean anything – like world peace or universal happiness or bread always falling butter-side-up?"

"I was thinking a little more personally. Isn't there anything you personally want or would like?"

"Like your Lamborghini Aventador?" Kit suggested. "It wouldn't be too much use to me, since I couldn't drive it. Or your gold Rolex Presidential wristwatch? Again, not too much use to a blind man. No, you see, one of the advantages of being blind is that you are not tempted by such possessions. A blind man can't see them or use them, and so cannot be tempted by them."

Minofel took a moment to think before replying. "If you were an obsessive about luxury cars, I suppose it is possible you might have been able to identify my car by the sound of its engine when I pulled up to the house, but there is no way you could have deduced the type of watch I wear from the imperceptible ticking of a Rolex. So you have surprised me and once again aroused my curiosity. Is this magic or can you see more than I thought?"

Kit laughed. "Sorry, no magic. And no fraud. I have been blind from birth – totally blind."

"Then how do you know what I own in such detail?"

"I think Jedwell must have mentioned the car. The watch, if you do indeed have a Rolex Presidential, was simply a lucky guess, but, given the type of car you drive, not an outrageously difficult one."

Minofel was unconvinced but decided to let the matter rest. "I bet you I can think of something you would want."

"I don't bet."

"Aha! That's what Adam said, but I've managed to persuade him to accept the odd wager."

"Well, you won't persuade me. I don't have the kind of money I would need for it even if I wanted to bet – which I don't."

"Fine! No bet. But I will still tell you what I think you want. I think you would like to be able to see."

It was Kit's turn to laugh. "You may be right, but I doubt it. I didn't lose my sight; I never had it. So of course I'm curious about the world of the sighted, but I don't miss it. You know, I thought it was normal to be blind until sighted children taught me it wasn't. And there are compensations to being blind: I hear more; I feel more when I touch the world. In many ways, I am in more direct contact with the world than a sighted person. And I don't have to hanker after Lamborghinis or Rolexes, which is quite a relief since they are beyond the reach of almost all of those who can see them. Music is important to me, perhaps more important than it is to most people. But no one owns Beethoven's 9th; you just hear it and enjoy it, and then it is gone. So even my luxuries are cheap or free."

"So if I offered you a way to have your sight restored, you would refuse."

"It's not possible, so there is no need for me to accept or refuse. And even if it were possible, why would you offer to pay for what would no doubt be an extraordinarily expensive operation?"

"Perhaps I would do it as a favour to Adam. I know he and you are close. I might even do it as an act of pure kindness."

"I don't wish to offend but you seem to me to be the type of man who expects a return on his investment."

Minofel chuckled. "You're right, of course. Civilisation depends on a self-centred sense of purpose. Altruism is self-destructive, and, if the self ceases to value itself, no one else will. Any society that is made up of those who lack confidence in their own self-worth collapses, or it is perverted by those few who are empowered by self-belief. Most people don't think; they are not capable of thought in any meaningful sense. Those who understand the challenge of existence tend to take control of it. *Cogito ergo vinco*"

"I disagree," said Kit sternly, "altruism is evidence of a higher mental state. Sacrifice of self for another: for another person or persons, or simply for the greater good, is evidence of a richer, not a weaker, consciousness."

Minofel didn't argue. "Why don't we resume this debate this evening when Adam joins us," was all he said.

When Minofel left, he had the uneasy feeling that, although Kit had done most of the talking, Kit had learned more about him than he had about the blind man.

49. Superimpositions

In the evening of the Saturday on which Adam had studied Dr Reed's dossier and David Minofel had attempted to explore Kit's character, Andrew Rimzil managed to slip away from the questors in Eve's house in Harrow and quietly make his way to the camper van, which was parked a few houses down the road.

Once inside, he took a small device with a ten-inch screen from one of the storage compartments in his corner of the van and plugged it into the paradox device, using a cigar-shaped connector. The screen blinked a couple of times and then began to focus. It displayed an outline map of the world, vibrant green against a black background. Andrew selected the UK and pressed the scan option. A light appeared in the tiny outline of the United Kingdom, roughly where London should have been. Andrew cleared the screen, selected Europe and pressed the scan option again. In addition to the London light, several lights now appeared. The map was too small to be precise, but, to Andrew, it looked as though there was now a light for every major capital in Europe. This time, before clearing the screen, he instructed the plug-in device to save a screenshot. He then repeated the process, having selected "All". There were now lights on every continent. In all cases, there was one light for each country, except for the United States where there were two. Andrew saved another screenshot. Later, he would compare the results with the screenshots he had saved on previous occasions, but, even without making a careful comparison, it was obvious to Andrew that the lights were stronger and more numerous than they had been in the past.

Andrew wasn't certain what the lights meant, but he suspected they were exactly what Prune had suggested. They were superimpositions of a different reality on top of our familiar world. What these different realities were, he had no idea. But the thought that anywhere in the world, there could be another reality coexistent and coincident with the one of which humanity was aware was deeply disconcerting. The map seemed to suggest that, in the very heart of most of the world's capital cities, there was a superimposition, possibly containing alien, or at least unknown, entities.

The question that troubled Andrew Rimzil most was simple enough: could these distinct realities interact? Andrew deduced that the answer was almost certainly yes. Otherwise, why would all the superimpositions be located over the world's capital cities? And if they were interacting, what were the superimpositions doing?

50. Minofel, Adam and Kit

That Saturday evening, after Adam had read the dossier on Dr Reed, and while he was still absorbing its contents, the telephone rang. It was Jedwell, who was waiting outside the apartment building. He had come to take Adam to dinner with David Minofel and a mystery guest.

"So who is it?" Adam asked. He assumed it would be one of David Minofel's friends or associates.

"All I can say," said the affable Jedwell, "is that it will be a pleasant surprise."

"That's not terribly informative. Don't you know who it is, or is it that you won't tell me?

"Mr Minofel told me to tell you it would be a pleasant surprise. And then he told me not to tell you anything else."

"I see," Adam laughed. "That's honest."

"I always try to be honest."

"And do exactly what David tells you?"

"Of course. He is my master."

"I wish you wouldn't call him your master. It's just a little bit creepy – as though he possesses you."

"He doesn't possess me, but it is true that I owe him everything."

Adam let the matter rest.

oooOooo

When they arrived at David's house, Jedwell dropped Adam off at the front door, so he could park the car in one of the garages. Adam rang the bell. Minofel opened the door immediately. They exchanged greetings, and then Minofel led Adam into the sitting room. In front of the empty fireplace stood Kit, a broad smile on his face.

"Kit," exclaimed an amazed Adam, "what on earth are you doing here?

"That's no way for one of my guests to greet the other?" Minofel intervened.

"No, I didn't mean… oh, never mind. Kit, it's really good to see you."

The two men embraced each other.

"I came to see you," said Kit. "I want to discuss a project with you. And I want to catch up on what you've been doing, and what you're doing now."

"I think he's here to make you an alternative offer," David laughed. "You're about to be head-hunted by a second head-hunter in the home of your first. I'm sure it's been said before, but head-hunters are a bit like buses: you wait for ages for one to come along, and then two or three arrive, one after another. Anyway, I'm sure the two of you have much to talk about, so I'll leave you for a while. You talk. We'll have a late dinner, more a supper."

David left the sitting room, closing the double doors after him.

"So what are you doing here?" Adam asked. Of course, he was pleased to see Kit, but he couldn't help feeling that something was wrong. Kit was out of place. He belonged to a different world in a past life.

"More to the point, what are you doing here?" Kit replied. "You left Eve alone in Harrow, not long after she had endured a traumatic experience – one you shared – to take a job in another country in an industry which, to the best of my knowledge, you know nothing about. Why are you here?

Why are you working for ZeD? Shouldn't you be with Eve, especially now she's pregnant?"

Not surprisingly, it was the last question that took precedence.

"Eve is pregnant?" was all Adam could muster.

"Yes, she is."

"She can't be. She would have told me."

"That's another question: why aren't you in contact with Eve? She hasn't told you because you sent an inexplicable text message saying you weren't to be disturbed. What is going on, Adam?"

"There's no mystery. I've somehow landed a high-powered and highly paid job here. It was too good an offer to turn down. Is Eve really pregnant?"

"Yes, she's really pregnant. And you should be with her. She needs you with her now. After what happened with Bella, this is going to be the most important time of her life. It's a new beginning – for her, for you, for both of you."

"I'll phone her."

"Well that's better than nothing, I suppose."

"I didn't know she was pregnant," said Adam defensively. "Of course I'll talk to her. But, if we're going to have another child, this job is even more important. Eve must have the best of everything and so must the child."

"I think she'd much prefer to have you with her."

"And I will be. I just need to concentrate on the job for a few more weeks. As you say, I'm no expert on pharmaceuticals, so I'm on an almost vertical learning curve. And we're launching a major new product in a few weeks. I just need to get the launch over, and then I can be with Eve – at least at weekends."

Kit shook his head. This wasn't the Adam he

remembered: the Adam who had set out on a quest to find the truth, who had endured an arduous trip through time and space, who had faced God, conversed with Prometheus and braved the first three great beginnings. No, something had happened to Adam. He had turned away from seeking truth to seeking money; it was an extraordinary and grotesquely banal conversion.

Kit and Adam talked until supper was served but both of them felt there was an invisible but impenetrable barrier between them.

At supper, David Minofel was in high spirits. He declared how delighted he was to have brought the two old friends together and urged Kit to stay in Geneva for a while, all expenses paid. Kit declined Minofel's offer, explaining that he was needed back in England. Adam felt relieved. He had enough on his plate without servings of guilt from the blind man.

When Kit had retired to bed, Adam and Minofel shared a whisky.

"I hope you enjoyed this evening," Minofel prompted.

"It was certainly a surprise – not just that Kit was your secret guest, but the news he brought."

"And what news was that?"

"Eve is pregnant."

"Very many congratulations!" declared Minofel, feigning surprise and delight.

"Thanks, but it complicates things," replied Adam, thoughtful and troubled.

Minofel said nothing, but he thought: 'You never spoke a truer word'.

oooOooo

When Adam had retired, Minofel summoned Jedwell.

"The blind man wishes to leave tomorrow. That is not going to happen. I need to spend a little more time with him."

"Am I right?" Jedwell asked. "Is he an emergent?"

"I can't be sure. He gives nothing away. Either he isn't an emergent or, if he is, he is an expert in cloaking his true nature. Unfortunately, the archives of the Praesidium remind us that one of the certain markers of emergents is their ability to conceal their true nature."

"So what should I do with him tomorrow?"

"Confine him to his suite. Tell him I have some important questions I wish to ask him. I have a meeting with the Praesidium tomorrow, but I shall be back in the evening. That is when I shall begin to ask my questions."

51. Review of progress

On Sunday at midday, David Minofel walked into the Praesidium building over Westminster. He went straight to the chairman's office. There he found John Noble, Simon Goodfellow and Manfred Bloch engaged in a heated discussion, a discussion which ended abruptly as soon as he entered the room.

"My ears are burning," he joked.

"We are discussing the progress you are making on your assignment," explained John Noble.

"We – or, more accurately, I – was querying whether you were making sufficient progress to justify the extortionate fees you are charging us," declared Manfred.

John Noble stepped in. "Gentlemen, let us observe the niceties appropriate to a senior Praesidium meeting; let us not be rude to our visitor."

"I'm simply summarising what we were saying before our visitor arrived," grumbled Bloch.

"Perhaps we should hear the practitioner's report before we assess progress," suggested Simon Goodfellow helpfully.

Simon was in an excellent mood. He had recently seduced Kathrin, the pretty young actress wife of Manfred Bloch, although, in Kathrin's case, 'seduce' was probably an imprecise use of the word. Kathrin maintained a level of promiscuity which was legendary in Praesidium circles.

Simon had been considering embarking on an affair with the wife of his rival for the Praesidium presidency for some time. He saw it as an insurance policy in the unlikely event that Bloch took the lead in the competition to replace

John Noble. He had refrained from embarking on this dangerous liaison for complex reasons. There had been little point until the time came to remove John Noble and, until recently, Noble's position had seemed unassailable. In any case, there were risks involved in dallying with Mrs Bloch. Manfred seemed oblivious to his wife's insatiable sexual appetite, but if, by any chance, he were to discover her infidelity, his rage would be uncontrollable and his response almost certainly violent. There was no reason to take such a risk until Kathrin's lover, whoever that might be, was in a position to pre-empt Manfred's outrage with greater and terminal violence – and then, by occupying the presidency, to avoid the consequences.

Simon's liaison with Kathrin had proved to be more pleasurable than he had imagined. Simon himself was no slouch in the art of love, but even he had been surprised at what Kathrin had been able to teach him. They were, of course, still in the first flush of lust, but Kathrin was so skilled that Simon was finding even fairly conventional love-making eminently pleasurable, without resorting to the darker aspects of the art which, in recent years, Simon had found essential to the achievement of any serious level of satisfaction.

"An excellent idea," said John Noble and David Minofel in unison, responding to Simon's suggestion they should hear Minofel's report.

"Progress with Adam has been excellent," David began. "He has settled well into his post at ZeD and is responding positively to the challenges he is facing. He is internalising the advice he is given, and I am more than satisfied that he is heading in the right direction. Without Adam, Eve and the motley collection of oddities who made up the questors are leaderless and ineffective.

"As for Kit – the blind man, the possible emergent – I am holding him in Geneva. I allowed a meeting between Adam and the blind man, and it went as badly as I had hoped. Adam has made such progress that they found it difficult to communicate, more difficult than if they had been strangers..."

Manfred interrupted. "Did I hear you say 'the possible emergent'? Our chairman assured us you were convinced the blind man was an emergent. It would not be honest to treble your fee on the basis of unproven speculation, now would it?"

Minofel was not in the mood to be lectured by Bloch. "Most speculations are unproven – otherwise they would be bereft of their speculative qualities, wouldn't they? More to the point, you are paying for me to determine whether or not the blind man is an emergent and to deal with him if he is. It's a fixed fee. If he turns out not to be an emergent, I make my money relatively easily. If, on the other hand, he is an emergent, the fee you are paying is derisory. It cuts both ways. I therefore find your use of the word 'extortionate' in relation to my fees to be both offensive and inaccurate. If, however, the Praesidium is unhappy with our arrangement, I will be perfectly happy to terminate the contract, subject to the terms we agreed for early termination."

"Which are as punitive as the fees themselves," snapped Bloch.

"Enough," Noble said, intervening again. "David, we need to hear more about Kit. What progress have you made in determining his nature?"

"As I said, I am holding him in Geneva, and I intend to begin the deconstruction process this evening. I have to say that, in the few hours I have spent with him, he has given no sign of emergent powers, but I would expect this to be so whether or not he is an emergent."

"So that's real progress," sniped Bloch.

Minofel ignored Bloch's provocation. "I shall know more when I apply pressure, although I should warn you, if he is an emergent, progress is likely to be slow. I have to move one step at a time. I'm sure you understand. If I make mistakes, if I fail, we shall all have cause to regret it."

There were murmurs of assent from Noble and Goodfellow.

"There is one other piece of news I must report," Minofel continued. "Eve is pregnant. I thought it might prove a distraction for Adam and it may yet prove to be so - but the initial signs are good. He is so obsessed with his job and the rewards it promises him that I think our chances of completely remoulding him are excellent."

This time, there were murmurs of approval from all three Praesidium executives.

"Before I leave, I should like to pay my respects to the monitaurs in the Chamber of the Crucible of Eternal Light," Minofel said, addressing the chairman.

Such visits to the Chamber were customary whenever a practitioner attended the Praesidium, as was the formal request for permission from the president to approach them. The profound bond between the monitaurs and the practitioners guaranteed an immediate rapport which allowed them to feed each other with purpose and confidence.

"Of course," Noble replied. "Enjoy."

oooOooo

When David Minofel had left the room, John Noble took Manfred Bloch to one side.

"Before the practitioner leaves, have a word with him," Noble urged. "I'm well aware that you are unhappy with our contract with him, but, since we are using his services, we should try to ensure he is committed to the goal we have set him. Your obvious hostility is unlikely to bring out the best in him."

"I'd be less unhappy if you hadn't agreed to pay him an amount not dissimilar to the annual budget I have to maintain the entire engineering division," grumbled Manfred.

"Nevertheless, I'd like you to have a word with him. Tell him we recognise that he is playing a crucial role that you, as much as anyone, understand how important it is that he succeeds."

oooOooo

When David Minofel entered the Chamber of the Crucible, there was a welcoming pulsing of light from the monitaurs in their wells. Waves of yellow, red, blue and grey light suffused the practitioner.

"It's good to see you too," Minofel said, returning the greeting. "I just want to say how much your work is appreciated by me and all my fellow practitioners. Yes, we are the ones who handle specific cases in the human world, but every one of us acknowledges that it is you, the monitaurs, who create the environment in which we operate. Without the exercise of your magnificently pernicious influence on all the affairs of men, our work would be so much harder."

The monitaurs responded with an impressive light show to indicate their appreciation of the practitioner's words.

There was much metaphorical mutual back-slapping.

"One more thing," said Minofel. "Currently I have a particularly challenging assignment. I have in my care a questor, a seeker after truth – or rather a man, Adam, who has in the past sought 'the truth'. Indeed, he and his wife, Eve, set out with the Storyteller on an epic journey and, believe it or not, they came close to initiating a beginning – a beginning which would, by my count, have been the fourth. Anyway, thankfully, all their efforts came to nothing. The Praesidium dealt with the anomaly and aborted it. But, to be sure that neither Adam nor his wife Eve can ever again threaten the establishment – by which I of course mean the Praesidium, you monitaurs, we practitioners, the Breakers and the Dawks – I have been set the task of satisfying this man's curiosity, not with '*the* truth' but with '*our* truth'. To achieve this end, when Adam is prepared, I plan to bring him here to the Praesidium, and then, eventually, to you in this chamber. I know you will overwhelm him with our truth."

To assure Minofel that they were willing, indeed enthusiastic, to help, the monitaurs sent waves of colour undulating across and around the chamber.

Minofel then set off round the chamber, dipping his hand into each of the wells and touching the pulsating liquid substance of each of the monitaurs, enjoying an all-too-brief moment of communion with the complex neuronal webs of depravity, extremism and corruption. He paused a little longer by the well containing the essence of Oliver Nates. Minofel had an especially high regard for Oliver's work in promoting obfuscation and negativity. Oliver's brief was, perhaps, not so obviously pernicious as those of Lotte Axelrod, Edgar Exton or Charlie Cornick, but David Minofel knew that, at the end of the day, obfuscation and negativity were the final defence of the Praesidium and all it stood for. "Good man," said David to his favourite monitaur, and then, acknowledging that he was addressing an indentation in the chamber floor, full of a glistening, gloopy substance, added with a laugh: "You know what I mean".

Minofel had considered telling the monitaurs about Kit, and the possibility that the blind man was an emergent, but eventually he thought better of it. What would be the point? He would simply alarm the monitaurs, perhaps unnecessarily. No, first he would deal with Adam, enlisting the monitaurs' assistance. Only then, if the blind man was a threat, would he tell them that he had to annihilate an emergent and that, if it came to it, he might well need them to risk every drop of their glistening, glutinous, neurally networked essence to help him.

oooOooo

As David left the Chamber, Manfred Bloch caught up with him.

"I do hope you didn't take my remarks at the meeting personally," said Manfred, attempting a conciliatory tone. "I certainly didn't intend to be rude."

"Please don't worry," said Minofel. "I never take anything personally, except late payment of my fees," he joked. "But seriously, we both have pretty tough jobs to do, and, in my opinion, a robust exchange of views is the sign of a healthy, constructive working relationship."

Manfred found himself shaking David's hand.

"And, in keeping with our healthy, constructive working relationship, and indeed as a friend, I think I should tell you to keep an eye on Simon Goodfellow," Minofel continued.

Manfred suddenly felt uneasy. "Why in particular, should I keep an eye on Goodfellow?" he asked.

"Why, because he intends to destroy you, old chap," said Minofel simply. "Utterly."

oooOooo

As David Minofel made his way back from the Chamber to start his return journey to Geneva, he passed John Noble's office. Cynthia, John Noble's secretary, intercepted him, with an invitation to say goodbye to the Chairman.

"There's a couple of things," said Noble, as soon as Minofel was seated. First, I must apologise for Manfred's outbursts. He lacks refinement, but he's a good technical man. I hope you will make allowances for him."

Minofel indicated with a gesture that Bloch's outbursts were a matter of no importance, then asked: "And the other thing?" Noble must have had some reason for summoning him to a private meeting, when, as far as he knew, they had dealt with all the current matters in the session with Bloch and Goodfellow.

"Yes, there is something else," Noble replied. "And it is worrying, very worrying. Someone in your world has found a way to locate the Praesidium's offices."

"Surely that's impossible? Nothing can break through the cloaking."

"That's what we have always believed. Nevertheless, we have conclusive proof that someone has found a way. We know our offices here have been scanned. It's a fairly crude scan at present. Probably, the operator knows only that there is a parallel entity in Westminster. It's unlikely he knows who we are, what we are or what we do, but he does know we are here."

"And who is this ingenious operator?" Minofel asked, although he suspected he already knew the answer.

"It's Andrew Rimzil, one of the questors."

"He wouldn't be using the paradox device by any chance?" Minofel had been intrigued when he had read the notes about how the questors had witnessed the creation of the universe. If the device could allow them to locate themselves in a lay-by outside time and space, it must have almost limitless potential.

"Yes," said Noble. "He's using the paradox device. We don't know how it works. We don't know how he is powering it. But it is evidently capable of breaking through a cloaking force field maintained by the most powerful of all energy sources."

"Do you want me to destroy the device?"

"No, I want you to find out everything you can about Andrew Rimzil. He clearly has a most extraordinary mind. We need to know how he created a device that can penetrate our cloaking, a device powered, we assume, by the battery in his van. It doesn't make any sense."

"It's a bit of a paradox, then!" said David Minofel, with a laugh, simultaneously working out how much he could reasonably increase his fees to take account of this additional assignment.

52. I'm leaving

It was Sunday morning, and Kit was sitting on the terrace, enjoying the sounds of summer. He had eaten a hearty breakfast, a full English, supplied by the Minofel house staff. Jedwell joined Kit as he drank his third cup of coffee.

"Please join me. Excellent service," said Kit as Jedwell entered.

"The staff do their best to please Mr Minofel's guests. He judges them by their success."

"That sounds a bit ominous," Kit suggested.

"No, no," Jedwell hastened to correct the misunderstanding. "It's a matter of bonuses, not punishments."

Kit smiled. "I'm glad to hear it."

"What would you like to do today?" asked Jedwell.

"I'd like to go to the airport to catch my plane. I thought I'd made it clear that I would like to fly back to the UK today. This was just a quick visit for me to talk to Adam. I've seen him; we've had our chat, and now I must go."

"Mr Minofel would really like you to stay a little longer. He wishes to know you better. In any case, you have seen nothing of Geneva." In accordance with his master's instructions, Jedwell was determined Kit should stay.

"I'm unlikely to see much of Geneva, however long I stay," said Kit. "But you don't need to worry. I've been to Geneva many times. I know the city well."

"But you haven't said goodbye to Mr Minofel."

"Please say good bye to him for me and thank him for his more than generous hospitality."

"He will be very upset if you leave." Jedwell was beginning to feel a little desperate. He wanted to avoid using coercion, if at all possible.

"You shouldn't even consider it," said Kit. "It would be inadvisable and entirely pointless."

"Sorry," said Jedwell. "What shouldn't I consider?"

"Never mind. Would you be kind enough to run me to the airport?"

Jedwell looked at Kit. He could read most people fairly easily – even those who made a living by deceit and trickery, but this blind man was something else. He had thought that Kit might just be concealing his true nature. Now a new explanation crossed his mind: perhaps the man wasn't concealing anything; perhaps he was an open book. Perhaps Jedwell couldn't read him because the book was in a language he didn't understand, or because the content was so complex that he couldn't comprehend it.

"I can't do that," said Jedwell eventually. "Mr Minofel wants you to stay."

Kit said nothing.

"Mr Minofel will be very angry if you leave. He will be very angry if I let you leave. I am sorry but I cannot allow you to leave."

Still Kit said nothing.

"I have no wish to use force, believe me, but if I have to, I will physically prevent you from leaving," said Jedwell flatly. He had done his best to persuade the blind man. Now he had made the situation clear.

"There is a salt cellar on the table, is there not?" Kit asked.

Jedwell shook his head in confusion but answered. "Yes, there is a salt cellar."

"How much do you think it weighs?"

"I have no idea. Maybe 200 grammes."

"So it is light enough for you to lift it without too much trouble?"

"Of course."

"Then lift it," Kit ordered. "If you lift it from the table even a few inches, I will stay. If you fail, you will take me to the airport. Is that a deal?"

Jedwell laughed. "Fair enough, although this all seems a bit silly."

"But you take the bet?" Kit persisted.

"Yes, I take the bet, and I'm really pleased we have been able to resolve the issue without any unpleasantness."

Jedwell stretched out his hand tentatively, as though expecting a mild electric shock.

"It's all right," Kit soothed. "It won't bite you."

Jedwell took hold of the salt cellar.

"Well, are you going to lift it?"

Jedwell tried. At first he used very little force, but when he found that the salt cellar seemed deeply attached to the table, he used all the strength in his right arm. Then he stood up and tried to yank the salt cellar from its anchorage, using both hands. Jedwell Boon was a very strong man – there was no doubt about that. Although of only medium height, he was powerfully built, big-boned with wide shoulders. And yet evidently he was having difficulty in lifting a 200-gramme salt cellar. Veins began to stand out on his forehead; beads of sweat appeared on his immaculately shaved head; his usually calm grey eyes screwed up with the exertion. He gave one final desperate heave; the table tilted and Kit's breakfast plates clattered to the ground, but the salt cellar remained bonded to the table.

Jedwell fell back into his chair. "That's one hell of a trick."

"It's not a trick," said Kit, reaching for the salt cellar. Jedwell had not replaced the table exactly where it had been before, so the salt cellar was a little out of position. Kit knocked it over, spilling a little salt on the table, then righted it and lifted it clear of the table.

"If it's not a trick, what is it?" asked Jedwell. "There must be some physical or psychological explanation."

"Now there's a question," Kit replied. "I think it's not so much a matter for explanation; it's more a moral issue, a matter of right and wrong. It would be wrong for Minofel to keep me here when my purpose in coming here has been fulfilled. So it was only right I should win our bet, which I am confident you will now honour. I'm sure that Mr Minofel will understand when you explain about our wager. I gather he's not averse to a bit of gambling himself."

"I'll bring the car round," said a chastened Boon.

When Jedwell had left, Kit took a few grains of the spilled salt and threw them over his left shoulder.

53. Man and wife

On Sunday evening, Adam phoned Eve. It was a difficult conversation.

When Adam phoned, Eve was sitting down to a meal prepared by Prune and Andrew. The two Irishmen had spent the entire cooking time arguing with each other, about every aspect of the dish: its ingredients, the order in which they should be added, the length of time they should be cooked.

"Who ever heard of putting chunks of bacon into an Irish stew?" demanded Prune.

"Almost everyone who has ever cooked one," replied Andrew dismissively.

"You'll be telling me you want to add carrots and turnips and suchlike next, I suppose."

"Absolutely. And pearl barley and a couple of cloves of garlic," said Andrew authoritatively.

"Bejesus!" exclaimed Prune. "I'm not saying it won't turn out to be edible, but I am saying that, if that's an Irish stew, I'm a leprechaun."

"Funnily enough," Andrew replied, "I've always thought of you as a bit of a leprechaun."

"Which bit?" enquired Prune. "No, don't answer that. Isn't it odd? You take an ancient Irish recipe, tried and tested down the centuries, imitated but never bettered, and, on a whim, you start adding ingredients which will destroy the perfect balance of mutton, potatoes, onion and water. But when it comes to the paradox device, you won't experiment with it in any way."

Andrew's eyes glanced up to the ceiling. Over the last

few days, whatever the subject under discussion, Prune had found some way to bring up the paradox device and Andrew's refusal to experiment with it. "Playing with the paradox device," said Andrew sharply, "could irrevocably damage the fabric of space-time. It could throw the laws of physics into chaos; it's not impossible it could suck the lifeblood out of reason. I really don't think that even you can compare such cataclysmic risks with chucking a couple of carrots and turnips into an Irish stew."

"At some point," mused Uncle Rambler, "someone must have taken a chance with the original recipe. It was not until the 17th century that the potato, originally a South American vegetable, became available in Ireland. An adventurous chef of the Emerald Isle must have decided to take a chance, no doubt against the advice of one of your forbears, Prune, and added potato to the original list of ingredients."

After the stew, now of indeterminate provenance, had been braising away for three hours, Andrew invited the others to taste it. All agreed it had an excellent flavour. Even Prune reluctantly approved of the dish, while insisting it was not quite as good as the pure Irish version.

It was just as the five of them sat down to eat that Adam phoned. Eve took the call and withdrew to the sitting room to talk.

After an awkward exchange of greetings, Adam asked Eve to confirm she was pregnant.

"Yes, I'm pregnant."

"Why didn't you tell me?"

"You sent me a text message saying you weren't to be disturbed."

"Oh come on, Eve. I didn't mean you shouldn't contact me if something like this happened."

"Well I'm sorry, but you didn't make that clear. As I recall, you just said you were too busy to take telephone calls. You didn't say "I'm prepared to make an exception if something like a pregnancy comes up".

"Eve, let's stop this. It's wonderful news that you're pregnant, isn't it? I know we didn't feel like having another child after Bella died, but this could be a new start for us. I'm just sorry I heard it from Kit, not you."

Eve thought of pointing out, once again, that it was his fault, that from the moment he'd been offered the job with ZeD their relationship had deteriorated, simply because he had shut her out; that the amazing closeness they had felt when the fourth beginning had begun now seemed so distant and so alien that it was as though it was a different couple who had felt it. She thought of saying all this and more, but in the end she didn't. What would be the point of it?

"So you've found time to meet with Kit? Or was it just a quick phone call?"

Adam ignored the goad. "I did have a late dinner with Kit yesterday despite the fact that I've had to wrestle with a major business problem over the last few days."

"How did that go?"

"It's difficult, Eve. I have never held a position like this. There are real problems that have to be resolved, and I have to take the decisions to solve them. People's jobs and futures depend on what I decide, and it's not easy. The issues are complicated, and sometimes you have to choose the lesser of two evils. I know I'm being paid a lot of money, but it's hard."

"I just meant how did your dinner with Kit go."

"It was fine. We did some catching up."

"Are you coming home next weekend?" Eve asked, even though she already knew the answer.

"Not next weekend. There's a meeting of all the drug reps next Saturday, and, as marketing director, I have to put in an appearance. But I'll try to get back the weekend after, I promise."

"I see," said Eve.

"Love you," said Adam.

Eve put the phone down.

54. Remorse, rebuke, review

David Minofel was none too pleased when he returned to his house in Geneva on Sunday evening only to find that his guest had departed. He had planned to spend a good deal of his precious time with the blind man.

"Mr Boon" he began, ominously using Jedwell's surname, "you really must make a greater effort to explain why you allowed my guest to depart. 'He wanted to leave' just doesn't cut it."

"He was most insistent," Jedwell replied. He always felt uneasy when his master summoned him to the study. There was something intimidating about the heavy oak furniture and the tall bookcases full of old leather-bound volumes. "I offered to show him round Geneva, but he said he knew the city well already. I told him you were eager to have another chat with him, but he said he had come to meet Adam, and that now he had met Adam, he felt it right he should leave."

"All perfectly understandable, except for one detail. Had I asked you why our guest had left, this would be a clear, succinct explanation. But that isn't what I asked. If memory serves me well, I gave you explicit instructions to keep the blind man here. I therefore asked you not why he had left, but why you had allowed him to leave."

Jedwell didn't know what to say. There was something about Kit that Jedwell found impossible to explain. First of all, although he had spent only a relatively short period of time with the man, it seemed to Jedwell that he had known Kit for a long time. It was almost as though he had always known him. Secondly, although Kit was blind and Jedwell himself was built like a battle-tank, Kit was not a man that Jedwell felt capable of compelling to do anything. Neither of these explanations would be acceptable to Minofel, nor, indeed, to Jedwell. Even though his role, his purpose in life was to serve his master, he had disobeyed a direct order.

Then there was the bet and the lifting of the salt cellar. The trouble with that explanation was that it was inexplicable.

"I'm waiting," said Minofel, a sharp edge to his voice.

"I lost a bet," said Jedwell eventually. "He agreed to stay if I won; I had to agree to let him go, if I lost."

"You took a bet?" Minofel was incredulous. "You gambled with a direct order? And I take it that you lost? You will understand why I am deeply dissatisfied."

Jedwell had seen often enough how Minofel's dissatisfaction with others expressed itself, and he had no wish to experience it himself. "It was a bet that I thought I couldn't lose. That's why I agreed: I thought I could keep him here without any need for force."

"And what was the bet?" asked Minofel. "What was this bet you felt sure you would win but which you lost?"

"He asked me to raise a salt cellar."

"He asked you to raise a salt cellar? To raise it in what sense? To raise it without touching it, perhaps. To raise it to the heavens? To infuse it with life, raising it from its inert state? What exactly do you mean?"

"He bet me I couldn't lift the salt cellar from the table on the terrace."

"And you failed? How could that be? Did he tie you up? Did he knock you out?"

Jedwell was embarrassed. "I tried but I couldn't lift it an inch. I used all my strength. I used both hands. In the end, I pulled the salt cellar so hard that I lifted the table itself off the ground, but still I couldn't shift the salt cellar."

"A man of your prodigious strength was unable to lift a salt cellar. Interesting. Your explanation?"

"I have none," Jedwell confessed. "I would say it was trickery, that he had somehow messed with my mind. But that would not explain why I could lift the table but not detach the salt cellar."

"And when you lost the bet, was it possible to move the salt cellar?"

"Yes, the blind man picked it up easily."

Minofel said nothing for a minute. Then he spoke, as though to himself. "So this is the first solid evidence that Kit is an emergent, or at least that he has emergent potential."

"Am I excused?" Jedwell asked nervously.

"No, not just yet. I have an assignment for you. I want you to go back to the Smith's house and bring the engineer, Andrew Rimzil, here to me. Don't harm him. He has a brilliant mind and I have some questions for him. I'm hoping he will prove better company than the blind man. I know that he will stay longer; I will personally ensure he has an extended stay."

"Yes, sir," said Jedwell, relieved that his master still trusted him with what must be an important task. Am I excused now?"

"Yes, yes, you are excused. Excused but not forgiven. As you know, I'm not much of a forgiver; it's not in my nature. And, to be frank, whatever the reason, you clearly failed to follow my orders. But don't let this failure weigh too heavily upon you. Personally I find guilt as useless as forgiveness. In any case, as you know, I have a soft spot for gambling, so that counts in your favour - although I have to say, when I place a bet, I, like Kit, prefer to win." And with that odd and ambiguous response, Minofel dismissed the contrite Jedwell.

David Minofel moved away from his desk and settled down into one of the leather armchairs provided for guests. He needed to take a few moments for reflection.

So the blind man had at least some abnormal powers and, what's more, he was aware that he had these powers and how to use them. Otherwise, he would not have offered Jedwell the bet. Nor was he afraid to reveal these powers to others. That was a surprise; Minofel had found Kit inscrutable during their chats. Either the blind man was determined to hide his true nature or, and this possibility worried the practitioner, his true nature was simply difficult to grasp. Whatever the truth, the odds that the man was indeed an emergent had increased. What had been just possible was now probable. Minofel concluded that it was likely he would have to earn his fee after all.

Before abandoning his moment of reflection, Minofel turned his thoughts to Jedwell Boon. He had been a good servant for many years, his loyalty unquestionable, his efficiency unsurpassed. But, just recently, and for the first time, David Minofel had heard warning bells. No, 'bells' was too strong a word. Distant, faint, warning tinkles, perhaps. On his mission to collect Kit and bring him back to Geneva, Jedwell had intervened in an incident on the Bakerloo line – an incident that had nothing to do with his brief. He had saved a young girl from the unwanted attentions of a menacing sex pest. Boon's motive for intervening was legitimate. He was determined to avoid involvement in an incident that might later require a police investigation. That was fair enough. No, it was not his actions that gave Minofel mild concern. It was Jedwell's feelings after the incident, feelings of satisfaction in having rescued the girl and punished the offender.

55. Learning curves

Adam was not looking forward to his meeting with Dr Reed, but he knew what he had to do, and he was keen to conclude the matter. Adam had summoned Dr Reed to his office. He felt it better to hold the meeting on the fifth floor within the marketing department so that Dr Reed would feel as much pressure as possible. Of course, Adam had the means to force the doctor to comply, but he had decided he would much prefer to persuade rather than coerce.

"Please make yourself comfortable," Adam said when Dr Reed was ushered into his office.

After furnishing the doctor with a cup of coffee, Adam began with a question: "Have you been able to give what we discussed further consideration?

Dr Reed was surprised. "I thought I had made my position clear."

The good doctor was not going to make life easy.

Adam used the line he had prepared over the weekend. "Given the consequences of delaying the launch of MC57 and your own admission that the death in the Basel trial almost certainly had nothing to do with our drug, surely you have at least given the matter some further thought?"

"As I explained," the doctor replied, "it is not a matter to be decided by 'further thought'. There are set procedures in the registration of drugs. I am not able to suppress one particular trial simply because the results are not to the company's liking. Any attempt by me to ignore or conceal the Basel trial, even if it were possible, would invalidate the registration process and vitiate my professionalism."

"You seem very concerned with your own self-image," Adam suggested. "Have you considered the self-image of many of our employees who will find themselves without a job in an overcrowded market if the launch does not go ahead and succeed?"

"Of course I'm aware of the implications if MC57 is blocked or delayed. But, as I keep explaining, there is nothing I can do about it."

"Alternatively, have you given any thought to what it will mean if the launch is a success? All employees will benefit. I will benefit. You, as medical director, will certainly benefit."

Dr Reed said nothing.

Adam continued. "Off the record, I'm expecting a bonus equivalent to my annual salary if MC57 succeeds. I'm pretty sure you will do at least as well."

Dr Reed shook his head in rejection of and contempt for what seemed to him to be Adam's unsubtle attempt at bribery. "I'm beginning to find this conversation unacceptable." Dr Reed was becoming angry. "I've explained my position to you. Now I think you had better explain your position to me. I fully understand that in your role as Marketing Director, you have to do your best to ensure the company is a commercial success. That said, I have to ask myself what kind of person would be prepared to put a possibly dangerous, even lethal, drug on the market in a misguided attempt to further his own and the company's financial interests. Good God, man, think what you are saying. We are here to heal not harm, much less kill, our customers."

Adam was taken aback by the vehemence of Dr Reed's tone. Dr Reed continued: "I must warn you that, if you persist in inviting me to disregard established procedures, to suppress somehow a perfectly valid trial result, to connive at falsifying our submission to the EMA – if you persist, I shall raise this matter with the managing director and demand your dismissal. And I can tell you now that, if I make that demand, Dr Dubois will accede to my demand."

Adam was silent for a moment. Dr Reed prepared to abort the meeting. Adam had hoped to avoid the need to use his final weapon, but it was clear that nothing else would have any chance of changing the good doctor's mind.

"I guess you see yourself as occupying the moral high ground in this situation," Adam began, with some reluctance.

"If you mean: do I think I am right and you are wrong, then yes," Dr Reed replied. He did not rise to leave; something told him that Adam hadn't finished with him.

"I touched earlier on the issue of remuneration," Adam continued. "You earn an excellent salary, is that not so?"

"I earn a salary commensurate with my experience and my responsibilities," Dr Reed replied warily.

"But, in my experience, salaries, however large, are never large enough. There are so many expenses, and costs always seem to rise to a level where they exceed income."

"Is that Adam's law?" Dr Reed asked. "You sound like Mr Micawber's financial advisor."

"In your own case," Adam continued, "you have a large mortgage and expensive school fees."

"I'm well aware of my financial commitments. I'm less clear on how the hell you know so much about my personal affairs."

"I'm coming to that in a minute," said Adam. He decided to make one more attempt to persuade the doctor without hitting him below the belt, literally and metaphorically. "If MC57 doesn't go ahead, I think all our jobs may be at risk. Even if you can afford your current lifestyle today, consider what it would mean if you lost your job. I'm sure you could get another appointment, but do you have sufficient reserves to see you through perhaps months until you find an acceptable position? Those demands for mortgage payments and for school fees just keep coming."

"Your job might be put at risk, but mine won't be," Dr Reed replied sharply. "Every pharmaceutical company needs a medical director. There would be no point in firing me, no advantage. If the company did so, it would need to seek and find an equally well qualified replacement. The costs of recruitment would simply add to the company's costs without any resultant savings when my replacement came on board. In any case, since I am more than competent at my job and am, as I think I have shown, determined to maintain the highest ethical standards in my professional life, I would have an unanswerable case for unfair dismissal, with a lucrative settlement at the end of it."

It was no good. Dr Reed was adamant and irritatingly complacent. In fact, he was so irritating that Adam felt much better about deploying his secret weapon. "You mentioned your personal affairs a few moments ago," Adam began. "Would you say that you hold the moral high ground in that sphere as clearly as you do in your professional life?"

Now Dr Reed was taken aback. Where was Adam heading?

Adam continued. "You see I find your high-minded and principled stand on the issue of a maverick clinical trial difficult to reconcile with your clandestine affair with a ZeD employee." Adam felt suffused by a mild wave of self-disgust, but he quickly set it aside. "I mean, your behaviour is not terribly good form even from a corporate viewpoint but, to your wife and children, I suspect it would seem a good deal worse. I assume your wife is unaware of your affair and would take it badly if she found out."

Dr Reed considered an outburst of outrage. He could demand an apology from Adam; he could emphatically deny the affair; he could accuse Adam of the most disgusting behaviour in trying to use a man's personal life against him. But he realised that none of these tactics would work. Geoffrey Reed loved his wife and he loved his children. He still didn't understand how he had become involved with Miss Tomic, but it had happened, and, despite his love for his family, he was unable to break with his mistress. On the other hand, he would rather die than lose his family. So this brash, unscrupulous, heartless new marketing director had won. It really was as simple as that.

"Do we understand each other?" Adam enquired.

"Oh yes, I understand you," Dr Reed replied. "I don't know how a man like you can sleep at night."

"Generally with my own wife," Adam turned the knife, "although currently, of necessity, we are separated by work commitments."

"I assume you have made arrangements for registration to proceed through your contact at the EMA," Dr Reed replied, ignoring Adam's riposte. "I can delay submission of the Basel trial."

"I think we need to invalidate it, rather than delay it. I'm sure you can find some irregularity in the protocol or its implementation; or some confusion in the patient coding; or some error in the administration of drugs or dosages."

"I will see what I can do," said Dr Reed.

Adam was satisfied. "I hope you won't allow this matter to damage our relationship. I'm sure we can work together constructively. I won't rehearse all the arguments for pressing on with MC57 without any distractions, but I will say that I'm sure, when you consider all the implications, you will come to see that we've decided on the right course. We're doing the right thing."

Dr Reed said nothing.

56. Philosophising

Meanwhile, at the Smith's house in Harrow, Numpty and Luke found themselves together.

"Do you fancy a walk?" Luke minded to Numpty.

"Certainly," Numpty replied. "I have something to discuss with you, and I find walking and thinking excellent companions."

The 'companionship of walking and thinking' was one of Uncle Rambler's favoured aphorisms, and Numpty greatly enjoyed quoting his uncle. He now had a deeper appreciation of his uncle's wisdom, although, if truth were told, he found some of his uncle's digressions a tad tedious.

Boy and dog set out on their walk along the leafy avenues of Harrow, heading in the general direction of Pinner.

"What is it you want to discuss?" minded Luke.

"It's simple really: I've been wondering if I exist," Numpty declared. "I mean, I know I have a body and a brain. But is there a 'me'? Is there an 'I'? Is there a self?"

"Wow!" minded Luke. "Where did that come from? Are you suffering some kind of identity crisis?"

"I was wondering if there is an 'I' that is continuous. When I asked my uncle, he said: '*Cogito ergo sum*,' which he said means 'I think, therefore I am'. But that begs the question because obviously it assumes there is an 'I' in 'I think' before it does the 'therefore I am' bit. It should be 'thinking therefore being' – which omits the 'I' from both the premise and the conclusion – but that doesn't make too much sense and doesn't answer my question."

"The problem with having enhanced mental capacity

is that you end up wrestling with enhanced philosophical issues," Luke commented, trying to be helpful.

"It crossed my mind that the self could be an illusion," Numpty continued, "an illusion sustained by memory alone. Because we experience event after event, and then remember what we have experienced, we may mistakenly conclude there is a continuous 'I' involved in all this experiencing. But it could be that the only thing that exists is the collection of memories. Of course, there is a brain and body in the present but that might just be a device for maintaining and adding to the archive of memories."

Luke didn't respond immediately. He recalled that Adam had wrestled with similar issues when his daughter Bella had been killed in the thunderstorm. Adam had, in the end, questioned whether there was any point in a self that tortured itself with painful memories. "You're swimming through deep, dark waters," was all Luke could offer.

"I prefer to think I am digging in dark, deep but hopefully fertile soil. My uncle has encouraged me to keep digging in the hope that nutrients of truth will seep up through my roots to the light of day to feed the leaves and flowers of my thoughts. I am an osmotic gouger."

"Jolly good!" was all Luke could manage. He might well be a brilliant superdog, endowed with extraordinary powers, but he was still a dog, and everyone knows that dogs are not much given to philosophising, still less to appreciating extended metaphors.

"Jolly good! Is that it?" enquired a disappointed Numpty. "I had hoped for more from you. You are after all a highly intelligent dog, and I thought that you had acquired new powers from the fourth beginning."

Numpty was right. After the fourth beginning, Luke had

found he could reach minds at considerable distances. He could even achieve long-distance, two-way communication with those (like the Storyteller, Kit and Numpty) who had always been able to hear what Luke minded to them when he was close by. Now proximity no longer mattered. He had chatted with Kit in Geneva.

With others who had never been able to pick up Luke's minded thoughts, two-way communication remained impossible but Luke had found he could still explore others' minds to some degree. After his talk with Kit in Geneva, Luke had briefly explored Adam's mind. What he had seen had frightened him. Adam's mind was being compartmentalised; some of the compartments were being sealed – permanently sealed – while others were being given greatly increased importance. As a result, Adam's personality and his identity were being remodelled.

"I don't have any great insight to impart about the nature of self," Luke began, "but I do know that whatever we think is the self can alter over time, and can be manipulated and changed. I have touched Adam's mind and he has changed or, rather, is being changed. I think this must mean that there is a self but that it is not a fixed entity."

"So will I still be the self I am today when I am an old man?" asked Numpty.

"It will be an older, more experienced and hopefully wiser self, but I guess it will still be you." As Luke gave his answer, he felt an inexplicable moment of unease.

Numpty seemed satisfied, at least for the moment.

Given what was happening to Adam, Luke had to accept the possibility that a self could be altered so radically that it became a different self. It was possible an individual's self could morph into a self so different from its previous states that it broke all links with its past.

There were two other reasons for Luke's unease. The first was that, after exploring Adam's mind, he had attempted to touch the mind of David Minofel. It had been an experience that, for Luke, had called into question the millennia-old bond between man and dog. The second reason for his unease; he was unable to imagine Numpty as very much older than he was.

57. The tangled web

On the Tuesday following his meeting with Dr Reed, Adam had set aside the morning for a meeting with David Minofel. The meeting was at Minofel's request.

Miss Tomic picked Adam up at 8.00 am. Adam was surprised: Tuesday was a working day, and, as he understood it, Miss Tomic worked for Yves Dubois., not David Minofel. But that, thought Adam, was just as he understood it. After all, as he understood it, Miss Tomic was engaged to be married to Giovanni Spinetti, despite the fact that, according to Dr Reed's personnel dossier, she was the good doctor's mistress.

As ever, Miss Tomic looked stunning. Adam frowned when he opened the door and saw her. She seemed so perfectly presented, so self-composed. He found it difficult to reconcile this cool, calm, extraordinarily beautiful woman with the ruthless, licentious, promiscuous female that her actions suggested her to be.

He also felt slightly irritated, although why he couldn't say. Perhaps disappointed came closer to the mark.

"David is looking forward to seeing you," said Miss Tomic, ignoring Adam's frown.

Adam grunted.

"He thinks you are making excellent progress."

"Does he?" snapped Adam. "He discusses my performance with you, does he? Obviously you have a very close, and not entirely transparent, relationship with Minofel."

For a moment Miss Tomic seemed severely discomfited,

then she said softly: "You and I are working for ZeD today, but we work for Slievins indefinitely. You will find that you will have a very close relationship with David, just as I do. That's how Slievins operates. And as time passes, the nature of the relationship with David, both yours and mine, will become less opaque. Believe me."

Neither spoke again for the rest of the journey to Minofel's house.

oooOooo

"Adam," Minofel beamed. "It's so good to see you. I must say you are making excellent progress."

"So I understand," Adam responded, without thinking.

Minofel smiled. "I particularly liked your closing remark to Dr Reed. Something about 'not letting the pressure you had put on him damage your working relationship'. There are not as many opportunities for humour as I would like in our line of work, but when one presents itself, we should seize it with both hands."

Adam joined Minofel in a chuckle, although he couldn't really see the humour in what he had said.

"We are going to get along splendidly," Minofel continued. "Anyone who can entirely shatter another man's life, compel him to betray everything he stands for, annihilate his self-image and then wrap it up in a banal expression of goodwill is my kind of guy. We are going to have a lot of fun."

Adam, now utterly confused, continued to grin.

"To business," said Minofel. "Today, we have to organise some paperwork."

"Paperwork?"

"Yes, paperwork, Adam. We have to wrap things up and

cover our backs. We need to strengthen Dr Reed's resolve a little. I think you more or less promised him a financial reward for losing the Basel trial. Now you should make good on your promise. You need to persuade Dr Dubois to pay the good doctor an appropriate bonus. There should be an accompanying memo referring to Dr Reed's assistance in dealing with the Basel issue."

"That could be a little difficult," said Adam. "I've kept the results of the Basel trial from Dr Dubois. As far as I know, he's unaware of any problem."

"Don't worry. Dubois relies on Miss Tomic to draft such memos. I'm sure you and she can work out a form of words which Dr Dubois will be happy to sign."

Adam nodded his assent. Dr Reed had agreed to cooperate but he might well have second thoughts. It would do no harm to stiffen his resolve with a financial sweetener, approved by the managing director.

"At the same time," Minofel continued, "we need some paperwork which makes it clear that it was Dr Reed's decision to kick the Basel trial into the long grass. Something like "after serious consideration of the available evidence, the Medical Director concluded that the Basel trial did not significantly affect the medical department's confidence in the EMA submission". Tell Guy McFall to arrange a meeting with Dr Reed. He's the product manager for MC57 so that's a perfectly appropriate thing for him to do. You shouldn't attend the meeting, but you should brief McFall on what we want and make sure he prepares the minutes of the meeting. You can do any subediting, if necessary, when you review the draft minutes."

"I'm not sure Dr Reed will sign off minutes that put all the responsibility on him. I think he feels a little bruised after my meeting with him; we shouldn't push him too far."

Minofel smiled. "In most circumstances, my friend, it is Slievins policy to push people all the way, long past 'too far', but in this case, there is no need. We don't need Dr Reed to sign the minutes. We just need a normal set of minutes filed in the company archive recording the substance of the meeting."

"Is all this really necessary?" Adam asked.

"Absolutely," Minofel replied at once. "We now have a clear run through to the launch of MC57. We have to make sure that the good doctor doesn't wobble at any point in the next few weeks. If he knows we have nailed him as the key decision-maker and that the company has already rewarded him for his 'flexibility', there is no way he can change his mind, either now or in the future."

Adam shrugged. He couldn't argue with that.

"It's too early for champagne," Minofel continued, "but let's celebrate with one of House Minofel's amazingly enlivening double expressos."

After the celebratory coffee, Adam stood up to leave.

"Could you do me a favour?" said Minofel. "I have a letter for Giovanni. Don't worry, there's no banker's draft in this one. It's just a note giving him some information that I think he will find interesting. It's already stamped and addressed. It will save me a trip to the post office."

"Yes, of course," Adam replied.

58. Suspicions and scepticism

Kit reached the Smith's house in Harrow on Monday morning. He had flown in the previous afternoon and had spent the evening in central London. As soon as he could, he took Eve to one side.

His first question was: "Has Adam made contact with you?"

"Yes, he phoned me yesterday."

"How did it go?"

"Not very well. He seemed strained and distant. We found it difficult to talk to each other. He seems to have changed."

"Did you tell him you were pregnant?"

"Yes. He was upset I hadn't told him before."

"That was hardly your fault."

"That's what I said. Anyway, how was your meeting with him? I'm sure you spent longer with him than I did on the phone."

Kit paused. What he had to say was likely to upset Eve, but it had to be said. So he said it. "Well, here's the thing. We have a problem. Adam is obsessed with his new job and the money he is earning. He is evidently under the influence of this David Minofel. And David Minofel is not a man I would trust. Is there anything more you can tell me about the man?"

He needed Eve to tell him in her own words about the burglary, the attempted rape and the deaths of the two burglars. But still she hesitated.

"Come on, Eve. There is something you're not telling

me," he said, knowing he could go no further without revealing what Luke had told him.

"There is something," said Eve. And then she told Kit everything.

"Wow!" was all Kit could manage when Eve had finished.

Eve felt as though a great weight had been lifted from her shoulders. She hadn't realised quite how much the events of that evening, and keeping those events to herself, had affected her. Of course, Adam had shared the experience with her, but that, in itself, was a problem. Talking with him about what had happened didn't give her any relief because he was part of it, not outside it. And, in any case, after the event, he had been more interested in what Slievins had to offer than in talking through the extraordinary incident with his wife.

"I don't know how you've held it all together," Kit said. "It was an appalling experience. And nothing happened afterwards? I mean, no press reports? No police enquiry? Surely the disappearance of two men, however reprehensible, must have registered with someone?"

"Not as far as I know. Minofel's man Boon disposed of the bodies and, without the bodies, there was no evidence of a crime. I guess the two burglars were the type who had previously 'disappeared' from time to time for other reasons. It's just that this time, they disappeared for good. Minofel assured us there were no loose ends and that there would be no repercussions."

"Quite a coincidence that Minofel was there to save you," observed Kit.

"It was just luck. He had an appointment to come here at 6.30 p.m. that evening to talk to Adam about his new job."

"Hmmm, are you sure he killed both men?"

"Absolutely. He broke one man's neck. The other, I think he cut off the blood to the man's brain; I saw him die. When Boon put the bodies in body bags, both of them were dead."

"In that case, I think you are in grave danger."

"Because Adam and I are accessaries after the fact? That's what I thought. We saw two men killed. One, you could argue, was justifiable homicide, but the other one was premeditated murder. He was the one who tried to rape me. He was defenceless, in agony. Minofel let him suffer for a bit and then murdered him. I guess we were both accessaries to one, if not two, murders…"

"That's not what I meant," Kit stopped her. "I can't prove this, but I think Minofel arranged the whole thing. If he really killed the two burglars, we have some indication of the type of organisation we are up against. I'm guessing the two burglars had been hired by Minofel. They were there so that Minofel could rescue you, establish himself as your protector and bind both of you to him by making you accessaries to murder."

"Kit, you can't be serious," said an astonished Eve. "He killed both men. What kind of a man or organisation would kill two people just to win the confidence of someone else? And why would anyone bother with us in the first place?"

"Hasn't it crossed your mind that all this: the burglary, Adam's new job, Minofel's involvement are connected with the quest, with the aborted fourth beginning?"

"I'm not much given to conspiracy theories," said Eve, but there was a hint of uncertainty in her voice. After all, before he had been consumed by his new job, Adam had speculated that his meteoric rise in executive status and pay might not be entirely unconnected to their journey in the company of the Storyteller.

"You must have considered the possibility that whoever aborted the fourth beginning would have been very tempted to ensure we couldn't ever – and I mean *ever* – try again," Kit suggested.

"What, by giving Adam a job and an employment package to die for?"

"Precisely."

"So, in order to neutralise me, they, whoever they are, are about to invite me to become editor of The Spectator?"

"No. They offered Adam the job in Geneva to split you up. And they chose him not you for special attention because they think he is easier to corrupt."

"So this is all about splitting up our marriage and corrupting Adam. If that's the case, they seem to be doing a pretty good job – on the splitting-up front, at least."

"I think they may be doing fairly well on the other front, too."

Eve was still not convinced. "It's a theory, but do you have any evidence - Adam checked Minofel out before he agreed to meet him? He's a *bona fide* consultant for Slievins, one of the oldest consultancy firms in the City. What would they have to do with our quest or the aborting of the fourth beginning? And what kind of a consultancy would set up a scam which, in passing, involved the execution of a couple of their employees? Isn't it more likely that Adam happened to be head-hunted by Slievins, and Minofel's offer turned his head? Adam has always been focused. He likes to pursue his latest project to the exclusion of everything else, just as he did when he decided to set out on the quest. Perhaps being a high-flying over-paid executive is just his latest project. As for the burglary and the part David Minofel played in it, it was just coincidence."

Kit was not persuaded. "When I said I wanted to leave Geneva, Minofel's man, Jedwell, tried to stop me. Don't you think it's odd that first they took me to Geneva and then they didn't want me to leave?"

"Not particularly. You wanted to see Adam. They want Adam to concentrate on his job. They thought that if they took you to him, it would be less disruptive than him flying back here to see you. And since, by your own account, your first meeting with Adam didn't go too well, they wanted you to stay to sort things out with your friend before you left."

"You've got an answer for everything," Kit laughed. "But there is something else; it's not evidence but, to me at least, it's compelling. I had a couple of meetings with Minofel. He's a very interesting man. He is clever and shrewd – and very, very evil. Yes, I know: it's just a feeling, but when you've been around as long as I have, you can tell."

"Even if you're right, what can we do about it?" Eve asked. Adam seemed content enough in Geneva. Kit's purpose in reconvening the questors was to reactivate the fourth beginning but, obviously, for Adam, the quest was something he now saw as another world, a world of long ago and far away. His world now was the world of ZeD, of ludicrously high salaries, of absurd bonuses, a world presided over by David Minofel and the Slievins Consultancy. If anyone could have persuaded him to come home and talk, it was Kit – and Kit had failed. Even the news of her pregnancy had taken second place in Adam's mind to an upcoming sales conference.

"We can't give up," said Kit softly. "We mustn't give up. We started something magnificent. We were part of something magnificent. It was important, so important that powers we don't understand intervened to stop it, so important that, if I'm right, they have gone to enormous trouble and extreme lengths to castrate one of the two key members of the team. Why would they do this if the fourth beginning wasn't important, and if there wasn't a chance we could succeed in reactivating it?"

Eve shrugged. He hadn't answered her question. In any case, she was far from certain that she wanted to re-engage with the quest. Kit was right: it had been an epic adventure. They had risked all, and they had succeeded – until the intervention. But Eve was pregnant now. She, like Adam, had a new world, a world which centred round the life growing inside her. Kit was single; he seemed to have no ties. Although he hadn't been part of the original decision to seek the truth – whatever that might be – he had joined the quest without a second thought and now seemed to be making it his own.

Eve made them both a cup of tea. "You know, if the quest is so important to you," she began tentatively, "you can pursue it without Adam and without me. I'm pretty sure Andrew and Prune would follow you to the ends of the earth. If you think Rambler could help, he will go with you, if only to fill another of his many notebooks. And where Uncle Rambler goes, Nephew Numpty follows."

Kit was shocked. "That wouldn't work. You and Adam are the key. It's your quest; you made everything possible."

"Not really," said Eve. "I've thought a good deal about the adventures we had on the quest, and I'm absolutely certain we wouldn't have survived them without you. You were the most effective, confident and driven of all of us."

"You're forgetting one thing," Kit replied. "The Storyteller. Nothing would have happened – nothing did happen – without the Storyteller. Even if I wanted to, which I don't, I couldn't resume the quest, I couldn't try to reactivate the fourth beginning, for a very simple reason."

"Which is?

Kit frowned. "Because it's not my story. It's yours."

59. Praesidium plots

The accommodation block for senior members of the Praesidium was connected to the main Praesidium building by a bridge, which was entirely encased in glass. Moving walkways carried the directors, executives and their staff to and fro between the two buildings. Off to the side of the walkways, at intervals of 50 metres, were benches on which Praesidium personnel could stop and chat, or simply enjoy the view.

As Simon Goodfellow was carried along, he glanced down at the parallel world of central London. He could see the citizens of that great city scurrying around, each pursuing his or her objectives with varying degrees of energy and efficiency. All of them thought that they were more or less free agents, exercising some degree of free will in pursuit of their chosen goals, under the protection of a generally decent, democratically elected government. It gave him great pleasure that, in the heart of the city, coincident with the Houses of Parliament, was the head office of the UK's Praesidium which, while being entirely cloaked from view, exercised real power over the entire country and all its citizenry.

When Simon entered his apartment, he found Kathrin waiting for him in the bedroom. She was sitting on the bed in white underwear, her blond hair hanging loosely around her shoulders. Her breasts were covered by her white top. Below the waist, all she wore was a white suspender belt and white-topped sheer nylon stockings.

Simon tended to prefer thin women but, for him,

Kathrin was the exception. She had a full, voluptuous figure with large breasts and a well-rounded bottom. He surveyed her form. The white top and suspender belt covered little of her smooth white body. She looked at him with innocent blue eyes, a trick she had perfected to rouse her many lovers, most of whom took added sexual pleasure from imagining that were despoiling something pure.

Simon sat beside Kathrin on the bed. "And what are you today, my pretty one? A young virgin, lost and alone in the big city? A maidservant, cleaning my room and caught unawares by her master? A dominatrix nurse hired to discipline a wayward husband?"

Kathrin laughed and her expression changed from ingénue to that of a woman well-versed in the arts of love. "I am the wife of your arch rival for the top job, and I have come to give you a thorough seeing-to."

With that, she pushed Simon back on to the bed and started to remove his clothes. When he tried to assist her, she smacked his hand and insisted he remained passive.

When he was naked, she stood in front of him. He was already fully aroused. "It makes a change for you to do as you're told," she said. "Now you must wait until I give you permission to move."

With that, she removed her top. Her breasts were full and firm. She leant over him and kissed him so that her blonde hair fell round his face and her nipples lightly touched his body. A scent of lavender and peaches hung in the air. He moved his hands to embrace her but she pulled back. "Did I say you could move?" she asked sharply. She turned away from him. He could see her beautifully smooth buttocks beneath the fastening of the suspender belt. "Now lie still," she commanded.

Kathrin stood up and finished the glass of wine she had been drinking before Simon Goodfellow arrived. "Now I shall mount you," she said, swinging a long, well-shaped leg over Simon's torso, so she straddled his belly. He could feel her but still couldn't enter her. If he strained upward she would shift forward a little.

"For goodness sake!" Simon exploded, "If you don't let me in, you will find the horse has bolted without you."

Even as he spoke, she eased herself down onto him.

What an extraordinary woman, Simon thought to himself when it was over. Having spent years exploring his own sexuality, he had recently found it increasingly difficult to achieve arousal, let alone satisfaction, without indulging in the more extreme forms of sensual stimulation. These extreme forms involved the exercise of power over his partner, usually in the form of violence and the infliction of sustained, exquisite pain. Yet Kathrin had the knack of somehow making him feel like a schoolboy having sex for the first time with a lubricious music teacher. His first sexual encounter had indeed been with his music teacher; even then, at the age of fourteen, he had felt the urge to dominate and inflict pain. At the time, he thought he had been driven by his dislike of music lessons but later he had realised it was an essential element of his sexual psyche. Yet Kathrin could bring him to climax by purely conventional love-play.

Of course, if the relationship were to last, Simon's natural inclinations would have to assert themselves, but then this was not an ordinary relationship. He knew it, and so did Kathrin. As she had said, she was the wife of his arch-rival for the presidency, and the battle for the presidency was close at hand. He had seduced Kathrin to give himself a psychological advantage over Manfred Bloch by doing as he pleased with Manfred's wife. There was power and pleasure in knowing that he had taken ownership of Manfred's most prized possession behind his rival's back.

The affair was also Simon's ultimate weapon. Manfred was besotted with his wife. Given her expertise in fornication, Simon was beginning to understand why. If it came to it, Simon would reveal the affair to Bloch. He was uncertain what Bloch's reaction would be - he might even try to kill his rival - but Simon would be well-prepared and the council would be unlikely to look favourably on an aspirant to the presidency who had attempted to murder the only other candidate. A more likely alternative was that the revelation of his wife's affair, and indeed of all the other sexual peccadilloes in which Kathrin had engaged but of which her husband remained blissfully ignorant, would reduce the head of engineering to a blubbering wreck.

And, as it happened, there was a degree of pleasure in the affair itself. Quite a high degree, thought Simon as he rolled Kathrin on to her stomach, spread her legs and entered her once again.

Kathrin, while using all her wiles to entertain her lover, still found time to consider the significance of the notes she had found in Goodfellow's desk while waiting for him to arrive. So he was planning to move against the president within weeks. He already had some support amongst council members, who clearly felt that John Noble somehow lacked the ruthlessness needed to deal with current problems. How little they knew their own president! She had memorised the name of every member of the board who would support Goodfellow. She would make sure John Noble had time to win over or neutralise those who were against him long before Goodfellow could act.

After all, for good or ill, her fate lay with the only man who had ever truly satisfied her.

60. Decision time

At the end of their talk, Eve had agreed that Kit should present his case for action to the others. She made it clear that she did not accept his interpretation of events but she was curious to hear what the others thought.

That evening, after dinner, Kit addressed the group. First he gave them a full account of his stay in Geneva, omitting only the incident with the salt cellar. Then he set out his theory that Adam's recruitment by Slievins was not simply a happy career advancement for Adam but was part of a plot to break up the questors and to prevent any possibility of an attempt to reactivate the fourth beginning.

"That's a bit of a stretch," said Prune Leach. "Why go to all the trouble of finding Adam a lucrative job in Geneva when, if you're right, they could have eliminated him here in Harrow?"

"That's a really good question," Kit conceded. "But I'm afraid you will find the answer an even bigger stretch. As you know, I've been to Geneva. I went in the company of Jedwell Boon, a man who works for David Minofel, the Slievins consultant – a man who refers to his boss as his master."

There was a murmur of confusion from the rest of the group at this seemingly irrelevant piece of information. Kit continued: "In Geneva I had a couple of meetings with David Minofel. In my opinion, he is evil."

Prune laughed. "What did you expect? A man who works for a city consultancy, advising companies on how to maximise profits and minimise taxes is unlikely to be a *duine maith*."

"That's 'good man' in Gaelic," offered Andrew Rimzil helpfully, for the benefit of those who knew no Gaelic.

"No," said Kit. "I don't mean he's not a good man. And I don't mean he is a bad man, although I certainly do think he is. I mean he is evil."

"What, evil personified?" asked Uncle Rambler. "That sounds a little melodramatic. Isn't this the man who has found Adam an excellent job working for one of the largest and most successful companies in the pharmaceutical industry? He seems powerful, well-connected and efficient but not necessarily or obviously evil. You've met him, Eve. Did you think he was evil?"

Eve refused to be drawn. "Listen to what Kit has to say and then form your own conclusions."

"So why do you think he is evil?" asked Prune.

"Two reasons, only one of which is conclusive. Adam has changed. If you recall, he and Eve were the driving force behind the quest. They wanted answers. They wanted to find the truth, or at least a truth. Eve wanted to know why Bella died? Adam wanted to know what his life was for. I have spent some time with Adam in Geneva. He is a changed man. He is concerned only with his new job, which now takes precedence over everything else, including Eve's pregnancy."

"That's wonderful news!" exclaimed Numpty. "Not the precedence thing, but the pregnancy." Numpty was the only one of them who had not already realised Eve was carrying.

"But isn't it perfectly normal for a business executive who lands an important job to devote all his time to making a success of it?" asked Rambler. "Examples of businessmen who have devoted their lives to their work – yes, at the expense of other things – are legion. In any case, people can change. Adam has always been goal-orientated. He has a new goal. It's not really surprising he's putting all his energies into his new project, is it?"

Kit shook his head. He was not making much headway.

"What's the other reason?" asked Prune. "You said there were two reasons."

Kit shook his head again. If he hadn't persuaded them with the first reason, there was even less chance that he would succeed with the second. "It's an intuition," he said lamely. "I feel – no, I'm certain – that I'm right."

The others seemed disappointed – all except Andrew Rimzil, that is. "There is something," he said, "something I think I should now share with you all. I have been experimenting with the paradox device…"

"You've what?" exploded Prune. "What do you mean you've been experimenting with the paradox device? You don't mean that, after all I've been saying, you've gone behind my back, without telling me…

"If he's gone behind your back, it would have to be without telling you," explained Numpty.

"Shut up!" shouted Prune at Numpty.

"Take it easy," Andrew said soothingly.

"There is no need to shout at the lad," said Rambler, defending his nephew.

"It's all right," said Numpty. "I was just having a bit of fun."

"There's nothing funny about what Rimzil has done," said Prune, still angry. "You all know I've been trying to persuade him to explore the uses of the paradox device. He refused, even though I helped him make the bloody thing. Now I find he's been lying to me."

"Perhaps if you let me tell you what I've found, you will understand," said Andrew.

"That sounds like a very good idea," said Eve.

"As you all know, I was very nervous about experimenting with the device. We used it to observe the first beginning. We set up a parking space for the van, so we could observe the creation of the universe. In effect, we managed to set up a parallel but coincident universe. I knew then that we had scarcely scratched the surface of the device's potential. But I also realised something else. If we could use the paradox device to set up a parallel, coincident universe, then others might have done the same. And that's what I must now tell you."

"What, that others have developed a paradox device?" asked Prune.

"No, that others could set up parallel, coincident universes; in fact, that others have set up such universes, and that one such parallel universe is now interfering in our own – and, I suspect, interfering in a comprehensive and probably malign way."

There were blank stares from all the others.

"I can't believe you experimented without telling me," said Prune, still angry and hurt. "I asked you about it a couple of days ago and you lied to me."

"I can understand your irritation, Prune," said Kit. "Andrew didn't tell you what he was doing, and you're upset. And that's important. But it's not as important as what Andrew has just told us." Kit turned to Andrew: "What evidence do you have?"

"I have set up a monitor to look for any rational anomalies anywhere in the world. It was simple really. I programmed the paradox device to sample for anomalies using all the forms of mass communication. At first the system found nothing. Then it identified a single anomaly in the Middle

East. I defined the anomaly's characteristics and then set the device to search for identical or at least similar anomalies. I have found dozens. There seems to be one in every capital city. Some countries have more than one. Switzerland, for example, has two: one in Berne; the other in Geneva."

"You call them anomalies," said Kit. "What kind of anomalies? What are they?"

"I don't know," said Andrew. "I'm working on a way of tuning in to them but I'm keen to do it without them knowing, and that makes it doubly difficult. I haven't had any success so far."

"Perhaps if you'd involved me, you might have made more progress," said Prune.

"I'm really sorry. I didn't tell you what I was doing because I was afraid you would push me too far and too quickly. I've been incredibly cautious in experimenting with the device. I've tested only its passive capabilities: scanning, for example. I haven't deployed it in active mode at all since the quest."

Prune was not to be mollified so easily. "So I'm not to be trusted. I'm too impetuous. I would jeopardise the space-time continuum on a whim."

"Come on, Prune," Andrew pleaded. "I'm not saying that. What I am saying is this: if an alien entity is operating without our knowledge in all the capitals of the world, we need to show the greatest caution before we let them know that we know they exist. Let's face it, if they wanted us to know, they would have told us."

"And why are you revealing this to us now?" asked Kit.

"Well, it may be nothing, but I've been monitoring the lights on my scanner that indicate the present of these anomalous constructs. I'm using a new, higher resolution, colour monitor. The light in Switzerland which is centred on Geneva has been particularly bright for the last few days and is pulsing in different colours – yellow, red, blue, before winking in white for a bit. And then the cycle begins again."

"Are any other indicator lights behaving in this way?" Prune asked, curiosity edging ahead of anger.

"Only one: London. The light for London has been behaving erratically. It's not in sync with the Swiss light but it's certainly not stable," Andrew Rimzil replied.

"What are you suggesting?" Eve asked.

"I think there might be a connection between the anomalous constructs and what is happening to Adam," Andrew replied.

"That doesn't make any sense," Eve responded. She suspected Andrew wanted to support Kit's theory but this was pure speculation. Andrew had said there were anomalous constructs everywhere. What that signified, she couldn't guess, except that it was extraordinary and very alarming. But why should their presence and whatever their purpose have anything to do with Adam? "Do you have any evidence? she asked.

"Only this," said Andrew. He pulled some sheets of paper from a folder. "When Kit went to meet Adam, I took readings on my monitor every half hour. This was the Friday that Kit went to Geneva. The light was normal until about 2.30 in the afternoon; then it became irregular and weaker. It stayed like that until the Sunday afternoon. Then, at about 2.30 pm on Sunday afternoon, it returned to normal, but only briefly. Then, in the evening, the coloured lights – yellow, red and blue – started pulsing. I think it was Kit's visit to Geneva that caused the light to become subdued. When he left, the light returned to normal, until someone

– I assume David Minofel – realised Kit had left without his host's permission. It's my guess that the different colours that became visible then indicated concern or anger, or some other intense emotion."

"What does all this mean?" Rambler asked, expressing the uncertainty that everyone felt. He was particularly anxious to have more information, so that, when he recorded the meeting in his notebook, it would have some semblance of a coherent narrative. He attempted a summary. "Are you saying you think there is a parallel existence or entity operational in every capital city around the world? But what it is and what it is doing is unknown."

"I'm working on that," said Andrew. "I'm gathering all the information these anomalous constructs are emitting and I'm trying to decipher what each bit of information means. I have made some progress: I'm pretty sure that a steady signal means all is running smoothly; irregular lights indicate a problem, a challenge or at least something unexpected; and that the intensity of light indicates levels of success in some way. I don't yet know what the different colours mean but I suspect they are measures of the activity of some distinct operation or function."

"When you say 'running smoothly' and 'success', I assume you mean from their point of view – the aliens or whatever?" Rambler queried. "Since we don't know what their purpose is, we have no idea whether success for them is good or bad for us."

"My guess is it's bad," Prune opined.

"It's too early to say for sure," Andrew replied, keen to discourage alarm. "If I can lock into their communication systems, I'll have a chance of finding out what they're up to, assuming I can understand their language."

“The real question from our point of view. or at least from mine, is this,” said Eve. “Do we think that Minofel’s intervention in our lives, Adam’s job in Geneva and the way in which, in Kit’s view, Adam is being changed are all connected with our quest, and are all part of plan to ensure we never again initiate a beginning?”

“And do we think these anomalous, coexistent entities which Andrew has discovered are connected in some way with Kit, Adam and the rest of us?” added Rambler.

“What do you think?” said Eve turning to the Storyteller. “What do you think? You must have an opinion.”

The Storyteller had listened attentively throughout the discussion but, until now, had made no comment. “Yes, I have an opinion. I think they are all connected. I think that Andrew has discovered one of the most exciting phenomena in human history. I think that this phenomenon probably constitutes a serious threat to us and to others. And I think we must now decide how we are to respond.”

There was a stunned silence. The Storyteller never answered important questions. He always told Adam and Eve that they had to find the answers themselves. Any hints he gave tended to be vague and ambiguous. True, he had organised the quest for Adam and Eve; he had provided the camper van that had taken them though space and time; he had introduced them to Andrew and Prune. But never before had he given a straight answer to a straight question.

“You seem very sure,” was all Eve could manage.

“That’s because I’ve received a message from David Minofel, delivered by his servant, Jedwell. Jedwell was most insistent I deliver the message precisely. That is what I am going to do.”

“Well,” prompted the others in unison.

"He said 'tell them to send Andrew Rimzil to Geneva at once,'" he began, then paused and added, placing great emphasis on his words, "and tell him to stop playing with his bloody paradox device before he wreaks havoc through this and any parallel universes that may or may not exist."

61. Genevan machinations

After his meeting with David Minofel, Adam had worked flat out for the next couple of weeks to prepare for the launch of MC57 – or Angeloma, as everyone now called the drug.

The sales conference had proved exhausting. Adam not only had to address some three hundred salesmen, he also had to take an active part in the various working groups set up to refine every aspect of the launch. His responsibilities included editing the text and visuals of all the printed promotional material; participating in doctor/drug rep role-playing in order to ensure that every rep could talk authoritatively on every technical aspect of Angeloma; and rehearsing prompt and convincing answers to tricky questions, such as 'what are the advantages of Angeloma over the market leader and why is it so expensive?' The aim was to make sure that every ZeD representative, however inexperienced, could answer any questions with the same confidence and fluency as the medical or marketing director. Conference participants were expected to work a twelve-hour day. The organisers, especially the marketing director, were lucky to grab four hours sleep a night.

Even after the sales conference ended, Adam was still expected to work all hours God sent. He had to liaise with all ZeD's head office departments to make sure they were fully prepared for the launch. As ZeD's most senior marketing man, he had to attend various meetings of industry working groups. He also had to make a tour of the Swiss cantons, each of which had its own regional manager and sales team.

Meetings with Dr Reed were difficult. The doctor was

performing his professional duties, as well as suppressing the results of the Basel trial, but he was not a happy man. It was clear to Adam that the good doctor was feeling the strain.

Of course Dr Reed was not alone in feeling the pressure. In his working life, Adam had never experienced anything like this. His job entirely encompassed his existence; the demands of the job were almost insupportable. And yet Adam felt a kind of release, a kind of freedom – even a kind of joy – that he found difficult to explain. He had power; when he decided on something, it happened. He had all the resources of a massive, efficiently run, pharmaceutical company at his disposal. His reward was commensurate with his effort and achievement. With his bonus for completing MC57's registration and for dealing with the Basel problem, he was earning money at a phenomenal and, for him, entirely unprecedented, rate. And he had a single, simple, achievable goal.

This last source of gratification puzzled Adam. After all, he and Eve had felt driven to accept the Storyteller's challenge. He had set out on a bizarre journey in search of the truth, but he had never really known what he meant by 'the truth'. Indeed, Nick Peters had told him from the start that there was no truth to be found. And they had never found 'the truth'. True, they had started something extraordinary, something that had promised to change the world, but it wasn't the truth, or at least not the kind of truth Adam thought he had been looking for. And, in any case, whatever it was that they had started had spluttered and died.

It puzzled Adam that he could find satisfaction – and if he was honest, it was complete satisfaction – in single-mindedly pursuing an utterly banal commercial objective, such as the launch of a mediocre pharmaceutical product. It crossed his mind that the satisfaction lay in what the pursuit of a goal could do for him, not what he could do for the goal. Then, there was the money. Again, he had the thought: it's not what I am doing for the money; it's what the money is doing for me. It is giving me confidence; it is proof of worth; it is power and it is freedom.

But these days, Adam had little time for introspection, although, to his surprise, he did feel stirrings of that question that had troubled him when Bella died. At one point, he had doubted his own existence – or, more precisely, the existence of a self. Eve had thought it was his way – a rather cowardly way – of refusing to feel the pain of Bella's death, but that was unfair. It had been more than that; it had been genuine existential doubt. Self-doubt: a condition he had now discovered could most effectively be assuaged by committing oneself to a demanding, well-paid, goal-orientated, self-satisfying job. It was while pondering this irony that Minofel's words at the beginning of their last meeting came to mind: "You are making excellent progress".

oooOooo

Towards the end of Adam's fourth week at ZeD, Yves Dubois summoned Adam to his office. It was a bight sunny morning, and Adam was in good spirits. All was going well. He had completed the busiest part of his pre-launch schedule and, although he certainly couldn't relax, he felt a little of the pressure lifting. It now seemed entirely possible the launch of Angeloma would proceed smoothly and successfully. As he made his way from the fifth to the ninth floor, the sun shone into the glass lift that ascended heavenwards. He felt positively cheerful.

When he entered Dubois's office, he gasped in surprise. Seated in the armchair opposite Yves Dubois's desk was Miss Tomic. She had a black eye, a cut on her cheek, and a bruised and swollen lower lip. For a very beautiful women, she looked shockingly unattractive.

Adam looked from Miss Tomic to Dr Dubois and back again.

"As you can see," said Dr Dubois, "Miss Tomic has been seriously assaulted. In normal circumstances, this would simply be a matter for the police, but, in this case, the circumstances are not entirely normal. That is why I have asked you to come to my office."

"What happened?" Adam asked, not sure whether to address the question to Miss Tomic or her employer.

Miss Tomic shook her head but was too upset to answer.

"It is complicated," said Dr Dubois. He spoke to Miss Tomic: "You may find it more comfortable to withdraw to the annex while I bring Adam up to speed."

Miss Tomic walked unsteadily into a private room adjacent to the Managing Director's office, a room Adam had never noticed before.

"I don't know how much you know about Miss Tomic's private life," Dr Dubois began, as soon as Miss Tomic had closed the door to the annex, but let's say it is rather complicated."

"I know she's engaged to Giovanni Spinetti," Adam responded. He said nothing of her long-standing affair with Dr Reed, but his discretion was unnecessary.

"She is also having an affair with Dr Reed," said Yves Dubois bluntly. "I hasten to add that the company frowns upon affairs between members of staff, but these things happen – and this relationship between Miss Tomic and Reed has happened. And we must deal with it."

Adam was at a loss. Obviously what had happened to Miss Tomic was shocking but, unless the perpetrator was a staff member or the assault had happened on company premises, he couldn't understand why the managing director of the company – or indeed, his marketing director – should need to deal with it.

"Spinetti has found out that his fiancée has not only had an affair with a senior member of ZeD staff – a man almost old enough to be her father, incidentally – but that she has not ended the relationship, despite her engagement."

Adam frowned. "Did Spinetti do this to her?"

"Yes, I'm afraid so," Dubois replied. "He's a very angry young man. He has told Miss Tomic that he feels betrayed and defiled. When she refused to agree never to see Reed again – an impossible demand in purely practical terms since their work necessitates contact – his anger turned to violence."

"Then surely she should break off the engagement and inform the police?" Adam said.

"I'm afraid that's not the end of it. Spinetti is threatening to expose Dr Reed."

"What, for having an affair with a very attractive personal assistant?" Then Adam thought for a moment and added: "Or does he want to punish Dr Reed by breaking up his marriage?" After all, that was the threat that had enabled Adam to persuade Reed to suppress the Basel trial.

And then suddenly it dawned on Adam why he was sitting in Dr Yves Dubois's office.

"Yes," said Yves Dubois in confirmation. "He's threatening to expose Dr Reed for suppressing the Basel trial."

"But he will ruin his own career," Adam objected. "He can't accuse Dr Reed without implicating himself. After all he's helped us at every stage."

"True, but according to Miss Tomic, he doesn't care. He's already beaten up his fiancée, which is enough for him to lose his job and possibly go to prison. He simply wants revenge. It seems we have a loose cannon on our hands."

Adam had a sinking feeling.

Dr Dubois continued: "I'm sorry to have to involve you in this matter; I know you are very busy with the launch. But, unless you can resolve the situation, there may well not be a launch. The company will provide whatever help we can, but I'm looking to you to devise a plan that will bring this affair to a satisfactory conclusion."

Adam's slight frown prompted Dr Yves Dubois to add: "Clearly, as managing director, I cannot be involved in your plan or its implementation. Indeed, it's best if I am kept in complete ignorance of both."

oooOooo

That evening, Adam met with David Minofel. Adam had phoned to request a meeting with Minofel, who had seemed delighted to hear from him and had insisted Adam come for dinner. Jedwell had collected Adam from his apartment at 7.00 p.m. and driven him to Minofel's house in the Lamborghini Aventador.

"I'm so glad you called," Minofel said when he arrived, as though Adam had done him a favour. He was holding two glasses in his hands. "Everything seems to be coming together, and I can't tell you how pleased I am with your progress."

Adam hadn't spoken to Minofel for a couple of weeks

but evidently his mentor was keeping a close eye on his performance.

"By the way, while I think of it," Minofel added. "I'm also impressed with Guy McFall. He's given you his full support. He's very competent, and I have plans for him. Always looking for new talent. I'd like you to explain to him who I am and tell him he's invited to dinner here next Saturday."

"Of course I will," said Adam, "I'm sure he'll be delighted, and I thank you for your confidence in me but there is a problem."

"Isn't there always?" Minofel responded affably. "If there weren't problems, they wouldn't need Slievins' people to solve them. And then where would we be?"

"It's a *big* problem," Adam said.

"Of course it is – which is why we will no doubt need a bold, decisive solution." Minofel sipped his whisky. "So what's the problem?"

"Giovanni Spinetti is the problem," said Adam, "and I suspect you can guess why. He's found out that his fiancée, the delectable Miss Gorgeous Tomic, is having an affair with Dr Reed – and, understandably, he's not very happy."

"Oh dear!" Minofel responded. "It's such a pity when people weave such tangled webs. I am sorry to hear Giovanni is unhappy, but I'm not sure why his unhappiness is our problem. Surely this is a matter for Spinetti and Miss Tomic to sort out?"

"Not such a good idea. He's already knocked six bells out of her. He doesn't seem to be in a conciliatory mood."

"He's beaten up Miss Tomic! That's a shame; such a beautiful creature."

"Absolutely," Adam agreed. "Terrible shame. But that's not the problem. He says he will expose Dr Reed for the fraudster and hypocrite he is. He will accuse him of betrayal in both his professional and personal life."

"He can expose infidelity in his personal life, but I don't see how he can accuse Reed of any professional misconduct without destroying his own career."

"Apparently, he doesn't care," Adam explained. "He is, or was, besotted with Miss Tomic. Her affair with Dr Reed, which, it seems, she is not prepared to end, has driven him to distraction."

"Well I can see that a continuing affair with the doctor would not be an ideal recipe for a stable marriage."

Adam was taken aback. Minofel didn't seem to be taking the situation seriously. "This really isn't a joking matter," Adam said, rebuking his host.

"Of course not," Minofel conceded. "Or, to be more precise, it really isn't a joking matter for you. For me, it is mildly amusing. Now, before you ask for my advice – indeed, perhaps instead of asking me for advice – why don't you apply the Slievins' method of problem-solving. Define the problem. Identify possible solutions. Explore their ramifications. Select the option with the most favourable outcomes. Act. That's all there is to it."

"Spinetti has to be stopped," said Adam.

"An excellent start," Minofel replied. "I tell you what," he continued with a benign, almost conspiratorial tone to his voice, "why don't we explore the possible solutions and the ramifications over dinner?"

oooOooo

After dinner, Jedwell took Adam back to his apartment. "I hope you had a good evening," Jedwell said as he dropped

Adam off. Adam was unable to answer.

When he reached his apartment, Adam poured himself a double whisky. He had already had quite a lot to drink; he knew well enough that another whisky was unwise, but he needed it.

He couldn't believe the conversation he had had over dinner with Minofel. Following Minofel's exposition of the Slievins problem-solving paradigm, they had discussed a number of possibilities, but eventually, after the main course of pot-roasted pheasant in cider, they had refined the options to three. Either Spinetti or Reed or both had to die. Minofel favoured killing both. Even if they killed Spinetti, he argued, there was still a danger, as Dr Reed couldn't be completely trusted. He had a conscience and, although his misgivings about suppressing the Basel trial were ill-judged, he could still be a risk – perhaps not in the short-term, but at some time in the future.

When Minofel had presented the case for a double murder, Adam had, at first, refused even to consider that either killing should happen. He had already conceded Spinetti had to be stopped; his assault on Miss Tomic rankled. But the cold-blooded killing, even of an unstable, fiancée-beating corrupt EMA official, was out of the question. That said, how else could they stop Spinetti? And, if they failed to stop him, not only would Dr Reed be destroyed, but others would be implicated and MC57 would probably never see the light of day.

"I'm not entirely sure you've got the hang of the Slievins problem-solving technique," David Minofel had said as the *crème brulee* arrived. "Have another glass of the Merlot. It's a Californian wine, blended, beautifully balanced and utterly consistent, just as our plans should be."

Adam drank.

"I really don't want you to worry about the details. Jedwell is always on hand to implement and clean up – that's his particular talent, as you well know. We just have to agree on policy and work out the logistics; Jedwell can do the rest."

"But killing?" was all Adam managed to say.

"Very well, if you object to killing, how do we stop Spinetti? Don't disappoint me, Adam. We know what the objective must be. Unless you have another way, it's obvious Spinetti at least must die, isn't it? And, because Slievins people are always inclined to minimise risk, it's probably best if we eliminate Reed as well."

The conversation had continued for at least another hour. Adam had found himself in the bizarre position of both conceding that they must kill Spinetti and arguing that Dr Reed should be spared. He had heard himself saying: "If Spinetti is dead, Dr Reed has every incentive to keep quiet. He can even continue his affair with Miss Tomic without the complication of her relationship with Spinetti. And Miss Tomic will be relieved that her violent fiancée has been removed from the scene."

In the end, Minofel had given way on Dr Reed. "I just hope you don't have cause to regret your decision," he had said.

That was it; Adam had made the decision. Adam had decided that Giovanni Spinetti should die. In one way, he couldn't believe it. In another way, the Slievins way, it was simply common sense.

"You look worried, Adam," Minofel had said. "There's nothing to worry about. Jedwell will help you with all operational matters and will make sure there are no loose ends. It will all run like clockwork. I'm prepared to bet on it."

"No bets," Adam had replied hurriedly. "Not on this."

Before he left, Minofel had given him another letter. This one was addressed to Dr Reed. "Make sure this reaches Dr Reed, in the middle of next week," he had said. "Don't worry. It is just a note to thank him for some medical advice he gave to a friend of mine. No cheque, no banker's draft; it wasn't even mates' rates. Dr Reed's help was free."

oooOooo

When Adam had left, David Minofel took the lift down to his underground complex. It was late, but he had promised to resume his conversation with Andrew Rimzil.

Persuading Rimzil to come to Geneva had been easy. The note that Minofel had sent to the Storyteller was enough. Mere mention of the paradox device and the clear implication that someone else knew more about the potential of the device than he did persuaded Andrew that he had no choice but to accept the invitation.

The others had agreed to Andrew's expedition with varying degrees of reluctance. Kit had warned him to be firm about leaving Geneva when he wanted to return to the UK and promised to come over to release him if Minofel tried to keep him there.

"That's a bit rum," Andrew had remarked, "although I believe you."

Prune had recovered from what he had construed to be Andrew's low regard for his character, if not his engineering prowess. He might have a hot temper, but it burnt itself out quickly. He wished his friend Godspeed, adding that, while he was away, he would have plenty of time to play with the paradox device himself, a suggestion which elicited howls of concern from Andrew and the others, until Prune added "Just kidding."

Rambler urged Andrew to keep a diary of his visit to Geneva, supplementing the record of events with technical notes whenever appropriate.

Numpty wished Andrew well but was more interested in what Luke had told him. Although Luke and Adam couldn't mind-meld, Luke now had the power to observe a person's state of mind at a distance. He had been able to communicate with Kit when he had been in Geneva. That morning he had tried to reach Adam but he had found nothing. It was as though Adam had ceased to exist, despite the fact that everyone knew he was working hard for ZeD, managing and interacting with many people. Either someone or something was blocking Luke's scanning efforts, or there was nothing there to observe – or the self that Luke was trying to access had somehow morphed into something so different that Luke was simply dialling the wrong number.

The following morning, Jedwell Boon had turned up and made all the arrangements for Andrew's visit. "I seem to be running a regular shuttle service," he had joked.

Before Andrew climbed into the Bentley Flying Star, Eve gave him a hug. Andrew was embarrassed but secretly rather pleased.

Yes, it had been easy to bring Andrew Rimzil to Geneva, but it was proving less easy to handle him now he was there.

David Minofel's objective was simple enough: he had to discover as much information as possible about the paradox device. The ability of the device to identify the Praesidium offices in London, and quite possibly around the world, had caused something close to panic amongst the Praesidium staff in their headquarters. Keeping the world ignorant of their presence was essential to the work of the Praesidium. To maintain the effective cloaking, they depended on the power of the Crucible of Eternal Light, the most powerful source of energy, as far as they knew, in this or any other universe. So the question that most troubled the Praesidium – and indeed David Minofel – was how an unknown engineer from Northern Ireland had somehow designed, manufactured and powered a device that could break through the Crucible's cloaking.

Minofel had considered using torture. It was often the quickest and most effective way of eliciting information. And the subterranean section of Minofel's house was well-equipped for all forms of interrogation. But he had decided against torture as soon as he met the tall, distinguished Andrew Rimzil. The Irishman had the demeanour of a military man. He was a person who possessed not only a powerful intellect, but also a high degree of self-discipline. His straight back, neatly trimmed white moustache and smart, well-tailored suit – all told Minofel the best approach would be to show respect, to tease out information. He would have to be careful but 'patience and flattery would almost certainly produce better results than assault and battery' (one of the many popular sayings in Slievens HR department).

Although it was late, Andrew Rimzil was still at work in Minofel's underground laboratory.

"Sorry to disturb you at this hour," said Minofel, in his most courteous voice, "but I just wanted to make sure you have everything you need.

"I could do with a strong cup of coffee," said Andrew, without looking up.

Andrew's disappointment that his host knew less about

the paradox device than he did had been mitigated by Minofel's generous welcome and the amazing facilities his host had put at his disposal. Andrew had never had access to such an array of tools and instruments. His head was buzzing with new ideas. Of course, Minofel kept pestering him with questions about the paradox device but his host would have to wait. Minofel would expect him to leave once he had revealed how the device worked, and then he would no longer have access to any of the laboratory's facilities.

62. Murder most foul

"I understand we have a project to work on together," said Jedwell Boon when he arrived at Adam's apartment the following evening. I have been told the plan is yours. My master was most insistent the plan should be implemented this Saturday evening."

Adam felt acutely embarrassed, but Jedwell's matter-of-fact approach reduced some of the tension.

"So soon," was all Adam could manage. He kept wondering if this was really happening.

"Yes, Mr Minofel was most insistent. 'Strike while the iron is hot' were his exact words. He certainly meant we should make haste, although he may simultaneously have been suggesting a possible *modus operandi*."

"For goodness' sake, keep your voice down!" exclaimed Adam.

Jedwell shrugged. There was no one to hear them. People were strange. 'For goodness' sake.' Really? "Spinetti will be ready to leave his apartment at 8.45 p.m. on Saturday evening. He is planning to meet Miss Tomic. She has told him she wants to talk things through. Do you wish to kill him in his apartment or out in the open?"

"I don't know," said Adam. "Which is best?"

"I would recommend killing him in his apartment. If he is killed anywhere else, the police will want to know where he was going and why he was going there. It just gives them something to work on. Best not to help them, eh?"

Adam thought of asking Jedwell whether he had done much of this sort of thing before, but he didn't because the answer was obvious. "So, in his apartment," said Adam quietly. "How will you do it?"

Jedwell smiled. "I think my master had it in mind that you should perform the act but he did say that I could lend a hand if you were a little squeamish. I'm perfectly happy to kill Mr Spinetti, so long as you take full ownership of the deed."

Adam nodded his assent and his gratitude, thus, he noted mentally, adding cowardice to murder on his moral CV.

"How will you do it?"

"I think I will use a knife. It's quiet and effective in the right hands. One thrust through the heart, and the pump stops. Minimal bleeding. Fast, neat and tidy. Do you agree?"

"Yes," said Adam. Suddenly he wondered if the two burglars who had burst into his home had discussed the operation in a similar vein. But the two cases were not similar. He and Eve had been entirely innocent, and the motives of both burglars had been pure evil; whereas Spinetti was a venal and violent man, and Adam's motives were at least in part benign. He wanted to ensure the success of Angeloma, protect thousands of jobs, increase the value of shareholders' shares, and save Dr Reed from personal and professional disaster. And it was Spinetti's fault anyway: if he hadn't been so ridiculously jealous and vengeful, none of this would have been necessary.

"I'll pick you up at 8.30 p.m.," said Jedwell Boon as he left.

oooOooo

Adam was shocked to learn how easy it was to kill a man. Of course, the involvement of a professional executioner was a considerable advantage, but even so, Adam couldn't believe how quickly the job was done. Jedwell, knocked with his gloved hand on the door of Spinetti's apartment at 8.40 on Saturday evening. Spinetti answered the door almost immediately. He was in the middle of tying his tie.

"Hello, Jedwell," he said as Jedwell entered the room, followed by Adam. "An unexpected surprise."

He was just finishing doing his tie, and both hands were lifted up. Jedwell said nothing. He simply stabbed Spinetti through his clean white shirt, between the third and fourth rib, straight into his heart.

Spinetti seemed more surprised than frightened as he died.

Jedwell left him where he fell. "Let's go," he said.

They took the lift to the ground floor. Adam was keen to leave but Jedwell stopped him.

"Just one more detail," he said. He knocked on the hall porter's door. The porter, who had been watching a football match on the television, was surprised at the interruption. He had not expected to be busy until later: at that time, most people were either out or watching the football. "We need to see the video footage on today's security tape." For some reason the porter didn't question Jedwell's credentials.

"It's in the machine over there. You can't view it at the moment; it's recording."

"That's fine," said Jedwell, stabbing the porter through the heart, just as he had stabbed Spinetti.

Jedwell took the tape from the machine. "Now we can go," he said.

They left the apartment at 8.46 p.m. It had taken six minutes to kill two men and part of that time had been spent in the lift.

63. A bright future

Guy McFall had been surprised and excited when Adam had told him that David Minofel wanted to see him – and not just to see him; he wanted him to come to dinner.

In his conversations with Guy, Adam had explained how Minofel, a partner in Slievins Consultancy, had approached him and arranged his appointment at ZeD. He had told Guy that he had mentioned him in despatches and that Minofel had been impressed. Adam had said: "All you have to do is confirm David's positive impression, and I'm pretty sure he will make you a very attractive offer. He has the power to change your life".

That Saturday evening, Guy asked his wife Jean what he should wear. Jean was a pretty woman in her mid-thirties. She had brown hair, sparkling brown eyes set in an oval face, and, despite having given birth to three children, she had a slim, trim figure. She and Guy had met at university, had become friends, then lovers and finally had married. There had been an inevitability about the process, simply because they were so well-matched. Each stage of development had seemed obvious to both of them, so obvious that Guy could not remember ever having asked Jean to marry him. They had both been 26 and had simply seen it as the next thing to do.

"I guess I had better wear a tie," said Guy. "If he's assessing me for a job, I guess I had better wear a tie."

"You should wear what you feel comfortable in," Jean replied. "You're not going to an interview. You haven't applied for a job. It might be better if you dressed smart casual. Smart to show you're interested, casual to show you're not desperate."

Guy laughed.

"The most important thing is to brush your hair. You should avoid the 'mad scientist' look if at all possible."

Guy picked out his best blazer, a pink shirt and light grey trousers. "What do you think?"

"I think I'd go for a white shirt. I said casual, not bisexual."

"I look good in pink," said Guy, a little hurt. He took out a white shirt.

"You'll be fine," said his wife. "If Adam has recommended you, and that's obviously why this Mr Minofel wants to see you, your home free. In any case, you've nothing to lose. You don't need a new job. Everything's good at ZeD."

Guy hadn't mentioned the Basel trial to Jean; at first because he hadn't wanted to worry her, and then because Adam had found a way of suppressing it. Guy still felt a little uneasy about how casually Adam had dismissed the trial, but Adam was the boss and Dr Reed had gone along with his decision.

"You're right," said Guy. "I've got nothing to lose."

oooOooo

When Guy left the Minofel house at 10.30 pm, he felt exceedingly pleased with himself. Minofel had set him at his ease as soon as he had walked through the door.

"I've asked you here tonight because I felt I had to meet you," Minofel had said. "Adam has told me how much help you have been to him, and how impressed he is – not only with your competence but also with your attitude."

"I've only done my job," Guy had replied.

Minofel had smiled. "It's your job I wanted to talk about."

Over dinner, Minofel had asked Guy about his background, his childhood, his education, his work experience, his marriage and his children. He had shown intense interest in every aspect of Guy's life, but he had elicited information naturally, in a non-intrusive way.

Towards the end of the meal, Minofel had stopped asking questions. Instead, he had begun to tell Guy about Slievins. When he had finished explaining his role as a head-hunter, he had asked Guy if he would be open to a job offer. He had said he couldn't be specific at this stage, but he could promise it would change Guy's life.

Guy had said that if the job would involve relocation, he would have to discuss it with his wife, but that he would certainly give any opportunity for advancement serious consideration.

Minofel had laughed as he shook Guy's hand. "I like that. Opportunity for advancement! Yes, that's exactly what Slievins offers."

64. The Enlightenment

It was around midday on Sunday that Minofel summoned Adam to his house.

Adam had spent the morning feeling spasms of guilt and elation. He understood why he felt guilt. He had been an instigator of one murder and an accessary to another. Oh yes, he understood the guilt. He was now a murderer; he had killed a man.

He had his reasons, but then every murderer has his reasons. He could deploy 'the lesser of two evils' argument: Spinetti could have damaged many lives; some might have been so damaged that, in despair at losing their job or their investments, they would have killed themselves.

Then again, he could share the blame with Spinetti himself. If Spinetti had not been so vindictive and so vengeful, so besotted with Miss Tomic, so insulted by her sexual preferences, none of this would have been necessary.

Nevertheless, he still felt guilty and suspected he always would.

No, it was not the guilt that puzzled him but the elation. He felt he had broken new ground. He had taken decisive action to solve a problem. He had assessed the situation, realised what had to be done and done it. He had opened up a whole world of possibilities from which he had previously been excluded by muddled thinking and moral qualms. At the moments of greatest elation, he thought there was now nothing he could not do.

It was in one of the intervals between guilt and elation that Jedwell arrived to take Adam to see David Minofel.

"Is everything all right?" enquired Adam. Funnily enough, although Adam had spent the whole morning feeling peaks and troughs of emotion, there was one emotion he had not felt – fear. Not for one moment had he worried that he might be caught, that the police might knock on his door, that he might be charged with two bloody murders.

"Everything's fine," said Jedwell. "My master is in particularly high spirits. I think this is going to be an important day, especially for you." He said nothing else on the journey from Adam's apartment to the Minofel house, and Adam thought it best to wait until Jedwell's 'master' could speak for himself.

oooOooo

David Minofel was seated on the terrace when Adam arrived. "Sit down. Would you like a coffee or something stronger? I tell you what – why don't we open a bottle of champagne? This is a day for many things, but, first and foremost, it is a day for celebration."

The murder of two people did not seem to Adam to be an obvious cause for celebration.

"No," said David, reading Adam's mind. "None of that! You have solved the Spinetti problem and, incidentally, done the delightful Miss Tomic a favour. We can be pretty sure Spinetti would not have confined his lust for revenge to Dr Reed. Who knows what he might have done to Miss Tomic if he hadn't been stopped. By the way, she's recovering well from his assault on her."

"I'm pleased to hear it," said Adam.

Minofel opened a bottle of Taittinger Comtes de Champagne Blanc de Blanc 2002 "This is a day for celebration and for frankness. You have learned much and made excellent progress; you have taken many steps, but today – well, today, you will take a leap."

They touched glasses and drank. "What do you think?" asked Minofel. "It's my favourite."

"It's very good," said Adam, although he thought one champagne tasted much as the next.

"So it should be, at more than £100 a bottle," said Minofel with a laugh.

Adam took another sip; this time he could taste the quality.

"The first thing I should tell you," said Minofel, settling back into his chair, "is that I have not been totally honest with you. I think you should read this." He gave Adam a folder."

Adam read. There were twelve pages. When he had read the twelve pages, he went back to the beginning and read them again. Then he said "I don't understand."

Minofel looked at him intently. "Open your mind to possibilities. Think like a strategist, not a tactician. And think like a Slievins man. Read them again."

The first six pages were the results of the Basel clinical trial. It was a draft of the original findings with a full disclosure of the death of one of the patients. The next three pages were the minutes of the meeting, convened by Guy McFall. These minutes included an expression of thanks to Dr Reed "for his cooperation in dealing with the Basel trial". The next page was the letter from Dr Dubois to Dr Reed, again thanking him for his help with the Basel trial. Then came a letter from Giovanni Spinetti to Dr Reed's wife, describing in considerable detail her husband's infidelity with Miss Tomic. Finally, there was a press release. The press release announced Adam Smith's resignation from his post as Marketing Director of ZeD. The reason he gave for this principled action was the unethical conduct of ZeD in suppressing the results of an adverse clinical trial of the new wonder drug Angeloma by means of a conspiracy involving senior members of the company, including the man at the top.

When he had finished his third reading he looked up. Minofel was smiling at him. "All these documents will be in the hands of the editors of every television news channel, every quality newspaper and some of the gutter press by this evening. Just watch the news broadcasts and the press tomorrow morning – and be ready to answer their questions."

Adam resisted the temptation to say he still didn't understand. It was clear Minofel planned to damage ZeD, possibly beyond repair. He would destroy Dr Dubois and Dr Reed, and even McFall would come under fire. Despite the unwillingness of governments to hold senior business executives personally accountable, especially when they worked for companies critical for governmental revenues, the evidence against Dr Dubois and Dr Reed was so blatant and compelling that they would both end up in jail. The damage to ZeD would be incalculable. Reputation is important to all companies, but especially so in the pharmaceutical industry: if there is any doubt about the medical integrity of a major pharmaceutical company, it is finished.

"You wish to bring ZeD down," said Adam lamely.

Minofel smiled.

"But why?" Adam continued. "I thought ZeD was a Slievins client. Why would you do this?"

"Dr Dubois retained Slievins to head-hunt a marketing director. That we did. And a fine, indeed exemplary, marketing director you have proved to be. You have prevented ZeD from launching a possibly lethal drug onto the market. With your appointment, our contract with ZeD ended. That allowed us to spend more time helping one of our other clients, a very important client, to fulfil its objectives."

"What client?" Adam asked, although he had a good idea of what the answer would be.

"PBS, of course," said Minofel. "Pharma BioSolex, manufacturers of Angiax, the drug that Angeloma hoped to topple."

"You mean that all this, all I have done, was simply a means of protecting Angiax? It doesn't make any sense. The patent on Angiax will expire soon. Why break a company for such a short-term advantage?"

Minofel, still smiling, replied "I don't know if Dr Reed or Miss Tomic mentioned to you that ZeD has a very promising anti-cancer drug in the pipeline. I'm no expert, but I believe it is a breakthrough. It's not a single drug; it's an entirely new approach to cancer treatment. If it works, it will spawn a whole family of pharmaceuticals that will be worth billions. PBS wants that range of drugs. It will buy ZeD if necessary. Let's face it, after tomorrow ZeD will be available at a knockdown price."

Adam was silent while it all sank in.

"One other thing," Minofel added. "We are going to be working together closely in future. Never again suggest that any of Slievins' plans don't make sense. You will find, Adam, that making sense is a Slievins' strong point, and you are now very much a Slievins' man."

I have one questions," said Adam. "If you have been planning all this for so long, why did I have to kill Spinetti?"

"Because an essential part of our plan is to establish you as a man of extraordinary integrity. It has to be you that reveals ZeD's skulduggery, not some star-crossed lover of Dr Dubois's personal assistant. He had to die so you could establish your credentials as a man of unimpeachable honour."

"I see."

"There were two other reasons," Minofel continued. "We want this story to dominate the news for weeks, long enough for the ZeD share price to hit rock bottom. In today's world, most top stories are about sex or money, but the very best news stories are about both. This one will run and run."

"And the other reason?"

Minofel paused, as though wondering whether or not to reveal his second reason. "Why not?" he said to himself. He poured Adam another glass of champagne. "Are you sitting comfortably?" he said to Adam, as though to a child. "Then I'll begin."

"You, Adam, are a truth seeker. You and Eve have spent much of your lives looking for truth, looking for meaning. Well, my role as your mentor is to reveal the truth, to provide your life with meaning. So far, you have barely scratched the surface, but already you have felt the freedom and power that I can give you."

"I thought so," Adam interrupted. "You know about the quest, about the fourth beginning, about what we started."

"Yes, I know and, more to the point, the Praesidium knows. The Praesidium knows, and they stopped it. You had no idea what you were doing. Indeed, if you're honest, you'll admit you've had no idea what you've been doing from the moment Bella died. When the branch of the tree struck your daughter, it killed Bella, but it also knocked you and Eve off course. You set out to find truth, without knowing what kind of truth you wanted. You searched for meaning without having set an objective. I'm going to show you that the only truth is the one you create in the life you have in the world of here and now; that meaning does not exist in its own right but has to be created in the process of moving from where you are to where you want to be. You want truth; I will give it to you. You want meaning; I will enable you to find it."

"Stop!" Adam was trying to take in what Minofel was saying but his mind was overloaded. "Wait. I need to absorb what you are telling me. I still don't understand why I had to kill Spinetti."

"It was your decision."

"Yes, but why me? It complicates matters. The police will be looking for the perpetrators. It could come back to me. Then where will I stand as a man of untarnished integrity?

"It won't come back to you," said Minofel. "Even as we speak, the police will be identifying the killer and preparing for his arrest."

"And who's the killer?"

"It will be obvious to anyone who reads the folder we are about to publish and who finds the answers to the following questions. Who has a motive? Who has no alibi? Who owns the murder weapon? And whose fingerprints will be the only ones on the murder weapon?

"So who is it?"

"Guy McFall," said Minofel. "He had a motive: Spinetti was about to scupper his brand new product. He owned the murder weapon: a long, silver paper knife. And his were the only fingerprints on the knife."

"Jedwell used Guy's paperknife?"

"That's what I said."

"But Guy has an alibi," Adam objected. "He had dinner with you last night, didn't he?" This was terrible. Minofel was trying to frame Guy, a man whom Adam had instinctively thought to be decent and honest.

"The purpose of my dinner with McFall was not to give him an alibi, Adam, but to ensure he didn't have one," said Minofel, in a tone that implied Adam should have understood the purpose of the dinner invitation much sooner. "He will claim he had dinner with me. When the police question me, I shall at first seem confused and will confirm that I had invited the man to dinner, but, as soon as I realise the seriousness of the charges against McFall, I shall emphatically deny that he kept his appointment for dinner. If he hadn't had dinner with me, he might well have had an alibi. Having had dinner with me will mean that he doesn't."

"But why Guy? And again, why me?"

"I realise I have given you much to ponder," said Minofel, "but there is no point in asking the same questions over and over again. Spinetti had to die so you could be the one to reveal the corruption at the heart of ZeD. If Spinetti had to die, there had to be a plausible culprit. Your praise of McFall's professionalism and commitment to MC57 suggested him as an obvious choice. And, if I'm honest, I took some satisfaction in destroying a man like McFall, an honest, unimaginative plodder for whom you had expressed profoundly misplaced admiration.

"As for 'why you?' it was important that you learned to take responsibility. We have great plans for you. There will be many times when you will have to take a decision which most would shy away from. That is not the Slievins way. Whatever is inevitable should be embraced, however appalling it is. Whatever must be done, however morally reprehensible, is right.

"Once you have dealt with the furore that will follow your revelations of ZeD's evil-doing, you will return to the UK. Your heroic whistle-blowing will almost certainly ensure you never again hold a top job in Switzerland, let alone in the Swiss pharmaceutical industry. No one likes a snitch! But you will not be going to Harrow. We are providing you with an apartment in the centre of London, in Westminster. It's not so much an apartment, more a small palace arranged on one floor – the top floor, of course…"

Minofel seemed inclined to further develop his eulogy of Adam's future lodgings, but Adam interrupted. "And what will I be doing in London?"

"Well, at the beginning you will be feted as a hero, for sacrificing your marketing career and your monolithic salary and benefits in the interests of medical ethics and commercial probity. As a result of your celebrity, you will meet the great and the good. These contacts will prove useful to you in your glittering future. But, if your future is truly to glitter, you will need some education and training. This will be provided by the Praesidium. I will personally introduce you to the Praesidium chairman, John Noble, and I will oversee your induction programme, but the courses will be managed by senior Praesidium staff. You'll love it. Not only will you be acquiring new skills every day, but you will also learn more and more about the truth you have always been looking for and the meaning that has always eluded you."

"What is the Praesidium? You keep mentioning the Praesidium. Is it part of Slievins?"

David Minofel laughed. "The Praesidium, dear boy, is what runs everything."

"I thought the Government ran everything, or the civil service, or the Establishment," said a puzzled Adam. "What do you mean 'the Praesidium runs everything'?"

"The Praesidium sets the strategy for world affairs, maintains order within countries or foments disorder from time to time, and keeps man in touch with his inner self. The Praesidium works through government, the civil service, the establishment; indeed, it infuses them with its ethos and then uses them to achieve its goals. Things are the way they are because the Praesidium ensures that it is so."

"So is Slievins part of the Praesidium?" Adam was trying to fit the pieces together.

"Slievins is an independent agency that the Praesidium finds useful. When called upon, we are the blood in the Praesidium's veins; we are the muscle in its limbs, we are the teeth in its jaws."

"'It sounds as though Slievins is bit more than an independent agency. It sounds as though Slievins is what keeps the Praesidium going."

"You will have to wait until you meet John Noble and his lieutenants. He will answer all your questions as part of your induction and training."

"And do I have say in any of this?" asked Adam.

"Of course you do," said Minofel affably. "As I said when I recruited you, you can terminate our agreement at any time. All Slievins people have the right to leave the organisation whenever they wish. Those who stay do so of their own free will. I should, however, advise you that, if you do decide to leave us, the consequences will be as dismal as your prospects, if you stay, will be bright. That is not a threat; it is a statement of fact. After Slievins, there is nothing but boredom, depression and defeat. I might add that, in almost all cases, once a man is a Slievins man, he will always live as a Slievins man and will almost certainly die as one. And you, my friend, are now, without a doubt, a Slievins man.

oooOooo

That evening, Adam phoned Eve. It was another difficult conversation. He told Eve to be ready for some dramatic developments. He told her he was leaving ZeD and Geneva, and coming back to London, where he had a new Slievins assignment.

"What do you mean you're leaving ZeD?" Eve asked. "You've only just started. You haven't even launched the new drug, the one you said was so important."

"It's complicated," Adam had replied. "You'll understand better when you read tomorrow's papers."

Eve was speechless.

"There's a big news story about to break. There's been some misconduct and corruption at ZeD. Not me," he added quickly. "I'm the hero apparently. But my job is finished. Anyway I'll be back in London soon. I'll be staying in an apartment in central London. As soon as I'm settled, I'll come over to see you."

Still Eve said nothing. He was talking to her as though she was a business contact, not his wife, the mother of their dead child and mother-to-be of their second child. What had happened to him? It's complicated, he'd said. What did that mean? Why couldn't he tell her what was happening? Then it all came out.

"What is the matter with you?" she exploded. "Why can't you talk to me? I mean really talk to me. I'm sick of you not contacting me. And I'm sick of you not talking to me on the odd occasion when you do. I think you need help. I don't know what Slievins or ZeD has done to you, but you're not well, I mean mentally. Can't you see you're not yourself? You're not Adam. We're going to have a child. For all I can tell, you don't care. You don't care about me or the child. I can't believe how you're behaving. There's something seriously wrong with you."

Adam knew she was not happy with the commitment he had given to his new career, but Eve's outburst came as a shock. She was really angry with him, and yet all he had done was take an opportunity that had presented itself. Yes, she was going to have a baby but you would have thought she would have been pleased to know that he was now earning enough to remove any possibility of money worries. It did cross his mind that, if Eve had known what he had done in Geneva, she might well have queried his integrity (she had always been rather stricter than he on moral issues) but she didn't know, so any suggestion there was something wrong with him, mentally or otherwise, was pretty much unreasonable.

In any case, it must be obvious to her, even from the little he had told her, that he had been under enormous pressure. Surely she should have been supportive, rather than throwing a hissy fit? After all, he was doing all this for her or, more precisely, for both of them.

"Wow!" was all he said.

"We need to talk when you're back," said Eve.

Then Adam said and did something that surprised him as much as it alienated Eve. He said: "Yes, we need to talk, when you're ready to listen."

And then he rang off.

65. Media frenzy

The next few days were chaotic and frenetic. The story of ZeD's misconduct became a top international story. It pushed almost every possible media button. First, it fed into the global consensus that the pharmaceutical industry was motivated entirely by money and was utterly ruthless in its pursuit. The core of the story alone would have ensured copious coverage in the quality press ("End of the line for ZeD?") and a splash in the redtops ("Digging for dirt down on the pharm!"). But, as the extent of the conspiracy became known and the violence and the sexual elements of the case were added to the mix, the story spread through the media like a tsunami. The arrest of Guy McFall for the murder of Giovanni Spinetti provided high drama. Despite the fact that the case against him was conclusive, especially when it was proved he had given a false alibi, he persisted in asserting his innocence. The photographs of the police taking him away, despite the tearful remonstrations of his distraught wife, Jean, evoked some sympathy for his partner but widespread public contempt for the man.

After a couple of days, pictures of Miss Tomic were published. They showed her attending various official functions, at leisure and on holiday; she looked extraordinarily beautiful on every occasion. Pictures of her in a swimsuit proved particularly popular.

Just when it seemed the story had achieved total saturation, news of Dr Reed's suicide lifted it to a new level. Spinetti's letter to Dr Reed was published in full. His vitriolic attack on Dr Reed, his lurid descriptions of his own intimate moments with Miss Tomic and his disgust at Dr Reed's perverted sexual predilections was considered by many journalists to be a masterpiece of both creative and destructive writing. It was a letter that would have driven most men in the good doctor's position to suicide. As David Minofel, the letter's true author, remarked to Adam, the letter's unwitting delivery boy: "Surely the pen is mightier than the sword."

The failure of the police to arrest Dr Dubois added a new dimension to the story. How was it that, every time a major scandal broke, the most senior person involved - often the one who carried the greatest responsibility - invariably escaped retribution? Were the police corrupt, or merely incompetent - or, which was more likely, both? Not that the police hadn't tried. As soon as they had proof of Dr Dubois's involvement, they had arrived in force to effect an arrest, but inexplicably, both Dr Dubois and all the money in his Swiss accounts had somehow dematerialised.

As for Adam, he found himself on an exceedingly steep learning curve. Preparation for the launch of Angeloma now seemed like gardening leave by comparison. Everyone wanted to talk to him. If Miss Tomic had not taken charge, he would have spent every waking moment being interviewed. The media appetite for him - and, indeed, for Miss Tomic - was insatiable, but she rationed their time with the media, ensuring that they spoke only to interviewers and journalists who could keep on message. Her task was easier than it would otherwise have been had the story not already been just about as sensational as anyone could imagine. The usual temptation for journalists to exaggerate or embellish was therefore greatly diminished.

"I've spent all my working life in business," Adam would

explain to a small army of bulbous microphones. "And, in my experience, most people in business are pretty honest. They know that a good deal is a fair deal; they know that, if you lie or cheat, you lose the trust and respect of others; they know that the customer is the last and most important link in the chain.

"I was therefore astonished when I joined ZeD to find that at this company all the principles on which I had based my professional life had been subverted. To be honest, once I had overcome my surprise, I didn't know what to do. My first instinct was to take my concerns to the managing director, but I learned fairly quickly that his office was the source of the corruption I found lower down.

"Then I knew what I had to do. Some have asked me if it was a difficult decision. Of course, I knew I would lose my job and that I might well end my career. Oh yes, I knew it was that serious! You think I did the right thing, and I thank you for your support. But, next time I apply for a job, they won't look at my work record; they won't give me credit for any courage or integrity; they will simply see the man who destroyed the last company that employed him.

"Yes, I've lost a good deal. I had an excellent salary, bonuses, and benefits. But it was not – I repeat, *not* – a difficult decision. I could not be part of an organisation that was prepared to put the lives of its customers at risk. ZeD's *raison d'etre* was to save lives and make the sick well, not to make them ill and kill them off."

Adam became expert in delivering this kind of homily.

"Keep control of the narrative," Minofel had advised him, "and make sure you slip in how big a sacrifice you have made. Miss Tomic will keep you on track. And while you're pumping out your story here, we are building you up in the

UK. 'Honest Brit exposes Swiss venality'; 'One man's stand against a global corporation'; 'David kills Goliath.' Every stereotype and caricature in the book. You will be a symbol of the English gentleman hero: decent, honest, brave. 'John Bull beats Swiss gnomes.'"

Adam queried the John Bull headline, concerned that the picture of a strapping rosy-cheeked Englishman beating up a number of vertically challenged, slightly deformed foreigners was not consistent with the image they wished to project but Minofel countered that no one cared about gnomes and that, in any case, a little fun at the expense of Johnny Foreigner was always popular with the English.

By the end of the second week ZeD's share price had fallen by 70%. Obviously, it's flagship beta blocker was dead. The failure of the drug on which ZeD had relied so much left the company exposed. But the real damage was the legal action that the Swiss government had initiated against the company. All clinical trials which the company used to promote its drugs were now suspect. ZeD was becoming a byword for disreputable practice in business. Indeed, the share price was so low that only someone who knew about the anti-cancer drugs in the pipeline would consider buying them.

But of course Pharma BioSolex knew – and so Pharma BioSolex did.

66. BREAKING UP

"What's happened?" Kit asked.

Eve was sitting alone in the bay window of the sitting room, staring out of the window.

It was the day after Adam's phone call when he had told her they could talk "when she was prepared to listen".

That morning, news of the ZeD scandal had broken. Adam's picture was everywhere. It was the top story on all national newscasts.

"Eve, what's the matter?"

"Have you seen the news?"

"No. I went for a walk with Numpty."

Eve turned on the television.

"Good God!" said Kit.

Eve sat through the report again so that Kit would know what had happened.

"It sounds as though Adam has done the right thing," Kit concluded when the report ended. "It must have taken a lot of guts. I'm no expert on big corporations but the rumour is that they're not too keen on whistle-blowers."

Eve shook her head.

"What?" Kit was puzzled.

"I spoke to Adam last night. He was..."

Eve trailed off. She didn't know how to describe Adam's behaviour. He had been reticent. He had been abrupt. He had been offensive. He had been arrogant. He hadn't been himself. There had been no hint of the Adam she knew. "He was... cruel," she said in the end.

"Cruel?" That was not what Kit had expected.

"Yes. Cold and cruel. He really doesn't seem to care about me or any of us. He has no interest in my pregnancy. When you saw him in Geneva, you knew he had changed, didn't you? Well, whatever he was changing into, the transformation is finished – and so, I think, is my marriage."

"Good God!" said Kit again. "Don't you think you're over-reacting just a little? Obviously, he had a lot on his mind yesterday and he's got a lot on his plate today. When things settle down, I'm sure you and Adam can sort things out."

"Oh yes," said Eve bitterly. "We can sort things out *when I'm prepared to listen.*"

67. Minofel's Report

David Minofel eased himself into his high-backed leather chair. He was sitting in his Slievens office on the top floor of a tall building in the City. It was a grey morning, dull but dry. Minofel swivelled round from his desk to look out of his window, down to the busy streets of London. This was one of those moments to be savoured. Beneath him, people scurrying around like ants, each confident that they were choosing their own path and in control of their own lives; above, the mighty Westminster PCC, invisibly monitoring, guiding, prompting and tempting each individual to make - through decadence, extremism, corruption, obfuscation and negativity - their own priceless contribution to the great organism of humanity.

And there, in the middle, was Slievens.

Many men have sought power. Emperors and Kings have ruled sizable portions of the world. City states in ancient times made a pretty good fist of conquest. Then, of course, nation states raised conquering to a new level. Was he not sitting in the capital of the British Empire on which, at its height, it was justifiably claimed that the sun never set?

And yet the power of these emperors and kings, these statesmen, these great leaders of their countries was nothing compared to the control on events exercised by the Praesidium. After all, from Hammurabi to Hitler, from Sargon to Stalin, from Tamburlaine to Tito, all had been in thrall to the Praesidium. They had all paid their dues. On their watch, and on the watch of all other leaders of peoples and nations, thousands had been butchered; corruption had flourished; depravity had thrived, mobs had rallied to the fanatic's flag. Why? Because, with the help of the Praesidium, man had been what man is. Given the historical record, who could deny that the Praesidium had been eminently successful in helping man to be true to his nature?

And behind the Praesidium was Slievens. Of course, the firm of Slievens was only a couple of hundred years old but there had always been a Slievens throughout recorded history. At all times, practitioners like David Minofel had been at work amongst men, identifying those, like Adam, with potential in order to encourage them, and identifying those few who threatened the Praesidium, like Kit, in order to destroy them.

David Minofel felt doubly honoured. In dealing with the questor Adam Smith and the blind man Kit Turner, he had been given the unique opportunity to nurture one exceptional individual and annihilate another. It was an intimidating task, even for an experienced practitioner, but he was handling both cases with his usual dexterity. Adam was now fully prepared for the Praesidium's induction programme. As for Kit Turner, the possible emergent, Minofel was confident that, by the time Adam reached his full potential, the blind man would be utterly destroyed.

Minofel opened a drawer in his desk and took out a single sheet of paper. He placed it on the large blotting pad which occupied the front of his desktop. The heading on the paper declared its function:

Progress Report
Adam Smith

The form offered a list of character qualities. The user was asked to enter crosses to denote where a subject was on a scale 1 to 10, where one meant a very low score and 10 a very high one. Minofel entered one cross in each row.

Qualities	1	2	3	4	5	6	7	8	9	10	Scores
Avarice									X		9
Disloyalty										X	10
Greed									X		9
Insensitivity										X	10
Mental cruelty								X			8
Pride								X			8
Ruthlessness									X		9
Totals								16	27	20	63

For entry to the Praesidium a candidate had to score 8 or above on all seven criteria. Adam had done well. A score of 63 out of a possible 70 was excellent. Mental cruelty and pride required further attention but clearly Adam was ready to progress to the next level.

Minofel then filled in the section which dealt with Crime Objectives. This set out the crimes which the Slievens consultant had aimed to persuade the subject to commit. There were three major crimes on Adam's sheet. With considerable satisfaction, Minofel put a cross by all three.

Crimes:	
Bribery	X
Blackmail	X
Murder	X

Minofel prepared to sign the completed form. He took a goose quill pen from the stand and dipped it in the adjacent inkpot. The nib took up too much ink and Minofel touched the tip to the blotting paper. A deep red circle spread quickly, then slowed and then stopped. The pen was now ready for use.

David Minofel signed the sheet, scrawling his name across the bottom. He smiled, poured some Taittinger champagne into a glass and said: "Here's to you Kevin, burglar, rapist and martyr. You gave your life to bring Adam and me together. Now my name, written in your blood, confirms that Adam is at last ready to move on with me to the next stage of his development. In neither case have you been aware of your contribution to our little schemes, but no matter. As Jedwell would say, a job well done. And that's the truth."

oooOooo

Some 12 miles to the north-west of the Slievens City office, Eve was at home resting, taking a short morning break. Just as David Minofel signed Adam's Progress Report, the baby kicked. Luke looked up from the comfort of his dog bed. He couldn't communicate his thoughts to Eve, so he padded over and gave her leg a lick. And then he minded to no one in particular. "This is not over, not by any stretch of the imagination."

Lightning Source UK Ltd.
Milton Keynes UK
UKOW06f0926100716

278002UK00020B/714/P

9 780993 110368